UNFORGET
GHOST STORIES
BY WOMEN WRITERS

EDITED AND WITH AN INTRODUCTION BY
MIKE ASHLEY

DOVER PUBLICATIONS, INC.
MINEOLA, NEW YORK

Acknowledgments

"The Lovely House" by Shirley Jackson: Copyright © 1968 Stanley Edgar Hyman, copyright renewed © 2008 Laurence Hyman, Barry Hyman, Jai Holly, and Sarah DeWitt, c/o Linda Allen Literary Agency.

"An Urban Paradox" by Joyce Carol Oates: Copyright © 1994 Ontario Review. Reprinted by Permission of John Hawkins & Associates, Inc.

"The Green Road" by Ruth Rendell: Copyright © 1981 Kingsmarkham Enterprises, Ltd.

"The Apartment" by Jessica Amanda Salmonson: Copyright © 1985 by Jessica Amanda Salmonson.

Copyright

Bibliographical Note

Unforgettable Ghost Stories by Women Writers, first published by Dover Publications, Inc., in 2008, is a new anthology of eighteen stories reprinted from standard texts. A new Introduction, written by Mike Ashley, has been specially prepared for the present edition.

Library of Congress Cataloging-in-Publication Data

Unforgettable ghost stories by women writers / edited and with an introduction by Mike Ashley.
    p. cm.
    ISBN-13: 978-0-486-46797-9
    ISBN-10: 0-486-46797-X
    1. Ghost stories, American. 2. Ghost stories, English. 3. American fiction—Women authors. 4. English fiction—Women authors. 5. American fiction—19th century. 6. American fiction—20th century. 7. English fiction—19th century. 8. English fiction—20th century. I. Ashley, Michael.

PS648.G48U54 2008
813'.0873308—dc22

2008024905

Manufactured in the United States of America
Dover Publications, Inc., 31 East 2nd Street, Mineola, N.Y. 11501

Contents

Introduction

It will not have escaped the attention of anyone with even a moderate interest in tales of ghosts and the supernatural that a significant number of writers are women. By the law of averages, one might expect at least half of the authors to be women, a figure supported by ghost-story experts Richard Dalby and Jessica Amanda Salmonson, but it goes beyond that. Women writers tended to be more prolific than men—especially in the nineteenth and early twentieth centuries—so for each story by a man you would encounter three or four by women.

So, what drew women to ghost stories? One might expect in their historical role of raising children that there would be a certain gift for storytelling, and indeed there is a similar magnitude of women writers of fairy tales and, in recent years, modern fantasy. But ghost stories, at least in their traditional image of moaning spectres and rattling chains, were designed to frighten and scarcely seemed appropriate as bedtime stories. Clearly, there was something about the ghost story that not only appealed to women, but also served a useful purpose.

What's more, women writers have long been associated with tales of the bizarre and the fantastic. Regardless of their true author, the *Arabian Nights* are inextricably linked with their ingenious storyteller, Scheherazade. When the mood for gothic fiction gripped the nation at the end of the eighteenth century, it was Clara Reeve and Ann Radcliffe who set the standards and eventually Jane Austen who pricked the bubble in *Northanger Abbey*. When horror met the new science, it was Mary Shelley— still not yet twenty—who wrote perhaps the most famous work of the whole gothic horror field, *Frankenstein*, published in 1818. And as the mood for more subtle ghosts took hold, there was a whole flock of women writers, led by Catherine Crowe and *The Night Side of Nature* in 1848, ready to meet the demand.

So what was the appeal?

The stories reprinted here go some way to answering this question. Whereas men liked to create stories of vengeful ghosts and sinister hauntings, women tended to go for something more subtle. For many women, ghost stories provided a medium to cope with loss—perhaps that of a husband or parent or, more often, the loss of a child. A significant proportion of stories by women writers concern the ghosts of children, far more than in stories by men. The stories included here by Mary E. Wilkins Freeman, Hildegarde Hawthorne, and Greye La Spina, are particularly powerful examples of this theme.

The ghost stories by women also focus strongly on relationships, ranging from blatant confrontation, evident in the stories by Edith Nesbit or May Sinclair, to more subtle but equally unsettling examples in the stories by Olivia Howard Dunbar, Shirley Jackson, or Ruth Rendell. The writers in this volume avoid the traditional image of the ghost and instead invoke spirits of place and memory. They question the nature of reality and sanity. Had the house viewed through a telescope in Harriet Prescott Spofford's story always existed or had it somehow appeared as part of an ancient haunting? Are we surrounded by creatures of fear that thankfully we are mostly unaware of, as suggested by Francis Stevens, or is it something even more dangerous than that, as Joyce Carol Oates explores? Ghost stories by women usually have a strong emphasis on the psychological aspects, often with an inherent fear of madness.

What becomes evident from all of these stories, written over a period of a hundred years, is that their authors understood the human condition, and that makes their stories chillingly realistic. It is to the legion of women ghost-story writers that we owe that depth of humanity in the ghost story. I'm sure we will all sympathize with the mother in Gwendolyn Wormser's story and even with the ghost in Olivia Dunbar's tale. These stories may unsettle you, but they will also leave you intrigued, fascinated, and perhaps even a little reassured.

—MIKE ASHLEY

Mary E. Wilkins Freeman
(1852–1930)

MARY ELEANOR WILKINS was born in Randolph, Massachusetts, and began writing soon after her mother's death in 1880. She became noted for her novels of New England life, many of which are haunted by a melancholic strangeness and decline. She wrote several stories dealing with premonitions and portents and a hint of witchcraft, which are collected in her much-overlooked volume, *Silence and Other Stories* (1898). She married Dr. Charles Freeman in 1902 and thereafter her work appeared under her married name. She produced a number of atmospheric ghost stories collected in *The Wind in the Rose-Bush* (1903), including "The Lost Ghost" (*Everybody's*, May 1903), a telling reminder of child neglect. Although Wilkins's reputation as a writer of regional novels has faded, it remains strong for her ghost stories. She continued to write them well into later life and although *The Collected Ghost Stories* (1974) includes a wide selection, a complete volume of all her supernatural stories has yet to be compiled.

The Lost Ghost

Mrs. John Emerson, sitting with her needlework beside the window, looked out and saw Mrs. Rhoda Meserve coming down the street, and knew at once by the trend of her steps and the cant of her head that she meditated turning in at her gate. She also knew by a certain something about her general carriage—a thrusting forward of the neck, a bustling hitch of the shoulders—that she had important news. Rhoda Meserve always had the news as soon as the news was in being, and generally Mrs. John Emerson was the first to whom she imparted it. The two women had been friends ever since Mrs. Meserve had married Simon Meserve and come to the village to live.

Mrs. Meserve was a pretty woman, moving with graceful flirts of ruffling skirts; her clearcut, nervous face, as delicately tinted as a shell, looked brightly from the plumy brim of a black hat at Mrs. Emerson in the window. Mrs. Emerson was glad to see her coming. She returned the greeting with enthusiasm, then rose hurriedly, ran into the cold parlour and brought out one of the best rocking-chairs. She was just in time, after drawing it up beside the opposite window, to greet her friend at the door.

"Good afternoon," said she. "I declare, I'm real glad to see you. I've been alone all day. John went to the city this morning. I thought of coming over to your house this afternoon, but I couldn't bring my sewing very well. I am putting the ruffles on my new black dress skirt."

"Well, I didn't have a thing on hand except my crochet work," responded Mrs. Meserve, "and I thought I'd just run over a few minutes."

"I'm real glad you did," repeated Mrs. Emerson. "Take your things right off. Here, I'll put them on my bed in the bedroom. Take the rocking-chair."

Mrs. Meserve settled herself in the parlour rocking-chair, while Mrs. Emerson carried her shawl and hat into the little adjoining bedroom. When she returned Mrs. Meserve was rocking peacefully and was already at work hooking blue wool in and out.

"That's real pretty," said Mrs. Emerson.

"Yes, I think it's pretty," replied Mrs. Meserve.

"I suppose it's for the church fair?"

"Yes. I don't suppose it'll bring enough to pay for the worsted, let alone the work, but I suppose I've got to make something."

"How much did that one you made for the fair last year bring?"

"Twenty-five cents."

"It's wicked, ain't it?"

"I rather guess it is. It takes me a week every minute I can get to make one. I wish those that bought such things for twenty-five cents had to make them. Guess they'd sing another song. Well, I suppose I oughtn't to complain as long as it is for the Lord, but sometimes it does seem as if the Lord didn't get much out of it."

"Well, it's pretty work," said Mrs. Emerson, sitting down at the opposite window and taking up her dress skirt.

"Yes, it is real pretty work. I just *love* to crochet."

The two women rocked and sewed and crocheted in silence for two or three minutes. They were both waiting. Mrs. Meserve waited for the other's curiosity to develop in order that her news might have, as it were, a befitting stage entrance. Mrs. Emerson waited for the news. Finally she could wait no longer.

"Well, what's the news?" said she.

"Well, I don't know as there's anything very particular," hedged the other woman, prolonging the situation.

"Yes, there is; you can't cheat me," replied Mrs. Emerson.

"Now, how do you know?"

"By the way you look."

Mrs. Meserve laughed consciously and rather vainly.

"Well, Simon says my face is so expressive I can't hide anything more than five minutes no matter how hard I try," said she. "Well, there is some news. Simon came home with it this noon. He heard it in South Dayton. He had some business over there this morning. The old Sargent place is let."

Mrs. Emerson dropped her sewing and stared.

"You don't say so!"

"Yes, it is."

"Who to?"

"Why, some folks from Boston that moved to South Dayton last year. They haven't been satisfied with the house they had there—it wasn't large enough. The man has got considerable property and can afford to live pretty well. He's got a wife and his unmarried sister in the family. The sister's got money, too. He does business in Boston and it's just as easy to get to Boston from here as from South Dayton, and so they're coming here. You know the old Sargent house is a splendid place."

"Yes, it's the handsomest house in town, but——"

"Oh, Simon said they told him about that and he just laughed. Said he wasn't afraid and neither was his wife and sister. Said he'd risk ghosts rather than little tucked-up sleeping-rooms without any sun, like they've had in the Dayton house. Said he'd rather risk *seeing* ghosts, than risk being ghosts themselves. Simon said they said he was a great hand to joke."

"Oh, well," said Mrs. Emerson, "it is a beautiful house, and maybe there isn't anything in those stories. It never seemed to me they came very straight anyway. I never took much stock in them. All I thought was—if his wife was nervous."

"Nothing in creation would hire me to go into a house that I'd ever heard a word against of that kind," declared Mrs. Meserve with emphasis. "I wouldn't go into that house if they would give me the rent. I've seen enough of haunted houses to last me as long as I live."

Mrs. Emerson's face acquired the expression of a hunting hound.

"Have you?" she asked in an intense whisper.

"Yes, I have. I don't want any more of it."

"Before you came here?"

"Yes; before I was married—when I was quite a girl."

Mrs. Meserve had not married young. Mrs. Emerson had mental calculations when she heard that.

"Did you really live in a house that was——" she whispered fearfully.

Mrs. Meserve nodded solemnly.

"Did you really ever—see—anything——"

Mrs. Meserve nodded.

"You didn't see anything that did you any harm?"

"No, I didn't see anything that did me harm looking at it in one way, but it don't do anybody in this world any good to see things that haven't any business to be seen in it. You never get over it."

There was a moment's silence. Mrs. Emerson's features seemed to sharpen.

"Well, of course I don't want to urge you," said she, "if you don't feel like talking about it; but maybe it might do you good to tell it out, if it's on your mind, worrying you."

"I try to put it out of my mind," said Mrs. Meserve.

"Well, it's just as you feel."

"I never told anybody but Simon," said Mrs. Meserve. "I never felt as if it was wise perhaps. I didn't know what folks might think. So many don't believe in anything they can't understand, that they might think my mind wasn't right. Simon advised me not to talk about it. He said he didn't believe it was anything supernatural, but he had to own up that he couldn't give any explanation for it to save his life. He had to own up that he didn't believe anybody could. Then he said he wouldn't talk about it. He said lots of folks would sooner tell folks my head wasn't right than to own up they couldn't see through it."

"I'm sure I wouldn't say so," returned Mrs. Emerson reproachfully. "You know better than that, I hope."

"Yes, I do," replied Mrs. Meserve. "I know you wouldn't say so."

"And I wouldn't tell it to a soul if you didn't want me to."

"Well, I'd rather you wouldn't."

"I won't speak of it even to Mr. Emerson."

"I'd rather you wouldn't even to him."

"I won't."

Mrs. Emerson took up her dress skirt again; Mrs. Meserve hooked up another loop of blue wool. Then she began:

"Of course," said she, "I ain't going to say positively that I believe or disbelieve in ghosts, but all I tell you is what I saw. I can't explain it. I don't pretend I can, for I can't. If you can, well and good; I shall be glad, for it will stop tormenting me as it has done and always will otherwise. There hasn't been a day nor a night since it happened that I haven't thought of it, and always I have felt the shivers go down my back when I did."

"That's an awful feeling," Mrs. Emerson said.

"Ain't it? Well, it happened before I was married, when I was a girl and lived in East Wilmington. It was the first year I lived there. You know my family all died five years before that. I told you."

Mrs. Emerson nodded.

"Well, I went there to teach school, and I went to board with a Mrs. Amelia Dennison and her sister, Mrs. Bird. Abby, her name was—Abby Bird. She was a widow; she had never had any children. She had a little money—Mrs. Dennison didn't have any—and she had come to East Wilmington and bought the house they lived in. It was a real pretty house, though it was very old and run down. It had cost Mrs. Bird a good deal to put it in order. I guess that was the reason they took me to board. I guess they thought it would help along a little. I guess what I paid for my board about kept us all in victuals. Mrs. Bird had enough to live on if they were careful, but she had spent so much fixing up the old house that they must have been a little pinched for awhile.

"Anyhow, they took me to board, and I thought I was pretty lucky to get in there. I had a nice room, big and sunny and furnished pretty, the paper and paint all new, and everything as neat as wax. Mrs. Dennison was one of the best cooks I ever saw, and I had a little stove in my room, and there was always a nice fire there when I got home from school. I thought I hadn't been in such a nice place since I lost my own home, until I had been there about three weeks.

"I had been there about three weeks before I found it out, though I guess it had been going on ever since they had been in the house, and that was 'most four months. They hadn't said anything about it, and I didn't wonder, for there they had just bought the house and been to so much expense and trouble fixing it up.

"Well, I went there in September. I begun my school the first Monday. I remember it was a real cold fall, there was a frost the middle of September, and I had to put on my winter coat. I remember when I came home that night (let me see, I began school on a Monday, and that was two weeks from the next Thursday), I took off my coat downstairs and laid it on the table in the front entry. It was a real nice coat—heavy black broadcloth trimmed with fur; I had had it the winter before. Mrs. Bird called after me as I went upstairs that I ought not to leave it in the front entry for fear somebody might come in and take it, but I only laughed and called back to her that I wasn't afraid. I never was much afraid of burglars.

"Well, though it was hardly the middle of September, it was a real cold night. I remember my room faced west, and the sun was getting low, and the sky was a pale yellow and purple, just as you see it sometimes in the winter when there is going to be a cold snap. I rather think that was the night the frost came the first time. I know Mrs. Dennison covered up some flowers she had in the front yard, anyhow. I remember looking out and seeing an old green plaid shawl of hers over the verbena bed. There was a fire in my little wood-stove. Mrs. Bird made it, I know. She was a real motherly sort of woman; she always seemed to be the happiest when she was doing something to make other folks happy and comfortable. Mrs. Dennison told me she had always been so. She said she had coddled her husband within an inch of his life. 'It's lucky Abby never had any children,' she said, 'for she would have spoilt them.'

"Well, that night I sat down beside my nice little fire and ate an apple. There was a plate of nice apples on my table. Mrs. Bird put them there. I was always very fond of apples. Well, I sat down and ate an apple, and was having a beautiful time, and thinking how lucky I was to have got board in such a place with such nice folks, when I heard a queer little sound at my door. It was such a little hesitating sort of sound that it sounded more like a fumble than a knock, as if some one very timid, with very little hands, was feeling along the door, not quite daring to knock. For a minute I thought it was a mouse. But I waited and it came again, and then I made up my mind it was a knock, but a very little scared one, so I said, 'Come in.'

"But nobody came in, and then presently I heard the knock again. Then I got up and opened the door, thinking it was very queer, and I had a frightened feeling without knowing why.

"Well, I opened the door, and the first thing I noticed was a draught of cold air, as if the front door downstairs was open, but there was a strange close smell about the cold draught. It smelled more like a cellar that had been shut up for years, than out-of-doors. Then I saw something. I saw my coat first. The thing that held it was so small that I couldn't see much of anything else. Then I saw a little white face with eyes so scared and wishful that they seemed as if they might eat a hole in anybody's heart. It was a dreadful little face, with something about it which made it different from any other face on earth, but it was so pitiful that somehow it did away a good deal with the dreadfulness. And there were two little hands spotted purple with the cold, holding up my winter coat, and a strange little far-away voice said: 'I can't find my mother.'

"'For Heaven's sake,' I said, 'who are you?'

"Then the little voice said again: 'I can't find my mother.'

"All the time I could smell the cold and I saw that it was about the child; that cold was clinging to her as if she had come out of some deadly cold place. Well, I took my coat, I did not know what else to do, and the cold was clinging to that. It was as cold as if it had come off ice. When I had the coat I could see the child more plainly. She was dressed in one little white garment made very simply. It was a nightgown, only very long, quite covering her feet, and I could see dimly through it her little thin body mottled purple with the cold. Her face did not look so cold; that was a clear waxen white. Her hair was dark, but it looked as if it might be dark only because it was so damp, almost wet, and might really be light hair. It clung very close to her forehead, which was round and white. She would have been very beautiful if she had not been so dreadful.

"'Who are you?' says I again, looking at her.

"She looked at me with her terrible pleading eyes and did not say anything.

"'What are you?' says I. Then she went away. She did not seem to run or walk like other children. She flitted, like one of those little filmy white butterflies, that don't seem like real ones they are so light, and move as if they had no weight. But she looked back from the head of the stairs. 'I can't find my mother,' said she, and I never heard such a voice.

"'Who is your mother?' says I, but she was gone.

"Well, I thought for a moment I should faint away. The room got dark and I heard a singing in my ears. Then I flung my coat onto the bed. My hands were as cold as ice from holding it, and I stood in my door, and called first Mrs. Bird and then Mrs. Dennison. I didn't dare go down over the stairs where that had gone. It seemed to me I should go mad if I didn't see somebody or something like other folks on the face of the earth. I thought I should never make anybody hear, but I could hear them stepping about downstairs, and I could smell biscuits baking for supper. Somehow the smell of those biscuits seemed the only natural thing left to keep me in my right mind. I didn't dare go over those stairs. I just stood there and called, and finally I heard the entry door open and Mrs. Bird called back:

"'What is it? Did you call, Miss Arms?'

"'Come up here; come up here as quick as you can, both of you,' I screamed out; 'quick, quick, quick!'

"I heard Mrs. Bird tell Mrs. Dennison: 'Come quick, Amelia, something is the matter in Miss Arms' room.' It struck me even then that she expressed herself rather queerly, and it struck me as very queer, indeed, when they both got upstairs and I saw that they knew what had happened, or that they knew of what nature the happening was.

"'What is it, dear?' asked Mrs. Bird, and her pretty, loving voice had a strained sound. I saw her look at Mrs. Dennison and I saw Mrs. Dennison look back at her.

"'For God's sake,' says I, and I never spoke so before—'for God's sake, what was it brought my coat upstairs?'

"'What was it like?' asked Mrs. Dennison in a sort of failing voice, and she looked at her sister again and her sister looked back at her.

"'It was a child I have never seen here before. It looked like a child,' says I, 'but I never saw a child so dreadful, and it had on a nightgown, and said she couldn't find her mother. Who was it? What was it?'

"I thought for a minute Mrs. Dennison was going to faint, but Mrs. Bird hung onto her and rubbed her hands, and whispered in her ear (she had the cooingest kind of voice), and I ran and got her a glass of cold water. I tell you it took considerable courage to go downstairs alone, but they had set a lamp on the entry table so I could see. I don't believe I could have spunked up enough to have gone downstairs in the dark, thinking every second that child might be close to me. The lamp and the smell of the biscuits baking seemed to sort of keep my courage up, but I tell you I didn't waste much time going down those stairs and out into the kitchen for a glass of water. I pumped as if the house was afire, and I grabbed the first thing I came across in the shape of a tumbler: it was a painted one that Mrs. Dennison's Sunday school class gave her, and it was meant for a flower vase.

"Well, I filled it and then ran upstairs. I felt every minute as if something would catch my feet, and I held the glass to Mrs. Dennison's lips, while Mrs. Bird held her head up, and she took a good long swallow, then she looked hard at the tumbler.

"'Yes,' says I, 'I know I got this one, but I took the first I came across, and it isn't hurt a mite.'

"'Don't get the painted flowers wet,' says Mrs. Dennison very feebly, 'they'll wash off if you do.'

"'I'll be real careful,' says I. I knew she set a sight by that painted tumbler.

"The water seemed to do Mrs. Dennison good, for presently she pushed Mrs. Bird away and sat up. She had been laying down on my bed.

"'I'm all over it now,' says she, but she was terribly white, and her eyes looked as if they saw something outside things. Mrs. Bird wasn't much better, but she always had a sort of settled sweet, good look that nothing could disturb to any great extent.

I knew I looked dreadful, for I caught a glimpse of myself in the glass, and I would hardly have known who it was.

"Mrs. Dennison, she slid off the bed and walked sort of tottery to a chair. 'I was silly to give way so,' says she.

"'No, you wasn't silly, sister,' says Mrs. Bird. 'I don't know what this means any more than you do, but whatever it is, no one ought to be called silly for being overcome by anything so different from other things which we have known all our lives.'

"Mrs. Dennison looked at her sister, then she looked at me, then back at her sister again, and Mrs. Bird spoke as if she had been asked a question.

"'Yes,' says she, 'I do think Miss Arms ought to be told—that is, I think she ought to be told all we know ourselves.'

"'That isn't much,' said Mrs. Dennison with a dying-away sort of sigh. She looked as if she might faint away again any minute. She was a real delicate-looking woman, but it turned out she was a good deal stronger than poor Mrs. Bird.

"'No, there isn't much we do know,' says Mrs. Bird, 'but what little there is she ought to know. I felt as if she ought to when she first came here.'

"'Well, I didn't feel quite right about it,' said Mrs. Dennison, 'but I kept hoping it might stop, and any way, that it might never trouble her, and you had put so much in the house, and we needed the money, and I didn't know but she might be nervous and think she couldn't come, and I didn't want to take a man boarder.'

"'And aside from the money, we were very anxious to have you come, my dear,' says Mrs. Bird.

"'Yes,' says Mrs. Dennison, 'we wanted the young company in the house; we were lonesome, and we both of us took a great liking to you the minute we set eyes on you.'

"And I guess they meant what they said, both of them. They were beautiful women, and nobody could be any kinder to me than they were, and I never blamed them for not telling me before, and, as they said, there wasn't really much to tell.

"They hadn't any sooner fairly bought the house, and moved into it, than they began to see and hear things. Mrs. Bird said they were sitting together in the sitting-room one evening when they heard it the first time. She said her sister was knitting lace (Mrs. Dennison made beautiful knitted lace) and she was reading the *Missionary Herald* (Mrs. Bird was very much interested in mission work), when all of a sudden they heard something. She heard it first and she laid down her *Missionary Herald* and listened, and then Mrs. Dennison she saw her listening and she drops her lace. 'What is it you are listening to, Abby?' says she. Then it came again and they both heard, and the cold shivers went down their backs to hear it, though they didn't know why. 'It's the cat, isn't it?' says Mrs. Bird.

"'It isn't any cat,' says Mrs. Dennison.

"'Oh, I guess it *must* be the cat; maybe she's got a mouse,' says Mrs. Bird, real cheerful, to calm down Mrs. Dennison, for she saw she was 'most scared to death, and she was always afraid of her fainting away. Then she opens the door and calls, 'Kitty, kitty, kitty!' They had brought their cat with them in a basket when they came to East Wilmington to live. It was a real handsome tiger cat, a tommy, and he knew a lot.

"Well, she called 'Kitty, kitty, kitty!' and sure enough the kitty came, and when he came in the door he gave a big yawl that didn't sound unlike what they had heard.

"'There, sister, here he is; you see it was the cat,' says Mrs. Bird. 'Poor kitty!'

"But Mrs. Dennison she eyed the cat, and she give a great screech.

"'What's that? What's that?' says she.

"'What's what?' says Mrs. Bird, pretending to herself that she didn't see what her sister meant.

"'Somethin's got hold of that cat's tail,' says Mrs. Dennison. 'Somethin's got hold of his tail. It's pulled straight out, an' he can't get away. Just hear him yawl!'

"'It isn't anything,' says Mrs. Bird, but even as she said that she could see a little hand holding fast to that cat's tail, and then the child seemed to sort of clear out of the dimness behind the hand, and the child was sort of laughing then, instead of looking sad, and she said that was a great deal worse. She said that laugh was the most awful and the saddest thing she ever heard.

"Well, she was so dumfounded that she didn't know what to

do, and she couldn't sense at first that it was anything supernatural. She thought it must be one of the neighbour's children
who had run away and was making free of their house, and was
teasing their cat, and that they must be just nervous to feel so
upset by it. So she speaks up sort of sharp.

"'Don't you know that you mustn't pull the kitty's tail?' says
she. 'Don't you know you hurt the poor kitty, and she'll scratch
you if you don't take care. Poor kitty, you mustn't hurt her.'

"And with that she said the child stopped pulling that cat's tail
and went to stroking her just as soft and pitiful, and the cat put
his back up and rubbed and purred as if he liked it. The cat
never seemed a mite afraid, and that seemed queer, for I had
always heard that animals were dreadfully afraid of ghosts; but
then, that was a pretty harmless little sort of ghost.

"Well, Mrs. Bird said the child stroked that cat, while she and
Mrs. Dennison stood watching it, and holding onto each other,
for, no matter how hard they tried to think it was all right, it
didn't look right. Finally Mrs. Dennison she spoke.

"'What's your name, little girl?' says she.

"Then the child looks up and stops stroking the cat, and says
she can't find her mother, just the way she said it to me. Then
Mrs. Dennison she gave such a gasp that Mrs. Bird thought she
was going to faint away, but she didn't. 'Well, who is your mother?' says she. But the child just says again 'I can't find my
mother—I can't find my mother.'

"'Where do you live, dear?' says Mrs. Bird.

"'I can't find my mother,' says the child.

"Well, that was the way it was. Nothing happened. Those two
women stood there hanging onto each other, and the child stood
in front of them, and they asked her questions, and everything
she would say was: 'I can't find my mother.'

"Then Mrs. Bird tried to catch hold of the child, for she
thought in spite of what she saw that perhaps she was nervous
and it was a real child, only perhaps not quite right in its head,
that had run away in her little nightgown after she had been put
to bed.

"She tried to catch the child. She had an idea of putting a
shawl around it and going out—she was such a little thing she

could have carried her easy enough—and trying to find out to which of the neighbours she belonged. But the minute she moved toward the child there wasn't any child there; there was only that little voice seeming to come from nothing, saying 'I can't find my mother,' and presently that died away.

"Well, that same thing kept happening, or something very much the same. Once in awhile Mrs. Bird would be washing dishes, and all at once the child would be standing beside her with the dish-towel, wiping them. Of course, that was terrible. Mrs. Bird would wash the dishes all over. Sometimes she didn't tell Mrs. Dennison, it made her so nervous. Sometimes when they were making cake they would find the raisins all picked over, and sometimes little sticks of kindling-wood would be found laying beside the kitchen stove. They never knew when they would come across that child, and always she kept saying over and over that she couldn't find her mother. They never tried talking to her, except once in awhile Mrs. Bird would get desperate and ask her something, but the child never seemed to hear it; she always kept right on saying that she couldn't find her mother.

"After they had told me all they had to tell about their experience with the child, they told me about the house and the people that had lived there before they did. It seemed something dreadful had happened in that house. And the land agent had never let on to them. I don't think they would have bought it if he had, no matter how cheap it was, for even if folks aren't really afraid of anything, they don't want to live in houses where such dreadful things have happened that you keep thinking about them. I know after they told me I should never have stayed there another night, if I hadn't thought so much of them, no matter how comfortable I was made; and I never was nervous, either. But I stayed. Of course, it didn't happen in my room. If it had I could not have stayed."

"What was it?" asked Mrs. Emerson in an awed voice.

"It was an awful thing. That child had lived in the house with her father and mother two years before. They had come—or the father had—from a real good family. He had a good situation: he was a drummer for a big leather house in the city, and they lived real pretty, with plenty to do with. But the mother was a real wicked woman. She was as handsome as a picture, and they said she came from good sort of people enough in Boston, but she was bad clean through, though she was real pretty spoken and 'most everybody liked her. She used to dress out and make a great show, and she never seemed to take much interest in the child, and folks began to say she wasn't treated right.

"The woman had a hard time keeping a girl. For some reason one wouldn't stay. They would leave and then talk about her awfully, telling all kinds of things. People didn't believe it at first; then they began to. They said that the woman made that little thing, though she wasn't much over five years old, and small and babyish for her age, do most of the work, what there was done; they said the house used to look like a pigsty when she didn't have help. They said the little thing used to stand on a chair and wash dishes, and they'd seen her carrying in sticks of wood 'most as big as she was many a time, and they'd heard her mother scolding her. The woman was a fine singer, and had a voice like a screech-owl when she scolded.

"The father was away most of the time, and when that happened he had been away out West for some weeks. There had been a married man hanging about the mother for some time, and folks had talked some; but they weren't sure there was anything wrong, and he was a man very high up, with money, so they kept pretty still for fear he would hear of it and make trouble for them, and of course nobody was sure, though folks did say afterward that the father of the child had ought to have been told.

"But that was very easy to say; it wouldn't have been so easy to find anybody who would have been willing to tell him such a thing as that, especially when they weren't any too sure. He set his eyes by his wife, too. They said all he seemed to think of was to earn money to buy things to deck her out in. And he about worshipped the child, too. They said he was a real nice man. The men that are treated so bad mostly are real nice men. I've always noticed that.

"Well, one morning that man that there had been whispers about was missing. He had been gone quite a while, though, before they really knew that he was missing, because he had gone away and told his wife that he had to go to New York on business and might be gone a week, and not to worry if he didn't get home, and not to worry if he didn't write, because he should be thinking from day to day that he might take the next train home and there would be no use in writing. So the wife waited, and she tried not to worry until it was two days over the week, then she run into a neighbour's and fainted dead away on the floor; and then they made inquiries and found out that he had skipped—with some money that didn't belong to him, too.

"Then folks began to ask where was that woman, and they found out by comparing notes that nobody had seen her since the man went away; but three or four women remembered that she had told them that she thought of taking the child and going to Boston to visit her folks, so when they hadn't seen her around, and the house shut, they jumped to the conclusion that was where she was. They were the neighbours that lived right around her, but they didn't have much to do with her, and she'd gone out of her way to tell them about her Boston plan, and they didn't make much reply when she did.

"Well, there was this house shut up, and the man and woman missing and the child. Then all of a sudden one of the women that lived the nearest remembered something. She remembered that she had waked up three nights running, thinking she heard a child crying somewhere, and once she waked up her husband, but he said it must be the Bisbees' little girl, and she thought it must be. The child wasn't well and was always crying. It used to have colic spells, especially at night. So she didn't think any more about it until this came up, then all of a sudden she did think of it. She told what she had heard, and finally folks began to think they had better enter that house and see if there was anything wrong.

"Well, they did enter it, and they found that child dead, locked in one of the rooms. (Mrs. Dennison and Mrs. Bird never used that room; it was a back bedroom on the second floor.)

"Yes, they found that poor child there, starved to death, and frozen, though they weren't sure she had frozen to death, for she was in bed with clothes enough to keep her pretty warm when she was alive. But she had been there a week, and she was nothing but skin and bone. It looked as if the mother had locked her into the house when she went away, and told her not to make any noise for fear the neighbours would hear her and find out that she herself had gone.

"Mrs. Dennison said she couldn't really believe that the woman had meant to have her own child starved to death. Probably she thought the little thing would raise somebody, or folks would try to get in the house and find her. Well, whatever she thought, there the child was, dead.

"But that wasn't all. The father came home, right in the midst of it; the child was just buried, and he was beside himself. And—he went on the track of his wife, and he found her, and he shot her dead; it was in all the papers at the time; then he disappeared. Nothing had been seen of him since. Mrs. Dennison said that she thought he had either made way with himself or got out of the country, nobody knew, but they did know there was something wrong with the house.

"'I knew folks acted queer when they asked me how I liked it when we first came here,' says Mrs. Dennison, 'but I never dreamed why till we saw the child that night.'"

"I never heard anything like it in my life," said Mrs. Emerson, staring at the other woman with awestruck eyes.

"I thought you'd say so," said Mrs. Meserve. "You don't wonder that I ain't disposed to speak light when I hear there is anything queer about a house, do you?"

"No, I don't, after that," Mrs. Emerson said.

"But that ain't all," said Mrs. Meserve.

"Did you see it again?" Mrs. Emerson asked.

"Yes, I saw it a number of times before the last time. It was lucky I wasn't nervous, or I never could have stayed there, much as I liked the place and much as I thought of those two women; they were beautiful women, and no mistake. I loved those women. I hope Mrs. Dennison will come and see me sometime.

"Well, I stayed, and I never knew when I'd see that child. I got so I was very careful to bring everything of mine upstairs, and not leave any little thing in my room that needed doing, for fear she would come lugging up my coat or hat or gloves or I'd find things done when there'd been no live being in the room to do them. I can't tell you how I dreaded seeing her; and worse than the seeing her was the hearing her say, 'I can't find my mother.' It was enough to make your blood run cold. I never heard a living child cry for its mother that was anything so pitiful as that dead one. It was enough to break your heart.

"She used to come and say that to Mrs. Bird oftener than to any one else. Once I heard Mrs. Bird say she wondered if it was possible that the poor little thing couldn't really find her mother in the other world, she had been such a wicked woman.

"But Mrs. Dennison told her she didn't think she ought to speak so nor even think so, and Mrs. Bird said she shouldn't wonder if she was right. Mrs. Bird was always very easy to put in the wrong. She was a good woman, and one that couldn't do things enough for other folks. It seemed as if that was what she lived on. I don't think she was ever so scared by that poor little ghost, as much as she pitied it, and she was 'most heartbroken because she couldn't do anything for it, as she could have done for a live child.

"'It seems to me sometimes as if I should die if I can't get that awful little white robe off that child and get her in some clothes and feed her and stop her looking for her mother,' I heard her say once, and she was in earnest. She cried when she said it. That wasn't long before she died.

"Now I am coming to the strangest part of it all. Mrs. Bird died very sudden. One morning—it was Saturday, and there wasn't any school—I went downstairs to breakfast, and Mrs. Bird wasn't there; there was nobody but Mrs. Dennison. She was pouring out the coffee when I came in. 'Why, where's Mrs. Bird?' says I.

"'Abby ain't feeling very well this morning,' says she; 'there isn't much the matter, I guess, but she didn't sleep very well, and her head aches, and she's sort of chilly, and I told her I thought she'd better stay in bed till the house gets warm.' It was a very cold morning.

"'Maybe she's got cold,' says I.

"'Yes, I guess she has,' says Mrs. Dennison. 'I guess she's got cold. She'll be up before long. Abby ain't one to stay in bed a minute longer than she can help.'

"Well, we went on eating our breakfast, and all at once a shadow flickered across one wall of the room and over the ceiling the way a shadow will sometimes when somebody passes the window outside. Mrs. Dennison and I both looked up, then out of the window; then Mrs. Dennison she gives a scream.

"'Why, Abby's crazy!' says she. 'There she is out this bitter cold morning, and—and—' She didn't finish, but she meant the child. For we were both looking out, and we saw, as plain as we ever saw anything in our lives, Mrs. Abby Bird walking off over the white snowpath with that child holding fast to her hand, nestling close to her as if she had found her own mother.

"'She's dead,' says Mrs. Dennison, clutching hold of me hard. 'She's dead; my sister is dead!'

"She was. We hurried upstairs as fast as we could go, and she was dead in her bed, and smiling as if she was dreaming, and one arm and hand was stretched out as if something had hold of it; and it couldn't be straightened even at the last—it lay out over her casket at the funeral."

"Was the child ever seen again?" asked Mrs. Emerson in a shaking voice.

"No," replied Mrs. Meserve; "that child was never seen again after she went out of the yard with Mrs. Bird."

Edith Wharton
(1862–1937)

EDITH WHARTON was born Edith Newbold Jones to a wealthy family whose name is believed to have lent itself to the phrase "keeping up with the Joneses." She is best known for her novels of New York society, notably the Pulitzer Prize-winning *The Age of Innocence* (1920). She was also a capable landscape gardener, and designed her mansion, The Mount, at Lenox, Massachusetts, in 1901. She had married Teddy Wharton in 1885, but he was a philanderer and they eventually divorced in 1913. Thereafter, Edith spent most of her time in France, continuing to live there during the First World War. Her ghost stories equal less than a tenth of her output, yet all are considered among the very best in the field. Her earliest was "The Fullness of Life," published in 1893, and her last was "All Souls," published posthumously in her final collection, *Ghosts* (1937). Her work is often compared to that of her friend and mentor Henry James, and certainly her ghost stories are the equal of his in their deceptive complexity. "Kerfol," which was published in *Scribner's* in May 1910, is set in her second home in France.

Kerfol

I

"You ought to buy it," said my host; "it's just the place for a solitary-minded devil like you. And it would be rather worth while to own the most romantic house in Brittany. The present people are dead broke, and it's going for a song—you ought to buy it."

It was not with the least idea of living up to the character my friend Lanrivain ascribed to me (as a matter of fact, under my unsociable exterior I have always had secret yearnings for domesticity) that I took his hint one autumn afternoon and went to Kerfol. My friend was motoring over to Quimper on business: he dropped me on the way, at a cross-road on a heath, and said: "First turn to the right and second to the left. Then straight ahead till you see an avenue. If you meet any peasants, don't ask your way. They don't understand French, and they would pretend they did and mix you up. I'll be back for you here by sunset—and don't forget the tombs in the chapel."

I followed Lanrivain's directions with the hesitation occasioned by the usual difficulty of remembering whether he had said the first turn to the right and second to the left, or the contrary. If I had met a peasant I should certainly have asked, and probably been sent astray; but I had the desert landscape to myself, and so stumbled on the right turn and walked on across the heath till I came to an avenue. It was so unlike any other avenue I have ever seen that I instantly knew it must be *the* avenue. The grey-trunked trees sprang up straight to a great height and then interwove their pale-grey branches in a long tunnel through which the autumn light fell faintly. I know most trees by name, but I haven't to this day been able to decide what those trees were. They had the tall curve of elms, the tenuity of poplars, the ashen colour of olives under a rainy sky; and they stretched ahead of me for half a mile or more without a break in their arch. If ever I saw an avenue that unmistakeably led to something, it was the avenue at Kerfol. My heart beat a little as I began to walk down it.

Presently the trees ended and I came to a fortified gate in a long wall. Between me and the wall was an open space of grass, with other grey avenues radiating from it. Behind the wall were tall slate roofs mossed with silver, a chapel belfry, the top of a keep. A moat filled with wild shrubs and brambles surrounded the place; the drawbridge had been replaced by a stone arch, and the portcullis by an iron gate. I stood for a long time on the hither side of the moat, gazing about me, and letting the influence of the place sink in. I said to myself: "If I wait long enough, the guardian will turn up and show me the tombs—" and I rather hoped he wouldn't turn up too soon.

I sat down on a stone and lit a cigarette. As soon as I had done it, it struck me as a puerile and portentous thing to do, with that great blind house looking down at me, and all the empty avenues converging on me. It may have been the depth of the silence that made me so conscious of my gesture. The squeak of my match sounded as loud as the scraping of a brake, and I almost fancied I heard it fall when I tossed it onto the grass. But there was more than that: a sense of irrelevance, of littleness, of futile bravado, in sitting there puffing my cigarette-smoke into the face of such a past.

I knew nothing of the history of Kerfol—I was new to Brittany, and Lanrivain had never mentioned the name to me till the day before—but one couldn't as much as glance at that pile without feeling in it a long accumulation of history. What kind of history I was not prepared to guess: perhaps only the sheer weight of many associated lives and deaths which gives a majesty to all old houses. But the aspect of Kerfol suggested something more—a perspective of stern and cruel memories stretching away, like its own grey avenues, into a blur of darkness.

Certainly no house had ever more completely and finally broken with the present. As it stood there, lifting its proud roofs and gables to the sky, it might have been its own funeral monument. "Tombs in the chapel? The whole place is a tomb!" I reflected. I hoped more and more that the guardian would not come. The details of the place, however striking, would seem trivial compared with its collective impressiveness; and I wanted only to sit there and be penetrated by the weight of its silence.

"It's the very place for you!" Lanrivain had said; and I was overcome by the almost blasphemous frivolity of suggesting to any living being that Kerfol was the place for him. "Is it possible that any one could *not* see—?" I wondered. I did not finish the thought: what I meant was undefinable. I stood up and wandered toward the gate. I was beginning to want to know more; not to *see* more—I was by now so sure it was not a question of seeing—but to feel more: feel all the place had to communicate. "But to get in one will have to rout out the keeper," I thought reluctantly, and hesitated. Finally I crossed the bridge and tried the iron gate. It yielded, and I walked under the tunnel formed by the thickness of the *chemin de ronde*. At the farther end, a wooden barricade had been laid across the entrance, and beyond it was a court enclosed in noble architecture. The main building faced me; and I now saw that one half was a mere ruined front, with gaping windows through which the wild growths of the moat and the trees of the park were visible. The rest of the house was still in its robust beauty. One end abutted on the round tower, the other on the small traceried chapel, and in an angle of the building stood a graceful well-head crowned with mossy urns. A few roses grew against the walls, and on an upper window-sill I remember noticing a pot of fuchsias.

My sense of the pressure of the invisible began to yield to my architectural interest. The building was so fine that I felt a desire to explore it for its own sake. I looked about the court, wondering in which corner the guardian lodged. Then I pushed open the barrier and went in. As I did so, a dog barred my way. He was such a remarkably beautiful little dog that for a moment he made me forget the splendid place he was defending. I was not sure of his breed at the time, but have since learned that it was Chinese, and that he was of a rare variety called the "Sleeve-dog." He was very small and golden brown, with large brown eyes and a ruffled throat: he looked rather like a large tawny chrysanthemum. I said to myself: "These little beasts always snap and scream, and somebody will be out in a minute."

The little animal stood before me, forbidding, almost menacing: there was anger in his large brown eyes. But he made no sound, he came no nearer. Instead, as I advanced, he gradually fell back, and I noticed that another dog, a vague rough brindled thing, had limped up on a lame leg. "There'll be a hubbub now," I thought; for at the same moment a third dog, a long-haired white mongrel, slipped out of a doorway and joined the others. All three stood looking at me with grave eyes; but not a sound came from them. As I advanced they continued to fall back on muffled paws, still watching me. "At a given point, they'll all charge at my ankles: it's one of the jokes that dogs who live together put up on one," I thought. I was not much alarmed, for they were neither large nor formidable. But they let me wander about the court as I pleased, following me at a little distance—always the same distance—and always keeping their eyes on me. Presently I looked across at the ruined façade, and saw that in one of its empty window-frames another dog stood: a large white pointer with one brown ear. He was an old grave dog, much more experienced than the others; and he seemed to be observing me with a deeper intentness.

"I'll hear from *him*," I said to myself; but he stood in the window-frame, against the trees of the park, and continued to watch me without moving. I stared back at him for a time, to see if the sense that he was being watched would not rouse him. Half the width of the court lay between us, and we stared at each other silently across it. But he did not stir, and at last I turned away. Behind me I found the rest of the pack, with a newcomer added: a small black greyhound with pale agate-coloured eyes. He was shivering a little, and his expression was more timid than that of the others. I noticed that he kept a little behind them. And still there was not a sound.

I stood there for fully five minutes, the circle about me—waiting, as they seemed to be waiting. At last I went up to the little golden-brown dog and stooped to pat him. As I did so, I heard myself give a nervous laugh. The little dog did not start, or growl, or take his eyes from me—he simply slipped back about a yard, and then paused and continued to look at me. "Oh, hang it!" I exclaimed, and walked across the court toward the well.

As I advanced, the dogs separated and slid away into different corners of the court. I examined the urns on the well, tried a locked door or two, and looked up and down the dumb façade; then I faced about toward the chapel. When I turned I perceived that all the dogs had disappeared except the old pointer, who still watched me from the window. It was rather a relief to be rid of that cloud of witnesses; and I began to look about me for a way to the back of the house. "Perhaps there'll be somebody in the garden," I thought. I found a way across the moat, scrambled over a wall smothered in brambles, and got into the garden. A few lean hydrangeas and geraniums pined in the flower-beds, and the ancient house looked down on them indifferently. Its garden side was plainer and severer than the other: the long granite front, with its few windows and steep roof, looked like a fortress-prison. I walked around the farther wing, went up some disjointed steps, and entered the deep twilight of a narrow and incredibly old box-walk. The walk was just wide enough for one person to slip through, and its branches met overhead. It was like the ghost of a box-walk, its lustrous green all turning to the shadowy greyness of the avenues. I walked on and on, the branches hitting me in the face and springing back with a dry rattle; and at length I came out on the grassy top of the *chemin de ronde*. I walked along it to the gate-tower, looking down into the court, which was just below me. Not a human being was in sight; and neither were the dogs. I found a flight of steps in the thickness of the wall and went down them; and when I emerged again into the court, there stood the circle of dogs, the golden-brown one a little ahead of the others, the black greyhound shivering in the rear.

"Oh, hang it—you uncomfortable beasts, you!" I exclaimed, my voice startling me with a sudden echo. The dogs stood motionless, watching me. I knew by this time that they would not try to prevent my approaching the house, and the knowledge left me free to examine them. I had a feeling that they must be horribly cowed to be so silent and inert. Yet they did not look hungry or ill-treated. Their coats were smooth and they were not thin, except the shivering greyhound. It was more as if they had lived a long time with people who never spoke to them or looked at them: as though the silence of the place had gradually benumbed their busy inquisitive natures. And this strange passivity, this almost human lassitude, seemed to me sadder than the misery of starved and beaten animals. I should have liked to rouse them for a minute, to coax them into a game or a scamper; but the longer I looked into their fixed and weary eyes the more preposterous the idea became. With the windows of that house looking down on us, how could I have imagined such a thing? The dogs knew better: *they* knew what the house would tolerate and what it would not. I even fancied that they knew what was passing through my mind, and pitied me for my frivolity. But even that feeling probably reached them through a thick fog of listlessness. I had an idea that their distance from me was as nothing to my remoteness from them. The impression they produced was that of having in common one memory so deep and dark that nothing that had happened since was worth either a growl or a wag.

"I say," I broke out abruptly, addressing myself to the dumb circle, "do you know what you look like, the whole lot of you? You look as if you'd seen a ghost—that's how you look! I wonder if there *is* a ghost here, and nobody but you left for it to appear to?" The dogs continued to gaze at me without moving. . . .

It was dark when I saw Lanrivain's motor lamps at the crossroads—and I wasn't exactly sorry to see them. I had the sense of having escaped from the loneliest place in the whole world, and of not liking loneliness—to that degree—as much as I had imagined I should. My friend had brought his solicitor back from Quimper for the night, and seated beside a fat and affable stranger I felt no inclination to talk of Kerfol. . . .

But that evening, when Lanrivain and the solicitor were clos-

eted in the study, Madame de Lanrivain began to question me
in the drawing-room.

"Well—are you going to buy Kerfol?" she asked, tilting up her
gay chin from her embroidery.

"I haven't decided yet. The fact is, I couldn't get into the
house," I said, as if I had simply postponed my decision, and
meant to go back for another look.

"You couldn't get in? Why, what happened? The family are
mad to sell the place, and the old guardian has orders—"

"Very likely. But the old guardian wasn't there."

"What a pity! He must have gone to market. But his
daughter—?"

"There was nobody about. At least I saw no one."

"How extraordinary! Literally nobody?"

"Nobody but a lot of dogs—a whole pack of them—who
seemed to have the place to themselves."

Madame de Lanrivain let the embroidery slip to her knee and
folded her hands on it. For several minutes she looked at me
thoughtfully.

"A pack of dogs—you *saw* them?"

"Saw them? I saw nothing else!"

"How many?" She dropped her voice a little. "I've always
wondered—"

I looked at her with surprise: I had supposed the place to be
familiar to her. "Have you never been to Kerfol?" I asked.

"Oh, yes: often. But never on that day."

"What day?"

"I'd quite forgotten—and so had Hervé, I'm sure. If we'd
remembered, we never should have sent you today—but then,
after all, one doesn't half believe that sort of thing, does one?"

"What sort of thing?" I asked, involuntarily sinking my voice
to the level of hers. Inwardly I was thinking: "I *knew* there was
something. . . ."

Madame de Lanrivain cleared her throat and produced a
reassuring smile. "Didn't Hervé tell you the story of Kerfol? An
ancestor of his was mixed up in it. You know every Breton house
has its ghost-story; and some of them are rather unpleasant."

"Yes—but those dogs?"

"Well, those dogs are the ghosts of Kerfol. At least, the peasants say there's one day in the year when a lot of dogs appear there; and that day the keeper and his daughter go off to Morlaix and get drunk. The women in Brittany drink dreadfully." She stooped to match a silk; then she lifted her charming inquisitive Parisian face. "Did you *really* see a lot of dogs? There isn't one at Kerfol," she said.

<h1 style="text-align:center">II</h1>

Lanrivain, the next day, hunted out a shabby calf volume from the back of an upper shelf of his library.

"Yes—here it is. What does it call itself? *A History of the Assizes of the Duchy of Brittany. Quimper, 1702*. The book was written about a hundred years later than the Kerfol affair; but I believe the account is transcribed pretty literally from the judicial records. Anyhow, it's queer reading. And there's a Hervé de Lanrivain mixed up in it—not exactly *my* style, as you'll see. But then he's only a collateral. Here, take the book up to bed with you. I don't exactly remember the details; but after you've read it I'll bet anything you'll leave your light burning all night!"

I left my light burning all night, as he had predicted; but it was chiefly because, till near dawn, I was absorbed in my reading. The account of the trial of Anne de Cornault, wife of the lord of Kerfol, was long and closely printed. It was, as my friend had said, probably an almost literal transcription of what took place in the court-room; and the trial lasted nearly a month. Besides, the type of the book was very bad. . . .

At first I thought of translating the old record. But it is full of wearisome repetitions, and the main lines of the story are forever straying off into side issues. So I have tried to disentangle it, and give it here in a simpler form. At times, however, I have reverted to the text because no other words could have conveyed so exactly the sense of what I felt at Kerfol; and nowhere have I added anything of my own.

III

It was in the year 16— that Yves de Cornault, lord of the domain
of Kerfol, went to the *pardon* of Locronan to perform his religious duties. He was a rich and powerful noble, then in his sixty-
second year, but hale and sturdy, a great horseman and hunter
and a pious man. So all his neighbours attested. In appearance
he was short and broad, with a swarthy face, legs slightly bowed
from the saddle, a hanging nose and broad hands with black
hairs on them. He had married young and lost his wife and son
soon after, and since then had lived alone at Kerfol. Twice a year
he went to Morlaix, where he had a handsome house by the
river, and spent a week or ten days there; and occasionally he
rode to Rennes on business. Witnesses were found to declare
that during these absences he led a life different from the one
he was known to lead at Kerfol, where he busied himself with
his estate, attended mass daily, and found his only amusement
in hunting the wild boar and water-fowl. But these rumours are
not particularly relevant, and it is certain that among people of
his own class in the neighbourhood he passed for a stern and
even austere man, observant of his religious obligations, and
keeping strictly to himself. There was no talk of any familiarity
with the women on his estate, though at that time the nobility
were very free with their peasants. Some people said he had
never looked at a woman since his wife's death; but such things
are hard to prove, and the evidence on this point was not worth
much.

Well, in his sixty-second year, Yves de Cornault went to the
pardon at Locronan, and saw there a young lady of Douarnenez,
who had ridden over pillion behind her father to do her duty to
the saint. Her name was Anne de Barrigan, and she came of
good old Breton stock, but much less great and powerful than
that of Yves de Cornault; and her father had squandered his
fortune at cards, and lived almost like a peasant in his little granite manor on the moors. . . . I have said I would add nothing of
my own to this bald statement of a strange case; but I must
interrupt myself here to describe the young lady who rode up to
the lych-gate of Locronan at the very moment when the Baron

de Cornault was also dismounting there. I take my description from a faded drawing in red crayon, sober and truthful enough to be by a late pupil of the Clouets, which hangs in Lanrivain's study, and is said to be a portrait of Anne de Barrigan. It is unsigned and has no mark of identity but the initials A. B., and the date 16—, the year after her marriage. It represents a young woman with a small oval face, almost pointed, yet wide enough for a full mouth with a tender depression at the corners. The nose is small, and the eyebrows are set rather high, far apart, and as lightly pencilled as the eyebrows in a Chinese painting. The forehead is high and serious, and the hair, which one feels to be fine and thick and fair, is drawn off it and lies close like a cap. The eyes are neither large nor small, hazel probably, with a look at once shy and steady. A pair of beautiful long hands are crossed below the lady's breast. . . .

The chaplain of Kerfol, and other witnesses, averred that when the Baron came back from Locronan he jumped from his horse, ordered another to be instantly saddled, called to a young page to come with him, and rode away that same evening to the south. His steward followed the next morning with coffers laden on a pair of pack mules. The following week Yves de Cornault rode back to Kerfol, sent for his vassals and tenants, and told them he was to be married at All Saints to Anne de Barrigan of Douarnenez. And on All Saints' Day the marriage took place.

As to the next few years, the evidence on both sides seems to show that they passed happily for the couple. No one was found to say that Yves de Cornault had been unkind to his wife, and it was plain to all that he was content with his bargain. Indeed, it was admitted by the chaplain and other witnesses for the prosecution that the young lady had a softening influence on her husband, and that he became less exacting with his tenants, less harsh to peasants and dependents, and less subject to the fits of gloomy silence which had darkened his widowhood. As to his wife, the only grievance her champions could call up in her behalf was that Kerfol was a lonely place, and that when her husband was away on business at Rennes or Morlaix—whither she was never taken—she was not allowed so much as to walk in the park unaccompanied. But no one asserted that she was unhappy, though one servant-woman said she had surprised her crying, and had heard her say that she was a woman accursed to have no child, and nothing in life to call her own. But that was a natural enough feeling in a wife attached to her husband; and certainly it must have been a great grief to Yves de Cornault that she bore no son. Yet he never made her feel her childlessness as a reproach—she herself admits this in her evidence—but seemed to try to make her forget it by showering gifts and favours on her. Rich though he was, he had never been open-handed; but nothing was too fine for his wife, in the way of silks or gems or linen, or whatever else she fancied. Every wandering merchant was welcome at Kerfol, and when the master was called away he never came back without bringing his wife a handsome present—something curious and particular—from Morlaix or Rennes or Quimper. One of the waiting-women gave, in cross-examination, an interesting list of one year's gifts, which I copy. From Morlaix, a carved ivory junk, with Chinamen at the oars, that a strange sailor had brought back as a votive offering for Notre Dame de la Clarté, above Ploumanac'h; from Quimper, an embroidered gown, worked by the nuns of the Assumption; from Rennes, a silver rose that opened and showed an amber Virgin with a crown of garnets; from Morlaix, again, a length of Damascus velvet shot with gold, bought of a Jew from Syria; and for Michaelmas that same year, from Rennes, a neck-let or bracelet of round stones—emeralds and pearls and rubies—strung like beads on a fine gold chain. This was the present that pleased the lady best, the woman said. Later on, as it happened, it was produced at the trial, and appears to have struck the Judges and the public as a curious and valuable jewel.

The very same winter, the Baron absented himself again, this time as far as Bordeaux, and on his return he brought his wife something even odder and prettier than the bracelet. It was a winter evening when he rode up to Kerfol and, walking into the hall, found her sitting by the hearth, her chin on her hand, look-ing into the fire. He carried a velvet box in his hand and, setting it down, lifted the lid and let out a little golden-brown dog.

Anne de Cornault exclaimed with pleasure as the little creature bounded toward her. "Oh, it looks like a bird or a butter-fly!" she cried as she picked it up; and the dog put its paws on her shoulders and looked at her with eyes "like a Christian's." After that she would never have it out of her sight, and petted and talked to it as if it had been a child—as indeed it was the nearest thing to a child she was to know. Yves de Cornault was much pleased with his purchase. The dog had been brought to him by a sailor from an East India merchantman, and the sailor had bought it of a pilgrim in a bazaar at Jaffa, who had stolen it from a nobleman's wife in China: a perfectly permissible thing to do, since the pilgrim was a Christian and the nobleman a heathen doomed to hellfire. Yves de Cornault had paid a long price for the dog, for they were beginning to be in demand at the French court, and the sailor knew he had got hold of a good thing; but Anne's pleasure was so great that, to see her laugh and play with the little animal, her husband would doubtless have given twice the sum.

So far, all the evidence is at one, and the narrative plain sailing; but now the steering becomes difficult. I will try to keep as nearly as possible to Anne's own statements; though toward the end, poor thing. . . .

Well, to go back. The very year after the little brown dog was brought to Kerfol, Yves de Cornault, one winter night, was found dead at the head of a narrow flight of stairs leading down from his wife's rooms to a door opening on the court. It was his wife who found him and gave the alarm, so distracted, poor wretch, with fear and horror—for his blood was all over her—that at first the roused household could not make out what she was saying, and thought she had suddenly gone mad. But there, sure enough, at the top of the stairs lay her husband, stone dead, and head foremost, the blood from his wounds dripping down to the steps below him. He had been dreadfully scratched and gashed about the face and throat, as if with curious pointed weapons; and one of his legs had a deep tear in it which had cut an artery, and probably caused his death. But how did he come there, and who had murdered him?

His wife declared that she had been asleep in her bed, and

hearing his cry had rushed out to find him lying on the stairs; but this was immediately questioned. In the first place, it was proved that from her room she could not have heard the struggle on the stairs, owing to the thickness of the walls and the length of the intervening passage; then it was evident that she had not been in bed and asleep, since she was dressed when she roused the house, and her bed had not been slept in. Moreover, the door at the bottom of the stairs was ajar, and it was noticed by the chaplain (an observant man) that the dress she wore was stained with blood about the knees, and that there were traces of small blood-stained hands low down on the staircase walls, so that it was conjectured that she had really been at the postern-door when her husband fell and, feeling her way up to him in the darkness on her hands and knees, had been stained by his blood dripping down on her. Of course it was argued on the other side that the blood-marks on her dress might have been caused by her kneeling down by her husband when she rushed out of her room; but there was the open door below, and the fact that the finger-marks in the staircase all pointed upward.

The accused held to her statement for the first two days, in spite of its improbability; but on the third day word was brought to her that Hervé de Lanrivain, a young nobleman of the neighbourhood, had been arrested for complicity in the crime. Two or three witnesses thereupon came forward to say that it was known throughout the country that Lanrivain had formerly been on good terms with the lady of Cornault; but that he had been absent from Brittany for over a year, and people had ceased to associate their names. The witnesses who made this statement were not of a very reputable sort. One was an old herb-gatherer suspected of witchcraft, another a drunken clerk from a neighbouring parish, the third a half-witted shepherd who could be made to say anything; and it was clear that the prosecution was not satisfied with its case, and would have liked to find more definite proof of Lanrivain's complicity than the statement of the herb-gatherer, who swore to having seen him climbing the wall of the park on the night of the murder. One way of patching out incomplete proofs in those days was to put some sort of pressure, moral or physical, on the accused person.

It is not clear what pressure was put on Anne de Cornault; but on the third day, when she was brought into court, she "appeared weak and wandering," and after being encouraged to collect herself and speak the truth, on her honour and the wounds of her Blessed Redeemer, she confessed that she had in fact gone down the stairs to speak with Hervé de Lanrivain (who denied everything), and had been surprised there by the sound of her husband's fall. That was better; and the prosecution rubbed its hands with satisfaction. The satisfaction increased when various dependents living at Kerfol were induced to say—with apparent sincerity—that during the year or two preceding his death their master had once more grown uncertain and irascible, and subject to the fits of brooding silence which his household had learned to dread before his second marriage. This seemed to show that things had not been going well at Kerfol; though no one could be found to say that there had been any signs of open disagreement between husband and wife.

Anne de Cornault, when questioned as to her reason for going down at night to open the door to Hervé de Lanrivain, made an answer which must have sent a smile around the court. She said it was because she was lonely and wanted to talk with the young man. Was this the only reason? she was asked; and replied: "Yes, by the Cross over your Lordships' heads." "But why at midnight?" the court asked. "Because I could see him in no other way." I can see the exchange of glances across the ermine collars under the Crucifix.

Anne de Cornault, further questioned, said that her married life had been extremely lonely: "desolate" was the word she used. It was true that her husband seldom spoke harshly to her; but there were days when he did not speak at all. It was true that he had never struck or threatened her; but he kept her like a prisoner at Kerfol, and when he rode away to Morlaix or Quimper or Rennes he set so close a watch on her that she could not pick a flower in the garden without having a waiting-woman at her heels. "I am no Queen, to need such honours," she once said to him; and he had answered that a man who has a treasure does not leave the key in the lock when he goes out. "Then take me with you," she urged; but to this he said that towns were pernicious places, and young wives better off at their own fire-sides.

"But what did you want to say to Hervé de Lanrivain?" the court asked; and she answered: "To ask him to take me away."

"Ah—you confess that you went down to him with adulterous thoughts?"

"No."

"Then why did you want him to take you away?"

"Because I was afraid for my life."

"Of whom were you afraid?"

"Of my husband."

"Why were you afraid of your husband?"

"Because he had strangled my little dog."

Another smile must have passed around the court-room: in days when any nobleman had a right to hang his peasants—and most of them exercised it—pinching a pet animal's wind-pipe was nothing to make a fuss about.

At this point one of the Judges, who appears to have had a certain sympathy for the accused, suggested that she should be allowed to explain herself in her own way; and she thereupon made the following statement.

The first years of her marriage had been lonely; but her husband had not been unkind to her. If she had had a child she would not have been unhappy; but the days were long, and it rained too much.

It was true that her husband, whenever he went away and left her, brought her a handsome present on his return; but this did not make up for the loneliness. At least nothing had, till he brought her the little brown dog from the East: after that she was much less unhappy. Her husband seemed pleased that she was so fond of the dog; he gave her leave to put her jewelled bracelet around its neck, and to keep it always with her.

One day she had fallen asleep in her room, with the dog at her feet, as his habit was. Her feet were bare and resting on his back. Suddenly she was waked by her husband: he stood beside her, smiling not unkindly.

"You look like my great-grandmother, Juliane de Cornault, lying in the chapel with her feet on a little dog," he said.

The analogy sent a chill through her, but she laughed and answered: "Well, when I am dead you must put me beside her, carved in marble, with my dog at my feet."

"Oho—we'll wait and see," he said, laughing also, but with his black brows close together. "The dog is the emblem of fidelity."

"And do you doubt my right to lie with mine at my feet?"

"When I'm in doubt I find out," he answered. "I am an old man," he added, "and people say I make you lead a lonely life. But I swear you shall have your monument if you earn it."

"And I swear to be faithful," she returned, "if only for the sake of having my little dog at my feet."

Not long afterward he went on business to the Quimper Assizes; and while he was away his aunt, the widow of a great nobleman of the duchy, came to spend a night at Kerfol on her way to the *pardon* of Ste. Barbe. She was a woman of piety and consequence, and much respected by Yves de Cornault, and when she proposed to Anne to go with her to Ste. Barbe no one could object, and even the chaplain declared himself in favour of the pilgrimage. So Anne set out for Ste. Barbe, and there for the first time she talked with Hervé de Lanrivain. He had come once or twice to Kerfol with his father, but she had never before exchanged a dozen words with him. They did not talk for more than five minutes now: it was under the chestnuts, as the procession was coming out of the chapel. He said: "I pity you," and she was surprised, for she had not supposed that any one thought her an object of pity. He added: "Call for me when you need me," and she smiled a little, but was glad afterward, and thought often of the meeting.

She confessed to having seen him three times afterward: not more. How or where she would not say—one had the impression that she feared to implicate some one. Their meetings had been rare and brief; and at the last he had told her that he was starting the next day for a foreign country, on a mission which was not without peril and might keep him for many months absent. He asked her for a remembrance, and she had none to give him but the collar about the little dog's neck. She was sorry afterward that she had given it, but he was so unhappy at going that she had not had the courage to refuse.

Her husband was away at the time. When he returned a few days later he picked up the animal to pet it, and noticed that its collar was missing. His wife told him that the dog had lost it in the undergrowth of the park, and that she and her maids had hunted a whole day for it. It was true, she explained to the court, that she had made the maids search for the necklet—they all believed the dog had lost it in the park. . . .

Her husband made no comment, and that evening at supper he was in his usual mood, between good and bad: you could never tell which. He talked a good deal, describing what he had seen and done at Rennes; but now and then he stopped and looked hard at her; and when she went to bed she found her little dog strangled on her pillow. The little thing was dead, but still warm; she stooped to lift it, and her distress turned to horror when she discovered that it had been strangled by twisting twice round its throat the necklet she had given to Lanrivain.

The next morning at dawn she buried the dog in the garden, and hid the necklet in her breast. She said nothing to her husband, then or later, and he said nothing to her; but that day he had a peasant hanged for stealing a faggot in the park, and the next day he nearly beat to death a young horse he was breaking.

Winter set in, and the short days passed, and the long nights, one by one; and she heard nothing of Hervé de Lanrivain. It might be that her husband had killed him; or merely that he had been robbed of the necklet. Day after day by the hearth among the spinning maids, night after night alone on her bed, she wondered and trembled. Sometimes at table her husband looked across at her and smiled; and then she felt sure that Lanrivain was dead. She dared not try to get news of him, for she was sure her husband would find out if she did: she had an idea that he could find out anything. Even when a witch-woman who was a noted seer, and could show you the whole world in her crystal, came to the castle for a night's shelter, and the maids flocked to her, Anne held back.

The winter was long and black and rainy. One day, in Yves de

Cornault's absence, some gypsies came to Kerfol with a troop of performing dogs. Anne bought the smallest and cleverest, a white dog with a feathery coat and one blue and one brown eye. It seemed to have been ill-treated by the gypsies, and clung to her plaintively when she took it from them. That evening her husband came back, and when she went to bed she found the dog strangled on her pillow.

After that she said to herself that she would never have another dog; but one bitter cold evening a poor lean greyhound was found whining at the castle-gate, and she took him in and forbade the maids to speak of him to her husband. She hid him in a room that no one went to, smuggled food to him from her own plate, made him a warm bed to lie on and petted him like a child.

Yves de Cornault came home, and the next day she found the greyhound strangled on her pillow. She wept in secret, but said nothing, and resolved that even if she met a dog dying of hunger she would never bring him into the castle; but one day she found a young sheep-dog, a brindled puppy with good blue eyes, lying with a broken leg in the snow of the park. Yves de Cornault was at Rennes, and she brought the dog in, warmed and fed it, tied up its leg and hid it in the castle till her husband's return. The day before, she gave it to a peasant woman who lived a long way off, and paid her handsomely to care for it and say nothing; but that night she heard a whining and scratching at her door, and when she opened it the lame puppy, drenched and shivering, jumped up on her with little sobbing barks. She hid him in her bed, and the next morning was about to have him taken back to the peasant woman when she heard her husband ride into the court. She shut the dog in a chest, and went down to receive him. An hour or two later, when she returned to her room, the puppy lay strangled on her pillow. . . .

After that she dared not make a pet of any other dog; and her loneliness became almost unendurable. Sometimes, when she crossed the court of the castle, and thought no one was looking, she stopped to pat the old pointer at the gate. But one day as she was caressing him her husband came out of the chapel; and the next day the old dog was gone. . . .

This curious narrative was not told in one sitting of the court, or received without impatience and incredulous comment. It was plain that the Judges were surprised by its puerility, and that it did not help the accused in the eyes of the public. It was an odd tale, certainly; but what did it prove? That Yves de Cornault disliked dogs, and that his wife, to gratify her own fancy, persistently ignored this dislike. As for pleading this trivial disagreement as an excuse for her relations—whatever their nature—with her supposed accomplice, the argument was so absurd that her own lawyer manifestly regretted having let her make use of it, and tried several times to cut short her story. But she went on to the end, with a kind of hypnotized insistence, as though the scenes she evoked were so real to her that she had forgotten where she was and imagined herself to be re-living them.

At length the Judge who had previously shown a certain kindness to her said (leaning forward a little, one may suppose, from his row of dozing colleagues): "Then you would have us believe that you murdered your husband because he would not let you keep a pet dog?"

"I did not murder my husband."

"Who did, then? Hervé de Lanrivain?"

"No."

"Who then? Can you tell us?"

"Yes, I can tell you. The dogs—" At that point she was carried out of the court in a swoon.

It was evident that her lawyer tried to get her to abandon this line of defense. Possibly her explanation, whatever it was, had seemed convincing when she poured it out to him in the heat of their first private colloquy; but now that it was exposed to the cold daylight of judicial scrutiny, and the banter of the town, he was thoroughly ashamed of it, and would have sacrificed her without a scruple to save his professional reputation. But the obstinate Judge—who perhaps, after all, was more inquisitive than kindly—evidently wanted to hear the story out, and she was ordered, the next day, to continue her deposition.

She said that after the disappearance of the old watch-dog

nothing particular happened for a month or two. Her husband was much as usual: she did not remember any special incident. But one evening a pedlar woman came to the castle and was selling trinkets to the maids. She had no heart for trinkets, but she stood looking on while the women made their choice. And then, she did not know how, but the pedlar coaxed her into buying for herself an odd pear-shaped pomander with a strong scent in it—she had once seen something of the kind on a gypsy woman. She had no desire for the pomander, and did not know why she had bought it. The pedlar said that whoever wore it had the power to read the future; but she did not really believe that, or care much either. However, she bought the thing and took it up to her room, where she sat turning it about in her hand. Then the strange scent attracted her and she began to wonder what kind of spice was in the box. She opened it and found a grey bean rolled in a strip of paper; and on the paper she saw a sign she knew, and a message from Hervé de Lanrivain, saying that he was at home again and would be at the door in the court that night after the moon had set. . . .

She burned the paper and sat down to think. It was nightfall, and her husband was at home. . . . She had no way of warning Lanrivain, and there was nothing to do but to wait. . . .

At this point I fancy the drowsy court-room beginning to wake up. Even to the oldest hand on the bench there must have been a certain relish in picturing the feelings of a woman on receiving such a message at nightfall from a man living twenty miles away, to whom she had no means of sending a warning. . . .

She was not a clever woman, I imagine; and as the first result of her cogitation she appears to have made the mistake of being, that evening, too kind to her husband. She could not ply him with wine, according to the traditional expedient, for though he drank heavily at times he had a strong head; and when he drank beyond its strength it was because he chose to, and not because a woman coaxed him. Not his wife, at any rate—she was an old story by now. As I read the case, I fancy there was no feeling for her left in him but the hatred occasioned by his supposed dishonour.

At any rate, she tried to call up her old graces; but early in the evening he complained of pains and fever, and left the hall to go up to the closet where he sometimes slept. His servant carried him a cup of hot wine, and brought back word that he was sleeping and not to be disturbed; and an hour later, when Anne lifted the tapestry and listened at his door, she heard his loud regular breathing. She thought it might be a feint, and stayed a long time barefooted in the passage, her ear to the crack; but the breathing went on too steadily and naturally to be other than that of a man in a sound sleep. She crept back to her room reassured, and stood in the window watching the moon set through the trees of the park. The sky was misty and starless, and after the moon went down the night was black as pitch. She knew the time had come, and stole along the passage, past her husband's door—where she stopped again to listen to his breathing—to the top of the stairs. There she paused a moment, and assured herself that no one was following her; then she began to go down the stairs in the darkness. They were so steep and winding that she had to go very slowly, for fear of stumbling. Her one thought was to get the door unbolted, tell Lanrivain to make his escape, and hasten back to her room. She had tried the bolt earlier in the evening, and managed to put a little grease on it; but nevertheless, when she drew it, it gave a squeak . . . not loud, but it made her heart stop; and the next minute, overhead, she heard a noise. . . .

"What noise?" the prosecution interposed.

"My husband's voice calling out my name and cursing me."

"What did you hear after that?"

"A terrible scream and a fall."

"Where was Hervé de Lanrivain at this time?"

"He was standing outside in the court. I just made him out in the darkness. I told him for God's sake to go, and then I pushed the door shut."

"What did you do next?"

"I stood at the foot of the stairs and listened."

"What did you hear?"

"I heard dogs snarling and panting." (Visible discouragement of the bench, boredom of the public, and exasperation of the lawyer for the defense. Dogs again—! But the inquisitive Judge insisted.)

"What dogs?"

She bent her head and spoke so low that she had to be told to repeat her answer: "I don't know."

"How do you mean—you don't know?"

"I don't know what dogs. . . ."

The Judge again intervened: "Try to tell us exactly what happened. How long did you remain at the foot of the stairs?"

"Only a few minutes."

"And what was going on meanwhile overhead?"

"The dogs kept on snarling and panting. Once or twice he cried out. I think he moaned once. Then he was quiet."

"Then what happened?"

"Then I heard a sound like the noise of a pack when the wolf is thrown to them—gulping and lapping."

(There was a groan of disgust and repulsion through the court, and another attempted intervention by the distracted lawyer. But the inquisitive Judge was still inquisitive.)

"And all the while you did not go up?"

"Yes—I went up then—to drive them off."

"The dogs?"

"Yes."

"Well—?"

"When I got there it was quite dark. I found my husband's flint and steel and struck a spark. I saw him lying there. He was dead."

"And the dogs?"

"The dogs were gone."

"Gone—where to?"

"I don't know. There was no way out—and there were no dogs at Kerfol."

She straightened herself to her full height, threw her arms above her head, and fell down on the stone floor with a long scream. There was a moment of confusion in the court-room. Some one on the bench was heard to say: "This is clearly a case for the ecclesiastical authorities"—and the prisoner's lawyer doubtless jumped at the suggestion.

After this, the trial loses itself in a maze of cross-questioning and squabbling. Every witness who was called corroborated Anne de Cornault's statement that there were no dogs at Kerfol: had been none for several months. The master of the house had taken a dislike to dogs, there was no denying it. But, on the other hand, at the inquest, there had been long and bitter discussions as to the nature of the dead man's wounds. One of the surgeons called in had spoken of marks that looked like bites. The suggestion of witchcraft was revived, and the opposing lawyers hurled tomes of necromancy at each other.

At last Anne de Cornault was brought back into court—at the instance of the same Judge—and asked if she knew where the dogs she spoke of could have come from. On the body of her Redeemer she swore that she did not. Then the Judge put his final question: "If the dogs you think you heard had been known to you, do you think you would have recognized them by their barking?"

"Yes."

"Did you recognize them?"

"Yes."

"What dogs do you take them to have been?"

"My dead dogs," she said in a whisper. . . . She was taken out of court, not to reappear there again. There was some kind of ecclesiastical investigation, and the end of the business was that the Judges disagreed with each other, and with the ecclesiastical committee, and that Anne de Cornault was finally handed over to the keeping of her husband's family, who shut her up in the keep of Kerfol, where she is said to have died many years later, a harmless mad-woman.

So ends her story. As for that of Hervé de Lanrivain, I had only to apply to his collateral descendant for its subsequent details. The evidence against the young man being insufficient, and his family influence in the duchy considerable, he was set free, and left soon afterward for Paris. He was probably in no mood for a worldly life, and he appears to have come almost immediately under the influence of the famous M. Arnauld d'Andilly and the gentlemen of Port Royal. A year or two later he was received into their Order, and without achieving any particular distinction he followed its good and evil fortunes till his death some twenty years later. Lanrivain showed me a portrait of him by a pupil of Philippe de Champaigne: sad eyes, an impulsive mouth and a narrow brow. Poor Hervé de Lanrivain: it was a grey ending. Yet as I looked at his stiff and sallow effigy, in the dark dress of the Jansenists, I almost found myself envying his fate. After all, in the course of his life two great things had happened to him: he had loved romantically, and he must have talked with Pascal. . . .

Ruth Rendell
(b. 1930)

RUTH RENDELL, who became Baroness Rendell of Babergh in 1997, is best known for her crime and suspense fiction. Since *From Doon with Death* (1964), she has written over twenty novels featuring Inspector Wexford plus over forty other books, including several superior suspense novels under the alias Barbara Vine. One of these, *A Fatal Inversion*, not only won the Crime Writers' Association Gold Dagger Award in 1987, it also went on to win the unique Dagger of Daggers Award during the Association's 50th celebration year. She has in fact won many awards, including the prestigious Edgar, first for her short story "The Fallen Curtain" in 1975 and then for her Barbara Vine novel, *A Dark Adapted Eye,* in 1987. Amidst all this splendor it is easy to overlook that she has also written several supernatural stories, ranging from the overtly ghostly "The Haunting of Shawley Rectory" (1979) to the rather more subtle "The Green Road," first published in *Ellery Queen's Mystery Magazine* for 1 January 1981.

The Green Road

There used to be, not long ago, a London suburban-line rail-way running up from Finsbury Park to Highgate, and farther than that for all I know. They closed it down before I went to live at Highgate and at some point they took up the sleepers and the rails. But the track remains and a very strange and interesting track it is. There are people living in the vicinity of the old line who say they can still hear, at night and when the wind is right, the sound of a train pulling up the slope to Highgate, and before it comes into the old disused station, giving its long, melancholy, hooting call. A ghost train, presumably, on rails that have long been lifted and removed.

But this is not a ghost story. Who could conceive of the ghost, not of a person but of a place, and that place having no existence in the natural world? Who could suppose anything of a supernatural or paranormal kind happening to a man like myself, who is quite unimaginative and not observant at all?

An observant person, for instance, could hardly have lived for three years only two minutes from the old station without knowing of the existence of the line. Day after day, on my way to the Underground, I passed it, glanced down unseeing at the weed-grown platforms, the broken canopies. Where did I suppose those trees were growing—rowans and Spanish chestnuts and limes that drop their sticky black juice like tar—that waved their branches in a long avenue high up in the air? What did I imagine that occasionally glimpsed valley was, lying between suburban back gardens?

You may enter or leave the line at the bridges where there are always places for scrambling up or down, and at some actual steps, much overgrown, and gates or at least gateposts. I had been walking under or over these bridges without ever asking myself what those bridges carried or crossed. It never even, I am sorry to say, occurred to me that there were rather a lot of bridges for a part of London where the only railway line, the Underground, ran deep in the bowels of the earth. I didn't think about them. As I walked under one of the brown-brick tunnels I didn't look up to question its presence or ever once glance over a parapet.

It was Arthur Kestrell who told me about the line, one evening while I was in his house.

Arthur was a novelist. I write "was," not because he has abandoned his profession for some other, but because he is dead. I am not even sure whether one would call his books novels. They truly belong in that curious category, a fairly popular genre, that is an amalgam of science fiction, fairy tale, and horror fantasy.

But Arthur, who used the pseudonym of Blaise Fastnet, was no Mervyn Peake and no Lovecraft either. Not that I had read any of his books at the time of which I am writing. But Elizabeth, my wife, had. Arthur used sometimes to give us one of them on publication, duly inscribed and handed to us, presented indeed, with the air of something very precious and uniquely desirable being bestowed.

I couldn't bring myself to read them. The titles alone were enough to repel me: *Kallinarth, the Cloudling; The Quest of Kallinarth; Lord of Quephanda; The Grail-Seeker's Guerdon,* and so forth. But I used somehow, without actually lying, to give Arthur the impression that I had read his latest, or I think I did. Perhaps, in fact, he saw through this, for he never inquired if I had enjoyed it or had any criticisms to make. Liz said they were "fun," and sometimes—with kindly intent, I know—would refer to an incident or portion of dialogue in one of the books in Arthur's presence.

"As Kallinarth might have said," she would say, or "Weren't those the flowers Kallinarth picked for Valaquen when she woke from her long sleep?"

This sort of thing only had the effect of making poor Arthur blush and look embarrassed. I believe that Arthur Kestrell was convinced in his heart that he was writing great literature, never perhaps to be recognized as such in his lifetime but for the appreciation of posterity. Liz, privately to me, used to call him "the poor man's Tolkien."

He suffered from periods of black and profound depression. When these came upon him he couldn't write or read or even bring himself to go out on those marathon walks ranging across north London which he dearly loved when he was well. He would shut himself up in his Gothic house in that district where Highgate and Crouch End merge, and there he would hide and suffer and pace the floors, not answering the door, still less the telephone until, after five or six days or more, the mood of wretched despair had passed.

His books were never reviewed in the press. How it comes about that some authors' work never receives the attention of the critics is a mystery, but the implication, of course, is that it is beneath their notice. This ignoring of a new publication, this bland passing over with neither a smile nor a sneer, implies that the author's work is a mere commercially motivated repetition of his last book, a slight variation on a tried and lucrative theme, another stereotyped bubbler in a long line of profitable potboilers. Arthur, I believe, took it hard. Not that he told me so. But soon after Liz had scanned the papers for even a solitary line to announce a new Fastnet novel, one of these depressions of his would settle on him and he would go into hiding behind his gray, crenelated walls.

Emerging, he possessed for a while a kind of slow cheerfulness combined with a dogged attitude to life. It was always a pleasure to be with him, if nothing else than for the experience of his powerful and strange imagination whose vividness colored those books of his, and in conversation gave an exotic slant to the observations he made and the opinions he uttered.

London, he always insisted, was a curious, glamorous, and sinister city, hung on slopes and valleys in the north of the world. Did I not understand the charm it held for foreigners who thought of it with wistfulness as a gray Eldorado?

I who had been born in it couldn't see its wonders, its contrasts, its wickednesses.

In summer Arthur got me to walk with him to Marx's tomb, to the house where Housman wrote *A Shropshire Lad,* to the pond in the Vale of Health where Shelley sailed boats. We walked the Heath and we walked the urban woodlands and then one day, when I complained that there was nowhere left to go, Arthur told me about the track where the railway line had used to be. A long green lane, he said, like a country lane, four and a half miles of it, and smiling in his cautious way, he told me where it went. Over Northwood Road, over Stanhope Road, under Crouch End Hill, over Vicarage Road, under Crouch Hill, under Mount View, over Mount Pleasant Villas, over Stapleton Hall, under Upper Tollington Park, over Oxford Road, under Stroud Green Road, and so to the station at Finsbury Park.

"How do you get onto it?" I said.

"At any of the bridges. Or at Holmesdale Road. You can get onto it from the end of my garden."

"Right," I said. "Let's go. It's a lovely day."

"There'll be crowds of people on a Saturday," said Arthur. "The sun will be bright like fire and there'll be hordes of wild people and their bounding dogs and their children with music machines and tinned drinks." This was the way Arthur talked, the words juicily or dreamily enunciated. "You want to go up there when it's quiet, at twilight, at dusk, when the air is lilac and you can smell the bitter scent of the tansy."

"Tomorrow night then. I'll bring Liz and we'll call for you and you can take us up there."

But on the following night when we called at Arthur's house and stood under the stone archway of the porch and rang his bell, there was no answer. I stepped back and looked up at the narrow latticed windows, shaped like inverted shields. This was something which, in these circumstances, I had never done before. Arthur's face looked back at me, blurred and made vague by the dark, diamond-paned glass, but unmistakably his small wizened face, pale and with its short sparse beard.

It is a disconcerting thing to be looked at like this by a dear friend who returns your smile and your mouthed greeting with a dead, blank, and unrecognizing stare. I suppose I knew then that poor Arthur wasn't quite sane any more. Certainly Liz and I both knew that he had entered one of his depressions and that it was useless to expect him to let us in.

We went off home, abandoning the idea of an exploration of the track that evening. But on the following day, work being rather slack at that time of the year, I found myself leaving the office early and getting out of the tube train at Highgate at half-past four. Liz, I knew, would be out. On an impulse, I crossed the street and turned into Holmesdale Road. Many a time, walking there before, I had noticed what seemed an unexpectedly rural meadow lying to the north of the street, a meadow overshadowed by broad trees, though no more than fifty yards from the roar and stench of the Archway Road. Now I understood what it was. I walked down the slope, turned southeastward where the meadow narrowed and came onto a grassy lane.

It was about the width of an English country lane and it was bordered by hedges of buddleia on which peacock and small tortoiseshell butterflies basked. And I might have felt myself truly in the country had it not been for the backs of houses glimpsed all the time between the long leaves and the purple spires of the buddleia bushes. Arthur's lilac hour had not yet come. It was windless sunshine up on the broad green track, the clear white light of a sun many hours yet from setting. But there was a wonderful warm and rural, or perhaps I should say pastoral, atmosphere about the place. I need Arthur's gift for words and Arthur's imagination to describe it properly and that I don't have. I can only say that there seemed, up there, to be a suspension of time and also of the hurrying, frenzied bustle, the rage to live, that I had just climbed up out of.

I went over the bridge at Northwood Road and over the bridge at Stanhope Road, feeling ashamed of myself for having so often walked unquestioningly *under* them. Soon the line began to descend, to become a valley rather than a causeway, with embankments on either side on which grew small delicate birch trees and the rosebay willow herb and the giant hogweed. But there were no tansy flowers, as far as I could see. These are bright yellow double daisies borne in clusters on long stems and they have the same sort of smell as chrysanthemums. For all I know, they may be a sort of chrysanthemum or belong to that family. Anyway, I couldn't see any or any lilac, but perhaps Arthur hadn't meant that and in any case it wouldn't be in bloom in July.

I went as far as Crouch End Hill that first time and then I walked home by road. If I've given the impression there were no people on the line, this wasn't so. I passed a couple of women walking a labrador, two boys with bikes, and a little girl in school uniform eating a choc ice.

Liz was intrigued to hear where I had been but rather cross that I hadn't waited until she could come too. So that evening, after we had had our meal, we walked along the line the way and the distance I had been earlier, and the next night we ventured into the longer section. A tunnel blocked up with barbed wire prevented us from getting quite to the end, but we covered nearly all of it and told each other we very likely hadn't missed much by this defeat.

The pastoral atmosphere disappeared after Crouch End Hill. Here there was an old station, the platforms alone still remaining, and under the bridge someone had dumped an old feather mattress—or plucked a dozen geese. The line became a rubbish dump for a hundred yards or so and then widened out into children's playgrounds with murals—and graffiti—on the old brick walls.

Liz looked back at the green valley. "What you gain on the swings," she said, "you lose on the roundabouts." A child in a rope seat swung past us, shrieking, nearly knocking us over.

All the prettiness and the atmosphere I have tried to describe was in that first section, Highgate station to Crouch End Hill. The next time I saw Arthur, when he was back in the world again, I told him we had explored the whole length of the line. He became quite excited.

"Have you now? All of it? It's beautiful, isn't it? Did you see the foxgloves? There must be a mile of foxgloves up there. And the mimosa? You wouldn't suppose mimosa could stand an English winter and I don't know of anywhere it grows, but it flourishes up there. It's sheltered, you see, sheltered from all the frost and the harsh winds."

Arthur spoke wistfully as if the frost and harsh winds were more metaphorical than actual, the coldness of life and fate and time rather than of climate. I didn't argue with him about the mimosa, though I had no doubt at all that he was mistaken. The line up there was exposed, not sheltered, and even if it had been sheltered, even if it had been in Cornwall or the warm Scilly Isles, it would still have been too cold for mimosa to survive. Foxgloves were another matter, though I hadn't seen any, only the hogweed with its bracts of dirty white flowers, garlic mustard and marestail, burdock and rosebay, and the pale leathery leaves of the coltsfoot. As the track grew rural again, past Mount View, hawthorn bushes, not mimosa, grew on the embankment slopes.

"It belongs to Haringey Council." Arthur's voice was always vibrant with expression and now it had become a drawl of scorn and contempt. "They want to build houses on it. They want to plaster it with a great red sprawl of council houses, a disfiguring red naevus." Poor Arthur's writing may not have been the effusion of genius he seemed to believe, but he certainly had a gift for the spoken word.

That August his annual novel was due to appear. Liz had been given an advance copy and had duly read it. Very much the same old thing, she said to me—Kallinarth, the hero-king in his realm composed of cloud; Valaquen, the maiden who sleeps, existing only in a dream life, until all evil has gone out of the world; Xadatel and Finrael, wizard and warrior, heavenly twins. The title this time was *The Fountains of Zond.*

Arthur came to dinner with us soon after Liz had read it. We had three other guests, and while we were having our coffee and brandy I happened to say that I was sorry not to have any drambuie as I knew he was particularly fond of it.

Liz said, "We ought to have Xadatel here, Arthur, to magic you some out of the fountains of Zond."

It was a harmless, even a rather sympathetic, remark. It showed she knew Arthur's work and was conversant with the properties of these miraculous fountains which apparently produced nectar, fabulous elixirs, or whatever was desired at a word from the wizard. Arthur, however, flushed and looked deeply offended. And afterward, in the light of what happened, Liz endlessly reproached herself for what she had said.

"How were you to know?" I asked.

"I should have known. I should have understood how serious and intense he was about his work. The fountains produced— well, holy waters, you see, and I talked about it making drambuie. Oh, I know it's absurd, but what he wrote meant everything to him. The same passion and inspiration, and muse if you like, affected Shakespeare and Arthur Kestrell—it's just the end product that's different."

Arthur, when she had made the remark about the fountains, had said very stiffly, "I'm afraid you're not very sensitive to imaginative literature, Elizabeth," and he left the party early. Liz and I were both rather cross at the time and Liz said she was sure Tolkien wouldn't have minded if someone had made a gentle joke to him about Frodo.

A week or so after this there was a story in the evening paper to the effect that the Minister for the Environment had finally decided to forbid Haringey's plans for putting council housing on the old railway line. The Parkland Walk, as the newspaper called it. Four and a half miles of a disused branch of the London and North-Eastern Railway, was the way it was described, from Finsbury Park to Highgate and at one time serving Alexandra Palace. It was to remain in perpetuity a walking place. The paper mentioned wild life inhabiting the environs of the line, including foxes. Liz and I said we would go up there one evening in the autumn and see if we could see a fox. We never did go. I had reasons for not going near the place, but when we planned it I didn't know I had things to fear.

This was August, the end of August. The weather, with its English vagaries, had suddenly become very cold, more like November with north winds blowing; but in the last days of the month the warmth and the blue skies came back. We had received a formal thank-you note for that dinner from Arthur, a few chilly lines written for politeness' sake, but since then neither sight nor sound of him.

The Fountains of Zond had been published, and as was always the case with Arthur's, or Blaise Fastnet's, books, had been ignored by the critics. I supposed that one of his depressions would have set in, but nevertheless I thought I should attempt to see him and patch up this breach between us. On September first, a Saturday, I set off in the afternoon to walk along the old railway line to his house.

I phoned first, but there was no answer. It was a beautiful afternoon and Arthur might well have been sitting in his garden where he couldn't hear the phone. It was the first time I had ever walked to his house by this route, though it was shorter and more direct than by road, and the first time I had been up on the Parkland Walk on a Saturday. I soon saw what he had meant about the crowds who used it at the weekends. There were teenagers with transistors, giggling schoolgirls, gangs of slouching youths, mobs of children, courting couples, middle-aged picnickers. At Northwood Road boys and girls were leaning against the parapet of the bridge, some with guitars, one with a drum, making enough noise for a hundred.

I remember that as I walked along, unable because of the noise and the press of people to appreciate nature or the view, that I turned my thoughts concentratedly on Arthur Kestrell. And I realized quite suddenly that although I thought of him as a close friend and liked him and enjoyed his company, I had never even tried to enter into his feelings or to understand him. If I had not actually laughed at his books, I had treated them in a light-hearted cavalier way, almost with contempt. I hadn't bothered to read a single one of them, a single page of one of them.

And it seemed to me, as I strolled along that grassy path toward the Stanhope Road bridge, that it must be a terrible thing to pour all your life and soul and energy and passion into works that are remaindered in the bookshops, ignored by the critics, dismissed by paperback publishers, and taken off library shelves only by those who are attracted by the jackets and are seeking escape.

I resolved there and then to read every one of Arthur's books that we had. I made a kind of vow to myself to show an interest in them to Arthur, to make him discuss them with me. And so fired was I by this resolve that I determined to start at once, the moment I saw Arthur. I would begin by apologizing for Liz and then I would tell him (without revealing, of course, that I had so far read nothing of his) that I intended to make my way carefully through all his books, treating them as an oeuvre, beginning with *Kallinarth, the Cloudling* and progressing through all fifteen, or however many there were, up to *The Fountains of Zond*. He might think this was sarcasm, but he wouldn't keep that up when he saw I was sincere. My enthusiasm might do him positive good; it might help cure those terrible depressions which lately had seemed to come more frequently.

Arthur's house stood on this side, the Highgate side, of Crouch End Hill. You couldn't see it from the line, though you could get onto the line from it. This was because the line had by then entered its valley out of which you had to climb into Crescent Road before the Crouch End Hill bridge. I climbed up and walked back and rang Arthur's bell but got no answer. So I looked up at those Gothic lattices as I had done on the day Liz was with me and though I didn't see Arthur's face this time, I was sure I saw a curtain move. I called up to him, something I had never done before, but I had never felt it mattered before, I had never previously had this sense of urgency and importance in connection with Arthur.

"Let me in, Arthur," I called to him. "I want to see you. Don't hide yourself, there's a good chap. This is important."

There was no sound, no further twitch of the curtain. I rang again and banged on the door. The house seemed still and wary, waiting for me to go away.

"All right," I said through the letterbox. "Be like that. But I'm coming back. I'll go for a bit of a walk and then I'll come back and I'll expect you to let me in."

I went back down on to the line, meeting the musicians from Northwood bridge who were marching in the Finsbury Park direction, banging their drum and joined now by two West Indian boys with zithers. A child had been stung by a bee that was on one of the buddleias and an alsatian and a yellow labrador were fighting under the bridge. I began to walk quickly toward Stanhope Road, deciding to ring Arthur as soon as I got home, and to keep on ringing until he answered.

Why was I suddenly so determined to see him, to break in on him, to make him know that I understood? I don't know why and I suppose I never will know, but this was all part of it, having some definite connection, I think, with what happened. It was as if, for those moments, perhaps half an hour all told, I became intertwined with Arthur Kestrell, part of his mind almost or he part of mine. He was briefly and for that one time the most important person in my world.

I never saw him again. I didn't go back. Some few yards before the Stanhope bridge, where the line rose once more above the streets, I felt an impulse to look back and see if from there I could see his garden or even seen him in his garden. But the hawthorn, small birches, the endless buddleia grew thick here and higher far than a man's height. I crossed to the right-hand, or northern, side and pushed aside with my arms the long purple flowers and rough dark leaves, sending up into the air a cloud of black-and-orange butterflies.

Instead of the gardens and backs of houses which I expected to see, there stretched before me, long and straight and raised like a causeway, a green road turning northward out of the old line. This debouching occurred, in fact, at my feet. Inadvertently, I had parted the bushes at the very point where a secondary branch left the line, the junction now overgrown with weeds and wild shrubs.

I stood staring at it in wonder. How could it be that I had never noticed it before, that Arthur hadn't mentioned it? Then I remembered that the newspaper story had said something about the line "serving Alexandra Palace." I had assumed this meant the line had gone on to Alexandra Palace after Highgate, but perhaps not, definitely not, for here was a branch line, leading northward, leading straight toward the palace and the park.

I hadn't noticed it, of course, because of the thick barrier of foliage. In winter, when the leaves were gone, it would be apparent for all to see. I decided to walk along it, check that it actually led where I thought it would, and catch a bus from Alexandra Palace home.

The grass underfoot was greener and far less worn than on the main line. This seemed to indicate that fewer people came along here, and I was suddenly aware that I had left the crowds behind. There was no one to be seen, not even in the far distance.

Which was not, in fact, so very far. I was soon wondering how I had got the impression when I first parted those bushes that the branch line was straight and treeless. For tall trees grew on either side of the path, oaks and beeches such as were never seen on the other line, and ahead of me their branches met overhead and their fine frondy twigs interlaced. Around their trunks I at last saw the foxgloves and the tansy Arthur had spoken of, and the farther I went the more the air seemed perfumed with the scent of wild flowers.

The green road—I found myself spontaneously and unaccountably calling this branch line the green road—began to take on the aspect of a grove or avenue and to widen. It was growing late in the afternoon and a mist was settling over London, as often happens after a warm day in late summer or early autumn. The slate roofs, lying a little beneath me, gleamed dully silver through this sleepy, goldshot mist. Perhaps, I thought, I should have the good luck to see a fox.

But I saw nothing, no living thing, not a soul passed me or overtook me, and when I looked back I could see only the smooth grassy causeway stretching back and back, deserted, still, serene and pastoral, with the mist lying in fine streaks beneath and beside it. No birds sang and no breeze ruffled the feather-light, golden, downy, sweet-scented tufts of the mimosa flowers. For, yes, there was mimosa here. I paused and looked at it and marveled.

It grew on either side of the path as vigorously and luxuriantly as it grows by the Mediterranean, the gentle swaying wattle. Its perfume filled the air, and the perfumes of the humbler foxglove and tansy were lost. Did the oaks shelter it from the worst of the frost? Was there by chance some warm spring that flowed under the earth here, in this part of north London where there are many patches of woodland and many green spaces? I picked a tuft of mimosa to take home to Liz, to prove I'd been here and seen it.

I walked for a very long way, it seemed to me, before I finally came into Alexandra Park. I hardly know this park, and apart from passing its gates by car my only experience of it till then had been a visit some years before to take Liz to an exhibition of paintings in the palace. The point in the grounds to which my green road had brought me was somewhere I had never seen before. Nor had I ever previously been aware of this aspect of Alexandra Palace, under whose walls the road led. It was more like Versailles than a Victorian greenhouse (which is how I had always thought of the palace) and in the oblong lakes which flanked the flight of steps before me were playing surely a hundred fountains.

I looked up this flight of steps and saw pillars and arches, a soaring elevation of towers. It was to here then, I thought, right up under the very walls, that the trains had come. People had used the line to come here for shows, for exhibitions, for concerts. I stepped off onto the stone stairs, descended a dozen of them to ground level, and looked out over the park.

London was invisible, swallowed now by the white mist which lay over it like cirrus. The effect was curious, something I had never seen before while standing on solid ground. It was the view you get from an airplane when it has passed above the clouds and you look down to the ruffled tops of them. I began to walk down over wide green lawns. Still there were no people, but I had guessed it likely that they locked the gates on pedestrians after a certain hour.

However, when I reached the foot of the hill the iron gates between their Ionic columns were still open. I came out into a street I had never been in before, in a district I didn't know, and there found a taxi which took me home. On the journey I remember thinking to myself that I would ask Arthur about this curious terminus to the branch line and get him to tell me something of the history of all that grandeur of lawns and pillars and ornamental water.

I was never to have the opportunity of asking him anything. Arthur's charwoman, letting herself into the Gothic house on Monday morning, found him hanging from one of the beams in his writing room. He had been dead, it was thought, since some-time on Saturday afternoon. There was a suicide note, written in Arthur's precise hand and in Arthur's wordy pedantic fashion: *Bitter disappointment at my continual failure to reach a sensi-tive audience or to attract understanding of my writings has led me to put an end to my life. There is no one who will suffer undue distress at my death. Existence has become insupportable and I cannot contemplate further sequences of despair.*

Elizabeth told me that in her opinion it was the only review she had ever known him to have which provoked poor Arthur to kill himself. She had found it in the paper herself on that Saturday afternoon while I was out and had read it with a sick feeling of dread for how Arthur would react. The critic, with perhaps nothing else at that moment to get his teeth into, had torn *The Fountains of Zond* apart and spat out the shreds.

He began by admitting he would not normally have wasted his typewriter ribbon (as he put it) on sci-fi fantasy trash, but he felt the time had come to campaign against the flooding of the fiction market with such stuff. Especially was it necessary in a case like this where a flavor of epic grandeur was given to the action, where there was much so-called "fine writing" and where heroic motives were attributed to stereotyped characters, so that innocent or young readers might be misled into believing that this was "good" or "valuable" literature.

There was a lot more in the same vein. With exquisite cruelty the reviewer had taken character after character and dissected each, holding the exposed parts up to stinging ridicule. If Arthur had read it, and it seemed likely that he had, it was no wonder he had felt he couldn't bear another hour of existence.

All this deflected my thoughts, of course, away from the green road. I had told Liz about it before we heard of Arthur's death and we had intended to go up there together; yet somehow, after that dreadful discovery in the writing room of the Gothic house, we couldn't bring ourselves to walk so close by his garden or to visit those places where he would have loved to take us. I kept wondering if I had really seen that curtain move when I had knocked at his door or if it had only been a flicker of the sunlight. Had he already been dead by then? Or had he perhaps been contemplating what he was about to do? Just as Liz reproached herself for that remark about the fountains, so I reproached myself for walking away, for not hammering on that door, breaking a window, getting in by some means. Yet, as I said to her, how could anyone have known?

In October I did go up on to the old railway line. Someone we knew living in Milton Road wanted to borrow my electric drill, and I walked over there with it, going down from the Stanhope Road bridge on the southern side. Peter offered to drive me back but it was a warm afternoon, the sun on the point of setting, and I had a fancy to look at the branch line once more. I climbed up on to the bridge and turned eastward.

For the most part the leaves were still on the bushes and trees, though turning red and gold. I calculated pretty well where the turnoff was and pushed my way through the buddleias. Or I thought I had calculated well, but when I stood on the ridge beyond the hedge all I could see were the gardens of Stanhope Road and Avenue Road. I had come to the wrong place, I thought, it must be farther along. But not much farther, for very soon what had been a causeway became a valley. My branch line hadn't turned out of that sort of terrain, I hadn't had to climb to reach it.

Had I made a mistake and had it been on the *other* side of the Stanhope Road bridge? I turned back, walking slowly, making sorties through the buddleias to look northward, but I couldn't find that turnoff to the branch line anywhere. It seemed to me then that, whatever I thought I remembered, I must in fact have climbed up the embankment to reach it, and the junction must be far nearer the bridge at Crouch End Hill than I had believed. By then it was getting dark. It was too dark to go back, I should have been able to see nothing.

"We'll find it next week," I said to Liz.

She gave me a rather strange look. "I didn't say anything at the time," she said, "because we were both so upset over poor Arthur, but I was talking to someone in the Highgate Society and she said there never was a branch line. The line to Alexandra Palace went on beyond Highgate."

"That's nonsense," I said. "I can assure you I walked along it. Don't you remember my telling you at the time?"

"Are you absolutely sure you couldn't have imagined it?"

"*Imagined it?* You know I haven't any imagination."

Liz laughed. "You're always saying that but I think you have. You're one of the most imaginative people I ever knew."

I said impatiently, "Be that as it may. I walked a good two miles along that line and came out in Alexandra Park, right under the palace, and walked down to Wood Green or Muswell Hill or somewhere and got a cab home. Are you and your Highgate Society friends saying I imagined oak trees and beech trees and mimosa? Look, that'll prove it—I picked a piece of mimosa. I put it in the pocket of my green jacket."

"Your green jacket went to the cleaners last month."

I wasn't prepared to accept that I had imagined or dreamed the green road. But the fact remains that I was never able to find it. Once the leaves were off the trees there was no question of delving about under bushes to hunt for it. The whole northern side of the old railway line lay exposed to the view and the elements and much of its charm was lost. It became what it really always was, nothing more or less than a ridge, a long strip of waste ground running across north London, over Northwood Road, over Stanhope Road, under Crouch End Hill, over Vicarage Road, under Crouch Hill, under Mount View, over Mount Pleasant Villas, over Stapleton Hall, under Upper Tollington Park, over Oxford Road, under Stroud Green Road, and so to the station at Finsbury Park. And nowhere along its length, for I explored every inch, was there a branch line running north to Alexandra Palace.

"You imagined it," said Liz, "and the shock of Arthur dying like that made you think it was real."

"But Arthur wasn't dead then," I said, "or I didn't know he was."

My invention, or whatever it was, of the branch line would have remained one of those mysteries which everyone, I suppose, has in his life—though I can't say I have any others in mine—had it not been for a rather curious and unnerving conversation which took place that winter between Liz and our

friends from Milton Park. In spite of my resolutions made on
that memorable Saturday afternoon, I had never brought myself
to read any of Arthur's books. What now would have been the
point? He was no longer there for me to talk to about them. And
there was another reason. I felt my memory of him might be
spoiled if there was truth in what the critic had said and his
novels were full of false heroics and sham fine writing. Better
feel with whatever poet it was who wrote:

> I wept as I remembered how often thou and I
> Have tired the sun with talking and sent him down the sky.

Liz, however, had had her interest in *The Chronicles of
Kallinarth* revived and had reread every book in the series, passing them on as she finished each to Peter and Jane. That winter
afternoon in the living room at Milton Park the three of them
were full of Kallinarth, cloud country, Valaquen, Xadatel, and it
was they who tired the sun with talking and sent him down the
sky. I sat silent, not taking part at all, but thinking of Arthur
whose house was not far from here and who would have marveled to hear of this detailed knowledge of his work.

I don't know which word of theirs it was that caught me or
what electrifying phrase jolted me out of my reverie so that I
leaned forward, intent. Whatever it was, it had sent a little
shiver through my body. In that warm room I felt suddenly
cold.

"No, it's not in *Kallinarth, the Cloudling,*" Jane was saying.
"It's in *The Quest of Kallinarth.* Kallinarth goes out hunting
early in the morning and he meets Xadatel and Finrael coming
on horseback up the green road to the palace."

"But that's not the first mention of it. In the first book there's
a long description of the avenue where the procession comes up
for Kallinarth to be crowned at the fountains of Zond and—"

"It's in all the books surely," interrupted Peter. "It's his
theme, his *leitmotiv*, the green road with the yellow wattle trees
that leads up to the royal palace of Quephanda—"

"Are you all right, darling?" Liz asked me quickly. "You've
gone as white as a ghost."

"White with boredom," said Peter. "It must be terrible for him, us talking about a book he's never even read."

"Somehow I feel I know it without having read it," I managed to say.

They changed the subject. I didn't take much part in that either, I couldn't. I could only think, it's fantastic, it's absurd, I couldn't have got into his mind or he into mine, that couldn't have happened at the point of his death. Yet what else?

And I kept repeating over and over to myself, he reached his audience, he reached his audience at last.

Jessica Amanda Salmonson
(b. 1950)

JESSICA SALMONSON is an American writer, editor, and book-
seller, who has a prodigious knowledge of the fields of fantasy
and supernatural fiction and, through diligent research, has rescued many lost works from oblivion and rediscovered the
careers of many overlooked writers. She has assembled several
volumes of the supernatural fiction of Harriet Prescott Spofford,
Olivia Howard Dunbar, Sarah Orne Jewett, Julian Hawthorne,
Vincent O'Sullivan, Marjorie Bowen, Georgia Wood Pangborn,
Thomas Burke, and many others. She has also edited several
anthologies, including *Amazons!* (1979), which won the World
Fantasy Award, and *What Did Miss Darrington See?* (1989), a
collection of feminist supernatural stories. Her own writing is no
less prolific and includes the *Tomoe Gozen* oriental fantasy saga
(3 volumes, 1981–84), a series of occult detective stories collected in *Harmless Ghosts* (1990), and a dozen other collections
and chapbooks, their contents ranging from folktales to dark
fantasy. Many of her best stories were reassembled in *The Deep
Museum* (2003), which includes this highly personal story, "The
Apartment," originally published in Salmonson's anthology of
rare ghost stories, *The Haunted Wherry* (1985).

The Apartment

In those, the darkest of my days, I was living in a horrid little suburban town. In past decades it had been the country, and gentle country at that; but it had aged badly. The area had become ugly and crowded by widening streets; filled-to-capacity parking lots in front of squat, wide shopping centers; old farm houses were abandoned, ultimately condemned, and replaced by housing that lacked charm or individuality and was grotesque even when it was new. The most recently added family dwellings consisted of row upon row, street upon street, of mobile homes. Few trees remained, though in my childhood there had been many. There were no longer any dairies or strawberry fields such as I recalled.

It had always been a poor part of the state; but it had had its saving graces in the form of wide spaces, dense woods, and wondrous bogs that the Audubon Society would visit regularly in order to observe rare species of duck or heron—with me, a local and uninvited tyke, tagging after. This rustic setting had the ill luck of reposing exactly halfway between two major urban centers, and of linking those cities by river and rail. Thus it became ideally suited to Industry with a capital I. The strawberry fields and pastures were paved; the bogs were drained; warehousing, aerospace, and military complexes sprung from the ground. Farmers sold out, or were zoned out of business. Population doubled, re-doubled, and doubled again, sprawling and despoiling in all directions.

Such is progress. And I had progressed from a smart-mouthed, dirty-skirted, rowdy little girl to a divorcée whose sexual excesses and perversities certainly had not led to happiness. My life, in short, had deteriorated much as the county where I was born.

Thus, upon a grey afternoon one winter, I sharpened up a carving knife, intending to stab myself in the jugular vein and bleed to death in the bathtub.

The sharpening was a ritual in itself. I drew out the process, savoring the sound of sharpening the blade, and not the least bit certain it would do the job of a razor that I happened not to own.

I had turned off all the electricity, except for a small lamp in the front of my dingy, two-room apartment. I wanted the rooms to be cold, for I did not want to rot very much before discovery. This was vanity. I wanted to look pathetic, drained white as the porcelain tub. I fancied something of my good looks, which in those young years were laudible to some, would linger, causing police and coroner to sense the tragedy of my life, and the loss to the world. This was ego. I had worked it through in my mind like this: If I was dead in a warm room for several days, I should smell and be covered with flies; and in such a case, no one who entered my impromptu tomb would think of the tragedy. Rather, they would be overwhelmed by the putrefaction and think of the tediously sickening job it was to deal with my remains. Hence, the apartment must be kept cold. It was winter, and I should be refrigerated, so to speak.

I know now, of course, that drained, and dead, and lax of muscle, I should have been hideous at all events. But, at the time, the only dead people I had ever seen were in funeral parlors or on the television. I believed it perfectly feasible to be at once dead, and passably good looking.

As you have no doubt surmised; I did not kill myself. Rather, I sat naked in the tub a very long time, knife pressed to throat, too afraid to push it through my skin. I did glance the blade across a wrist, enough to draw a bit of blood, but insufficient to damage tendons or veins. I watched my wrist drip blood onto my belly. I felt fascinated and detached. In a while, I got out of the tub, wrapped my scratched wrist in a bandage, and got dressed. Something in me had determined to start life anew, and I had left that terrible apartment within the week.

I repaired to the city, where, after a slow adjustment and gradual recovery of my peace of mind, I began to live happily in Bohemian society. I wrote poetry for numerous journals, much of it about the agony I no longer felt. I met a woman slightly older than myself who was a potter and a grand companion for coffee in the morning and wine at night. I forgot such things as suburban ugliness and horror.

Perhaps three years later, in a coffeehouse one morning, I overheard a strange conversation at a nearby table. A queer little man obviously delighted in recounting grim happenings to his friends. He was repeating some bit of news he had caught in that morning's paper. It was about a suicide in the town where I was born, so his overloud retelling of the news story caught my attention. Her name was Louisa something-or-other, no one I knew, but I recognized the description of the apartment block: a homely affair that was actually a converted motel. The odd thing was that it was the third suicide in as many years to occur in that same apartment.

I left the coffeehouse before the queer man had finished his version of the events, and I purchased a paper for myself. On the inside page, I established all too certainly that the repeating tragedies had been occurring in the apartment that had once been mine.

I couldn't get it out of my mind. I caught a bus to the sub-urbs—an hour and a half ride—then walked the short distance from the bus stop to my old apartment. I stood outside it a long while, afraid of the sight of it, the memories it brought back to me. As I stood there, I fancied that a white face looked out of the small, dark window. It was my own face! I gasped, wheeled about, and almost ran away. But I gathered my wits, climbed the stoop, pressed the bell, and a small, pale woman came to the door to say, "Yes?"

Her tone was flat and vacant. She was young and probably attractive, but had been so long without sleep, and apparently suffered long bouts of tears, so that her visage was almost frightening.

Then I said, crudely I realized afterward, "I heard about . . . the accident."

The girl tried to close the door. I set my hand against it, not pressing hard, but enough to make her listen a minute.

"I—I used to live here," I said. "Do you live here now?"

"It was my sister's apartment," said the pale woman. "I was living with her. I'm packing to go. The police and reporters were around here all day yesterday, so I had to leave. Please don't drive me away before I get the work done."

"Do you know . . ." I began, stammering, "that others have killed themselves . . . here?"

"If I didn't know it before," she said, somewhat curtly, "I certainly do after this morning's papers, don't you think?"

She finished closing the door.

I stood there a while, not knowing why I'd come, but at length reaching out to turn the doorknob. The girl hadn't locked it. I walked in and she looked over her shoulder at me, not as put off as I might have been in a similar circumstance. She was putting things in boxes.

"Let me help," I said, and took up an empty cardboard box.

She relented, frankly needing company, though not needing any further questions such as police and reporters ask. I couldn't help but look repeatedly at the bathroom door, which was closed. She took as much pity on me as I did upon her; and she asked at last, "How long did you live here?"

"I left about four years ago," I said. "I must have lived here almost two years. I was miserable and lonely the whole time. I nearly killed myself in there." I pointed toward the bathroom. "I thought about it, at least. With a carving knife, no less."

I tried to laugh at myself, but couldn't. The young woman, Betty, became twice as pale.

"They all used knives," she said. "My sister, too. As for me . . ." She rolled back her sleeve and showed me the line of a half-healed scratch. It was not a scar, but one of those "practice" cuts suicides often do experimentally, such as I had done. "I lost my nerve," she said.

"So did I," I said, then asked, "You did it in the tub?"

"Where else."

We hurried with the packing. Betty's father was, she said, driving up with a van, from the south part of the state, to get the things which were Betty's and her sister's. When it was all packed, Betty wanted to get out of the place, as did I. We took the key to the landlady in case Betty's father came while we were gone.

Betty had no car, so we walked several long blocks to a road-side restaurant and sat over the kind of horrid coffee made only in the suburbs, "cooked" coffee rather than steamed, barely drinkable to someone who has spent a few years in the city. We sat there, facing each other across the dull table, as dour a pair of girls as you may imagine.

"It's something in that apartment," said Betty. "It's just too gloomy to live with it, whatever it is."

I said, "I don't think there was anything there when I first moved in. It was ugly, but cheap. A rather giddy young woman had moved out; and she never seemed to experience anything. I met her where I was working at the time, and she was getting married, so I took over the apartment. There was nothing wrong with it at first."

"But . . ." Betty didn't know what to say. She was rather fond of her theory. "But, it does seem haunted now."

"A ghost, you mean?"

"Or ghosts," she said. "There was a sense I had right from the start that there were other people in the place. It was too small for anyone to be hiding anywhere, but the first day when I came to stay with Louisa, I asked her if she didn't already have company. I felt there were three of them. I didn't know why I thought so. Now I think there are four."

"Did you tell the reporters that?"

"Of course not." She grinned sourly. "Anyway, there were only two other women who killed themselves that way—my sister was the third. So four ghosts is an overestimate, don't you think? To tell the truth, I felt like I was a ghost, a fifth one! That's how I felt today at least."

"Do you still feel that you could . . . that you could . . ."

"Kill myself? No. I mean, it's going to take a while getting over what my sister did. We were pretty close. And I found her in the tub like that, sitting in her blood. If I didn't have a reason to feel so depressed before, I certainly do now. All the same, the only way I could kill myself would be if . . . if I kept living there. And it's not related to what my sister did. It's the place itself. I should have made her move out the day I came to stay for a few months! I knew there was something strange."

"I remember," I began, "lying on my bed day after day, rarely eating, rarely even thinking. But I didn't think of blaming the apartment. It was certainly gloomy and dingy and contributed to my depression; but even now, I can't think it was haunted while I was there. I had outside reasons, outside things to deal with. I still deal with them a bit, but I never think of killing myself."

"Maybe it started after you left, then," she said quietly.

"Or while I was there?"

"You think so?"

"I don't know what to think," I said. "I feel somehow responsible for it. I may have impregnated the place with my emotional stress during the two years I lived there. I tell you, I think I was close to mad. But I got hold of myself somehow, I pulled myself out of it at the last possible minute, before I was either dead, or commitable."

"I don't think you should feel responsible," she said.

I said, "I hope you're right."

We walked back to the apartment and saw Betty's father's van parked in front. He wasn't around. The door was still locked.

"He must be off to the landlady's to get the key," said Betty.

But she had guessed wrong. He'd gone around to the back part of the apartment building, apparently to try the back window. While we were standing on the front doorstep, he came around to the front again, a burly man who looked very sad, which was to be expected. When he saw us standing there, he suddenly looked startled, mistaking me, I realized, for his older daughter; for the light was dim. When he realized I was some friend of Betty's—how recent a friend, he could hardly know— his expression changed once more, to a sort of anger that men like to wear when they're sad or afraid.

"Why didn't you open the door when I knocked!" the rough man said sharply.

Betty was used to his abruptness. "I was gone," she said. "I left the spare key with the landlady for you." As she said this, she was using her own key to open the door. Her father came up the steps while answering her statement:

"Nonsense! I saw you looking from the window at me. I went around in back and you looked at me from the bathroom window, too. You must have been standing on something."

We all went inside and started to carry out boxes to the van. At one point, Betty's father had gotten very distraught and tried to avoid us, lest we see his tears. As he was rearranging things deep in the cavity of the van, Betty whispered to me, "How could he have thought such a thing?" Then she answered her own query, "I told you there were ghosts."

I said, "When I was coming up to the place this afternoon, I thought I saw a face look out at me. I supposed it was you, after I saw you. But to tell the truth, the first thing I thought was that . . . that it was me."

Betty nodded as though it made sense to her. Then she went to heft a few more boxed things.

Betty's father agreed to take me home, at Betty's insistence, though it was out of the way and I could have taken a bus. As we all piled into the front of the van and started to drive away, Betty and I were both looking in the big right-hand-door mirror. We both saw it, but neither of us made a comment. I never saw her again, either, despite that I had rather liked her and intended to get in touch a second time. So we were never able to talk of what we saw. It was pretty dark by then, and a single lamp burned in the apartment window—though we had left the place bare. The lamp reminded me grimly of one I had owned at the time of my own depression. But more than the lamp, there were the faces. At both of the front windows, faces watched us driving away. There were five faces in all. Three of them I didn't recognize, though I supposed one to be Betty's sister. Of the two I recognized, one was Betty and the other myself. We were as pale and sorrow-stricken as the ones who had actually killed themselves, the ones who had succeeded. How could we have been with them though we're still alive? It's difficult and painful to ponder. More difficult for me than for Betty has to be the fact that it really does seem to have begun with me. Well, I don't feel I should be punished for it. Some part of my soul obviously *is* being punished, lingering with those other victims of melancholy.

That old row of apartments converted from motel rooms, lacking the least semblance of hominess, were torn down a few years later to make room for a parking lot adjacent to a new shopping mall. In the meantime, there had been no more suicides in that apartment that I ever heard about. For that, at least, I try to feel grateful.

May Sinclair
(1863–1946)

MAY SINCLAIR was born in Rock Ferry, Cheshire, where her father was a wealthy shipowner. He fell on hard times, however, and became an alcoholic, and young May was left to look after her mother and brothers, all of whom had heart problems and died young. Sinclair moved to the outskirts of London, where she remained after her mother's death. She became fascinated by the works of Sigmund Freud, exploring psychological depths in many of her stories. She was also an active suffragette, writing the pamphlet, *Feminism,* in 1912. She joined the Society for Psychical Research and her later work increasingly reflected her fascination for the life beyond. Her strange tales are collected in *Uncanny Stories* (1923) and *The Intercessor* (1931). "The Victim," which for its day has a revolutionary view on its attitude to murder, first appeared in *The Criterion* for October 1922.

The Victim

I

Steven Acroyd, Mr. Greathead's chauffeur, was sulking in the garage.

Everybody was afraid of him. Everybody hated him except Mr. Greathead, his master, and Dorsy, his sweetheart.

And even Dorsy now, after yesterday!

Night had come. On one side the yard gates stood open to the black tunnel of the drive. On the other the high moor rose above the wall, immense, darker than the darkness. Steven's lantern in the open doorway of the garage and Dorsy's lamp in the kitchen window threw a blond twilight into the yard between. From where he sat, slantways on the step of the car, he could see, through the lighted window, the table with the lamp and Dorsy's sewing huddled up in a white heap as she left it just now, when she had jumped up and gone away. Because she was afraid of him.

She had gone straight to Mr. Greathead in his study, and Steven, sulking, had flung himself out into the yard.

He stared into the window, thinking, thinking. Everybody hated him. He could tell by the damned spiteful way they looked at him in the bar of the King's Arms; kind of sideways and slink-eyed, turning their dirty tails and shuffling out of his way.

He had said to Dorsy he'd like to know what he'd done. He'd just dropped in for his glass as usual; he'd looked round and said "Good evening," civil, and the dirty tykes took no more notice of him than if he'd been a toad. Mrs. Oldishaw, Dorsy's aunt, *she* hated him, boiled-ham-face, swelling with spite, shoving his glass at the end of her arm, without speaking, as if he'd been a bloody cockroach.

All because of the thrashing he'd given young Ned Oldishaw. If she didn't want the cub's neck broken she'd better keep him out of mischief. Young Ned knew what he'd get if he came meddling with *his* sweetheart.

It had happened yesterday afternoon, Sunday, when he had gone down with Dorsy to the King's Arms to see her aunt. They were sitting out on the wooden bench against the inn wall when young Ned began it. He could see him now with his arm round Dorsy's neck and his mouth gaping. And Dorsy laughing like a silly fool and the old woman snorting and shaking.

He could hear him. "She's my cousin if she *is* your sweetheart. You can't stop me kissing her." *Couldn't* he!

Why, what did they think? When he'd given up his good job at the Darlington Motor Works to come to Eastthwaite and black Mr. Greathead's boots, chop wood, carry coal and water for him, and drive his shabby secondhand car. Not that he cared what he did so long as he could live in the same house with Dorsy Oldishaw. It wasn't likely he'd sit like a bloody Moses, looking on, while Ned—

To be sure, he had half killed him. He could feel Ned's neck swelling and rising up under the pressure of his hands, his fingers. He had struck him first, flinging him back against the inn wall, then he had pinned him—till the men ran up and dragged him off.

And now they were all against him. Dorsy was against him. She had said she was afraid of him.

"Steven," she had said, "tha med 'a killed him."

"Well—p'r'aps next time he'll knaw better than to coom meddlin' with *my* lass."

"I'm not thy lass, ef tha canna keep thy hands off folks. I should be feared for my life of thee. Ned wurn't doing naw 'arm."

"Ef he doos it again, ef he cooms between thee and me, Dorsy, I shall do 'im in."

"Naw, tha maunna talk that road."

"It's Gawd's truth. Anybody that cooms between thee and me, loove, I shall do 'im in. Ef 'twas thy aunt, I should wring 'er neck, same as I wroong Ned's."

"And ef it was me, Steven?"

"Ef it wur thee, ef tha left me—Aw, doan't tha assk me, Dorsy."

"There—that's 'ow tha scares me."

"But tha' 'astna left me—'tes thy wedding claithes tha'rt making."

"Aye, 'tes my wedding claithes."

She had started fingering the white stuff, looking at it with her head on one side, smiling prettily. Then all of a sudden she had flung it down in a heap and burst out crying. When he tried to comfort her she pushed him off and ran out of the room, to Mr. Greathead.

It must have been half an hour ago and she had not come back yet.

He got up and went through the yard gates into the dark drive. Turning there, he came to the house front and the lighted window of the study. Hidden behind a clump of yew he looked in.

Mr. Greathead had risen from his chair. He was a little old man, shrunk and pinched, with a bowed narrow back and slender neck under his grey hanks of hair.

Dorsy stood before him, facing Steven. The lamplight fell full on her. Her sweet flower-face was flushed. She had been crying.

Mr. Greathead spoke.

"Well, that's my advice," he said. "Think it over, Dorsy, before you do anything."

That night Dorsy packed her boxes, and the next day at noon, when Steven came in for his dinner, she had left the Lodge. She had gone back to her father's house in Garthdale.

She wrote to Steven saying that she had thought it over and found she daren't marry him. She was afraid of him. She would be too unhappy.

II

That was the old man, the old man. He had made her give him up. But for that, Dorsy would never have left him. She would never have thought of it herself. And she would never have got away if he had been there to stop her. It wasn't Ned. Ned was going to marry Nancy Peacock down at Morfe. Ned hadn't done any harm.

It was Mr. Greathead who had come between them. He hated Mr. Greathead.

His hate became a nausea of physical loathing that never ceased. Indoors he served Mr. Greathead as footman and valet, waiting on him at meals, bringing the hot water for his bath, helping him to dress and undress. So that he could never get away from him. When he came to call him in the morning, Steven's stomach heaved at the sight of the shrunken body under the bedclothes, the flushed, pinched face with its peaked, finicking nose upturned, the thin silver tuft of hair pricked up above the pillow's edge. Steven shivered with hate at the sound of the rattling, old-man's cough, and the "shoob-shoob" of the feet shuffling along the flagged passages.

He had once had a feeling of tenderness for Mr. Greathead as the tie that bound him to Dorsy. He even brushed his coat and hat tenderly, as if he loved them. Once Mr. Greathead's small, close smile—the greyish bud of the lower lip pushed out, the upper lip lifted at the corners—and his kind, thin "Thank you, my lad," had made Steven smile back, glad to serve Dorsy's master. And Mr. Greathead would smile again and say, "It does me good to see your bright face, Steven." Now Steven's face writhed in a tight contortion to meet Mr. Greathead's kindliness, while his throat ran dry and his heart shook with hate.

At meal-times from his place by the sideboard he would look on at Mr. Greathead eating, in a long contemplative disgust. He could have snatched the plate away from under the slow, fumbling hands that hovered and hesitated. He would catch words coming into his mind: "He ought to be dead. He ought to be dead." To think that this thing that ought to be dead, this old, shrivelled skin-bag of creaking bones should come between him and Dorsy, should have power to drive Dorsy from him.

One day when he was brushing Mr. Greathead's soft felt hat a paroxysm of hatred gripped him. He hated Mr. Greathead's hat. He took a stick and struck at it again and again; he threw it on the flags and stamped on it, clenching his teeth and drawing in his breath with a sharp hiss. He picked up the hat, looking round furtively, for fear lest Mr. Greathead or Dorsy's successor, Mrs. Blenkiron, should have seen him. He pinched and pulled it back into shape and brushed it carefully and hung it on the stand. He was ashamed, not of his violence, but of its futility.

Nobody but a damned fool, he said to himself, would have done that. He must have been mad.

It wasn't as if he didn't know what he was going to do. He had known ever since the day when Dorsy left him.

"I shan't be myself again till I've done him in," he thought.

He was only waiting till he had planned it out; till he was sure of every detail; till he was fit and cool. There must be no hesitation, no uncertainty at the last minute, above all, no blind, headlong violence. Nobody but a fool would kill in mad rage, and forget things, and be caught and swing for it. Yet that was what they all did. There was always something they hadn't thought of that gave them away.

Steven had thought of everything, even the date, even the weather.

Mr. Greathead was in the habit of going up to London to attend the debates of a learned Society he belonged to that held its meetings in May and November. He always travelled up by the five o'clock train, so that he might go to bed and rest as soon as he arrived. He always stayed for a week and gave his housekeeper a week's holiday. Steven chose a dark, threatening day in November, when Mr. Greathead was going up to his meeting and Mrs. Blenkiron had left Eastthwaite for Morfe by the early morning bus. So that there was nobody in the house but Mr. Greathead and Steven.

Eastthwaite Lodge stands alone, grey, hidden between the shoulder of the moor and the ash-trees of its drive. It is approached by a bridle-path across the moor, a turning off the road that runs from Eastthwaite in Rathdale to Shawe in Westleydale, about a mile from the village and a mile from Hardraw Pass. No tradesmen visited it. Mr. Greathead's letters and his newspapers were shot into a post-box that hung on the ash-tree at the turn.

The hot water laid on in the house was not hot enough for Mr. Greathead's bath, so that every morning, while Mr. Greathead shaved, Steven came to him with a can of boiling water.

Mr. Greathead, dressed in a mauve and grey striped sleeping-suit, stood shaving himself before the looking-glass that hung on the wall beside the great white bath. Steven waited with his hand on the cold tap, watching the bright curved rod of water falling with a thud and a splash.

In the white, stagnant light from the muffed window-pane the knife-blade flame of a small oil-stove flickered queerly. The oil sputtered and stank.

Suddenly the wind hissed in the water-pipes and cut off the glittering rod. To Steven it seemed the suspension of all move-ment. He would have to wait there till the water flowed again before he could begin. He tried not to look at Mr. Greathead and the lean wattles of his lifted throat. He fixed his eyes on the long crack in the soiled green distemper of the wall. His nerves were on edge with waiting for the water to flow again. The fumes of the oil-stove worked on them like a rank intoxicant. The soiled green wall gave him a sensation of physical sickness.

He picked up a towel and hung it over the back of a chair. Thus he caught sight of his own face in the glass above Mr. Greathead's; it was livid against the soiled green wall. Steven stepped aside to avoid it.

"Don't you feel well, Steven?"

"No, sir." Steven picked up a small sponge and looked at it.

Mr. Greathead had laid down his razor and was wiping the lather from his chin. At that instant, with a gurgling, spluttering haste, the water leaped from the tap.

It was then that Steven made his sudden, quiet rush. He first gagged Mr. Greathead with the sponge, then pushed him back and back against the wall and pinned him there with both hands round his neck, as he had pinned Ned Oldishaw. He pressed in on Mr. Greathead's throat, strangling him.

Mr. Greathead's hands flapped in the air, trying feebly to beat Steven off; then his arms, pushed back by the heave and thrust of Steven's shoulders, dropped. Then Mr. Greathead's body sank, sliding along the wall, and fell to the floor, Steven still keeping his hold, mounting it, gripping it with his knees. His fingers tightened, pressing back the blood. Mr. Greathead's face swelled up; it changed horribly. There was a groaning and rattling sound in his throat. Steven pressed in till it had ceased.

Then he stripped himself to the waist. He stripped Mr. Greathead of his sleeping-suit and hung his naked body face downwards in the bath. He took the razor and cut the great arteries and veins in the neck. He pulled up the plug of the waste-pipe, and left the body to drain in the running water.

He left it all day and all night.

He had noticed that murderers swung just for want of attention to little things like that; messing up themselves and the whole place with blood; always forgetting something essential. He had no time to think of horrors. From the moment he had murdered Mr. Greathead his own neck was in danger; he was simply using all his brain and nerve to save his neck. He worked with the stern, cool hardness of a man going through with an unpleasant, necessary job. He had thought of everything.

He had even thought of the dairy.

It was built on to the back of the house under the shelter of the high moor. You entered it through the scullery, which cut it off from the yard. The window-panes had been removed and replaced by sheets of perforated zinc. A large corrugated glass sky-light lit it from the roof. Impossible either to see in or to approach it from the outside. It was fitted up with a long, black slate shelf, placed, for the convenience of butter-makers, at the height of an ordinary work-bench. Steven had his tools, a razor, a carving-knife, a chopper and a meat-saw, laid there ready, beside a great pile of cotton waste.

Early the next day he took Mr. Greathead's body out of the bath, wrapped a thick towel round the neck and head, carried it down to the dairy and stretched it out on the slab. And there he cut it up into seventeen pieces.

These he wrapped in several layers of newspaper, covering the face and the hands first, because, at the last moment, they frightened him. He sewed them up in two sacks and hid them in the cellar.

He burnt the towel and the cotton waste in the kitchen fire; he cleaned his tools thoroughly and put them back in their places; and he washed down the marble slab. There wasn't a spot on the floor except for one flagstone where the pink rinsing of the slab had splashed over. He scrubbed it for half an hour, still seeing the rusty edges of the splash long after he had scoured it out.

He then washed and dressed himself with care.

As it was war-time Steven could only work by day, for the light in the dairy roof would have attracted the attention of the police. He had murdered Mr. Greathead on a Tuesday; it was now three o'clock on Thursday afternoon. Exactly at ten minutes past four he had brought out the car, shut in close with its black hood and side curtains. He had packed Mr. Greathead's suit-case and placed it in the car with his umbrella, railway rug, and travelling cap. Also, in a bundle, the clothes that his victim would have gone to London in.

He stowed the body in the two sacks beside him on the front.

By Hardraw Pass, half-way between Eastthwaite and Shawe, there are three round pits, known as the Churns, hollowed out of the grey rock and said to be bottomless. Steven had thrown stones, big as a man's chest, down the largest pit, to see whether they would be caught on any ledge or boulder. They had dropped clean, without a sound.

It poured with rain, the rain that Steven had reckoned on. The Pass was dark under the clouds and deserted. Steven turned his car so that the headlights glared on the pit's mouth. Then he ripped open the sacks and threw down, one by one, the seventeen pieces of Mr. Greathead's body, and the sacks after them, and the clothes.

It was not enough to dispose of Mr. Greathead's dead body;

he had to behave as though Mr. Greathead were alive. Mr. Greathead had disappeared and he had to account for his disappearance. He drove on to Shawe station to the five o'clock train, taking care to arrive close to its starting. A troop-train was due to depart a minute earlier. Steven, who had reckoned on the darkness and the rain, reckoned also on the hurry and confusion on the platform.

As he had foreseen, there were no porters in the station entry; nobody to notice whether Mr. Greathead was or was not in the car. He carried his things through on to the platform and gave the suit-case to an old man to label. He dashed into the booking-office and took Mr. Greathead's ticket, and then rushed along the platform as if he were following his master. He heard himself shouting to the guard, "Have you see Mr. Greathead?" And the guard's answer, "Naw!" And his own inspired statement, "He must have taken his seat in the front, then." He ran to the front of the train, shouldering his way among the troops. The drawn blinds of the carriages favoured him.

Steven thrust the umbrella, the rug, and the travelling cap into an empty compartment, and slammed the door to. He tried to shout something through the open window; but his tongue was harsh and dry against the roof of his mouth, and no sound came. He stood, blocking the window, till the guard whistled. When the train moved he ran alongside with his hand on the window ledge, as though he were taking the last instructions of his master. A porter pulled him back.

"Quick work, that," said Steven.

Before he left the station he wired to Mr. Greathead's London hotel, announcing the time of his arrival.

He felt nothing, nothing but the intense relief of a man who has saved himself by his own wits from a most horrible death. There were even moments, in the week that followed, when, so powerful was the illusion of his innocence, he could have believed that he had really seen Mr. Greathead off by the five o'clock train. Moments when he literally stood still in amazement before his own incredible impunity. Other moments when a sort of vanity uplifted him. He had committed a murder that for sheer audacity and cool brain work surpassed all murders celebrated in the history of crime. Unfortunately the very perfection of his achievement doomed it to oblivion. He had left not a trace.

Not a trace.

Only when he woke in the night a doubt sickened him. There was the rusted ring of that splash on the dairy floor. He wondered, had he really washed it out clean. And he would get up and light a candle and go down to the dairy to make sure. He knew the exact place; bending over it with the candle, he could imagine that he still saw a faint outline.

Daylight reassured him. *He* knew the exact place, but nobody else knew. There was nothing to distinguish it from the natural stains in the flagstone. Nobody would guess. But he was glad when Mrs. Blenkiron came back again.

On the day that Mr. Greathead was to have come home by the four o'clock train Steven drove into Shawe and bought a chicken for the master's dinner. He met the four o'clock train and expressed surprise that Mr. Greathead had not come by it. He said he would be sure to come by the seven. He ordered dinner for eight; Mrs. Blenkiron roasted the chicken, and Steven met the seven o'clock train. This time he showed uneasiness.

The next day he met all the trains and wired to Mr. Greathead's hotel for information. When the manager wired back that Mr. Greathead had not arrived, he wrote to his relatives and gave notice to the police.

Three weeks passed. The police and Mr. Greathead's relatives accepted Steven's statements, backed as they were by the evidence of the booking office clerk, the telegraph clerk, the guard, the porter who had labelled Mr. Greathead's luggage and the hotel manager who had received his telegram. Mr. Greathead's portrait was published in the illustrated papers with requests for any information which might lead to his discovery. Nothing happened, and presently he and his disappearance were forgotten. The nephew who came down to Eastthwaite to look into his affairs was satisfied. His balance at his bank was low owing to the non-payment of various dividends, but the accounts and the contents of Mr. Greathead's cash-box and bureau were in order and Steven had put down every penny he had spent.

The nephew paid Mrs. Blenkiron's wages and dismissed her and arranged with the chauffeur to stay on and take care of the house. And as Steven saw that this was the best way to escape suspicion, he stayed on.

Only in Westleydale and Rathdale excitement lingered. People wondered and speculated. Mr. Greathead had been robbed and murdered in the train (Steven said he had had money on him). He had lost his memory and wandered goodness knew where. He had thrown himself out of the railway carriage. Steven said Mr. Greathead wouldn't do *that*, but he shouldn't be surprised if he had lost his memory. He knew a man who forgot who he was and where he lived. Didn't know his own wife and children. Shell-shock. And lately Mr. Greathead's memory hadn't been what it was. Soon as he got it back he'd turn up again. Steven wouldn't be surprised to see him walking in any day.

But on the whole people noticed that he didn't care to talk much about Mr. Greathead. They thought this showed very proper feeling. They were sorry for Steven. He had lost his master and he had lost Dorsy Oldishaw. And if he *did* half kill Ned Oldishaw, well, young Ned had no business to go meddling with his sweetheart. Even Mrs. Oldishaw was sorry for him. And when Steven came into the bar of the King's Arms everybody said "Good evening, Steve," and made room for him by the fire.

III

Steven came and went now as if nothing had happened. He made a point of keeping the house as it would be kept if Mr. Greathead were alive. Mrs. Blenkiron, coming in once a fortnight to wash and clean, found the fire lit in Mr. Greathead's study and his slippers standing on end in the fender. Upstairs his bed was made, the clothes folded back, ready. This ritual guarded Steven not only from the suspicions of outsiders, but from his own knowledge. By behaving as though he believed that Mr. Greathead was still living he almost made himself believe it.

By refusing to let his mind dwell on the murder he came to forget it. His imagination saved him, playing the play that kept him sane, till the murder became vague to him and fantastic like a thing done in a dream. He had waked up and this was the reality; this round of caretaking, this look the house had of waiting for Mr. Greathead to come back to it. He had left off getting up in the night to examine the place on the dairy floor. He was no longer amazed at his impunity.

Then suddenly, when he really had forgotten, it ended. It was on a Saturday in January, about five o'clock. Steven had heard that Dorsy Oldishaw was back again, living at the King's Arms with her aunt. He had a mad, uncontrollable longing to see her again.

But it was not Dorsy that he saw.

His way from the Lodge kitchen into the drive was through the yard gates and along the flagged path under the study window. When he turned on to the flags he saw it shuffling along before him. The lamplight from the window lit it up. He could see distinctly the little old man in the long, shabby black overcoat, with the grey woollen muffler round his neck hunched up above his collar, lifting the thin grey hair that stuck out under the slouch of the black hat.

In the first moment that he saw it Steven had no fear. He simply felt that the murder had not happened, that he really *had* dreamed it, and that this was Mr. Greathead come back, alive among the living. The phantasm was now standing at the door of the house, its hand on the door-knob as if about to enter.

But when Steven came up to the door it was not there.

He stood, fixed, staring at the space which had emptied itself so horribly. His heart heaved and staggered, snatching at his breath. And suddenly the memory of the murder rushed at him. He saw himself in the bathroom, shut in with his victim by the soiled green walls. He smelt the reek of the oil-stove; he heard the water running from the tap. He felt his feet springing forward, and his fingers pressing, tighter and tighter, on Mr. Greathead's throat. He saw Mr. Greathead's hands flapping helplessly, his terrified eyes, his face swelling and discoloured, changing horribly, and his body sinking to the floor.

He saw himself in the dairy, afterwards; he could hear the thudding, grinding, scraping noises of his tools. He saw himself on Hardraw Pass and the headlights glaring on the pit's mouth. And the fear and the horror he had not felt then came on him now.

He turned back; he bolted the yard gates and all the doors of the house, and shut himself up in the lighted kitchen. He took up his magazine, *The Autocar,* and forced himself to read it. Presently his terror left him. He said to himself it was nothing. Nothing but his fancy. He didn't suppose he'd ever see anything again.

Three days passed. On the third evening, Steven had lit the study lamp and was bolting the window when he saw it again.

It stood on the path outside, close against the window, looking in. He saw its face distinctly, the greyish, stuck-out bud of the under-lip, and the droop of the pinched nose. The small eyes peered at him, glittering. The whole figure had a glassy look between the darkness behind it and the pane. One moment it stood outside, looking in; and the next it was mixed up with the shimmering picture of the lighted room that hung there on the blackness of the trees. Mr. Greathead then showed as if reflected, standing with Steven in the room.

And now he was outside again, looking at him, looking at him through the pane.

Steven's stomach sank and dragged, making him feel sick. He pulled down the blind between him and Mr. Greathead, clamped the shutters to and drew the curtains over them. He locked and double-bolted the front door, all the doors, to keep Mr. Greathead out. But, once that night, as he lay in bed, he heard the "shoob-shoob" of feet shuffling along the flagged passages, up the stairs, and across the landing outside his door. The door handle rattled; but nothing came. He lay awake till morning, the sweat running off his skin, his heart plunging and quivering with terror.

When he got up he saw a white, scared face in the looking-glass. A face with a half-open mouth, ready to blab, to blurt out his secret; the face of an idiot. He was afraid to take that face into Eastthwaite or into Shawe. So he shut himself up in the house, half starved on his small stock of bread, bacon and groceries.

Two weeks passed; and then it came again in broad daylight.

It was Mrs. Blenkiron's morning. He had lit the fire in the study at noon and set up Mr. Greathead's slippers in the fender. When he rose from his stooping and turned round he saw Mr. Greathead's phantasm standing on the hearthrug close in front of him. It was looking at him and smiling in a sort of mockery, as if amused at what Steven had been doing. It was solid and completely lifelike at first. Then, as Steven in his terror backed and backed away from it (he was afraid to turn and feel it there behind him), its feet became insubstantial. As if undermined, the whole structure sank and fell together on the floor, where it made a pool of some whitish glistening substance that mixed with the pattern of the carpet and sank through.

That was the most horrible thing it had done yet, and Steven's nerve broke under it. He went to Mrs. Blenkiron, whom he found scrubbing out the dairy.

She sighed as she wrung out the floor-cloth.

"Eh, these owd yeller stawnes, scroob as you will they'll navver look clean."

"Naw," he said. "Scroob and scroob, you'll navver get them clean."

She looked up at him.

"Eh, lad, what ails 'ee? Ye've got a faace like a wroong dish-clout hanging ower t' sink."

"I've got the colic."

"Aye, an' naw woonder wi' the damp, and they misties, an' your awn bad cooking. Let me roon down t' King's Arms and get you a drop of whisky."

"Naw, I'll gaw down mysen."

He knew now he was afraid to be left alone in the house. Down at the King's Arms Dorsy and Mrs. Oldishaw were sorry for him. By this time he was really ill with fright. Dorsy and Mrs. Oldishaw said it was a chill. They made him lie down on the settle by the kitchen fire and put a rug over him, and gave him stiff hot grog to drink. He slept. And when he woke he found Dorsy sitting beside him with her sewing.

He sat up and her hand was on his shoulder.

"Lay still, lad."

"I maun get oop and gaw."

"Nay, there's naw call for 'ee to gaw. Lay still and I'll make thee a coop o' tea."

He lay still.

Mrs. Oldishaw had made up a bed for him in her son's room, and they kept him there that night and till four o'clock the next day.

When he got up to go Dorsy put on her coat and hat.

"Is tha gawing out, Dorsy?"

"Aye. I canna let thee gaw and set there by thysen. I'm cooming oop to set with 'ee till night time."

She came up and they sat side by side in the Lodge kitchen by the fire as they used to sit when they were together there, holding each other's hands and not talking.

"Dorsy," he said at last, "what astha coom for? Astha coom to tell me tha'll navver speak to me again?"

"Nay. Tha knaws what I've coom for."

"To saay tha'll marry me?"

"Aye."

"I maunna marry thee, Dorsy. 'Twouldn' be right."

"Right? What dostha mean? 'Twouldn't be right for me to coom and set wi' thee this road ef I doan't marry thee."

"Nay. I darena'. Tha said tha was afraid of me, Dorsy. I doan't want 'ee to be afraid. Tha said tha'd be unhappy. I doan't want 'ee to be unhappy."

"That was lasst year. I'm not afraid of 'ee, now, Steve."

"Tha doan't knaw me, lass."

"Aye, I knaw thee. I knaw tha's sick and starved for want of me. Tha canna live wi'out thy awn lass to take care of 'ee."

She rose.

"I maun gaw now. But I'll be oop tomorrow and the next day."

And tomorrow and the next day and the next, at dusk, the hour that Steven most dreaded, Dorsy came. She sat with him till long after the night had fallen.

Steven would have felt safe so long as she was with him, but for his fear that Mr. Greathead would appear to him while she was there and that she would see him. If Dorsy knew he was being haunted she might guess why. Or Mr. Greathead might take some horrible blood-dripping and dismembered shape that would show her how he had been murdered. It would be like him, dead, to come between them as he had come when he was living.

They were sitting at the round table by the fireside. The lamp was lit and Dorsy was bending over her sewing. Suddenly she looked up, her head on one side, listening. Far away inside the house, on the flagged passage from the front door, he could hear the "shoob-shoob" of the footsteps. He could almost believe that Dorsy shivered. And somehow, for some reason, this time he was not afraid.

"Steven," she said, "didsta 'ear anything?"

"Naw. Nobbut t' wind oonder t' roogs."

She looked at him; a long wondering look. Apparently it satisfied her, for she answered: "Aye. Mebbe 'tes nobbut wind," and went on with her sewing.

He drew his chair nearer to her to protect her if it came. He could almost touch her where she sat.

The latch lifted. The door opened, and, his entrance and his passage unseen, Mr. Greathead stood before them.

The table hid the lower half of his form; but above it he was steady and solid in his terrible semblance of flesh and blood.

Steven looked at Dorsy. She was staring at the phantasm with an innocent, wondering stare that had no fear in it at all. Then she looked at Steven. An uneasy, frightened, searching look, as though to make sure whether he had seen it.

That was her fear—that *he* should see it, that *he* should be frightened, that *he* should be haunted.

He moved closer and put his hand on her shoulder. He thought, perhaps, she might shrink from him because she knew that it *was* he who was haunted. But no, she put up her hand and held his, gazing up into his face and smiling.

Then, to his amazement, the phantasm smiled back at them; not with mockery, but with a strange and terrible sweetness. Its face lit up for one instant with a sudden, beautiful, shining light; then it was gone.

"Did tha see 'im, Steve?"

"Aye."

"Astha seen annything afore?"

"Aye, three times I've seen 'im."

"Is it that 'as scared thee?"

"'Oo tawled 'ee I was scared?"

"I knawed. Because nowt can 'appen to thee but I maun knaw it."

"What dostha think, Dorsy?"

"I think tha needna be scared, Steve. 'E's a kind ghawst. Whatever 'e is 'e doan't mean thee no 'arm. T' owd gentleman navver did when he was alive."

"Didn' 'e? Didn' 'e? 'E served me the woorst turn 'e could when 'e coomed between thee and me."

"Whatever makes 'ee think that, lad?"

"I doan' think it. I *knaw*."

"Nay, loove, tha dostna."

"'E did. 'E did, I tell thee."

"Doan' tha say that," she cried. "Doan' tha say it, Stevey."

"Why shouldn't I?"

"Tha'll set folk talking that road."

"What do they knaw to talk about?"

"Ef they was to remember what tha said."

"And what did I say?"

"Why, that ef annybody was to coom between thee and me, tha'd do them in."

"I wasna thinking of *'im*. Gawd knaws I wasna."

"*They* doan't," she said.

"*Tha* knaws? Tha knaws I didna mean 'im?"

"Aye, *I* knaw, Steve."

"An', Dorsy, tha 'rn't afraid of me? Tha 'rn't afraid of me anny more?"

"Nay, lad. I loove thee too mooch. I shall navver be afraid of 'ee again. Would I coom to thee this road ef I was afraid?"

"Tha'll be afraid now."

"And what should I be afraid of?"

"Why—*'im*."

"*'Im?* I should be a deal more afraid to think of 'ee setting with 'im oop 'ere, by thysen. Wuntha coom down and sleep at aunt's?"

"That I wunna. But I shall set 'ee on t' road passt t' moor."

He went with her down the bridle-path and across the moor and along he main road that led through Eastthwaite. They parted at the turn where the lights of the village came in sight.

The moon had risen as Steven went back across the moor. The ash-tree at the bridle-path stood out clear, its hooked, bending branches black against the grey moor-grass. The shadows in the ruts laid stripes along the bridle-path, black on grey. The house was black-grey in the darkness of the drive. Only the lighted study window made a golden square in its long wall.

Before he could go up to bed he would have to put out the study lamp. He was nervous; but he no longer felt the sickening and sweating terror of the first hauntings. Either he was getting used to it, or—something had happened to him.

He had closed the shutters and put out the lamp. His candle made a ring of light round the table in the middle of the room. He was about to take it up and go when he heard a thin voice calling his name: "Steven." He raised his head to listen. The thin thread of sound seemed to come from outside, a long way off, at the end of the bridle-path.

"Steven, Steven——"

This time he could have sworn the sound came from inside his head, like the hiss of air in his ears.

"Steven——"

He knew the voice now. It was behind him in the room. He turned, and saw the phantasm of Mr. Greathead sitting, as he used to sit, in the arm-chair by the fire. The form was dim in the dusk of the room outside the ring of candlelight. Steven's first movement was to snatch up the candlestick and hold it between him and the phantasm, hoping that the light would cause it to disappear. Instead of disappearing the figure became clear and solid, indistinguishable from a figure of flesh and blood dressed in black broadcloth and white linen. Its eyes had the shining transparency of blue crystal; they were fixed on Steven with a look of quiet, benevolent attention. Its small, narrow mouth was lifted at the corners, smiling.

It spoke.

"You needn't be afraid," it said.

The voice was natural now, quiet, measured, slightly quavering. Instead of frightening Steven it soothed and steadied him.

He put the candle on the table behind him and stood up before the phantasm, fascinated.

"*Why* are you afraid?" it asked.

Steven couldn't answer. He could only stare, held there by the shining, hypnotizing eyes.

"You are afraid," it said, "because you think I'm what you call a ghost, a supernatural thing. You think I'm dead and that you killed me. You think you took a horrible revenge for a wrong you thought I did you. You think I've come back to frighten you, to revenge myself in my turn.

"And every one of those thoughts of yours, Steven, is wrong. I'm real, and my appearance is as natural and real as anything in this room—*more* natural and more real if you did but know. You didn't kill me, as you see; for here I am, as alive, more alive than you are. Your revenge consisted in removing me from a state which had become unbearable to a state more delightful than you can imagine. I don't mind telling you, Steven, that I was in serious financial difficulties (which, by the way, is a good thing for you, as it provides a plausible motive for my disappearance). So that, as far as revenge goes, the thing was a complete frost. You were my benefactor. Your methods were somewhat violent, and I admit you gave me some disagreeable moments before my actual deliverance; but as I was already developing rheumatoid arthritis there can be no doubt that in your hands my death was more merciful than if it had been left to Nature. As for the subsequent arrangements, I congratulate you, Steven, on your coolness and resource. I always said you were equal to any emergency, and that your brains would pull you safe through any scrape. You committed an appalling and dangerous crime, a crime of all things the most difficult to conceal, and you contrived so that it was not discovered and never will be discovered. And no doubt the details of this crime seemed to you horrible and revolting to the last degree; and the more horrible and the more revolting they were, the more you piqued yourself on your nerve in carrying the thing through without a hitch.

"I don't want to put you entirely out of conceit with your performance. It was very creditable for a beginner, very creditable indeed. But let me tell you, this idea of things being horrible and revolting is all illusion. The terms are purely relative to your limited perceptions.

"I'm speaking now to your intelligence—I don't mean that practical ingenuity which enabled you to dispose of me so neatly. When I say intelligence I mean intelligence. All you did, then, was to redistribute matter. To our incorruptible sense matter never takes any of those offensive forms in which it so often appears to you. Nature has evolved all this horror and repulsion just to prevent people from making too many little experiments like yours. You mustn't imagine that these things have any eternal importance. Don't flatter yourself you've electrified the universe. For minds no longer attached to flesh and blood, that horrible butchery you were so proud of, Steven, is simply silly. No more terrifying than the spilling of red ink or the rearrangement of a jig-saw puzzle. I saw the whole business, and I can assure you I felt nothing but intense amusement. Your face, Steven, was so absurdly serious. You've no idea what you looked like with that chopper. I'd have appeared to you then and told you so, only I knew I should frighten you into fits.

"And there's another grand mistake, my lad—your thinking that I'm haunting you out of revenge, that I'm trying to frighten you. . . . My dear Steven, if I'd wanted to frighten you I'd have appeared in a very different shape. I needn't remind you what shape I *might* have appeared in. . . . What do you suppose I've come for?"

"I don't know," said Steven in a husky whisper. "Tell me."

"I've come to forgive you. And to save you from the horror you *would* have felt sooner or later. And to stop your going on with your crime."

"You needn't," Steven said. "I'm not going on with it. I shall do no more murders."

"There you are again. Can't you understand that I'm not talking about your silly butcher's work? I'm talking about your *real* crime. Your real crime was hating me.

"And your very hate was a blunder, Steven. You hated me for something I hadn't done."

"Aye, what did you do? Tell me that."

"You thought I came between you and your sweetheart. That night when Dorsy spoke to me, you thought I told her to throw you over, didn't you?"

"Aye. And what did you tell her?"

"I told her to stick to you. It was you, Steven, who drove her away. You frightened the child. She said she was afraid for her life of you. Not because you half killed that poor boy, but because of the look on your face before you did it. The look of hate, Steven.

"I told her not to be afraid of you. I told her that if she threw you over you might go altogether to the devil; that she might even be responsible for some crime. I told her that if she married you and was faithful—*if she loved you*—I'd answer for it you'd never go wrong.

"She was too frightened to listen to me. Then I told her to think over what I'd said before she did anything. You heard me say that."

"Aye. That's what I heard you say. I didn't knaw. I didn't knaw. I thought you'd set her agen me."

"If you don't believe me, you can ask her, Steven."

"That's what she said t'other night. That you navver coom between her and me. Navver."

"Never," the phantasm said. "And you don't hate me now."

"Naw. Naw. I should navver 'a hated 'ee. I should navver 'a laid a finger on thee, ef I'd knawn."

"It's not your laying fingers on me, it's your hatred that matters. If that's done with, the whole thing's done with."

"Is it? Is it? Ef it was knawn, I should have to hang for it. Maunna I gie mysen oop? Tell me, maun I gie mysen oop?"

"You want me to decide that for you?"

"Aye. Doan't gaw," he said. "Doan't gaw."

It seemed to him that Mr. Greathead's phantasm was getting a little thin, as if it couldn't last more than an instant. He had never so longed for it to go, as he longed now for it to stay and help him.

"Well, Steven, any flesh-and-blood man would tell you to go and get hanged tomorrow; that it was no more than your plain duty. And I daresay there are some mean, vindictive spirits even in my world who would say the same, not because *they* think death important but because they know *you* do, and want to get even with you that way.

"It isn't *my* way. I consider this little affair is strictly between ourselves. There isn't a jury of flesh-and-blood men who would understand it. They all think death so important."

"What do you want me to do, then? Tell me and I'll do it! Tell me!"

He cried it out loud; for Mr. Greathead's phantasm was getting thinner and thinner; it dwindled and fluttered, like a light going down. Its voice came from somewhere away outside, from the other end of the bridle-path.

"Go on living," it said. "Marry Dorsy."

"I darena. She doan' knaw I killed 'ee."

"Oh, yes"—the eyes flickered up, gentle and ironic—"she does. She knew all the time."

And with that the phantasm went out.

Olivia Howard Dunbar

(1873–1953)

OLIVIA HOWARD DUNBAR was born in West Bridgewater, Massachusetts, but after graduating from Smith College in 1894, she moved to New York, where she worked first as a journalist and later as a feature writer for magazines. Although she married Ridgeley Torrence in 1914, she kept her maiden name for all her writings. She subsequently became heavily involved in both black rights and women's suffrage. Her name is virtually forgotten today, but was mercifully rescued from oblivion by Jessica Salmonson, who collected together a few of her supernatural stories in *The Shell of Sense* (1997). The title story first appeared in *Harper's Monthly Magazine* for December 1908.

The Shell of Sense

It was intolerably unchanged, the dim, dark-toned room. In an agony of recognition my glance ran from one to another of the comfortable, familiar things that my earthly life had been passed among. Incredibly distant from it all as I essentially was, I noted sharply that the very gaps that I myself had left in my bookshelves still stood unfilled; that the delicate fingers of the ferns that I had tended were still stretched futilely toward the light; that the soft agreeable chuckle of my own little clock, like some elderly woman with whom conversation has become automatic, was undiminished.

Unchanged—or so it seemed at first. But there were certain trivial differences that shortly smote me. The windows were closed too tightly; for I had always kept the house very cool, although I had known that Theresa preferred warm rooms. And my work-basket was in disorder; it was preposterous that so small a thing should hurt me so. Then, for this was my first experience of the shadow-folded transition, the odd alternation of my emotions bewildered me. For at one moment the place seemed so humanly familiar, so distinctly my own proper envelope, that for love of it I could have laid my cheek against the wall; while in the next I was miserably conscious of strange new shrillnesses. How could they be endured—and had I ever endured them?—those harsh influences that I now perceived at the window; light and color so blinding that they obscured the form of the wind, tumult so discordant that one could scarcely hear the roses open in the garden below?

But Theresa did not seem to mind any of these things.

97

Disorder, it is true, the dear child had never minded. She was sitting all this time at my desk—at *my* desk,—occupied, I could only too easily surmise how. In the light of my own habits of precision it was plain that that sombre correspondence should have been attended to before; but I believe that I did not really reproach Theresa, for I knew that her notes, when she did write them, were perhaps less perfunctory than mine. She finished the last one as I watched her, and added it to the heap of black-bordered envelopes that lay on the desk. Poor girl! I saw now that they had cost her tears. Yet, living beside her day after day, year after year, I had never discovered what deep tenderness my sister possessed. Toward each other it had been our habit to display only a temperate affection, and I remember having always thought it distinctly fortunate for Theresa, since she was denied my happiness, that she could live so easily and pleasantly without emotions of the devastating sort. . . . And now, for the first time, I was really to behold her. . . . Could it be Theresa, after all, this tangle of subdued turbulences? Let no one suppose that it is an easy thing to bear, the relentlessly lucid understanding that I then first exercised; or that, in its first enfranchisement, the timid vision does not yearn for its old screens and mists.

Suddenly, as Theresa sat there, her head, filled with its tender thoughts of me, held in her gentle hands, I felt Allan's step on the carpeted stair outside. Theresa felt it, too—but how? for it was not audible. She gave a start, swept the black envelopes out of sight, and pretended to be writing in a little book. Then I forgot to watch her any longer in my absorption in Allan's coming. It was he, of course, that I was awaiting. It was for him that I had made this first lonely, frightened effort to return, to recover. . . . It was not that I had supposed he would allow himself to recognize my presence, for I had long been sufficiently familiar with his hard and fast denials of the invisible. He was so reasonable always, so sane—so blindfolded. But I had hoped that because of his very rejection of the ether that now contained me I could perhaps all the more safely, the more secretly, watch him, linger near him. He was near now, very near—but why did Theresa, sitting there in the room that had never belonged to her, appropriate for herself his coming? It was so manifestly I who had drawn him, I whom he had come to seek.

The door was ajar. He knocked softly at it "Are you there, Theresa?" he called. He expected to find her, then, there in my room? I shrank back, fearing, almost, to stay.

"I shall have finished in a moment," Theresa told him, and he sat down to wait for her.

No spirit still unreleased can understand the pang that I felt with Allan sitting almost within my touch. Almost irresistibly the wish beset me to let him for an instant feel my nearness. Then I checked myself, remembering—oh, absurd, piteous human fears!—that my too unguarded closeness might alarm him. It was not so remote a time that I myself had known them, those blind, uncouth timidities. I came, therefore, somewhat nearer— but I did not touch him. I merely leaned toward him and with incredible softness whispered his name. That much I could not have forborne: the spell of life was still too strong in me.

But it gave him no comfort, no delight. "Theresa!" he called, in a voice dreadful with alarm—and in that instant the last veil fell, and desperately, scarce believingly, I beheld how it stood between them, those two.

She turned to him that gentle look of hers.

"Forgive me," came from him hoarsely. "But I had suddenly the most—unaccountable sensation. Can there be too many windows open? There is such a—chill—about."

"There are no windows open," Theresa assured him. "I took care to shut out the chill. You are not well, Allan!"

"Perhaps not." He embraced the suggestion. "And yet I feel no illness apart from this abominable sensation that persists— persists. . . . Theresa, you must tell me: do I fancy it, or do you, too, feel—something—strange here?"

"Oh, there is something very strange here," she half sobbed. "There always will be."

"Good heavens, child, I didn't mean that!" He rose and stood looking about him. "I know, of course, that you have your beliefs, and I respect them, but you know equally well that I have nothing of the sort! So—don't let us conjure up anything inexplicable."

I stayed impalpably, imponderably near him. Wretched and bereft though I was, I could not have left him while he stood denying me.

"What I mean," he went on, in his low, distinct voice, "is a special, an almost ominous sense of cold. Upon my soul, Theresa,"—he paused—"if I *were* superstitious, if I *were* a woman, I should probably imagine it to seem—a presence!"

He spoke the last word very faintly, but Theresa shrank from it nevertheless.

"*Don't* say that, Allan!" she cried out. "Don't think it, I beg of you! I've tried so hard myself not to think it—and you must help me. You know it is only perturbed, uneasy spirits that wander. With her it is quite different. She has always been so happy— she must still be."

I listened, stunned, to Theresa's sweet dogmatism. From what blind distances came her confident misapprehensions, how dense, both for her and for Allan, was the separating vapor!

Allan frowned. "Don't take me literally, Theresa," he explained; and I, who a moment before had almost touched him, now held myself aloof and heard him with a strange untried pity, new born in me. "I'm not speaking of what you call—spirits. It's something much more terrible." He allowed his head to sink heavily on his chest. "If I did not positively know that I had never done her any harm, I should suppose myself to be suffering from guilt, from remorse. . . . Theresa, you know better than I, perhaps. Was she content, always? Did she believe in me?"

"Believe in you?—when she knew you to be so good!—when you adored her!"

"She thought that? She said it? Then what in Heaven's name ails me?—unless it is all as you believe, Theresa, and she knows now what she didn't know then, poor dear, and minds—"

"Minds what? What do you mean, Allan?"

I, who with my perhaps illegitimate advantage saw so clear, knew that he had not meant to tell her: I did him that justice, even in my first jealousy. If I had not tortured him so by clinging near him, he would not have told her. But the moment came, and overflowed, and he did tell her—passionate, tumultuous story that it was. During all our life together, Allan's and mine, he had spared me, had kept me wrapped in the white cloak of an unblemished loyalty. But it would have been kinder, I now bitterly thought, if, like many husbands, he had years ago found for the story he now poured forth some clandestine listener; I should not have known. But he was faithful and good, and so he waited till I, mute and chained, was there to hear him. So well did I know him, as I thought, so thoroughly had he once been mine, that I saw it in his eyes, heard it in his voice, before the words came. And yet, when it came, it lashed me with the whips of an unbearable humiliation. For I, his wife, had not known how greatly he could love.

And that Theresa, soft little traitor, should, in her still way, have cared too! Where was the iron in her, I moaned within my stricken spirit, where the steadfastness? From the moment he bade her, she turned her soft little petals up to him—and my last delusion was spent. It was intolerable; and none the less so that in another moment she had, prompted by some belated thought of me, renounced him. Allan was hers, yet she put him from her; and it was my part to watch them both.

Then in the anguish of it all I remembered, awkward, untutored spirit that I was, that I now had the Great Recourse. Whatever human things were unbearable, I had no need to bear. I ceased, therefore, to make the effort that kept me with them. The pitiless poignancy was dulled, the sounds and the light ceased, the lovers faded from me, and again I was mercifully drawn into the dim, infinite spaces.

There followed a period whose length I cannot measure and during which I was able to make no progress in the difficult, dizzying experience of release. "Earth-bound" my jealousy relentlessly kept me. Though my two dear ones had forsworn each other, I could not trust them, for theirs seemed to me an affectation of a more than mortal magnanimity. Without a ghostly sentinel to prick them with sharp fears and recollections, who could believe that they would keep to it? Of the efficacy of my own vigilance, so long as I might choose to exercise it, I could have no doubt, for I had by this time come to have a dreadful exultation in the new power that lived in me. Repeated delicate experiment had taught me how a touch or a breath, a wish or a whisper, could control Allan's acts, could keep him from Theresa. I could manifest myself as palely, as transiently, as a thought. I could produce the merest necessary flicker, like the shadow of a just-opened leaf, on his trembling, tortured consciousness. And these unrealized perceptions of me he interpreted, as I had known that he would, as his soul's inevitable penance. He had come to believe that he had done evil in silently loving Theresa all these years, and it was my vengeance to allow him to believe this, to prod him ever to believe it afresh.

I am conscious that this frame of mind was not continuous in me. For I remember, too, that when Allan and Theresa were safely apart and sufficiently miserable I loved them as dearly as I ever had, more dearly perhaps. For it was impossible that I should not perceive, in my new emancipation, that they were, each of them, something more and greater than the two beings I had once ignorantly pictured them. For years they had practiced a selflessness of which I could once scarcely have conceived, and which even now I could only admire without entering into its mystery. While I had lived solely for myself, these two divine creatures had lived exquisitely for me. They had granted me everything, themselves nothing. For my undeserving sake their lives had been a constant torment of renunciation—a torment they had not sought to alleviate by the exchange of a single glance of understanding. There were even marvellous moments when, from the depths of my newly informed heart, I pitied them:—poor creatures, who, withheld from the infinite solaces that I had come to know, were still utterly within that

> Shell of sense
> So frail, so piteously contrived for pain.

Within it, yes; yet exercising qualities that so sublimely transcended it. Yet the shy, hesitating compassion that thus had birth in me was far from being able to defeat the earlier, earthlier emotion. The two, I recognized, were in a sort of conflict;

and I, regarding it, assumed that the conflict would never end; that for years, as Allan and Theresa reckoned time, I should be obliged to withhold myself from the great spaces and linger suffering, grudging, shamed, where they lingered.

It can never have been explained, I suppose, what, to devitalized perception such as mine, the contact of mortal beings with each other appears to be. Once to have exercised this sense-freed perception is to realize that the gift of prophecy, although the subject of such frequent marvel, is no longer mysterious. The merest glance of our sensitive and uncloyed vision can detect the strength of the relation between two beings, and therefore instantly calculate its duration. If you see a heavy weight suspended from a slender string, you can know, without any wizardry, that in a few moments the string will snap; well, such, if you admit the analogy, is prophecy, is foreknowledge. And it was thus that I saw it with Theresa and Allan. For it was perfectly visible to me that they would very little longer have the strength to preserve, near each other, the denuded impersonal relation that they, and that I, behind them, insisted on; and that they would have to separate. It was my sister, perhaps the more sensitive, who first realized this. It had now become possible for me to observe them almost constantly, the effort necessary to visit them had so greatly diminished; so that I watched her, poor, anguished girl, prepare to leave him. I saw each reluctant movement that she made. I saw her eyes, worn from self-searching; I heard her step grown timid from inexplicable fears; I entered her very heart and heard its pitiful, wild beating. And still I did not interfere.

For at this time I had a wonderful, almost demoniacal sense of disposing of matters to suit my own selfish will. At any moment I could have checked their miseries, could have restored happiness and peace. Yet it gave me, and I could weep to admit it, a monstrous joy to know that Theresa thought she was leaving Allan of her own free intention, when it was I who was contriving, arranging, insisting. . . . And yet she wretchedly felt my presence near her; I am certain of that.

A few days before the time of her intended departure my

sister told Allan that she must speak with him after dinner. Our beautiful old house branched out from a circular hall with great arched doors at either end; and it was through the rear doorway that always in summer, after dinner, we passed out into the garden adjoining. As usual, therefore, when the hour came, Theresa led the way. That dreadful daytime brilliance that in my present state I found so hard to endure was now becoming softer. A delicate, capricious twilight breeze danced inconsequently through languidly whispering leaves. Lovely pale flowers blossomed like little moons in the dusk, and over them the breath of mignonette hung heavily. It was a perfect place—and it had so long been ours, Allan's and mine. It made me restless and a little wicked that those two should be there together now.

For a little they walked about together, speaking of common, daily things. Then suddenly Theresa burst out:

"I am going away, Allan. I have stayed to do everything that needed to be done. Now your mother will be here to care for you, and it is time for me to go."

He stared at her and stood still. Theresa had been there so long, she so definitely, to his mind, belonged there. And she was, as I also had jealously known, so lovely there, the small, dark, dainty creature, in the old hall, on the wide staircases, in the garden. . . . Life there without Theresa, even the intentionally remote, the perpetually renounced Theresa—he had not dreamed of it, he could not, so suddenly, conceive of it.

"Sit here," he said, and drew her down beside him on a bench, "and tell me what it means, why you are going. Is it because of something that I have been—have done?"

She hesitated. I wondered if she would dare tell him. She looked out and away from him, and he waited long for her to speak.

The pale stars were sliding into their places. The whispering of the leaves was almost hushed. All about them it was still and shadowy and sweet. It was that wonderful moment when, for lack of a visible horizon, the not yet darkened world seems infinitely greater—a moment when anything can happen, anything be believed in. To me, watching, listening, hovering, there came a dreadful purpose and a dreadful courage. Suppose, for one moment, Theresa should not only feel, but see me—would she dare to tell him then?

There came a brief space of terrible effort, all my fluttering, uncertain forces strained to the utmost. The instant of my struggle was endlessly long and the transition seemed to take place outside me—as one sitting in a train, motionless, sees the leagues of earth float by. And then, in a bright, terrible flash I knew I had achieved it—I had *attained visibility*. Shuddering, insubstantial, but luminously apparent, I stood there before them. And for the instant that I maintained the visible state I looked straight into Theresa's soul.

She gave a cry. And then, thing of silly, cruel impulses that I was, I saw what I had done. The very thing that I wished to avert I had precipitated. For Allan, in his sudden terror and pity, had bent and caught her in his arms. For the first time they were together; and it was I who had brought them.

Then, to his whispered urging to tell the reason of her cry, Theresa said:

"Frances was here. You did not see her, standing there, under the lilacs, with no smile on her face?"

"My dear, my dear!" was all that Allan said. I had so long now lived invisibly with them, he knew that she was right.

"I suppose you know what it means?" she asked him, calmly.

"Dear Theresa," Allan said, slowly, "if you and I should go away somewhere, could we not evade all this ghostliness? And will you come with me?"

"Distance would not banish her," my sister confidently asserted. And then she said, softly: "Have you thought what a lonely, awesome thing it must be to be so newly dead? Pity her, Allan. We who are warm and alive should pity her. She loves you still—that is the meaning of it all, you know—and she wants us to understand that for that reason we must keep apart. Oh, it was so plain in her white face as she stood there. And you did not see her?"

"It was your face that I saw," Allan solemnly told her—oh, how different he had grown from the Allan that I had known!—"and yours is the only face that I shall ever see." And again he drew her to him.

She sprang from him. "You are defying her, Allan!" she cried. "And you must not. It is her right to keep us apart, if she wishes. It must be as she insists. I shall go, as I told you. And, Allan, I beg of you, leave me the courage to do as she demands!"

They stood facing each other in the deep dusk, and the wounds that I had dealt them gaped red and accusing. "We must pity her," Theresa had said. And as I remembered that extraordinary speech, and saw the agony in her face, and the greater agony in Allan's, there came the great irreparable cleavage between mortality and me. In a swift, merciful flame the last of my mortal emotions—gross and tenacious they must have been—was consumed. My cold grasp of Allan loosened and a new unearthly love of him bloomed in my heart.

I was now, however, in a difficulty with which my experience in the newer state was scarcely sufficient to deal. How could I make it plain to Allan and Theresa that I wished to bring them together, to heal the wounds that I had made?

Pityingly, remorsefully, I lingered near them all that night and the next day. And by that time had brought myself to the point of a great determination. In the little time that was left, before Theresa should be gone and Allan bereft and desolate, I saw the one way that lay open to me to convince them of my acquiescence in their destiny.

In the deepest darkness and silence of the next night I made a greater effort than it will ever be necessary for me to make again. When they think of me, Allan and Theresa, I pray now that they will recall what I did that night, and that my thousand frustrations and selfishnesses may shrivel and be blown from their indulgent memories.

Yet the following morning, as she had planned, Theresa appeared at breakfast dressed for her journey. Above in her room there were the sounds of departure. They spoke little during the brief meal, but when it was ended Allan said:

"Theresa, there is half an hour before you go. Will you come upstairs with me? I had a dream that I must tell you of."

"Allan!" She looked at him, frightened, but went with him. "It was of Frances you dreamed," she said, quietly, as they entered the library together.

"Did I say it was a dream? But I was awake—thoroughly awake. I had not been sleeping well, and I heard, twice, the striking of the clock. And as I lay there, looking out at the stars, and thinking—thinking of you, Theresa—she came to me, stood there before me, in my room. It was no sheeted spectre, you understand; it was Frances, literally she. In some inexplicable fashion I seemed to be aware that she wanted to make me know something, and I waited, watching her face. After a few moments it came. She did not speak, precisely. That is, I am sure I heard no sound. Yet the words that came from her were definite enough. She said: 'Don't let Theresa leave you. Take her and keep her.' Then she went away. Was that a dream?"

"I had not meant to tell you," Theresa eagerly answered, "but now I must. It is too wonderful. What time did your clock strike, Allan?"

"One, the last time."

"Yes; it was then that I awoke. And she had been with me. I had not seen her, but her arm had been about me and her kiss was on my cheek. Oh, I knew; it was unmistakable. And the sound of her voice was with me."

"Then she bade you, too—"

"Yes, to stay with you. I am glad we told each other." She smiled tearfully and began to fasten her wrap.

"But you are not going—*now!*" Allan cried. "You know that you cannot, now that she has asked you to stay."

"Then you believe, as I do, that it was she?" Theresa demanded.

"I can never understand, but I know," he answered her. "And now you will not go?"

I am freed. There will be no further semblance of me in my old home, no sound of my voice, no dimmest echo of my earthly self. They have no further need of me, the two that I have brought together. Theirs is the fullest joy that the dwellers in the shell of sense can know. Mine is the transcendent joy of the unseen spaces.

Mary Molesworth
(1839–1921)

MARY MOLESWORTH—or Mary Stewart, as she was born—was a Scottish writer, primarily of children's books. She had been born in Rotterdam, where her father was a merchant, but returned to Britain and a rather strict Victorian upbringing. She married Major Richard Molesworth in 1861, but it was an unhappy marriage and they eventually separated. She turned to writing in 1869 after the death of two of her children and though her first two books were written for adults, she soon turned to writing for children. Her best-known books, especially *The Cuckoo Clock* (1877) and *The Tapestry Room* (1879), were among the favorite readings of Edith Nesbit and greatly influenced her writing. Mary Molesworth wrote several ghost stories spread over most of her long writing career, with the majority collected in *Four Ghost Stories* (1888) and *Uncanny Tales* (1896). It was not until 2002 that John Smith published a complete *Collected Ghost Stories*. "The Shadow in the Moonlight," which first appeared in *Uncanny Tales*, is both the longest and the best of her ghost stories. Although told through the viewpoint of teenage children, it is not a children's story.

The Shadow in the Moonlight

PART I

We never thought of Finster St. Mabyn's being haunted. We really never did. This may seem strange, but it is absolutely true. It was such an extremely interesting and curious place in many ways that it required nothing extraneous to add to its attractions. Perhaps this was the reason. Nowadays, immediately that you hear of a house being "very old," the next remark is sure to be "I hope it is"—or "is not"—that depends on the taste of the speaker—"haunted."

But Finster was more than very old; it was *ancient* and, in a modest way, historical. I will not take up time by relating its history, however, or by referring my readers to the chronicles in which mention of it may be found. Nor shall I yield to the temptation of describing the room in which a certain royalty spent one night, if not two or three nights, four centuries ago, or the tower, now in ruins, where an even more renowned personage was imprisoned, for several months. All these facts—or legends—have nothing to do with what I have to tell. Nor, strictly speaking, has Finster itself, except as a sort of prologue to my narrative.

We heard of the house through friends living in the same county, though some distance farther inland. They—Mr. and Miss Miles, it is convenient to give their name at once, knew that we had been ordered to leave our own home for some months, to get over the effects of a very trying visitation of influenza, and that sea-air was specially desirable.

We grumbled at this. Seaside places are often so dull and

commonplace. But when we heard of Finster we grumbled no longer.

"Dull" in a sense it might be, but assuredly not "commonplace." Janet Miles's description of it, though she was not particularly clever at description, read like a fairy tale, or one of Longfellow's poems.

"A castle by the sea—how perfect!" we all exclaimed. "Do, oh, do fix for it, Mother!"

The objections were quickly over-ruled. It was rather isolated, said Miss Miles, standing, as was not difficult to trace in its name, on a point of land—a corner rather—with sea on two sides. It had not been lived in, save spasmodically, for some years, for the late owner was one of those happy, or unhappy people, who have more houses than they can use, and the present one was a minor. Eventually it was to be overhauled and some additions and alterations made, but the trustees would be glad to let it at a moderate rent for some months, and had intended putting it into some agents' hands when Mr. Miles happened to meet one of them, who mentioned it to him. There was nothing against it; it was absolutely healthy. But the furniture was old and shabby, and there was none too much of it. If we wanted to have visitors we should certainly require to add to it. This, however, could easily be done, our informant went on to say. There was a very good upholsterer and furniture dealer at Raxtrew, the nearest town, who was in the habit of hiring out things to the officers at the fort. "Indeed," she added, "we often pick up charming old pieces of furniture from him for next to nothing, so you could both hire and buy."

Of course, we should have visitors—and our own house would not be the worse for some additional chairs and tables here and there, in place of some excellent monstrosities Phil and Nugent and I had persuaded Mother to get rid of.

"If I go down to spy the land with Father," I said, "I shall certainly go to the furniture dealer's and have a good look about me."

I did go with Father. I was nineteen—it is four years ago—and a capable sort of girl. Then I was the only one who had not

been ill, and Mother had been the worst of all, Mother and
Dormy—poor little chap—for he nearly died.

He is the youngest of us—we are four boys and two girls.
Sophy was then fifteen. My own name is Leila.

If I attempted to give any idea of the impression Finster St.
Mabyn's made upon us, I should go on for hours. It simply took
our breath away. It really felt like going back a few centuries
merely to enter within the walls and gaze round you. And yet we
did not see it to any advantage, so at least said the two Miles's
who were our guides. It was a gloomy day, with the feeling of
rain not far off, early in April. It might have been November,
though it was not cold.

"You can scarcely imagine what it is on a bright day," said
Janet, eager, as people always are in such circumstances, to
show off her trouvaille. "The lights and shadows are so
exquisite."

"I love it as it is," I said. "I don't think I shall ever regret having seen it first on a grey day. It is just perfect."

She was pleased at my admiration, and did her utmost to
facilitate matters. Father was taken with the place, too, I could
see, but he hummed and hawed a good deal about the bareness
of the rooms—the bedrooms especially. So Janet and I went
into it at once in a businesslike way, making lists of the actually
necessary additions, which did not prove very formidable after
all.

"Hunter will manage all that easily," said Miss Miles, upon
which Father gave in—I believe he had meant to do so all the
time. The rent was really so low that a little furniture-hire could
be afforded, I suggested. And Father agreed. "It is extremely
low," he said, "for a place possessing so many advantages."

But even then it did not occur to any of us to suggest "suspi-
ciously low."

We had the Miles's guarantee for it all, to begin with. Had
there been any objection they must have known it. We spent the
night with them and the next morning at the furniture dealer's.
He was a quick, obliging little man, and took in the situation at
a glance. And his terms were so moderate that Father said to me
amiably: "There are some quaint odds and ends here, Leila. You

might choose a few things, to use at Finster in the first place, and then to take home with us."

I was only too ready to profit by the permission, and with Janet's help a few charmingly quaint chairs and tables, a three-cornered wall cabinet, and some other trifles were soon put aside for us. We were just leaving, when at one end of the shop some tempting-looking draperies caught my eye.

"What are these?" I asked the upholsterer. "Curtains! Why, this is real old tapestry!"

The obliging Hunter drew out the material in question.

"They are not exactly curtains, miss," he said. "I thought they would make nice *portières*. You see the tapestry is set into cloth. It was so frail when I got it that it was the only thing to do with it."

He had managed it very ingeniously. Two panels, so to say, of old tapestry, very charming in tone, had been lined and framed with dull green cloth, making a very good pair of *portières,* indeed.

"Oh, Papa!" I cried, "do let us have these. There are sure to be draughty doors at Finster, and afterwards they would make perfect *portières* for the two side doors in the hall at home."

Father eyed the tapestry appreciatively, but first prudently inquired the price. It seemed higher in proportion than Hunter's other charges.

"You see, sir," he said half apologetically, "the panels are real antique work, though so much the worse for wear."

"Where did they come from?" asked Father.

Hunter hesitated.

"To tell you the truth, sir," he replied, "I was asked not to name the party that I bought it from. It seems a pity to part with heir-looms, but—it happens sometimes—I bought several things together of a family quite lately. The *portières* have only come out of the workroom this morning. We hurried on with them to stop them fraying more; you see where they were before, they must have been nailed to the wall."

Janet Miles, who was something of a connoisseur, had been examining the tapestry.

"It is well worth what he asks," she said, in a low voice. "You don't often come across such tapestry in England."

So the bargain was struck, and Hunter promised to see all

that we had chosen, both purchased and hired, delivered at Finster the week before we proposed to come.

Nothing interfered with our plans. By the end of the month we found ourselves at our temporary home—all of us except Nat, our third brother, who was at school. Dormer, the small boy, still did lessons with Sophy's governess. The two older "boys," as we called them, happened to be at home for different reasons—one, Nugent, on leave from India; Phil, forced to miss a term at college through an attack of the same illness which had treated Mother and Dormy so badly.

But now that everybody was well again, and going to be much better, thanks to Finster air, we thought the ill wind had brought us some very distinct good. It would not have been half such fun had we not been a large family party to start with, and before we had been a week at the place we had added to our numbers by the first detachment of the guests we had invited.

It was not a very large house; besides ourselves we had not room for more than three or four others. For some of the rooms—those on the top storey—were really too dilapidated to suit anyone but rats—rats or ghosts—said someone laughingly one day, when we had been exploring them. Afterwards the words returned to my memory.

We had made ourselves very comfortable, thanks to the invaluable Hunter. And every day the weather grew milder and more spring-like. The woods on the inland side were full of primroses. It promised to be a lovely season. There was a gallery along one side of the house, which soon became a favourite resort; it made a pleasant lounging-place, in the day-time especially, though less so in the evening, as the fireplace at one end warmed it but imperfectly, and besides this it was difficult to light up. It was draughty, too, as there was a superfluity of doors, two of which, one at each end, we at once condemned. They were not needed, as the one led by a very long spiral staircase to the unused attic rooms, the other to the kitchen and offices. And when we did have afternoon tea in the gallery, it was easy to bring it through the dining or drawing-rooms, long rooms, lighted at their extreme ends, which ran parallel to the gallery lengthways, both of which had a door opening onto it as well as from the hall on the other side. For all the principal rooms at Finster were on the first floor, not on the ground floor.

The closing of these doors got rid of a great deal of draught, and, as I have said, the weather was really mild and calm.

One afternoon—I am trying to begin at the beginning of our strange experiences; even at the risk of long-windedness it seems better to do so—we were all assembled in the gallery at tea-time. The "children," as we called Sophy and Dormer, much to Sophy's disgust, and their governess, were with us, for rules were relaxed at Finster, and Miss Larpent was a great favourite with us all.

Suddenly Sophy gave an exclamation of annoyance.

"Mamma," she said, "I wish you would speak to Dormer. He has thrown over my tea-cup—only look at my frock! If you cannot sit still," she added, turning herself to the boy, "I don't think you should be allowed to come to tea here."

"What is the matter, Dormy?" said Mother.

Dormer was standing beside Sophy, looking very guilty, and rather white.

"Mamma," he said, "I was only drawing a chair out. It got so dreadfully cold where I was sitting, I really could not stay there," and he shivered slightly.

He had been sitting with his back to one of the locked-up doors. Phil, who was nearest, moved his hand slowly across the spot.

"You are fanciful, Dormy," he said, "there is really no draught whatever."

This did not satisfy Mother.

"He must have got a chill, then," she said, and she went on to question the child as to what he had been doing all day, for, as I have said, he was still delicate.

But he persisted that he was quite well, and no longer cold.

"It wasn't exactly a draught," he said, "it was—oh! just icy, all of a sudden. I've felt it before—sitting in that chair."

Mother said no more, and Dormer went on with his tea, and when bed-time came he seemed just as usual, so that her anxiety faded. But she made thorough investigation as to the possibility of any draught coming up from the back stairs, with which this door communicated. None was to be discovered—the door fitted fairly well, and beside this, Hunter had tacked felt round the edges—furthermore, one of the thick heavy *portières* had been hung in front. An evening or two later we were sitting in the drawing-room after dinner, when a cousin who was staying with us suddenly missed her fan.

"Run and fetch Muriel's fan, Dormy," I said, for Muriel felt sure it had slipped under the dinner table. None of the men had as yet joined us.

"Why, where are you going, child?" I said as he turned towards the farther door. "It is much quicker by the gallery." He said nothing, but went out, walking rather slowly, by the gallery door. And in a few minutes he returned, fan in hand, but by the other door.

He was a sensitive child, and though I wondered what he had got into his head against the gallery, I did not say anything before the others. But when, soon after, Dormy said "Good night," and went off to bed, I followed him. "What do you want, Leila?" he said rather crossly. "Don't be vexed, child," I said. "I can see there is something the matter. Why do you not like the gallery?"

He hesitated, but I had laid my hand on his shoulder, and he knew I meant to be kind.

"Leila," he said, with a glance round, to be sure that no one was within hearing—we were standing, he and I, near the inner dining-room door, which was open—"you'll laugh at me, but—there's something queer there—sometimes!"

"What? And how do you mean 'sometimes'?" I asked, with a slight thrill at his tone.

"I mean not always, I've felt it several times—there was the cold the day before yesterday, and besides that, I've felt a—a sort of breaving"—Dormy was not perfect in his "th's"—"like somebody very unhappy."

"Sighing?" I suggested.

"Like sighing in a whisper," he replied, "and that's always near the door. But last week—no, not so long ago, it was on Monday—I went round that way when I was going to bed. I didn't want to be silly. But it was moonlight—and—Leila, a shadow went all along the wall on that side, and stopped at the

door. I saw it waggling about—its hands" and here he shivered—"on that funny curtain that hangs up, as if it were feeling
for a minute or two, and then—"

"Well—what then?"

"It just went out," he said simply. "But it's moonlight again
tonight, sister, and I daren't see it again. I just daren't."

"But you did go to the dining-room that way," I reminded
him.

"Yes, but I shut my eyes and ran, and even then I felt as if
something cold was behind me."

"Dormy, dear," I said, a good deal concerned, "I do think it's
your fancy. You are not quite well yet, you know."

"Yes, I am," he replied sturdily. "I'm not a bit frightened anywhere else. I sleep in a room alone, you know. It's not me, sister,
it's somefing in the gallery."

"Would you be frightened to go there with me now? We can
run through the dining-room; there's no one to see us," and I
turned in that direction as I spoke.

Again my little brother hesitated.

"I'll go with you if you'll hold hands," he said, "but I'll shut my
eyes. And I won't open them till you tell me there's no shadow
on the wall. You must tell me truly."

"But there must be some shadows," I said, "in this bright
moonlight, trees and branches, or even clouds scudding across—
something of that kind is what you must have seen, dear."

He shook his head.

"No, no, of course I wouldn't mind that. I know the difference. No—you couldn't mistake. It goes along, right along, in a
creeping way, and then at the door its hands come farther out,
and it feels."

"Is it like a man or a woman?" I said, beginning to feel rather
creepy myself.

"I think it's most like a rather little man," he replied, "but I'm
not sure. Its head has got something fuzzy about it—oh, I know,
like a sticking-out wig. But lower down it seems wrapped up,
like in a cloak. Oh, it's horrid."

And again he shivered—it was quite time all this nightmare
nonsense was put out of his poor little head.

I took his hand and held it firmly; we went through the dining-room. Nothing could have looked more comfortable and less ghostly. For the lights were still burning on the table, and the flowers in their silver bowls, some wine gleaming in the glasses, the fruit and pretty dishes, made a pleasant glow of colour. It certainly seemed a curiously sudden contrast when we found ourselves in the gallery beyond, cold and unillumined, save by the pale moonlight streaming through the unshuttered windows. For the door closed with a bang as we passed through—the gallery was a draughty place.

Dormy's hold tightened.

"Sister," he whispered, "I've shut my eyes now. You must stand with your back to the windows—between them, or else you'll think it's our own shadows—and watch."

I did as he said, and I had not long to wait.

It came—from the farther end, the second condemned door, whence the winding stair mounted to the attics—it seemed to begin or at least take form there, creeping along, just as Dormy said—stealthily but steadily—right down to the other extremity of the long room. And then it grew blacker—more concentrated—and out from the vague outline came two bony hands, and, as the child had said, too, you could see that they were feeling—all over the upper part of the door.

I stood and watched. I wondered afterwards at my own courage, if courage it was. It was the shadow of a small man, I felt sure. The head seemed large in proportion, and—yes—it—the original of the shadow—was evidently covered by an antique wig. Half mechanically I glanced round—as if in search of the material body that must be there. But no; there was nothing, literally nothing, that could throw this extraordinary shadow.

Of this I was instantly convinced; and here I may as well say once for all, that never was it maintained by anyone, however previously sceptical, who had fully witnessed the whole, that it could be accounted for by ordinary, or, as people say, "natural" causes. There was this peculiarity at least about our ghost.

Though I had fast hold of his hand, I had almost forgotten Dormy—I seemed in a trance.

Suddenly he spoke, though in a whisper.

"You see it, sister, I know you do," he said.

"Wait, wait a minute, dear," I managed to reply in the same tone, though I could not have explained why I waited. Dormer had said that after a time—after the ghastly and apparently fruitless feeling all over the door—"it"—"went out."

I think it was this that I was waiting for. It was not quite as he had said. The door was in the extreme corner of the wall, the hinges almost in the angle, and as the shadow began to move on again, it looked as if it disappeared; but no, it was only fainter. My eyes, preternaturally sharpened by my intense gaze, still saw it, working its way round the corner, as assuredly no shadow in the real sense of the word ever did nor could do. I realized this, and the sense of horror grew all but intolerable; yet I stood still, clasping the cold little hand in mine tighter and tighter. And an instinct of protection of the child gave me strength. Besides, it was coming on so quickly—we could not have escaped—it was coming, nay, it was behind us.

"Leila!" gasped Dormy, "the cold—you feel it now?"

Yes, truly—like no icy breath that I had ever felt before was that momentary but horrible thrill of utter cold. If it had lasted another second I think it would have killed us both. But, mercifully, it passed, in far less time than it has taken me to tell it, and then we seemed in some strange way to be released.

"Open your eyes, Dormy," I said, "you won't see anything, I promise you. I want to rush across to the dining-room."

He obeyed me. I felt there was time to escape before that awful presence would again have arrived at the dining-room door, though it was coming—ah, yes, it was coming, steadily pursuing its ghastly round. And, alas! the dining-room door was closed. But I kept my nerve to some extent. I turned the handle without over much trembling, and in another moment, the door shut and locked behind us, we stood in safety, looking at each other, in the bright cheerful room we had left so short a time ago.

Was it so short a time? I said to myself. It seemed hours! And through the door open to the hall came at that moment the sound of cheerful laughing voices from the drawing-room. Someone was coming out. It seemed impossible, incredible, that within a few feet of the matter-of-fact pleasant material life, this horrible inexplicable drama should be going on, as doubtless it still was.

Of the two I was now more upset than my little brother. I was older and took in more. He, boy-like, was in a sense triumphant at having proved himself correct and no coward, and though he was still pale, his eyes shone with excitement and a queer kind of satisfaction.

But before we had done more than look at each other, a figure appeared at the open doorway. It was Sophy.

"Leila," she said, "Mamma wants to know what you are doing with Dormy? He is to go to bed at once. We saw you go out of the room after him, and then a door banged. Mamma says if you are playing with him it's very bad for him so late at night."

Dormy was very quick. He was still holding my hand, and he pinched it to stop my replying.

"Rubbish!" he said. "I am speaking to Leila quietly, and she is coming up to my room while I undress. Good night, Sophy."

"Tell Mamma Dormy really wants me," I added, and then Sophy departed.

"We mustn't tell her, Leila," said the boy. "She'd have 'sterics."

"Whom shall we tell?" I said, for I was beginning to feel very helpless and upset.

"Nobody, tonight," he replied sensibly. "You mustn't go in there," and he shivered a little as he moved his head towards the gallery; "you're not fit for it, and they'd be wanting you to. Wait till the morning and then I'd—I think I'd tell Philip first. You needn't be frightened tonight, sister. It won't stop you sleeping. It didn't me the time I saw it before."

He was right. I slept dreamlessly. It was as if the nervous strain of those few minutes had utterly exhausted me.

PART II

Phil is our soldier brother. And there is nothing fanciful about *him!* He is a rock of sturdy common-sense and unfailing good nature. He was the very best person to confide our strange secret to, and my respect for Dormy increased.

We did tell him—the very next morning. He listened very attentively, only putting in a question here and there, and though, of course, he was incredulous—had I not been so myself?—he was not mocking.

"I am glad you have told no one else," he said, when we had related the whole as circumstantially as possible. "You see Mother is not very strong yet, and it would be a pity to bother Father, just when he's taken this place and settled it all. And for goodness' sake, don't let a breath of it get about among the servants; there'd be the—something to pay, if you did."

"I won't tell anybody," said Dormy.

"Nor shall I," I added. "Sophy is far too excitable, and if she knew, she would certainly tell Nannie." Nannie is our old nurse.

"If we tell anyone," Philip went on, "that means," with a rather irritating smile of self-confidence, "if by any possibility I do not succeed in making an end of your ghost and we want another opinion about it, the person to tell would be Miss Larpent."

"Yes," I said, "I think so, too."

I would not risk irritating him by saying how convinced I was that conviction awaited *him* as surely it had come to myself, and I knew that Miss Larpent, though far from credulous, was equally far from stupid scepticism concerning the mysteries "not dreamt of" in ordinary "philosophy."

"What do you mean to do?" I went on. "You have a theory, I see. Won't you tell me what it is?"

"I have two," said Phil, rolling up a cigarette as he spoke. "It is either some queer optical illusion, partly the effect of some odd reflection outside—or it is a clever trick."

"A trick!" I exclaimed; "what *possible* motive could there be for a trick?"

Phil shook his head.

"Ah," he said, "that I cannot at present say."

"And what are you going to do?"

"I shall sit up tonight in the gallery and see for myself."

"Alone?" I exclaimed, with some misgiving. For big, sturdy fellow as he was, I scarcely liked to think of him—of *any one*—alone with that awful thing.

"I don't suppose you or Dormy would care to keep me company," he replied, "and on the whole I would rather not have you."

"I wouldn't do it," said the child honestly, "not for—for nothing."

"I shall keep Tim with me," said Philip, "I would rather have him than anyone."

Tim was Phil's bull-dog, and certainly, I agreed, much better than nobody.

So it was settled.

Dormy and I went to bed unusually early that night, for as the day wore on we both felt exceedingly tired. I pleaded headache, which was not altogether a fiction, though I repented having complained at all when I found that poor Mamma immediately began worrying herself that "after all," I too, was to fall a victim to the influenza.

"I shall be all right in the morning," I assured her.

I knew no further details of Phil's arrangements. I fell asleep almost at once. I usually do. And it seemed to me that I had slept a whole night when I was awakened by a glimmering light at my door, and heard Philip's voice speaking softly.

"Are you awake, Lel?" he said, as people always say when they awake you in any untimely way. Of course, *now* I was awake, very much awake indeed.

"What is it?" I exclaimed eagerly, my heart beginning to beat very fast.

"Oh, nothing, nothing at all," said my brother, advancing a little into the room. "I just thought I'd look in on my way to bed to reassure you I have seen *nothing*, absolutely nothing."

I do not know if I was relieved or disappointed.

"Was it moonlight?" I asked abruptly.

"No," he replied, "unluckily the moon did not come out at all, though it is nearly at the full. I carried in a small lamp, which made things less eerie. But I should have preferred the moon."

I glanced up at him. Was it the reflection of the candle he held, or did he look paler than usual?

"And," I added suddenly, "did you *feel* nothing?"

He hesitated.

"It—it was chilly, certainly," he said. "I fancy I must have dozed a little, for I did feel pretty cold once or twice."

"Ah, indeed!" thought I to myself. "And how about Tim?"

Phil smiled, but not very successfully.

"Well," he said, "I must confess Tim did not altogether like it. He started snarling, then he growled, and finished up with whining in a decidedly unhappy way. He's rather upset—poor old chap!"

And then I saw that the dog was beside him—rubbing up close to Philip's legs—a very dejected, reproachful Tim—all the starch taken out of him.

"Good night, Phil," I said, turning round on my pillow. "I'm glad you are satisfied. Tomorrow morning you must tell me which of your theories holds most water. Good night, and many thanks."

He was going to say more, but my manner for the moment stopped him, and he went off.

Poor old Phil!

We had it out the next morning. He and I alone. He was not satisfied. Far from it. In the bottom of his heart I believe it was a strange yearning for a breath of human companionship, for the sound of a human voice, that had made him look in on me the night before.

For he had felt the cold passing him.

But he was very plucky.

"I'll sit up again tonight, Leila," he said.

"Not tonight," I objected. "This sort of adventure requires one to be at one's best. If you take my advice you will go to bed early and have a good stretch of sleep, so that you will be quite fresh by tomorrow. There will be a moon for some nights still."

"Why do you keep harping on the moon?" said Phil rather crossly for him.

"Because—I have some idea that it is only in the moonlight that—that anything is to be *seen*."

"Bosh!" said my brother politely—he was certainly rather discomposed—"we are talking at cross-purposes. You are satisfied—"

"Far from satisfied," I interpolated.

"Well, convinced, whatever you like to call it—that the whole thing is supernatural, whereas I am equally sure it is a trick; a clever trick, I allow, though I haven't yet got at the motive of it."

"You need your nerves to be at their best to discover a trick of this kind, if a trick it be," I said quietly.

Philip had left his seat, and walked up and down the room; his way of doing so gave me a feeling that he wanted to walk off some unusual consciousness of irritability. I felt half provoked and half sorry for him.

At that moment—we were alone in the drawing-room—the door opened and Miss Larpent came in.

"I cannot find Sophy," she said, peering about through her rather short-sighted eyes, which, nevertheless, see a great deal sometimes; "do you know where she is?"

"I saw her setting off somewhere with Nugent," said Philip, stopping his quarter-deck exercise for a moment.

"Ah, then it is hopeless. I suppose I must resign myself to very irregular ways for a little longer," Miss Larpent replied with a smile.

She is not young, and not good looking, but she is gifted with a delightful way of smiling, and she is—well, the dearest and almost the wisest of women.

She looked at Philip as she spoke. She had known as nearly since our babyhood.

"Is there anything the matter?" she said suddenly. "You look fagged, Leila, and Philip seems worried."

I glanced at Philip. He understood me.

"Yes," he replied, "I am irritated, and Leila is—" he hesitated.

"What?" asked Miss Larpent.

"Oh, I don't know—obstinate, I suppose. Sit down, Miss Larpent, and hear our story. Leila, you can tell it."

I did so—first obtaining a promise of secrecy, and making Phil relate his own experience.

Our new *confidante* listened attentively, her face very grave.
When she had heard all, she said quietly, after a moment's
silence: "It's very strange, very. Philip, if you will wait till tomorrow night, and I quite agree with Leila that you had better do
so, I will sit up with you. I have pretty good nerves, and I have
always wanted an experience of that kind."

"Then you don't think it is a trick?" I said eagerly. I was like
Dormer, divided between my real underlying longing to explain
the thing, and get rid of the horror of it, and a half childish wish
to prove that I had not exaggerated its ghastliness.

"I will tell you that the day after tomorrow," she said. I could
not repress a little shiver as she spoke.

She *had* good nerves, and she was extremely sensible.

But I almost blamed myself afterwards for having acquiesced
in the plan. For the effect on her was very great. They never told
me exactly what happened; "You *know*," said Miss Larpent. I
imagine their experience was almost precisely similar to Dormy's
and mine, intensified, perhaps, by the feeling of loneliness. For
it was not till all the rest of the family was in bed that this second
vigil began. It was a bright moonlight night—they had the whole
thing complete.

It was impossible to throw off the effect; even in the daytime
the four of us who had seen and heard, shrank from the gallery,
and made any conceivable excuse for avoiding it.

But Phil, however convinced, behaved consistently. He examined the closed door thoroughly, to detect any possible trickery.
He explored the attics, he went up and down the staircase leading to the offices, till the servants must have thought he was
going crazy. He found nothing—no vaguest hint even as to why
the gallery was chosen by the ghostly shadow for its nightly
round.

Strange to say, however, as the moon waned, our horror
faded, so that we almost began to hope the thing was at an end,
and to trust that in time we should forget about it. And we congratulated ourselves that we had kept our own counsel and not
disturbed any of the others even Father, who would, no doubt,
have hooted at the idea—by the baleful whisper that our charming castle by the sea was haunted!

And the days passed by, growing into weeks. The second detachment of our guests had left, and a third had just arrived, when one morning as I was waiting at what we called "the sea-door" for some of the others to join me in a walk along the sands, someone touched me on the shoulder. It was Philip.

"Leila," he said, "I am not happy about Dormer. He is looking ill again, and—"

"I thought he seemed so much stronger," I said, surprised and distressed, "quite rosy, and so much merrier."

"So he was till a few days ago," said Philip. "But if you notice him well you'll see that he's getting that white look again. And I've got it into my head—he is an extraordinarily sensitive child—that it has something to do with the moon. It's getting on to the full."

For the moment I stupidly forgot the association.

"Really, Phil," I said, "you are too absurd! Do you actually— oh," as he was beginning to interrupt me, and my face fell, I feel sure—"you don't mean about the gallery."

"Yes, I do," he said.

"How? Has Dormy told you anything?" and a sort of sick feeling came over me. "I had begun to hope," I went on, "that somehow it had gone; that, perhaps, it only comes once a year at a certain season, or possibly that newcomers see it at the first and not again. Oh, Phil, we *can't* stay here, however nice it is, if it is really haunted."

"Dormy hasn't said much," Philip replied. "He only told me he had *felt the cold* once or twice, since the moon came again," he said. "But I can see the fear of more is upon him. And this determined me to speak to you. I have to go to London for ten days or so, to see the doctors about my leave, and a few other things. I don't like it for you and Miss Larpent if—if this thing is to return—with no one else in your confidence, especially on Dormy's account. Do you think we must tell Father before I go?"

I hesitated. For many reasons I was reluctant to do so.

Father would be exaggeratedly sceptical at first, and then, if he were convinced, as I knew he would be, he would go to the other extreme and insist upon leaving Finster, and there would be a regular upset, trying for Mother and everybody concerned. And Mother liked the place, and was looking so much better!

"After all," I said, "it has not hurt any of us. Miss Larpent got a shake, so did I. But it wasn't as great a shock to us as to you, Phil, to have to believe in a ghost. And we can avoid the gallery while you are away. No, except for Dormy, I would rather keep it to ourselves—after all, we are not going to live here always. Yet it is so nice, it seems such a pity."

It was such an exquisite morning; the air, faintly breathing of the sea, was like elixir; the heights and shadows on the cliffs, thrown out by the darker woods behind, were indeed, as Janet Miles had said, "wonderful."

"Yes," Phil agreed, "it is an awful nuisance. But as for Dormy," he went on, "supposing I get Mother to let me take him with me? He'd be as jolly as a sand-boy in London, and my old landlady would look after him like anything if ever I had to be out late. And I'd let my doctor see him—quietly, you know—he might give him a tonic or something."

I heartily approved of the idea. So did Mamma when Phil broached it—she, too, had thought her "baby" looked quite pale lately. A London doctor's opinion would be such a satisfaction. So it was settled, and the very next day the two set off, Dormer, in his "old-fashioned," reticent way, in the greatest delight, though only by one remark did the brave little fellow hint at what was, no doubt, the principal cause of his satisfaction.

"The moon will be long past the full when we come back," he said. "And after that there'll only be one other time before we go, won't there, Leila? We've only got this house for three months?"

"Yes," I said, "Father only took it for three," though in my heart I knew it was with the option of three more—six in all.

And Miss Larpent and I were left alone, not with the ghost, certainly, but with our fateful knowledge of its unwelcome proximity. We did not speak of it to each other, but we tacitly avoided the gallery, even, as much as possible, in the day-time. I felt, and so, she has since confessed, did she, that it would be impossible to endure *that cold* without betraying ourselves.

And I began to breathe more freely, trusting that the dread of the shadows' possible return was really only due to the child's over-wrought nerves.

Till—one morning—my fools paradise was abruptly destroyed. Father came in late to breakfast—he had been for an early walk, he said, to get rid of a headache. But he did not look altogether as if he had succeeded in doing so.

"Leila," he said, as I was leaving the room after pouring out his coffee—Mamma was not yet allowed to get up early—"Leila, don't go. I want to speak to you."

I stopped short, and turned towards the table. There was something very odd about his manner. He is usually hearty and eager, almost impetuous in his way of speaking.

"Leila," he began again, "you are a sensible girl, and your nerves are strong, I fancy. Besides, you have not been ill like the others. Don't speak of what I am going to tell you."

I nodded in assent; I could scarcely have spoken. My heart was beginning to thump. Father would not have commended my nerves had he known it.

"Something odd and inexplicable happened last night," he went on. "Nugent and I were sitting in the gallery. It was a mild night, and the moon magnificent. We thought the gallery would be pleasanter than the smoking-room, now that Phil and his pipes are away. Well—we were sitting quietly. I had lighted my reading-lamp on the little table at one end of the room, and Nugent was half lying in his chair, doing nothing in particular except admiring the night, when all at once he started violently with an exclamation, and, jumping up, came towards me. Leila, his teeth were chattering, and he was blue with cold. I was very much alarmed—you know how ill he was at college. But in a moment or two he recovered.

"What on earth is the matter?" I said to him. He tried to laugh. "I really don't know," he said; "I felt as if I had had an electric shock of *cold*—but I'm all right again now."

"I went into the dining-room, and made him take a little brandy and water, and sent him off to bed. Then I came back, still feeling rather uneasy about him, and sat down with my book, when, Leila—you will scarcely credit it—I myself felt the same shock exactly. A perfectly *hideous* thrill of cold. That was how it began. I started up, and then, Leila, by degrees, in some instinctive way, I seemed to realize what had caused it. My dear child, you will think I have gone crazy when I tell you that there was a shadow—a shadow in the moonlight—*chasing* me, so to say, round the room, and once again it caught me up, and again came that appalling sensation. I would not give in. I dodged it after that, and set myself to watch it, and then—"

I need not quote my father further; suffice to say his experience matched that of the rest of us entirely—no, I think it surpassed them. It was the worst of all.

Poor Father! I shuddered for him. I think a shock of that kind is harder upon a man than upon a woman. Our sex is less sceptical, less imaginative, or whatever you like to call the readiness to believe what we cannot explain. And it was astounding to me to see how my father at once capitulated— never even *alluding* to a possibility of trickery. Astounding, yet at the same time not without a certain satisfaction in it. It was almost a relief to find others in the same boat with ourselves. I told him at once all we had to tell, and how painfully exercised we had been as to the advisability of keeping our secret to ourselves. I never saw Father so impressed; he was awfully kind, too, and so sorry for us. He made me fetch Miss Larpent, and we held a council of—I don't know what to call it!—not "war," assuredly, for none of us thought of fighting the ghost. How could one fight a shadow? We decided to do nothing beyond endeavouring to keep the affair from going further. During the next few days Father arranged to have some work done in the gallery which would prevent our sitting there, without raising any suspicions on Mamma's or Sophy's part.

"And then," said Father, "we must see. Possibly this extraordinary influence only makes itself felt periodically."

"I am almost certain it is so," said Miss Larpent.

"And in this case," he continued, "we may manage to evade it. But I do not feel disposed to continue my tenancy here after three months are over. If once the servants get hold of the story, and they are sure to do so sooner or later, it would be unendurable—the worry and annoyance would do your mother far more harm than any good effect the air and change have had upon her."

I was glad to hear this decision. Honestly, I did not feel as if I could stand the strain for long, and it might kill poor little Dormy.

But where should we go? Our own home would be quite uninhabitable till the autumn, for extensive alterations and repairs were going on there. I said this to Father.

"Yes," he agreed, "it is not convenient"—and he hesitated. "I cannot make it out," he went on, "Miles would have been sure to know if the house had a bad name in any way. I think I will go over and see him today, and tell him all about it—at least I shall inquire about some other house in the neighbourhood— and perhaps I will tell him our reason for leaving this."

He did so—he went over to Raxtrew that very afternoon, and, as I quite anticipated would be the case, he told me on his return that he had taken both our friends into his confidence.

"They are extremely concerned about it," he said, "and very sympathising, though, naturally, inclined to think us a parcel of very weak-minded folk indeed. But I am glad of one thing—the Rectory there is to be let from the first of July for three months. Miles took me to see it. I think it will do very well—it is quite out of the village, for you really can't call it a town—and a nice little place in its way. Quite modern, and as unghost-like as you could wish, bright and cheery."

"And what will Mamma think of our leaving so soon?" I asked.

But as to this Father assured me. He had already spoken of it to her, and somehow she did not seem disappointed. She had got it into her head that Finster did not suit Dormy, and was quite disposed to think that three months of such strong air were enough at a time.

"Then have you decided upon Raxtrew Rectory?" I asked.

"I have the refusal of it," said my father. "But you will be almost amused to hear that Miles begged me not to fix abso- lutely for a few days. He is coming to us tomorrow, to spend the night."

"You mean to see for himself?"

Father nodded.

"Poor Mr. Miles!" I ejaculated. "You won't sit up with him, I hope, Father?"

"I offered to do so, but he won't hear of it," was the reply. "He is bringing one of his keepers with him—a sturdy, trustworthy young fellow, and they two with their revolvers are going to nab the ghost, so he says. We shall see. We must manage to prevent our servants suspecting anything."

This *was* managed. I need not go into particulars. Suffice to say that the sturdy keeper reached his own home before dawn on the night of the vigil, no endeavours of his master having succeeded in persuading him to stay another moment at Finster, and that Mr. Miles himself looked so ill the next morning when he joined us at the breakfast-table that we, the initiated, could scarcely repress our exclamations, when Sophy, with the curious instinct of touching a sore place which some people have, told him that he looked exactly, "as if he had seen a ghost."

His experience had been precisely similar to ours. After that we heard no more from him—about the pity it was to leave a place that suited us so well, etc., etc. On the contrary, before he left, he told my father and myself that he thought us uncommonly plucky for staying out the three months, though at the same time he confessed to feeling completely nonplussed.

"I have lived near Finster St. Mabyn's all my life," he said, "and my people before me, and never, do I honestly assure you, have I heard one breath of the old place being haunted. And in a shut-up neighbourhood like this, such a thing would have leaked out."

We shook our heads, but what could we say?

PART III

We left Finster St. Mabyn's towards the middle of July. Nothing worth recording happened during the last few weeks. If the ghostly drama were still re-enacted night after night, or only during some portion of each month, we took care not to assist at the performance. I believe Phil and Nugent planned another vigil, but he gave it up by my father's expressed wish, and on one pretext or another he managed to keep the gallery locked off without arousing any suspicion in my mother or Sophy, or any of our visitors.

It was a cold summer—those early months of it at least—and that made it easier to avoid the room.

Somehow none of us were sorry to go. This was natural, so far as several were concerned, but rather curious as regards those of the family who knew no drawback to the charms of the place. I suppose it was due to some instinctive consciousness of the influence which so many of the party had felt it impossible to resist or explain.

And the Rectory at Raxtrew was really a dear little place. It was so bright and open and sunny. Dormy's pale face was rosy with pleasure the first afternoon when he came rushing in to tell us that there were tame rabbits and a pair of guinea-pigs in an otherwise empty loose box in the stableyard.

"Do come and look at them," he begged, and I went with him, pleased to see him so happy.

I did not care for the rabbits, but I always think guinea-pigs rather fascinating, and we stayed playing with them some little time.

"I'll show you another way back into the house," said Dormy, and he led me through a conservatory into a large, almost unfurnished room, opening again into a tiled passage leading to the offices.

"This is the Warden boys' play-room," he said. "They keep their cricket and football things here, you see, and their tricycle. I wonder if I might use it?"

"We must write and ask them," I said. "But what are all these big packages?" I went on. "Oh, I see, it's our heavy luggage from Finster. There is not room in this house for our odds and ends of furniture, I suppose. It's rather a pity they have put it in here, for we could have had some nice games in this big room on a wet day, and see, Dormy, here are several pairs of roller-skates! Oh, we must have this place cleared."

We spoke to Father about it—and he came and looked at the room and agreed with us that it would be a pity not to have the full use of it. Roller-skating would be good exercise for Dormy, he said, and even for Nat, who would be joining us before long for his holidays.

So our big cases, and the chairs and tables we had bought from Hunter, in their careful swathings of wisps and matting, were carried out to an empty barn—a perfectly dry and weather-tight barn—for everything at the Rectory was in excellent repair. In this, as in all other details, our new quarters were a complete contrast to the picturesque abode we had just quitted.

The weather was charming for the first two or three weeks—much warmer and sunnier than at Finster. We all enjoyed it, and seemed to breathe more freely. Miss Larpent, who was staying through the holidays this year, and I congratulated each other more than once, when sure of not being overheard, on the cheerful, wholesome atmosphere in which we found ourselves.

"I do not think I shall ever wish to live in a very old house again," she said one day. We were in the play-room, and I had been persuading her to try her hand—or feet—at rollerskating. "Even now," she went on, "I own to you, Leila, though it may sound very weak-minded, I cannot think of that horrible night without a shiver. Indeed, I could fancy I feel that thrill of indescribable cold at the present moment."

She was shivering and extraordinary to relate, as she spoke, her tremor communicated itself to me. Again, I could swear to it, again I felt that blast of unutterable, unearthly cold.

I started up. We were seated on a bench against the wall—a bench belonging to the play-room, and which we had not thought of removing, as a few seats were a convenience.

Miss Larpent caught sight of my face. Her own, which was very white, grew distressed in expression. She grasped my arm.

"My dearest child," she exclaimed, "you look blue, and your teeth are chattering! I do wish I had not alluded to that fright we had. I had no idea you were so nervous."

"I did not know it myself," I replied. "I often think of the Finster ghost quite calmly, even in the middle of the night. But just then, Miss Larpent, do you know, I really *felt* that horrid cold again!"

"So did I—or rather my imagination did," she replied, trying to talk in a matter-of-fact way. She got up as she spoke, and went to the window. "It can't be *all* imagination," she added. "See, Leila, what a gusty, stormy day it is—not like the beginning of August. It really is cold."

"And this play-room seems nearly as draughty as the gallery at Finster," I said. "Don't let us stay here—come into the drawing-room and play some duets. I wish we could quite forget about Finster."

"Dormy has done so, I hope," said Miss Larpent.

That chilly morning was the commencement of the real break-up in the weather. We women would not have minded it so much, as there are always plenty of indoor things we can find to do. And my two grown-up brothers were away. Raxtrew held no particular attractions for them, and Phil wanted to see some of our numerous relations before he returned to India. So he and Nugent started on a round of visits. But, unluckily, it was the beginning of the public school holidays, and poor Nat—the fifteen-years-old boy—had just joined us. It was very disappointing for him in more ways that one. He had set his heart on seeing Finster, impressed by our enthusiastic description of it when we first went there, and now his anticipations had to come down to a comparatively tame and uninteresting village, and every probability—so said the wise—of a stretch of rainy, unsummerlike weather.

Nat was a good-natured, cheery fellow, however—not nearly as clever or as impressionable as Dormy, but with the same common-sense. So he wisely determined to make the best of things, and as we were really sorry for him, he did not, after all, come off very badly.

His principal amusement was roller-skating in the playroom. Dormy had not taken to it in the same way—the greater part of his time was spent with the rabbits and guinea-pigs, where Nat, when he himself had had skating enough, was pretty sure to find him.

I suppose it is with being the eldest sister that it always seems my fate to receive the confidences of the rest of the family, and it was about this time, a fortnight or so after his arrival, that it began to strike me that Nat looked as if he had something on his mind.

"He is sure to tell me what it is, sooner or later," I said to myself. "Probably he has left some small debts behind him at school—only he did not look worried or anxious when he first came home.

The confidence was given. One afternoon Nat followed me into the library, where I was going to write some letters, and said he wanted to speak to me. I put my paper aside and waited.

"Leila," he began, "you must promise not to laugh at me."

This was not what I expected.

"Laugh at you—no, certainly not," I replied, "especially if you are in any trouble. And I have thought you were looking worried, Nat."

"Well, yes," he said, "I don't know if there is anything coming over me I feel quite well, but—Leila," he broke off, "do you believe in ghosts?"

I started.

"Has anyone—" I was beginning rashly, but the boy interrupted me.

"No, no," he said eagerly, "no one has put anything of the kind into my head—no one. It is my own senses that have seen—felt it—or else, if it is fancy, I must be going out of my mind, Leila—I do believe there is a ghost here *in the play-room*."

I sat silent, an awful dread creeping over me, which, as he went on, grew worse and worse. Had the thing—the Finster shadow—attached itself to us—I had read of such cases—had it journeyed with us to this peaceful, healthful house? The remembrance of the cold thrill experienced by Miss Larpent and myself flashed back upon me. And Nat went on.

Yes, the cold was the first thing he had been startled by, followed, just as in the gallery of our old castle, by the consciousness of the terrible, shadow-like presence gradually taking form in the moonlight. For there had been moonlight the last night or two, and Nat, in his skating ardour, had amused himself alone in the play-room after Dormy had gone to bed.

"The night before last was the worst," he said. "It stopped

raining, you remember, Leila, and the moon was very bright—I noticed how it glistened on the wet leaves outside. It was by the moonlight I saw the—the shadow. I wouldn't have thought of skating in the evening but for the light, for we've never had a lamp in there. It came round the walls, Leila, and then it seemed to stop and fumble away in one corner—at the end where there is a bench, you know."

Indeed I did know; it was where our governess and I had been sitting.

"I got so awfully frightened," said Nat honestly, "that I ran off. Then yesterday I was ashamed of myself, and went back there in the evening with a candle. But I saw nothing: the moon did not come out. Only—I felt the cold again. I believe it was there—though I could not see it. Leila, what *can* it be? If only I could make you understand! It is so much worse than it sounds to tell."

I said what I could to soothe him, I spoke of odd shadows thrown by the trees outside swaying in the wind, for the weather was still stormy. I repeated the time-worn argument about optical illusions, etc. etc., and in the end he gave in a little. It *might* have been his fancy. And he promised me most faithfully to breathe no hint—not the very faintest—of the fright he had had, to Sophy or Dormy, or anyone.

Then I had to tell my father. I really shrank from doing so, but there seemed no alternative. At first, of course, he pooh-poohed it at once by saying Dormy must have been talking to Nat about the Finster business, or if not Dormy, someone—Miss Larpent even! But when all such explanations were entirely set at nought, I must say poor Father looked rather blank. I was sorry for him, and sorry for myself—the idea of being *followed* by this horrible presence was too sickening.

Father took refuge at last in some brain-wave theory—involuntary impressions had been made on Nat by all of us, whose minds were still full of the strange experience. He said he felt sure, and no doubt he tried to think he did, that this theory explained the whole. I felt glad for him to get any satisfaction out of it, and I did my best to take it up too. But it was no use. I felt that Nat's experience had been an "objective" one, as Miss

Larpent expressed it—or, as Dormy had said at first at Finster: "No, no, sister—it's something *there*—it's nothing to do with *me*."

And earnestly I longed for the time to come for our return to our own familiar home.

"I don't think I shall ever wish to leave it again," I thought. But after a week or two the feeling began to fade again. And Father very sensibly discovered that it would not do to leave our spare furniture and heavy luggage in the barn—it was getting all dusty and cobwebby. So it was all moved back again to the play-room, and stacked as it had been at first, making it impossible for us to skate or amuse ourselves in any way there, at which Sophy grumbled, but Nat did not.

Father was very good to Nat. He took him about with him as much as he could to get the thought of that horrid thing out of his head. But yet it could not have been half as bad for Nat as for the rest of us, for we took the greatest possible precautions against any whisper of the dreadful and mysterious truth reaching him, that the ghost had *followed us* from Finster.

Father did not tell Mr. Miles or Jenny about it. They had been worried enough, poor things, by the trouble at Finster, and it would be too bad for them to think that the strange influence was affecting us in the *second* house we had taken at their recommendation.

"In fact," said Father with a rather rueful smile, "if we don't take care, we shall begin to be looked upon askance as a haunted family! Our lives would have been in danger in the good old witchcraft days."

"It is really a mercy that none of the servants have got hold of the story," said Miss Larpent, who was one of our council of three. "We must just hope that no further annoyance will befall us till we are safe at home again."

Her hopes were fulfilled. Nothing else happened while we remained at the Rectory—it really seemed as if the unhappy shade was limited locally, in one sense. For at Finster, even, it had never been seen or felt save in the one room.

The vividness of the impression of poor Nat's experience had almost died away when the time came for us to leave. I felt now that I should rather enjoy telling Phil and Nugent about it, and hearing what *they* could bring forward in the way of explanation.

We left Raxtrew early in October. Our two big brothers were awaiting us at home, having arrived there a few days before us. Nugent was due at Oxford very shortly.

It was very nice to be in our own house again, after several months' absence, and it was most interesting to see how the alterations, including a good deal of new papering and painting, had been carried out. And as soon as the heavy luggage arrived we had grand consultations as to the disposal about the rooms of the charming pieces of furniture we had picked up at Hunter's. Our rooms are large and nicely shaped, most of them. It was not difficult to make a pretty corner here and there with a quaint old chair or two and a delicate spindle-legged table, and when we had arranged them all—Phil, Nugent and I were the movers—we summoned Mother and Miss Larpent to give their opinion.

They quite approved, Mother even saying that she would be glad of a few more odds and ends.

"We might empower Janet Miles," she said, "to let us know if she sees anything very tempting. Is that really all we have? They looked so much more important in their swathings."

The same idea struck me. I glanced round.

"Yes," I said, "that's all. Except—oh, yes, there are the tapestry *portières*—the best of all. We can't have them in the drawing-room, I fear. It is too modern for them. Where shall we hang them?"

"You are forgetting, Leila," said Mother. "We spoke of having them in the hall. They will do beautifully to hang before the two side doors, which are seldom opened. And in cold weather the hall is draughty, though nothing like the gallery at Finster."

Why did she say that? It made me shiver, but then, of course, she did not know.

Our hall is a very pleasant one. We sit there a great deal. The side doors Mother spoke of are second entrances to the dining-room and library, quite unnecessary, except when we have a large party, a dance or something of that sort. And the *portières*

certainly seemed the very thing, the mellow colouring of the
tapestry showing to great advantage. The boys—Phil and
Nugent, I mean—set to work at once, and in an hour or two the
hangings were placed.

"Of course," said Philip, "if ever these doors are to be opened,
this precious tapestry must be taken down, or very carefully
looped back. It is very worn in some places, and in spite of the
thick lining it should be tenderly handled. I am afraid it has suffered a little from being so long rolled up at the Rectory. It
should have been hung up!"

Still, it looked very well indeed, and when Father, who was
away at some magistrates' meeting, came home that afternoon,
I showed him our arrangements with pride.

He was very pleased.

"Very nice, very nice indeed," he said, though it was almost
too dusk for him to judge quite fully of the effect of the tapestry.
"But, dear me, child, this hall is very cold. We must have a
larger fire. Only October! What sort of a winter are we going to
have?"

He shivered as he spoke. He was standing close to one of the
portières—smoothing the tapestry half absently with one hand.
I looked at him with concern.

"I *hope* you have not got a chill, Papa," I said.

But he seemed all right again when we went into the library,
where tea was waiting—an extra late tea for his benefit.

The next day Nugent went to Oxford. Nat had already
returned to school. So our home party was reduced to Father
and Mother, Miss Larpent, Phil and I, and the children.

We were very glad to have Phil settled at home for some time.
There was little fear of his being tempted away, now that the
shooting had begun. We were expecting some of our usual
guests at this season; the weather was perfect autumn weather;
we had thrown off all remembrance of influenza and other
depressing "influences," and were feeling bright and cheerful,
when again—ah, yes, even now it gives me a faint, sick sensation
to recall the horror of that *third* visitation!

But I must tell it simply, and not give way to painful remem-
brances.

It was the very day before our first visitors were expected that the blow fell, the awful fear made itself felt. And, as before, the victim was a new one, the one—who, for reasons already mentioned, we had specially guarded from any breath of the gruesome terror—poor little Sophy!

What she was doing alone in the hall late that evening I cannot quite recall—yes, I think I remember her saying she had run downstairs when half-way up to bed, to fetch a book she had left there in the afternoon. She had no light, and the one lamp in the hall—we never sat there after dinner—was burning feebly. *It was bright moonlight.*

I was sitting at the piano, where I had been playing in a rather sleepy way—when a sudden touch on my shoulder made me start, and, looking up, I saw my sister standing beside me, white and trembling.

"Leila," she whispered, "come with me quickly. I don't want Mamma to notice."

For Mother was still nervous and delicate.

The drawing-room is very long, and has two or three doors. No one else was at our end. It was easy to make our way out unperceived. Sophy caught my hand and hurried me upstairs without speaking till we reached my own room, where a bright fire was burning cheerfully.

Then she began.

"Leila," she said, "I have had such an awful fright. I did not want to speak until we were safe up here."

"What was it?" I exclaimed breathlessly. Did I already suspect the truth? I really do not know, but my nerves were not what they had been.

Sophy gasped and began to tremble. I put my arm round her.

"It does not sound so bad," she said. "But—oh, Leila, what *could* it be? It was in the hall," and then I think she explained how she had come to be there. "I was standing near the side door into the library that we never use—and—all of a sudden a sort of darkness came along the wall, and seemed to settle on the door—where the old tapestry is, you know. I thought it was the shadow of something outside, for it was bright moonlight, and the windows were not shuttered. But in a moment I saw it could not be that—there is nothing to throw such a shadow. It seemed to wriggle about—like—like a monstrous spider, or—" and there she hesitated—"almost like a deformed sort of human being. And all at once, Leila, my breath went and I fell down. I really did. I was *choked* with cold. I think my senses went away, but I am not sure. The next thing I remember was rushing across the hall and then down the south corridor to the drawing-room, and then I was so thankful to see you there by the piano."

I drew her down on my knee, poor child.

"It was very good of you, dear," I said, "to control yourself, and not startle Mamma."

This pleased her, but her terror was still uppermost.

"Leila," she said piteously, "can't you explain it? I did so hope you could."

What *could* I say?

"I—one would need to go to the hall and look well about to see what could cast such a shadow," I said vaguely, and I suppose I must involuntarily have moved a little, for Sophy started, and clutched me fast.

"Oh, Leila, don't go—you don't mean you are going now?" she entreated.

Nothing truly was farther from my thoughts, but I took care not to say so.

"I won't leave you if you'd rather not," I said, "and I tell you what, Sophy, if you would like very much to sleep here with me tonight, you shall. I will ring and tell Freake to bring your things down and undress you—on one condition."

"What?" she said eagerly. She was much impressed by my amiability.

"That you won't say *one word* about this, or give the least shadow of a hint to anyone that you have had a fright. You don't know the trouble it will cause."

"Of course I will promise to let no one know, if you think it better, for you are so kind to me," said Sophy. But there was a touch of reluctance in her tone. "You—you mean to do something about it though, Leila," she went on. "I shall never be able to forget it if you don't."

"Yes," I said, "I shall speak to Father and Phil about it tomorrow. If anyone has been trying to frighten us," I added unguardedly, "by playing tricks, they certainly must be exposed."

"Not us," she corrected, "it was only me," and I did not reply. Why I spoke of the possibility of a trick I scarcely know. I had no hope of any such explanation.

But another strange, almost incredible idea was beginning to take shape in my mind, and with it came a faint, very faint touch of relief. Could it be not the *houses,* nor the *rooms,* nor, worst of all, we ourselves that were haunted, but some thing or things among the old furniture we had bought at Raxtrew?

And lying sleepless that night a sudden flash of illumination struck me—could it—whatever the "it" was—could it have something to do with the tapestry hangings?

The more I thought it over the more striking grew the coincidences at Finster. It had been on one of the closed doors that the shadow seemed to settle, as again here in our own hall. But in both cases the *portière* had hung in front!

And at the Rectory? The tapestry, as Philip had remarked, had been there rolled up all the time. Was it possible that it had never been taken out to the barn at all? What *more* probable than that it should have been left, forgotten, under the bench where Miss Larpent and I had felt for the second time that hideous cold? And, stay, something else was returning to my mind in connection with that bench. Yes—I had it—Nat had said "it seemed to stop and fumble away in one corner—at the end where there is a bench, you know."

And then to my unutterable thankfulness at last I fell asleep.

PART IV

I told Philip the next morning. There was no need to bespeak his attention. I think he felt nearly as horrified as I had done myself at the idea that our own hitherto bright, cheerful home was to be haunted by this awful thing—influence or presence, call it what you will. And the suggestions which I went on to make struck him, too, with a sense of relief.

He sat in silence for some time after making me recapitulate as precisely as possible every detail of Sophy's story.

"You are sure it was the door into the library?" he said at last.

"Quite sure," I replied; "and, oh, Philip," I went on, "it has just occurred to me that *Father* felt a chill there the other evening."

For till that moment the little incident in question had escaped my memory.

"Do you remember which of the *portières* hung in front of the door at Finster?" said Philip.

I shook my head.

"Dormy would," I said, "he used to examine the pictures in the tapestry with great interest. I should not know one from the other. There is an old castle in the distance in each, and a lot of trees, and something meant for a lake."

But in his turn Philip shook his head.

"No," he said, "I won't speak to Dormy about it if I can possibly help it. Leave it to me, Leila, and try to put it out of your own mind as much as you possibly can, and don't be surprised at anything you may notice in the next few days. I will tell you, first of anyone, whenever I have anything to tell."

That was all I could get out of him. So I took his advice. Luckily, as it turned out, Mr. Miles, the only outsider, so to say (except the unfortunate keeper), who had witnessed the ghostly drama, was one of the shooting party expected that day. And Philip at once determined to consult him about this new and utterly unexpected manifestation.

He did not tell me this. Indeed, it was not till fully a week later that I heard anything, and then in a letter—a very long letter from my brother, which, I think, will relate the sequel of our strange ghost story better than any narration at secondhand, of my own.

Mr. Miles only stayed two nights with us. The very day after he came he announced that, to his great regret, he was obliged—most unexpectedly—to return to Raxtrew on important business.

"And," he continued, "I am afraid you will all feel much vexed with me when I tell you I am going to carry off Phil with me."

Father looked very blank indeed.

"Phil!" he exclaimed, "and how about our shooting?"

"You can easily replace us," said my brother, "I have thought of that," and he added something in a lower tone to Father. He—Phil—was leaving the room at the time. I thought it had reference to the real reason of his accompanying Mr. Miles, but I was mistaken. Father, however, said nothing more in opposition to the plan, and the next morning the two went off.

We happened to be standing at the hall door—several of us— for we were a large party now—when Phil and his friend drove away. As we turned to re-enter the house, I felt someone touch me. It was Sophy. She was going out for a constitutional with Miss Larpent, but had stopped a moment to speak to me.

"Leila," she said in a whisper, "why have they—did you know that the tapestry had been taken down?"

She glanced at me with a peculiar expression. I had not observed it. Now, looking up, I saw that the two locked doors were visible in the dark polish of their old mahogany as of yore—no longer shrouded by the ancient *portières*. I started in surprise.

"No," I whispered in return, "I did not know. Never mind, Sophy. I suspect there is a reason for it which we shall know in good time."

I felt strongly tempted—the moon being still at the full—to visit the hall that night—in hopes of feeling and seeing—*nothing*. But when the time drew near, my courage failed; besides I had tacitly promised Philip to think as little as I possibly could about the matter, and any vigil of the kind would certainly not have been acting in accordance with the spirit of his advice. I think I will now copy, as it stands, the letter from Philip which I received a week or so later. It was dated from his club in London.

My Dear Leila,

I have a long story to tell you and a very extraordinary one. I think it is well that it should be put into writing, so I will devote this evening to the task especially as I shall not be home for ten days or so.

You may have suspected that I took Miles into my confidence as soon as he arrived. If you did you were right. He was the best person to speak to for several reasons. He looked, I must say, rather—well, "blank" scarcely expresses it—when I told him of the ghost's re-appearance, not only at the Rectory, but in our own house, and on both occasions to persons—Nat, and then Sophy—who had not heard a breath of the story. But when I went on to propound your suggestion, Miles cheered up. He had been, I fancy, a trifle touchy about our calling Finster haunted, and it was evidently a satisfaction to him to start another theory. We talked it well over, and we decid-ed to test the thing again—it took some resolution, I own, to do so. We sat up that night—bright moonlight luckily—and—well, I needn't repeat it all. Sophy was quite correct. It came again—the horrid creeping shadow—poor wretch, I'm rather sorry for it now— just in the old way—quite as much at home in ——shire, appar-ently, as in the Castle. It stopped at the closed library door, and fumbled away, then started off again—ugh! We watched it closely, but kept well in the middle of the room, so that the cold did not strike us so badly. We both noted the special part of the tapestry where its hands seemed to sprawl, and we meant to stay for another round; but—when it came to the point we funked it, and went to bed.

Next morning, on pretence of examining the date of the tapestry, we had it down—you were all out—and we found—*something*. Just where the hands felt about, there had been a cut—three cuts, three sides of a square, as it were, making a sort of door in the stuff, the fourth side having evidently acted as a hinge, for there was a mark where it had been folded back. And just where—treating the thing as a door—you might expect to find a handle to open it by, we found a distinct dint in the tapestry, as if a button or knob had once been there. We looked at each other. The same idea had struck us. The tapestry had been used to conceal a small door in the wall—the door of a secret cupboard probably. The ghostly fingers had been vainly seeking for the spring which in the days of their flesh and bone they had been accustomed to press.

"The first thing to do," said Miles, "is to look up Hunter and make him tell where he got the tapestry from. Then we shall see."

"Shall we take the *portière* with us?" I said.

But Miles shuddered, though he half laughed too.

"No, thank you," he said. "I'm not going to travel with the evil thing."

"We can't hang it up again, though," I said, "after this last experience."

In the end we rolled up the two *portières*, not to attract attention by only moving one, and—well, I thought it just possible the ghost might make a mistake, and I did not want any more scares while I was away—we rolled them up together, first carefully measuring the cut, and its position in the curtain, and then we hid them away in one of the lofts that no one ever enters, where they are at this moment, and where the ghost may have been disporting himself, for all I know, though I fancy he has given it up by this time, for reasons you shall hear.

Then Miles and I, as you know, set off for Raxtrew. I smoothed my father down about it, by reminding him how good-natured they had been to us, and telling him Miles really needed me. We went straight to Hunter. He hummed and hawed a good deal—he had not distinctly promised not to give the name of the place the tapestry had come from, but he knew the gentleman he had bought it from did not want it known.

"Why?" said Miles. "Is it some family that has come down in the world and is forced to part with things to get some ready money?"

"Oh, dear no!" said Hunter. "It is not that, at all. It was only that—I suppose I must give you the name Captain Devereux—did not want any gossip to get about, as to—"

"Devereux!" repeated Miles, "you don't mean the people at Hallinger?"

"The same," said Hunter. "If you know them, sir, you will be careful, I hope, to assure the Captain that I did my best to carry out his wishes?"

"Certainly," said Miles, "I'll exonerate you."

And then Hunter told us that Devereux, who only came into the Hallinger property a few years ago, had been much annoyed by stories getting about of the place being haunted, and this had led to his dismantling one wing, and—Hunter thought, but was not quite clear as to this—pulling down some rooms altogether. But he, Devereux, was very touchy on the subject—he did not want to be laughed at.

"And the tapestry came from him—you are certain as to that?" Miles repeated.

"Positive, sir. I took it down with my own hands. It was fitted onto two panels in what they call the round room at Hallinger—there were, oh, I daresay, a dozen of them, with tapestry nailed on, but I only bought these two pieces—the others were sold to a London dealer."

"The round room," I said. Leila, the expression struck me. Miles, it appeared, knew Devereux fairly well. Hallinger is only ten miles off. We drove over there, but found he was in London. So our next move was to follow him there. We called twice at his club, and then Miles made an appointment, saying he wanted to see him on private business.

He received us civilly, of course. He is quite a young fellow—in the Guards. But when Miles began to explain to him what we had come about, he stiffened.

"I suppose you belong to the Psychical Society?" he said. "I can only repeat that I have nothing to tell, and I detest the whole subject."

"Wait a moment," said Miles, and as he went on I saw that Devereux had changed. His face grew intent with interest and a queer sort of eagerness, and at last he started to his feet. "Upon my soul," he said, "I believe you've run him to earth for me—the ghost, I mean, and if so, you shall have my endless gratitude. I'll go down to Hallinger with you at once—this afternoon, if you like, and see it out."

He was so excited that he spoke almost incoherently, but after a bit he calmed down, and told us all he had to tell—and that was a good deal—which would indeed have been nuts for the Psychical Society. What Hunter had said was but a small part of the whole. It appeared that on succeeding to Hallinger, on the death of an uncle, young Devereux had made considerable changes in the house. He had, among others, opened out a small wing—a sort of round tower—which had been completely dismantled and bricked up for, I think he said, over a hundred years. There was some story about it. An ancestor of his—an awful gambler—had used the principal room in this wing for his orgies. Very queer things went on there, the finish up being the finding of old Devereux dead there one night, when his servants were summoned by the man he had been playing with— with whom he had had an awful quarrel. This man, a low fellow, probably a professional cardsharper, vowed that he had been robbed of a jewel which his host had staked, and it was said that a ring of great value had disappeared. But it was all hushed up—Devereux had really died in a fit—though soon after, for reasons only hinted at, the round tower was shut up, until the present man rashly opened it again.

Almost at once, he said, the annoyances, to use a mild term, began. First one, then another of the household were terrified out of their wits, just as we were, Leila. Dereveux himself had seen it two or three times, the "it," of course, being his miserable old ancestor. A small

man, with a big wig, and long, thin, claw-like fingers. It all correspond-
ed. Mrs. Devereux is young and nervous. She could not stand it. So in
the end the round tower was shut up again, all the furniture and hangings sold, and locally speaking, the ghost laid. That was all Devereux
knew.

We started, the three of us, that very afternoon, as excited as a party
of schoolboys. Miles and I kept questioning Devereux, but he had
really no more to tell. He had never thought of examining the walls of
the haunted room—it was wainscoted, he said—and might be lined all
through with secret cupboards for all he knew. But he could not get
over the extraordinariness of the ghost's sticking to the *tapestry*—and
indeed it does rather lower one's idea of ghostly intelligence.

We went at it at once—the tower was not bricked up again, luckily—we got in without difficulty the next morning—Devereux making
some excuse to the servants, a new set who had not heard of the ghost,
for our eccentric proceedings. It was a tiresome business. There were
so many panels in the room, as Hunter had said, and it was impossible
to tell in which *the* tapestry had been fixed. But we had sure measures,
and we carefully marked a line as near as we could guess at the height
from the floor that the cut in the *portière* must have been. Then we
tapped and pummelled and pressed imaginary springs till we were
nearly sick of it—there was nothing to guide us. The wainscotting was
dark and much shrunk and marked with age, and full of joins in the
wood any one of which might have meant a door.

It was Devereux himself who found it at last. We heard an exclamation from where he was standing by himself at the other side of the
room. He was quite white and shaky.

"Look here," he said, and we looked.

"Yes—there was a small deep recess, or cupboard in the thickness
of the wall, excellently contrived. Devereux had touched the spring at
last, and the door, just matching the cut in the tapestry, flew open.

Inside lay what at first we took for a packet of letters, and I hoped
to myself they contained nothing that would bring trouble to poor
Devereux. They were not letters, however, but two or three incomplete packs of cards—grey and dust-thick with age—and as Miles
spread them out, certain markings on them told their own tale.
Devereux did not like it, naturally—their supposed owner had been a
member of his house.

"The ghost has kept a conscience," he said, with an attempt at a
laugh. "Is there nothing more?"

Yes—a small leather bag—black and grimy, though originally, I fancy, of chamois skin. It drew with strings. Devereux pulled it open, and felt inside.

"By George!" he exclaimed. And he held out the most magnificent diamond ring I have ever seen—sparkling away as if it had only just come from the polisher's. "This must be the ring," he said.

And we all stared—too astonished to speak.

Devereux closed the cupboard again, after carefully examining it to make sure nothing had been left behind. He marked the exact spot where he had pressed the spring so as to find it at any time. Then we all left the round room, locking the door securely after us.

Miles and I spent that night at Hallinger. We sat up late, talking it all over. There are some queer inconsistencies about the thing which will probably never be explained. First and foremost—why has the ghost stuck to the tapestry instead of to the actual spot he seemed to have wished to reveal? Secondly, what was the connection between his visits and the full moon—or is it that only by the moonlight the shade becomes perceptible to human sense? Who can say?

As to the story itself—what was old Devereux's motive in concealing his own ring? Were the marked cards his, or his opponent's, of which he had managed to possess himself, and had secreted as testimony against the other fellow?

I incline, and so does Miles, to this last theory, and when we suggested it to Devereux, I could see it was a relief to him. After all, one likes to think one's ancestors were gentlemen!

"But what, then, has he been worrying about all this century or more?" he said. "If it were that he wanted the ring returned to its real owner—supposing the fellow *had* won it—I could understand it, though such a thing would be impossible. There is no record of the man at all—his name was never mentioned in the story."

"He may want the ring restored to its proper owner all the same," said Miles. "You are its owner, as the head of the family, and it has been your ancestor's fault that it has been hidden all these years. Besides, we cannot take upon ourselves to explain motives in such a case. Perhaps—who knows?—the poor shade could not help himself. His peregrinations may have been of the nature of punishment."

"I hope they are over now," said Devereux, "for his sake and everybody else's. I should be glad to think he wanted the ring restored to us, but besides that, I should like to do something—something *good* you know—if it would make him easier, poor old chap. I must consult Lilias." Lilias is Mrs. Devereux.

This is all I have to tell you at present, Leila. When I come home we'll have the *portières* up again and see what happens. I want you now to read all this to my father, and if he has no objections—he and my mother, of course, I should like to invite Captain and Mrs. Devereux to stay a few days with us—as well as Miles, as soon as I come back.

Philip's wish was acceded to. It was with no little anxiety and interest that we awaited his return.

The tapestry *portières* were restored to their place—and on the first moonlight night, my father, Philip, Captain Devereux and Mr. Miles held their vigil.

What happened?

Nothing—the peaceful rays lighted up the quaint landscape of the tapestry, undisturbed by the poor groping fingers—no gruesome unearthly chill as of worse than death made itself felt to the midnight watchers—the weary, may we not hope repentant, spirit was at rest at last!

And never since has anyone been troubled by the shadow in the moonlight.

"I cannot help hoping," said Mrs. Devereux, when talking it over, "that what Michael has done may have helped to calm the poor ghost."

And she told us what it was. Captain Devereux is rich, though not immensely so. He had the ring valued—it represented a very large sum, but Philip says I had better not name the figures—and then he, so to say, bought it from himself. And with this money he—no, again Phil says I must not enter into particulars beyond saying that with it he did something very good, and very useful, which had long been a pet scheme of his wife's.

Sophy is grown up now and she knows the whole story. So does our mother. And Dormy too has heard it all. The horror of it has quite gone. We feel rather proud of having been the actual witnesses of a ghostly drama.

Edith Nesbit

(1858–1924)

EDITH NESBIT was a remarkably tolerant woman, prepared to accommodate her husband, Hubert Bland, and his mistress, and live as a *ménage a trois* for many years, raising his illegitimate children as her own. They were both free thinkers and were among the earliest members of the Fabian Society, which included H. G. Wells, George Bernard Shaw, and the suffragette Emmeline Pankhurst. Nesbit is best known for her children's books, especially *The Railway Children* (1904) and *Five Children and It* (1902). Her supernatural stories written for adults are often overlooked, even though these were among her earliest writings. Some were collected as *Grim Tales* (1893) and *Something Wrong* (1893), collections reworked as *Fear* (1910). Nesbit's weird fiction is far from traditional, and includes some modern concepts. She was one of the first to write about a haunted car in "The Violet Car" (1910). In 2000, Hugh Lamb compiled a volume of her best weird tales, *In the Dark*. Nesbit would sometimes frighten herself with her stories, most of which feature her own phobias of the dark, dead bodies, and premature burial. There are elements of her fears and echoes of her private life in "From the Dead," which first appeared in the *Illustrated London News* for 3 September 1892.

From the Dead

I

"But true or not true, your brother is a scoundrel. No man—no decent man—tells such things."

"He did not tell me. How dare you suppose it? I found the letter in his desk; and since she was my friend and your sweetheart, I never thought there could be any harm in my reading anything she might write to my brother. Give me back the letter. I was a fool to tell you."

Ida Helmont held out her hand for the letter.

"Not yet," I said, and I went to the window. The dull red of a London sunset burned on the paper, as I read in the pretty handwriting I knew so well, and had kissed so often:

DEAR: I do—I do love you; but it's impossible. I must marry Arthur. My honour is engaged. If he would only set me free—but he never will. He loves me foolishly. But as for me—it is you I love—body, soul, and spirit. There is no one in my heart but you. I think of you all day, and dream of you all night. And we must part. Goodbye—Yours, yours, yours,

ELVIRA

I had seen the handwriting, indeed, often enough. But the passion there was new to me. That I had not seen.

I turned from the window. My sitting-room looked strange to me. There were my books, my reading-lamp, my untasted dinner still on the table, as I had left it when I rose to dissemble my surprise at Ida Helmont's visit—Ida Helmont, who now sat looking at me quietly.

"Well—do you give me no thanks?"

151

"You put a knife in my heart, and then ask for thanks?"

"Pardon me," she said, throwing up her chin. "I have done nothing but show you the truth. For that one should expect no gratitude—may I ask, out of pure curiosity, what you intend to do?"

"Your brother will tell you—"

She rose suddenly, very pale, and her eyes haggard.

"You will not tell my brother?"

She came towards me—her gold hair flaming in the sunset light.

"Why are you so angry with me?" she said. "Be reasonable. What else could I do?"

"I don't know."

"Would it have been right not to tell you?"

"I don't know. I only know that you've put the sun out, and I haven't got used to the dark yet."

"Believe me," she said, coming still nearer to me, and laying her hands in the lightest touch on my shoulders, "believe me, she never loved you."

There was a softness in her tone that irritated and stimulated me. I moved gently back, and her hands fell by her sides.

"I beg your pardon," I said. "I have behaved very badly. You were quite right to come, and I am not ungrateful. Will you post a letter for me?"

I sat down and wrote:

I give you back your freedom. The only gift of mine that can please you now.——

ARTHUR

I held the sheet out to Miss Helmont, but she would not look at it. I folded, sealed, stamped, and addressed it.

"Goodbye," I said then, and gave her the letter. As the door closed behind her, I sank into my chair, and cried like a child, or a fool, over my lost play-thing—the little, dark-haired woman who loved someone else with "body, soul, and spirit."

I did not hear the door open or any foot on the floor, and therefore I started when a voice behind me said:

"Are you so very unhappy? Oh, Arthur, don't think I am not sorry for you!"

"I don't want anyone to be sorry for me, Miss Helmont," I said.

She was silent a moment. Then, with a quick, sudden, gentle movement she leaned down and kissed my forehead—and I heard the door softly close. Then I knew that the beautiful Miss Helmont loved me.

At first that thought only fleeted by—a light cloud against a grey sky—but the next day reason woke, and said:

"Was Miss Helmont speaking the truth? Was it possible that——"

I determined to see Elvira, to know from her own lips whether by happy fortune this blow came, not from her, but from a woman in whom love might have killed honesty.

I walked from Hampstead to Gower Street. As I trod its long length, I saw a figure in pink come out of one of the houses. It was Elvira. She walked in front of me to the corner of Store Street. There she met Oscar Helmont. They turned and met me face to face, and I saw all I needed to see. They loved each other. Ida Helmont had spoken the truth. I bowed and passed on. Before six months were gone, they were married, and before a year was over, I had married Ida Helmont.

What did it, I don't know. Whether it was remorse for having, even for half a day, dreamed that she could be so base as to forego a lie to gain a lover, or whether it was her beauty, or the sweet flattery of the preference of a woman who had half her acquaintance at her feet, I don't know; anyhow, my thoughts turned to her as to their natural home. My heart, too, took that road, and before very long I loved her as I never loved Elvira. Let no one doubt that I loved her—as I shall never love again—please God!

There never was anyone like her. She was brave and beautiful, witty and wise, and beyond all measure adorable. She was the only woman in the world. There was a frankness—a largeness of heart—about her that made all other women seem small and contemptible. She loved me and I worshipped her. I married her, I stayed with her for three golden weeks, and then I left her. Why?

Because she told me the truth. It was one night—late—we had sat all the evening in the veranda of our sea-side lodging, watching the moonlight on the water, and listening to the soft sound of the sea on the sand. I have never been so happy; I shall never be happy any more, I hope.

"My dear, my dear," she said, leaning her gold head against my shoulder, "how much do you love me?"

"How much?"

"Yes—how much? I want to know what place I hold in your heart. Am I more to you than anyone else?"

"My love!"

"More than yourself?"

"More than my life."

"I believe you," she said. Then she drew a long breath, and took my hands in hers. "It can make no difference. Nothing in heaven or earth can come between us now."

"Nothing," I said. "But, my dear one, what is it?"

For she was trembling, pale.

"I must tell you," she said; "I cannot hide anything now from you, because I am yours—body, soul, and spirit."

The phrase was an echo that stung.

The moonlight shone on her gold hair, her soft, warm, gold hair, and on her pale face.

"Arthur," she said, "you remember my coming to Hampstead with that letter."

"Yes, my sweet, and I remember how you——"

"Arthur!" she spoke fast and low—"Arthur, that letter was a forgery. She never wrote it. I——"

She stopped, for I had risen and flung her hands from me, and stood looking at her. God help me! I thought it was anger at the lie I felt. I know now it was only wounded vanity that smarted in me. That *I* should have been tricked, that *I* should have been deceived, and *I* should have been led on to make a fool of myself. That *I* should have married the woman who had befooled me. At that moment she was no longer the wife

I adored—she was only a woman who had forged a letter and tricked me into marrying her.

I spoke: I denounced her; I said I would never speak to her again. I felt it was rather creditable in me to be so angry. I said I would have no more to do with a liar and a forger.

I don't know whether I expected her to creep to my knees and implore forgiveness. I think I had some vague idea that I could by-and-by consent with dignity to forgive and forget. I did not mean what I said. No, oh no, no; I did not mean a word of it. While I was saying it, I was longing for her to weep and fall at my feet, that I might raise her and hold her in my arms again.

But she did not fall at my feet; she stood quietly looking at me.

"Arthur," she said, as I paused for breath, "let me explain— she—I——"

"There is nothing to explain," I said hotly, still with that foolish sense of there being something rather noble in my indignation, the kind of thing one feels when one calls one's self a miserable sinner. "You are a liar and a forger, that is enough for me. I will never speak to you again. You have wrecked my life——"

"Do you mean that?" she said, interrupting me, and leaning forward to look at me. Tears lay on her cheeks, but she was not crying now.

I hesitated. I longed to take her in my arms and say: "What does all that old tale matter now? Lay your head here, my darling, and cry here, and know how I love you."

But instead I said nothing.

"*Do* you mean it?" she persisted.

Then she put her hand on my arm. I longed to clasp it and draw her to me.

Instead, I shook it off, and said:

"Mean it? Yes—of course I mean it. Don't touch me, please. You have ruined my life."

She turned away without a word, went into our room, and shut the door.

I longed to follow her, to tell her that if there was anything to forgive, I forgave it.

Instead, I went out on the beach, and walked away under the cliffs.

The moonlight and the solitude, however, presently brought me to a better mind. Whatever she had done, had been done for love of me—I knew that. I would go home and tell her so—tell her that whatever she had done, she was my dear life, my heart's one treasure. True, my ideal of her was shattered, at least I felt I ought to think that it was shattered, but, even as she was, what was the whole world of women compared to her? And to be loved like that . . . was that not sweet food for vanity? To be loved more than faith and fair dealing, and all the traditions of honesty and honour? I hurried back, but in my resentment and evil temper I had walked far, and the way back was very long. I had been parted from her for three hours by the time I opened the door of the little house where we lodged. The house was dark and very still. I slipped off my shoes and crept up the narrow stairs, and opened the door of our room quite softly. Perhaps she would have cried herself to sleep, and I would lean over her and waken her with my kisses, and beg her to forgive me. Yes, it had come to that now.

I went into the room—I went towards the bed. She was not there. She was not in the room, as one glance showed me. She was not in the house, as I knew in two minutes. When I had wasted a precious hour in searching the town for her, I found a note on my pillow:

"Goodbye! Make the best of what is left of your life. I will spoil it no more."

She was gone, utterly gone. I rushed to town by the earliest morning train, only to find that her people knew nothing of her. Advertisement failed. Only a tramp said he had seen a white lady on the cliff, and a fisherman brought me a handkerchief, marked with her name, which he had found on the beach.

I searched the country far and wide, but I had to go back to London at last, and the months went by. I won't say much about those months, because even the memory of that suffering turns me faint and sick at heart. The police and detectives and the

Press failed me utterly. Her friends could not help me, and were, moreover, wildly indignant with me, especially her brother, now living very happily with my first love.

I don't know how I got through those long weeks and months. I tried to write; I tried to read; I tried to live the life of a reasonable human being. But it was impossible. I could not endure the companionship of my kind. Day and night I almost saw her face—almost heard her voice. I took long walks in the country, and her figure was always just round the next turn of the road—in the next glade of the wood. But I never quite saw her, never quite heard her. I believe I was not all together sane at that time. At last, one morning, as I was setting out for one of those long walks that had no goal but weariness, I met a telegraph boy, and took the red envelope from his hand.

On the pink paper inside was written:

Come to me at once I am dying you must come IDA
Apinshaw Farm Mellor Derbyshire.

There was a train at twelve to Marple, the nearest station. I took it. I tell you there are some things that cannot be written about. My life for those long months was one of them, that journey was another. What had her life been for those months? That question troubled me, as one is troubled in every nerve by the sight of a surgical operation, or a wound inflicted on a being dear to one. But the overmastering sensation was joy—intense, unspeakable joy. She was alive. I should see her again. I took out the telegram and looked at it: "I am dying." I simply did not believe it. She could not die till she had seen me. And if she had lived all these months without me, she could live now, when I was with her again, when she knew of the hell I had endured apart from her, and the heaven of our meeting. She must live; I could not let her die.

There was a long drive over bleak hills. Dark, jolting, infinitely wearisome. At last we stopped before a long, low building, where one or two lights gleamed faintly. I sprang out.

The door opened. A blaze of light made me blink and draw back. A woman was standing in the doorway.

"Art thee Arthur Marsh?" she said.

"Yes."

"Then th'art ower late. She's dead."

II

I went into the house, walked to the fire, and held out my hands
to it mechanically, for though the night was May, I was cold to
the bone. There were some folks standing round the fire, and
lights flickering. Then an old woman came forward, with the
northern instinct of hospitality.

"Thou'rt tired," she said, "and mazed-like. Have a sup o' tea."

I burst out laughing. I had travelled two hundred miles to see
her. And she was dead, and they offered me tea. They drew back
from me as if I had been a wild beast, but I could not stop laughing. Then a hand was laid on my shoulder and someone led me
into a dark room, lighted a lamp, set me in a chair, and sat down
opposite me. It was a bare parlour, coldly furnished with rush
chairs and much-polished tables and presses. I caught my
breath, and grew suddenly grave, and looked at the woman who
sat opposite me.

"I was Miss Ida's nurse," said she, "and she told me to send
for you. Who are you?"

"Her husband——"

The woman looked at me with hard eyes, where intense surprise struggled with resentment.

"Then may God forgive you!" she said. "What you've done I
don't know, but it'll be hard work forgivin' *you*, even for *Him!*"

"Tell me," I said, "my wife——"

"Tell you!" The bitter contempt in the woman's tone did not
hurt me. What was it to the self-contempt that had gnawed my
heart all these months. "Tell you! Yes, I'll tell you. Your wife was
that ashamed of you she never so much as told me she was married. She let me think anything I pleased sooner than that. She
just come 'ere, an' she said, 'Nurse, take care of me, for I am in
mortal trouble. And don't let them know where I am,' says she.
An' me being well married to an honest man, and well-to-do
here, I was able to do it, by the blessing."

"Why didn't you send for me before?" It was a cry of anguish wrung from me.

"I'd *never* 'a sent for you. It was *her* doin'. Oh, to think as God A'mighty's made men able to measure out such-like pecks o' trouble for us womenfolk! Young man, I don't know what you did to 'er to make 'er leave you; but it muster bin something cruel, for she loved the ground you walked on. She useter sit day after day a-lookin' at your picture, an' talkin' to it, an' kissin' of it, when she thought I wasn't takin' no notice, and cryin' till she made me cry too. She useter cry all night 'most. An' one day, when I tells 'er to pray to God to 'elp 'er through 'er trouble, she outs with *your* putty face on a card, she does, an', says she, with her poor little smile, 'That's my god, Nursey,' she says."

"Don't!" I said feebly, putting out my hands to keep off the torture; "not any more. Not now."

"*Don't!*" she repeated. She had risen, and was walking up and down the room with clasped hands. "Don't, indeed! No, I won't; but I shan't forget you! I tell you, I've had you in my prayers time and again, when I thought you'd made a light-o'-love of my darling. I shan't drop you outer them now, when I know she was your own wedded wife, as you chucked away when you tired of her, and left 'er to eat 'er 'eart out with longin' for you. Oh! I pray to God above us to pay you scot and lot for all you done to 'er. You killed my pretty. The price will be required of you, young man, even to the uttermost farthing. Oh God in Heaven, make him suffer! Make him feel it!"

She stamped her foot as she passed me. I stood quite still. I bit my lip till I tasted the blood hot and salt on my tongue.

"She was nothing to you," cried the woman, walking faster up and down between the rush chairs and the table; "any fool can see that with half an eye. You didn't love her, so you don't feel nothin' now; but some day you'll care for someone, and then you shall know what she felt—if there's any justice in Heaven."

I, too, rose, walked across the room, and leaned against the wall. I heard her words without understanding them.

"Can't you feel *nothin?* Are you mader stone? Come an' look at 'er lyin' there so quiet. She don't fret arter the likes o' you no more now. She won't sit no more a-lookin' outer winder an' sayin' nothin'—only droppin' 'er tears one by one, slow, slow on 'er lap. Come an' see 'er; come an' see what you done to my pretty—an' then you can go. Nobody wants you 'ere. *She* don't want you now. But p'raps you'd like to see 'er safe under ground afore yer go? I'll be bound you'll put a big stone slab on 'er—to make sure she don't rise again."

I turned on her. Her thin face was white with grief and rage. Her claw-like hands were clenched.

"Woman," I said, "have mercy."

She paused and looked at me.

"Eh?" she said.

"Have mercy!" I said again.

"Mercy! You should 'a thought o' that before. You 'adn't no mercy on 'er. She loved you—she died loving you. An' if I wasn't a Christian woman, I'd kill you for it—like the rat you are! That I would, though I 'ad to swing for it afterwards."

I caught the woman's hands and held them fast, though she writhed and resisted.

"Don't you understand?" I said savagely. "We loved each other. She died loving me. I have to live loving her. And it's *her* you pity. I tell you it was all a mistake—a stupid, stupid mistake. Take me to her, and for pity's sake, let me be left alone with her."

She hesitated; then said, in a voice only a shade less hard: "Well, come along, then."

We moved towards the door. As she opened it, a faint, weak cry fell on my ear. My heart stood still.

"What's that?" I asked, stopping on the threshold.

"Your child," she said shortly.

That too! Oh, my love! oh, my poor love! All these long months!

"She allus said she'd send for you when she'd got over 'er trouble," the woman said, as we climbed the stairs. "'I'd like him to see his little baby, nurse,' she says; 'our little baby. It'll be all right when the baby's born,' she says. 'I know he'll come to me then. You'll see.' And I never said nothin', not thinkin' you'd come if she was your leavin's and not dreamin' you could be 'er 'usband an' could stay away from 'er a hour—'er bein' as she was. Hush!"

She drew a key from her pocket and fitted it to a lock. She opened the door, and I followed her in. It was a large, dark room, full of old-fashioned furniture and a smell of lavender, camphor, and narcissus.

The big four-post bed was covered with white.

"My lamb—my poor, pretty lamb!" said the woman, beginning to cry for the first time as she drew back the sheet. "Don't she look beautiful?"

I stood by the bedstead. I looked down on my wife's face. Just so I had seen it lie on the pillow beside me in the early morning, when the wind and the dawn came up from beyond the sea. She did not look like one dead. Her lips were still red, and it seemed to me that a tinge of colour lay on her cheek. It seemed to me, too, that if I kissed her she would awaken, and put her slight hand on my neck, and lay her cheek against mine—and that we should tell each other everything, and weep together, and understand, and be comforted.

So I stooped and laid my lips to hers as the old nurse stole from the room.

But the red lips were like marble, and she did not waken. She will not waken now ever any more.

I tell you again there are some things that cannot be written.

III

I lay that night in a big room, filled with heavy dark furniture, in a great four-poster hung with heavy, dark curtains—a bed, the counterpart of that other bed from whose side they had dragged me at last.

They fed me, I believe, and the old nurse was kind to me. I think she saw now that it is not the dead who are to be pitied most.

I lay at last in the big, roomy bed, and heard the household noises grow fewer and die out, the little wail of my child sounding latest. They had brought the child to me, and I had held it in my arms, and bowed my head over its tiny face and frail fingers. I did not love it then. I told myself it had cost me her life.

But my heart told me it was I who had done that. The tall clock at the stair-head sounded the hours—eleven, twelve, one, and still I could not sleep. The room was dark and very still.

I had not yet been able to look at my life quietly. I had been full of the intoxication of grief—a real drunkenness, more merciful than the sober calm that comes afterwards.

Now I lay still as the dead woman in the next room, and looked at what was left of my life. I lay still, and thought, and thought, and thought. And in those hours I tasted the bitterness of death. It must have been about three when I first became aware of a slight sound that was not the ticking of a clock. I say I first became aware, and yet I knew perfectly that I had heard that sound more than once before, and had yet determined not to hear it, *because it came from the next room*—the room where the corpse lay.

And I did not wish to hear that sound, because I knew it meant that I was nervous—miserably nervous—a coward, and a brute. It meant that I, having killed my wife as surely as though I had put a knife in her breast, had now sunk so low as to be afraid of her dead body—the dead body that lay in the next room to mine. The heads of the beds were placed against the same wall: and from that wall I had fancied that I heard slight, slight, almost inaudible sounds. So that when I say I became aware of them, I mean that I, at last, heard a sound so definite as to leave no room for doubt or question. It brought me to a sitting position in the bed, and the drops of sweat gathered heavily on my forehead and fell on my cold hands, as I held my breath and listened.

I don't know how long I sat there—there was no further sound—and at last my tense muscles relaxed, and I fell back on the pillow.

"You fool!" I said to myself; "dead or alive, is she not your darling, your heart's heart? Would you not go near to die of joy, if she came back to you? Pray God to let her spirit come back and tell you she forgives you!"

"I wish she would come," myself answered in words, while every fibre of my body and mind shrank and quivered in denial.

I struck a match, lighted a candle, and breathed more freely as I looked at the polished furniture—the commonplace details of an ordinary room. Then I thought of her, lying alone so near me, so quiet under the white sheet. She was dead; she would not wake or move. But suppose she did move? Suppose she turned back the sheet and got up and walked across the floor, and turned the door-handle?

As I thought it, I heard—plainly, unmistakably heard—the door of the chamber of death open slowly. I heard slow steps in the passage, slow, heavy steps. I heard the touch of hands on my door outside, uncertain hands that felt for the latch.

Sick with terror, I lay clenching the sheet in my hands.

I knew well enough what would come in when that door opened—that door on which my eyes were fixed. I dreaded to look, yet dared not turn away my eyes. The door opened slowly, slowly, slowly, and the figure of my dead wife came in. It came straight towards the bed, and stood at the bed foot in its white grave-clothes, with the white bandage under its chin. There was a scent of lavender and camphor and white narcissus. Its eyes were wide open, and looked at me with love unspeakable.

I could have shrieked aloud.

My wife spoke. It was the same dear voice that I had loved so to hear, but it was very weak and faint now; and now I trembled as I listened.

"You aren't afraid of me, darling, are you, though I am dead? I heard all you said to me when you came, but I couldn't answer. But now I've come back from the dead to tell you. I wasn't really so bad as you thought me. Elvira had told me she loved Oscar. I only wrote the letter to make it easier for you. I was too proud to tell you when you were so angry, but I am not proud any more now. You'll love again now, won't you, now I am dead. One always forgives dead people."

The poor ghost's voice was hollow and faint. Abject terror paralysed me. I could answer nothing.

"Say you forgive me," the thin, monotonous voice went on, "say you love me again."

I had to speak. Coward as I was, I did manage to stammer: "Yes; I love you. I have always loved you, God help me."

The sound of my own voice reassured me, and I ended more firmly than I began. The figure by the bed swayed a little, unsteadily.

"I suppose," she said wearily, "you would be afraid, now I am dead, if I came round to you and kissed you?"

She made a movement as though she would have come to me.

Then I did shriek aloud, again and again, and covered my face with all my force. There was a moment's silence. Then I heard my door close, and then a sound of feet and of voices, and I heard something heavy fall. I disentangled my head from the sheet. My room was empty. Then reason came back to me. I leaped from the bed.

"Ida, my darling, come back! I am not afraid! I love you. Come back! Come back!"

I sprang to my door and flung it open. Someone was bringing a light along the passage. On the floor, outside the door of the death chamber, was a huddled heap—the corpse, in its grave-clothes. Dead, dead, dead.

She is buried in Mellor churchyard, and there is no stone over her.

Now, whether it was catalepsy, as the doctor said, or whether my love came back, even from the dead, to me who loved her, I shall never know; but this I know, that if I had held out my arms to her as she stood at my bed-foot—if I had said, "Yes, even from the grave, my darling—from hell itself, come back, come back to me!"—if I had had room in my coward's heart for anything but the unreasoning terror that killed love in that hour, I should not now be here alone. I shrank from her—I feared her—I would not take her to my heart. And now she will not come to me anymore.

Why do I go on living?

You see, there is the child. It is four years old now, and it has never spoken and never smiled.

Harriet Prescott Spofford
(1835–1921)

HARRIET ELIZABETH PRESCOTT was born in Calais, Maine, and was a precocious if melancholic child. She was encouraged in her writing by Thomas Wentworth Higginson, who was her local Unitarian minister, and who later became literary mentor to Emily Dickinson. Thanks to Higginson, Prescott sold "In a Cellar" to the *Atlantic Monthly* (February 1859) and her career was launched. Her first novel, the gothic *Sir Rohan's Ghost*, appeared the following year as did her haunting dark tale, "Circumstance" (*Atlantic Monthly*, May 1860), the story which established her name. Her early stories were collected as *The Amber Gods* (1863), a much-overlooked yet important landmark in the development of weird fiction in America. She married Richard Spofford, a young attorney, in 1865. He was extremely supportive of her writing and she continued to produce stories and poetry for the next fifty years. "The Mad Lady" was her very last ghost story, written when she was eighty years old. It appeared in *Scribner's Magazine* for February 1916.

The Mad Lady

Certainly there was a house there, half-way up Great Hill, a mansion of pale cream-colored stone, built with pillared porch and wings, vines growing over some parts of it, a sward like velvet surrounding it; the sun was flashing back from the windows—but—Why? Why had none of the Godsdale people seen that house before? Could the work of building have gone on sheltered by the thick wood in front, the laborers and the materials coming up the other side of the hill? It would not be visible now if, overnight, vistas had not been cut in the wood.

The Godsdale people seldom climbed the hill; there were rumors of ill-doing there in long past days, there were perhaps rattlesnakes, it was difficult except from the other side, there was nothing to see when you arrived, and few ever wandered that way. Why any one should wish to build there was a mystery. As the villagers stared at the place they saw, or thought they saw, swarthy turbaned servitors moving about, but so far off as to be indistinct. In fact, it was all very indistinct; so much so that Parson Solewise even declared there was no house there at all. But when Mr. Dunceby, the schoolmaster, opened his spy-glass and saw a lady—who, he said, was tall, was dark, was beautiful, with flowing draperies about her of black and filmy stuff—come down the terrace-steps and enter a waiting automobile that speedily passed round the scarp of the hill and went down the other side, the thing was proved. Mr. Ditton, the village lawyer, also saw it without having recourse to the spy-glass; but as Mr. Ditton had but lately had what he called a nip, and indeed several of them, he was in that happy state of sweet good nature which agrees with the last speaker.

Every day for several days, even weeks, the lady was seen to enter the automobile, and be taken round the side of the hill and down to the plain intersected by many roads and ending in a marsh bounded by the great river. The car would go some distance, and then, apparently at an order given through the long speaking-tube, would turn about and take a different course, only to be as quickly reversed and sent to another road on the right or on the left. Sometimes it would seem to certain of the adventurous youth coming and going on the great plain that the chauffeur remonstrated, but evidently the more she insisted, and the car went on swiftly in the new direction, wrecklessly plunging and rocking over deep-rutted places as if both driver and passenger were mad. Indeed they came to call the woman the Mad Lady. She seemed to be on a wild search for something that lay she knew not where, or for the right road to it in all the tangle of roads. One day, it was Mr. Dunceby and Mr. Ditton who, coming from a fishing-trip—Mr. Ditton's flask quite empty—saw a ride which they averred was the wildest piece of daredeviltry ever known, or would have been but for the black tragedy at its end.

The car was speeding down Springwood way, as if running a race with the wind, when suddenly it swerved, backed, and turned about, going diagonally opposite into Blueberry lane, crossed over from that by a short cut to Commoners, only to reverse again—the lady inside, as well as they could see, giving contradictory and excited orders—and after one or two more turns and returns and zigzags, the car shot forward with incredible swiftness, as if the right way were found at last, straight down the long dike or causeway over which the farmers hauled their salt hay from the marsh in winter—the marsh now swollen to a morass by the high tides and recent rains. And then, as if in the accelerating speed the chauffeur found himself helpless, they saw the car bound into the air—at least Mr. Ditton did— the lady flung the door open, crying: "It is here! It is here!" pitching forward at the words and tossed out like a leaf, the chauffeur thrown off as violently, and all plunged into the morass, sucked down by the quicksand, and seen no more.

When a deputation of the Godsdale people, the constable,

the parson, the schoolmaster, Mr. Ditton, and some others, climbed the path to Great Hill top, they found the house there quite empty, no living soul to be seen, and without furnishing of any kind. Was it possible that every one had absconded during the time in which the people had exclaimed and discussed and delayed, and that they had taken rugs and hangings and paintings and statuary with them? Or, as Parson Solewise conjectured, had there never been anything of the sort there? Yet there were others who, on returning to the village, vowed that the rich rugs, the soft draperies, the wonderful pictures they had seen were something not known by them to exist before, and that turbaned slaves were packing them away with celerity.

One thing certainly was strange: a wing of the house had vanished, the porch and the eastern wing were there, but there was no west wing; if there ever had been the grass was growing over it. The schoolmaster said it was due to the perspective; they would see it when down in the village again. And so they did. Mr. Ditton, however, went back to review the case; but, on the spot again, there was no western wing to that strange building.

The automobile was raised by some friendly hands, chiefly boys, cleansed, and taken up Great Hill and left in its place. After that, for some years the good people of Godsdale talked of the mansion, and marvelled, and borrowed the schoolmaster's spy-glass to look at it. But at last it was as an old story, and half forgotten at that; and then one and another had died; and no one came to claim the place; and other things filled the mind.

It so chanced that Mary Solewise, the old parson's daughter, one afternoon in her rambles with her lover, came out on the half-forgotten house and, stepping across the terrace, looked in at one of the windows that at a little distance had seemed to stare at them. Her lover was the young poet who had come to Godsdale for the sake of its quiet, that he might finish his epic to the resonance of no other noise than the tune in his thought. The epic is quite unknown now; but we all know and sing his songs, which are pieces of perfection. But he himself said Mary Solewise was the best poem he had found.

With a little money, some talent, and plenty of time, he was content till this song of Mary began to sing in his heart; and then when he found she was his for this life and all life to come, he found also that his small income needed to be trebled; it was too narrow a mantle to stretch over himself and Mary too. He could, after a fashion, make the little money sufficient, perhaps his verses would bring in something—verse had made more poets than Tennyson rich—but there was no roof to shelter her. And so in the midst of his happiness he was wretched. He could not enjoy the sunshine for fear of a weather-breeder. Of course if he chose to go back, if he chose to submit—but that sacrifice of honor was not to be dreamed. He lived in the hope that his epic would bring immediate fame and fortune, but, alas, his life and thought were so taken up by Mary that he could not work on the epic at all. They went off and sat down on the edge of the terrace. The great house, in the flickering afternoon sunshine through the shadows of leaves, seemed to tremble. One felt it might melt away. There was to the poet something really appealing about it. "This forsaken place has a personality," he said. "It seems as if it were asking some one to come and companion it, to save it from itself and the doom of forsaken things."

It was very evidently, indeed, by way of falling to pieces: bricks had toppled from the chimney-stacks, spiders had spun their webs everywhere, and one might expect to find a brother to dragons in the great halls. "To live in it?" asked Mary. "Why, the very thing! Let the creepers cover all the main part and hold it up with their strong ropes if need be. But there in the east wing the rooms are reasonable. You have such a knack with carpentry and machines and things, you could turn that long window into a door, we could bolt off the main part—and—and there we are!"

"It is God-given!" said the lover. "But would you not be afraid of ghosts? This is a place to be known of these shadowy people."

"I would give anything to see one!" she exclaimed, and then began to shiver as if fearing to be taken at her word. Her hair had fallen down in her struggles with bushes and boughs and briers on the way up; she was braiding it in a shining rope of gold.

"It will grow and shroud you in gold in your grave," he said, passing a tress of it across his lips.

The color mounted in her cheeks, exquisite as that on a rose-petal; nothing could be more the opposite of ghostliness than she, the very picture of vital strength.

All at once it seemed to the poet that here was a way to put fresh being into this dead place, to suspend its decay, till it gathered force and new meaning and became instead of a suspected apparition a thing glowing with life. He went to the window and looked in; it gave way under his hand, and he stepped across. "This shall be the door," he said.

"And this the living-room," she replied. And they went through the wing.

"It is quite ample enough," he exclaimed.

"More than enough," she said.

"It will do very well," he continued. "I will come up with old Will and brooms and pails, and clear out the dust and cobwebs and litter, and mop and scour. I can do it."

"And I can help. Oh, how I can help!"

"Here will be your sewing-room. Here will be my writing-room—only you will sit there, too. Here is our own room. How fine a great fire roaring up this chimney will be! Here can be pantry and kitchen. See—there is water running from some spring higher up the hill. It is really quite perfect. Why did we never think of it before? No one claims it. We shall be married now the moment it is ready to receive a bride. A fine place, those great halls, for children to romp in. I hear them now with their piping silver voices!"

"And I will have a garden on this side, with rows of lilies, with rows of roses, with white sweet-william against blue larkspur, with gillyflowers and pansies—oh, why *didn't* we think of this before!"

"We will need some furnishing—"

"Not a great deal. Mother and father will give us things they don't use. And we can make tables and dressers—you can."

"And I shall be paid for my verses the *Magazine of Light* accepted, some time."

"And there is the old automobile—though I don't know if I would like to ride in that, even if I could."

"I think I can furbish it up. I'll take a look at it. I always had a way with tools. Oh, yes, you will like to ride in it. It won't be quite—the same—may need some new parts."

"But—the poor Mad Lady—won't we be afraid?"

"Of what? She wouldn't hurt us if she could, and she couldn't if she would. She will be glad to have her limousine give pleasure to a young wife and her adoring man-at-arms. Oh, Mary, we have a home! But it's too good to be true. Come, let us hurry down before the whole thing fades like a dream!"

The parson and the schoolmaster and Mr. Ditton all went up the next day to look over the possibilities, and they all agreed that the plan was feasible. "The main building," said the schoolmaster, "could be used for a boarding-school," and he pictured himself a delighted headmaster there in no time.

"A fine place for one of those retreats where people invite heaven into their souls," said the parson.

"A place for much revelry unseen by the curious. I wonder it has not been utilized," said Mr. Ditton. And then they all did their kind best to help the poet and his sweetheart.

It was the prettiest wedding under the sun. All the village took note, and part of the people followed the pleasant procession up the hill. They had turned out in a body two or three weeks before and made the path up the hill wide and smooth; and all the furnishings and belongings had been taken up some days ago. The bridegroom, dark and straight, prouder that morning than if the Iliad had been his achievement, walked with his wife who, a little pale, found some strength in leaning on his arm, her veil flowing about her, half veil, half scarf, the rose in her hair the beginning of a long garland of roses that the schoolchildren had braided for her, that fell on her shoulder and trailed to her feet. A group of the children followed, marshalled by the schoolmaster, all prettily demure, but full of the suspended spirit of gambol and outcry. Then came the glad young friends and companions, and next them the parson and his wife, solemn as if they were ascending the mount of sacrifice, which indeed they were doing in giving their child to an almost unknown man. After these came all who wished them well sufficiently to climb the steep; while the music of a flute-blower went all the way along from the sheltering wood.

A passing cloud obscured the main building, but the sun lay full on the east wing, which seemed to give a smiling welcome. On the terrace was a fine banquet spread, and a wedding-cake for the bride to cut; and after the dainties had been enjoyed and Billy Biggs's pockets stuffed as full as his stomach, and the flute-blower had come out of the wood, they all swarmed through the east wing and over the great house; and the schoolmaster formed a class there and told them in his own way the story of a wedding where one of the guests, a person of deific quality, had turned jars of water into wine. "That," said he, "is what marriage does. It gives to those who have drunk only water the wine of life." It is to be doubted if the little people understood him, but the poet did.

After this came dancing; and presently sunset was casting ruby fires over all the world. And the old parson went to the new husband and wife, and blessed them as if all power were given him to bless, and he kissed them both, and led the way home.

Then Mary went inside and divested herself of her lovely finery, and made the tea, and they supped together, and then sat on the door-stone and watched the moon come up and silver the great morass in the distance; and at last they went inside, and the husband locked the door. "Oh," said Mary, "when I heard you turn the key I knew that we had left the world outside!"

"And that you and I are one!" said her husband.

The poet did not do much with his epic, after all, that year; but he gave us that charming masque of "Mornings in Arcady" that haunts its lovers as remembered strains of music do. And he made the beginnings of his wife's garden, and he wrought with his carpentry tools, and did some repairing on the motor-car; sooth to say, it needed a good deal of renewing, and it took all the amount of the check for his poem to replace the useless parts, and from other verses, too.

And by and by came the little child, as if a small angel had wandered out of heaven. And Mary began to have a strange

foreboding about the main building, as of some baleful influence there that might harm the child. So her husband took the
child with her and went all over the main building, and showed
her there was nothing there but emptiness, not even gloom; for
how could gloom live in a place flooded with sunshine through
all its many windows? After the twin babies came, Mary had the
clothes hung there to dry.

Sometimes now they had the flute-blower come up, and all
their friends from the village, to make merry in the spacious
places of the main building, which seemed to put on a brighter
face in welcome. And again, when there was rumor of war the
women gathered there to scrape lint and roll bandages, while
their children played about. Sometimes in summer the Sunday-
school received their lessons there and sang their hymns, and
had their fest. And the poet had his wish of seeing his children
at play there. Once in a while the visiting village children found
themselves storm-bound there, staying for days together, and
the wide rooms rang with their glad voices. The place was full
of life.

One day when her mother was there, the poet came to his
wife, heralded by a great puffing and blowing, sliding to the
door in the motor-car. "It is quite regenerated," he said. "I have
run it down the road and back to make assurance doubly sure.
Now mother will keep the babies, and we will follow the poor
Mad Lady's way. Oh, I have had motors before. I could have
them again if I chose to accept the conditions."

"Oh, I shall be afraid!" she said.

"Of what?" he asked, as he had asked before. "The machine
is all right. Shabby, but can go like blazes. A pity I had not
attended to it when we first set up our gods here. What a thing
it is to have a wife!" as she obediently took her seat.

"What a thing it is to have a limousine," she answered, "and a
chauffeur!"

As the car slid along Mary idly took up the speaking-tube
through which one gives orders to the man outside. It seemed
to her that she heard murmurs in it like a voice. At first faint,
then the murmurs swelled till they were not only distinct but
startling. Mary dropped the tube, but caught it up again, and

put it to her ear. It was a woman's voice evidently. "Down this way," it seemed to say. "No, no, try the first turn to the left. Oh, did I say the left? I mean the right. Don't go by it! Now, straight ahead. Oh, stop, stop, let me think—this is not right! The Springwood way, the Commoners, now the third from the forks. Why should it be so difficult to reach the road where they bring in the hay? Oh, shall we never arrive? Shall we never find it? It might be lost! It might be water-soaked! It is at the roots of the big tree that leans over the marsh. Oh, here, here! Put on more speed! Hurry, hurry, faster! It is precious, it is priceless, lives depend upon it!"

It was Mary's turn to try to say "Stop!" But she could not bring herself to use that speaking-tube. She flung herself against the glass between herself and her husband. He turned and saw her terror, and stopped instantly. "What is it, what is it?" he cried. "Oh, Mary, what is the matter?"

"The car is haunted! By the Mad Lady's voice!" she exclaimed. "I hear it in the tube there! Oh, it is dreadful!"

"Nonsense, my darlingest! It is the wind you hear. Let me try it. I hear nothing. You see we are not moving now."

"Then move!" cried Mary, "and put your ear where you would hear me if I used it. I will go and sit with you."

She did so, and he reseated himself, and the car moved on, and the poet listened. "By George, it is saying something," he exclaimed presently. "'The third from the forks.' Why, that is just where we are. 'It is such a small thing it might be lost.' By George, Mary, what does this mean? There it goes again, 'Speed, hurry, hurry, it is precious, it is priceless, lives depend—' This is the weirdest thing I ever came across," he said, as he wiped his forehead. "Look here, suppose we obey the directions, go where she says and see what will happen?"

Mary was trembling in every limb; her teeth chattered, but she tried not to have it seen. They began to go forward, turning the corner, coming out on the straight road to the marsh.

It was a season of low tides, and except for a short but terrific thunder-storm there had been no rain for weeks, so that the marsh had visibly shrunk. "There's no danger, we won't go out on the marsh, of course. That chauffeur, the Mad Lady's, must have lost control, he was going at such a horrific rate, they say."

"There is the big tree on the edge!" cried Mary, still in a tremor, her very voice shaking.

"Let us look. We will find some sticks and turn up the earth," said her husband.

"Oh, it is the most awful thing!" murmured Mary. "I feel as if we were meddling in some terrible conspiracy, as if—as if—"

"As if the Prince of the Powers of the Air had it in for you. Never fear, sweetheart, I'm here."

He worked out the foot-rest of the car and began to break with it the soil about the roots of the tree. And then he saw that the earth had been torn up by a thunderbolt fallen there not long since, stripping the bark off the tree, too, but making his work more easy.

"There's nothing there at all!" cried Mary. "It's all our imagination."

"There's nothing like effort," he replied. "Aha, what is this?" And there resounded a slight metallic clang, and he wrenched out and brought to light a small japanned box covered with rust and mould.

"It may contain a fortune in priceless stones," he said.

"She said it was priceless," Mary answered. But they had nothing with which to open it; and he turned the car and they went home, feeling as if they had a weight of lead with them.

The parson had come up for his wife, and was as interested as Mary and the poet. It took only a few minutes with a chisel to open the box. Inside was a fast-locked ebony casket. "It is too bad to break it," said Mary.

"There is nothing else to do," he said, prying it open. They found then a lock of curling hair, a slender gold ring, and a piece of thin parchment on which was written something illegible, neither name nor place being decipherable, but yet which had an air of marriage lines.

"Now what does this mean?" asked the poet. "A house takes shape out of the air apparently, a woman lives in it, and drives round wildly in search of this box that has perhaps been stolen from her, whose contents were needed to prove innocence, descent, rights to property, and what-not, and loses her life searching for it. We must get out of this, Mary! The whole thing is a baseless fabric and will melt away, and for all I know melt us with it."

The schoolmaster and Mr. Ditton coming up on their afternoon stroll in which they usually discussed points of the cabala, had heard the poet's words. "You are doubting the stability of the house?" said the schoolmaster. "You need not. It is written in the Zohar that thought is the source of all that is, and searching the Sephiroth we find that matter is only a form of thought. In fact the soul builds the body—"

"Many a castle in the air has been made solid by putting in the underpinning," said Mr. Ditton.

"My children," said the parson, "if the Mad Lady was able to project herself and her palace to this spot, for reasons of her own, you have projected into it yourselves. Your innocent and happy lives have filled it with vitality, and have fixed a dream into a home. It is as strong as the foundations of the earth. Stay here in safety, the house and the home are permanent. The poor Mad Lady! Come, wife."

But Mary was still trembling a little.

Shirley Jackson
(1916–1965)

SHIRLEY JACKSON provides an interesting link between the West Coast writers, like Gertrude Atherton, and the New England writers, like Mary E. Wilkins Freeman. Jackson was born in San Francisco in 1916 (not 1919, as she subsequently claimed) but later settled in Rochester, New York, and then Bennington, Vermont, where she died at the age of 48 in 1965. Most of her stories are set in New England, including her best-known, "The Lottery" (1948), about a small American town that holds a violent annual tradition. Not all of Jackson's work involves the supernatural, but she did have a fascination for the formidable hold a particular place may have over individuals. This was most evident in her best-known novel, *The Haunting of Hill House* (1959), but is equally present in *The Sundial* (1958), *We Have Always Lived in the Castle* (1962), and that novel's literary predecessor, "The Lovely House," first published in *New World Writing* in 1952.

The Lovely House

I

The house in itself was, even before anything had happened there, as lovely a thing as she had ever seen. Set among its lavish grounds, with a park and a river and a wooded hill surrounding it, and carefully planned and tended gardens close upon all sides, it lay upon the hills as though it were something too precious to be seen by everyone; Margaret's very coming there had been a product of such elaborate arrangement, and such letters to and fro, and such meetings and hopings and wishings, that when she alighted with Carla Montague at the doorway of Carla's home, she felt that she too had come home, to a place striven for and earned. Carla stopped before the doorway and stood for a minute, looking first behind her, at the vast reaching gardens and the green lawn going down to the river, and the soft hills beyond, and then at the perfect grace of the house, showing so clearly the long-boned structure within, the curving staircases and the arched doorways and the tall thin lines of steadying beams, all of it resting back against the hills, and up, past rows of windows and the flying lines of the roof, on, to the tower—Carla stopped, and looked, and smiled, and then turned and said, "Welcome, Margaret."

"It's a lovely house," Margaret said, and felt that she had much better have said nothing.

The doors were opened and Margaret, touching as she went the warm head of a stone faun beside her, passed inside. Carla, following, greeted the servants by name, and was welcomed with reserved pleasure; they stood for a minute on the rose and white tiled floor. "Again, welcome, Margaret," Carla said.

Far ahead of them the great stairway soared upward, held to the hall where they stood by only the slimmest of carved balustrades; on Margaret's left hand a tapestry moved softly as the door behind was closed. She could see the fine threads of the weave, and the light colors, but she could not have told the picture unless she went far away, perhaps as far away as the staircase, and looked at it from there; perhaps, she thought, from halfway up the stairway this great hall, and perhaps the whole house, is visible, as a complete body of story together, all joined and in sequence. Or perhaps I shall be allowed to move slowly from one thing to another, observing each, or would that take all the time of my visit?

"I never saw anything so lovely," she said to Carla, and Carla smiled.

"Come and meet my mama," Carla said.

They went through doors at the right, and Margaret, before she could see the light room she went into, was stricken with fear at meeting the owners of the house and the park and the river, and as she went beside Carla she kept her eyes down.

"Mama," said Carla, "this is Margaret, from school."

"Margaret," said Carla's mother, and smiled at Margaret kindly. "We are very glad you were able to come."

She was a tall lady wearing pale green and pale blue, and Margaret said as gracefully as she could, "Thank you, Mrs. Montague; I am very grateful for having been invited."

"Surely," said Mrs. Montague softly, "surely my daughter's friend Margaret from school should be welcome here; surely we should be grateful that she has come."

"Thank you, Mrs. Montague," Margaret said, not knowing how she was answering, but knowing that she was grateful.

When Mrs. Montague turned her kind eyes on her daughter, Margaret was at last able to look at the room where she stood next to her friend; it was a pale green and a pale blue long room with tall windows that looked out onto the lawn and the sky, and thin colored china ornaments on the mantel. Mrs. Montague had left her needlepoint when they came in and from where Margaret stood she could see the pale sweet pattern from the underside; all soft colors it was, melting into one another end-

lessly, and not finished. On the table nearby were books, and
one large book of sketches that were most certainly Carla's;
Carla's harp stood next to the windows, and beyond one window
were marble steps outside, going shallowly down to a fountain,
where water moved in the sunlight. Margaret thought of her
own embroidery—a pair of slippers she was working for her
friend—and knew that she should never be able to bring it into
this room, where Mrs. Montague's long white hands rested on
the needlepoint frame, soft as dust on the pale colors.

"Come," said Carla, taking Margaret's hand in her own.
"Mama has said that I might show you some of the house."

They went out again into the hall, across the rose and white
tiles which made a pattern too large to be seen from the floor,
and through a doorway where tiny bronze fauns grinned at them
from the carving. The first room that they went into was all gold,
with gilt on the window frames and on the legs of the chairs and
tables, and the small chairs standing on the yellow carpet were
made of gold brocade with small gilded backs, and on the wall
were more tapestries showing the house as it looked in the sunlight with even the trees around it shining, and these tapestries
were let into the wall and edged with thin gilded frames.

"There is so much tapestry," Margaret said.

"In every room," Carla agreed. "Mama has embroidered all
the hangings for her own room, the room where she writes her
letters. The other tapestries were done by my grandmamas and
my great-grandmamas and my great-great-grandmamas."

The next room was silver, and the small chairs were of silver
brocade with narrow silvered backs, and the tapestries on the
walls of this room were edged with silver frames and showed the
house in moonlight, with the white light shining on the stones
and the windows glittering.

"Who uses these rooms?" Margaret asked.

"No one," Carla said.

They passed then into a room where everything grew smaller
as they looked at it: the mirrors on both sides of the room
showed the door opening and Margaret and Carla coming
through, and then, reflected, a smaller door opening and a
small Margaret and a smaller Carla coming through, and then,

reflected again, a still smaller door and Margaret and Carla, and so on, endlessly, Margaret and Carla diminishing and reflecting. There was a table here and nesting under it another lesser table, and under that another one, and another under that one, and on the greatest table lay a carved wooden bowl holding within it another carved wooden bowl, and another within that, and another within that one. The tapestries in this room were of the house reflected in the lake, and the tapestries themselves were reflected, in and out, among the mirrors on the wall, with the house in the tapestries reflected in the lake.

This room frightened Margaret rather, because it was so difficult for her to tell what was in it and what was not, and how far in any direction she might easily move, and she backed out hastily, pushing Carla behind her. They turned from here into another doorway which led them out again into the great hall under the soaring staircase, and Carla said, "We had better go upstairs and see your room; we can see more of the house another time. We have *plenty* of time, after all," and she squeezed Margaret's hand joyfully.

They climbed the great staircase, and passed, in the hall upstairs, Carla's room, which was like the inside of a shell in pale colors, with lilacs on the table, and the fragrance of the lilacs followed them as they went down the halls.

The sound of their shoes on the polished floor was like rain, but the sun came in on them wherever they went. "Here," Carla said, opening a door, "is where we have breakfast when it is warm; here," opening another door, "is the passage to the room where Mama does her letters. And that—" nodding, "—is the stairway to the tower, and *here* is where we shall have dances when my brother comes home."

"A real tower?" Margaret said.

"And *here,*" Carla said, "is the old schoolroom, and my brother and I studied here before he went away, and I stayed on alone studying her until it was time for me to come to school and meet *you.*"

"Can we go up into the tower?" Margaret asked.

"Down here, at the end of the hall," Carla said, "is where all my grandpapas and my grandmamas and my great-great-grandpapas and grandmamas live." She opened the door to the long gallery, where pictures of tall old people in lace and pale waistcoats leaned down to stare at Margaret and Carla. And then, to a walk at the top of the house, where they leaned over and looked at the ground below and the tower above, and Margaret looked at the gray stone of the tower and wondered who lived there, and Carla pointed out where the river ran far below, far away, and said they should walk there tomorrow.

"When my brother comes," she said, "he will take us boating on the river."

In her room, unpacking her clothes, Margaret realized that her white dress was the only one possible for dinner, and thought that she would have to send home for more things; she had intended to wear her ordinary gray downstairs most evenings before Carla's brother came, but knew she could not when she saw Carla in light blue, with pearls around her neck. When Margaret and Carla came into the drawing room before dinner Mrs. Montague greeted them very kindly, and asked had Margaret seen the painted room, or the room with the tiles?

"We had no time to go near that part of the house at all," Carla said.

"After dinner, then," Mrs. Montague said, putting her arm affectionately around Margaret's shoulders, "we will go and see the painted room and the room with the tiles, because they are particular favorites of mine."

"Come and meet my papa," Carla said.

The door was just opening for Mr. Montague, and Margaret, who felt almost at ease now with Mrs. Montague, was frightened again of Mr. Montague, who spoke loudly and said, "So this is m'girl's friend from school? Lift up your head, girl, and let's have a look at you." When Margaret looked up blindly, and smiled weakly, he patted her cheek and said, "We shall have to make you look bolder before you leave us," and then he tapped his daughter on the shoulder and said she had grown to a monstrous fine girl.

They went in to dinner, and on the walls of the dining room were tapestries of the house in the seasons of the year, and the dinner service was white china with veins of gold running through it, as though it had been mined and not molded. The fish was one Margaret did not recognize, and Mr. Montague very generously insisted upon serving her himself without smiling at her ignorance. Carla and Margaret were each given a glassful of pale spicy wine.

"When my brother comes," Carla said to Margaret, "we will not dare be so quiet at table." She looked across the white cloth to Margaret, and then to her father at the head, to her mother at the foot, with the long table between them, and said, "My brother can make us laugh all the time."

"Your mother will not miss you for these summer months?" Mrs. Montague said to Margaret.

"She has my sisters, ma'am," Margaret said, "and I have been away at school for so long that she has learned to do without me."

"We mothers never learn to do without our daughters," Mrs. Montague said, and looked fondly at Carla. "Or our sons," she added with a sigh.

"When my brother comes," Carla said, "you will see what this house can be like with life in it."

"When does he come?" Margaret asked.

"One week," Mr. Montague said, "three days, and four hours."

When Mrs. Montague rose, Margaret and Carla followed her, and Mr. Montague rose gallantly to hold the door for them all.

That evening Carla and Margaret played and sang duets, although Carla said that their voices together were too thin to be appealing without a deeper voice accompanying, and that when her brother came they should have some splendid trios. Mrs. Montague complimented their singing, and Mr. Montague fell asleep in his chair.

Before they went upstairs Mr. Montague reminded herself of her promise to show Margaret the painted room and the room with the tiles, and so she and Margaret and Carla, holding their long dresses up away from the floor in front so that their skirts whispered behind them, went down a hall and through a passage and down another hall, and through a room filled with books and then through a painted door into a tiny octagonal room where each of the sides were paneled and painted, with pink and blue and green and gold small pictures of shepherds and nymphs, lambs and fauns, playing on the broad green lawns by the river, with the house standing lovely behind them. There was nothing else in the little room, because seemingly the paintings were furniture enough for one room, and Margaret felt surely that she could stay happily and watch the small painted people playing, without ever seeing anything more of the house. But Mrs. Montague led her on, into the room of the tiles, which was not exactly a room at all, but had one side all glass window looking out onto the same lawn of the pictures in the octagonal room. The tiles were set into the floor of this room, in tiny bright spots of color which showed, when you stood back and looked at them, that they were again a picture of the house, only now the same materials that made the house made the tiles, so that the tiny windows were tiles of glass, and the stones of the tower were chips of gray stone, and the bricks of the chimneys were chips of brick.

Beyond the tiles of the house Margaret, lifting her long skirt as she walked, so that she should not brush a chip of the tower out of place, stopped and said, "What is *this?*" And stood back to see, and then knelt down and said, "*What* is this?"

"Isn't she enchanting?" said Mrs. Montague, smiling at Margaret, "I've always loved her."

"I was wondering what Margaret would say when she saw it," said Carla, smiling also.

It was a curiously made picture of a girl's face, with blue chip eyes and a red chip mouth, staring blindly from the floor, with long light braids made of yellow stone chips going down evenly on either side of her round cheeks.

"She is pretty," said Margaret, stepping back to see her better. "What does it say underneath?"

She stepped back again, holding her head up and back to read the letters, pieced together with stone chips and set unevenly in the floor. "Here was Margaret," it said, "who died for love."

II

There was, of course, not time to do everything. Before Margaret had seen half the house, Carla's brother came home. Carla came running up the great staircase one afternoon calling, "Margaret, Margaret, he's come," and Margaret, running down to meet her, hugged her and said, "I'm so glad."

He had certainly come, and Margaret, entering the drawing room shyly behind Carla, saw Mrs. Montague with tears in her eyes and Mr. Montague standing straighter and prouder than before, and Carla said, "Brother, here is Margaret."

He was tall and haughty in uniform, and Margaret wished she had met him a little later, when she had perhaps been to her room again, and perhaps tucked up her hair. Next to him stood his friend, a captain, small and dark and bitter, and smiling bleakly upon the family assembled. Margaret smiled back timidly at them both, and stood behind Carla.

Everyone then spoke at once. Mrs. Montague said, "We've missed you so," and Mr. Montague said, "Glad to have you back, m'boy," and Carla said "We shall have such times—I've promised Margaret—" and Carla's brother said "So this is Margaret?" and the dark captain said "I've been wanting to come."

It seemed that they all spoke at once, every time; there would be a long waiting silence while all of them looked around with joy at being together, and then suddenly everyone would have found something to say. It was so at dinner. Mrs. Montague said "You're not eating enough," and "You used to be more fond of pomegranates," and Carla said "We're to go boating," and "We'll have a dance, won't we?" and "Margaret and I insist upon a picnic," and "I saved the river for my brother to show to Margaret." Mr. Montague puffed and laughed and passed the wine, and Margaret hardly dared lift her eyes. The black captain said "Never realized what an attractive old place it could be, after all," and Carla's brother said "There's much about the house I'd like to show Margaret."

After dinner they played charades, and even Mrs. Montague did Achilles with Mr. Montague, holding his heel and both of them laughing and glancing at Carla and Margaret and the captain. Carla's brother leaned on the back of Margaret's chair and once she looked up at him and said, "No one ever calls you by name. Do you actually have a name?"

"Paul," he said.

The next morning they walked on the lawn, Carla with the captain and Margaret with Paul. They stood by the lake, and Margaret looked at the pure reflection of the house and said, "It almost seems as though we could open a door and go in."

"There," said Paul, and he pointed with his stick at the front entrance, "there is where we shall enter, and it will swing open for us with an underwater crash."

"Margaret," said Carla, laughing, "you say odd things, sometimes. If you tried to go into *that* house, you'd be in the lake."

"Indeed, and not like it much, at all," the captain added.

"Or would you have the side door?" asked Paul, pointing with his stick.

"I think I prefer the front door," said Margaret.

"But you'd be drowned," Carla said. She took Margaret's arm as they started back toward the house, and said, "We'd make a scene for a tapestry right now, on the lawn before the house."

"Another tapestry?" said the captain, and grimaced.

They played croquet, and Paul hit Margaret's ball toward a wicket, and the captain accused her of cheating prettily. And they played word games in the evening, and Margaret and Paul won, and everyone said Margaret was so clever. And they walked endlessly on the lawns before the house, and looked into the still lake, and watched the reflection of the house in the water, and Margaret chose a room in the reflected house for her own, and Paul said she should have it.

"That's the room where Mama writes her letters," said Carla, looking strangely at Margaret.

"Not in our house in the lake," said Paul.

"And I suppose if you like it she would lend it to you while you stay," Carla said.

"Not at all," said Margaret amiably. "I think I should prefer the tower anyway."

"Have you seen the rose garden?" Carla asked.

"Let me take you there," said Paul.

Margaret started across the lawn with him, and Carla called to her," Where are you off to now, Margaret?"

"Why, to the rose garden," Margaret called back, and Carla said, staring, "You ae really very odd, sometimes, Margaret. And it's growing colder, far too cold to linger among the roses," and so Margaret and Paul turned back.

Mrs. Montague's needlepoint was coming on well. She had filled in most of the outlines of the house, and was setting in the windows. After the first small shock of surprise, Margaret no longer wondered that Mrs. Montague was able to set out the house so well without a pattern or a plan; she did it from memory and Margaret, realizing this for the first time, thought "How amazing," and then "But of course how else *would* she do it?"

To see a picture of the house, Mrs. Montague needed only to lift her eyes in any direction, but, more than that, she had of course never used any other model for her embroidery; she had of course learned the faces of the house better than the faces of her children. The dreamy life of the Montagues in the house was most clearly shown Margaret as she watched Mrs. Montague surely and capably building doors and windows, carvings and cornices, in her embroidered house, smiling tenderly across the room to where Carla and the captain bent over a book together, while her fingers almost of themselves turned the edge of a carving Margaret had forgotten or never known about until, leaning over the back of Mrs. Montague's chair, she saw it form itself under Mrs. Montague's hands.

The small thread of days and sunlight, then, that bound Margaret to the house, was woven here as she watched. And Carla, lifting her head to look over, might say, "Margaret, do come and look, here. Mother is always at her work, but my brother is rarely home."

They went for a picnic, Carla and the captain and Paul and Margaret, and Mrs. Montague waved to them from the doorway as they left, and Mr. Montague came to his study window and lifted his hand to them. They chose to go to the wooded hill beyond the house, although Carla was timid about going too far away—"I always like to be where I can see the roofs, at least," she said—and sat among the trees, on moss greener than Margaret had ever seen before, and spread out a white cloth and drank red wine.

It was a very proper forest, with neat trees and the green moss, and an occasional purple or yellow flower growing discreetly away from the path. There was no sense of brooding silence, and there sometimes is with trees about, and Margaret realized, looking up to see the sky clearly between the branches, that she had seen this forest in the tapestries in the breakfast room, with the house shining in the sunlight beyond.

"Doesn't the river come through here somewhere?" she asked, hearing, she thought, the sound of it through the trees. "I feel so comfortable here among these trees, so at home."

"It is possible," said Paul, "to take a boat from the lawn in front of the house and move without sound down the river, through the trees, past the fields and then, for some reason, around past the house again. The river, you see, goes almost around the house in a great circle. We are very proud of that."

"The river *is* nearby," said Carla. "It goes almost completely around the house."

"Margaret," said the captain. "You must not look rapt on a picnic unless you are contemplating nature."

"I was, as a matter of fact," said Margaret. "I was contemplating a caterpillar approaching Carla's foot."

"Will you come and look at the river?" said Paul, rising and holding his hand out to Margaret. "I think we can see much of its great circle from near here."

"Margaret," said Carla as Margaret stood up, "you are *always* wandering off."

"I'm coming right back," Margaret said, with a laugh. "It's only to look at the river."

"Don't be away long," Carla said. "We must be getting back before dark."

The river as it went through the trees was shadowed and cool, broadening out into pools where only the barest movement disturbed the ferns along its edge, and where small stones made it possible to step out and see the water all around, from a precarious island, and where without sound a leaf might be carried from the limits of sight to the limits of sight, moving swiftly but imperceptibly and turning a little as it went.

"Who lives in the tower, Paul?" asked Margaret, holding a fern and running it softly over the back of her hand. "I know someone lives there, because I saw someone moving at the window once."

"Not *lives* there," said Paul, amused. "Did you think we kept a political prisoner locked away?"

"I thought it might be the birds, at first," Margaret said, glad to be describing this to someone.

"No," said Paul, still amused. "There's an aunt, or a great-aunt, or perhaps even a great-great-great-aunt. She doesn't live there, at all, but goes there because she says she cannot *endure* the sight of tapestry." He laughed. "She has filled the tower with books, and a huge old cat, and she may practice alchemy there, for all anyone knows. The reason you've never seen her would be that she has one of her spells of hiding away. Sometimes she is downstairs daily."

"Will I ever meet her?" Margaret asked wonderingly.

"Perhaps," Paul said. "She might take it into her head to come down formally one night to dinner. Or she might wander carelessly up to you where you sat on the lawn, and introduce herself. Or you might never see her, at that."

"Suppose I went up to the tower?"

Paul glanced at her strangely. "I suppose you could, if you wanted to," he said. "*I've* been there."

"Margaret," Carla called through the woods. "Margaret, we shall be late if you do not give up brooding by the river."

All this time, almost daily, Margaret was seeing new places in the house: the fan room, where the most delicate filigree fans had been set into the walls with their fine ivory sticks painted in exquisite miniature; the small room where incredibly perfect wooden and glass and metal fruits and flowers and trees stood on glittering glass shelves, lined up against the windows. And daily she passed and repassed the door behind which lay the stairway to the tower, and almsot daily she stepped carefully around the tiles on the floor which read "Here was Margaret, who died for love."

It was no longer possible, however, to put off going to the tower. It was no longer possible to pass the doorway several times a day and do no more than touch her hand secretly to the panels, or perhaps set her head against them and listen, to hear if there were footsteps up or down, or a voice calling her. It was not possible to pass the doorway once more, and so in the early morning Margaret set her hand firmly to the door and pulled it open, and it came easily, as though relieved that at last, after so many hints and insinuations, and so much waiting and such helpless despair, Margaret had finally come to open it.

The stairs beyond, gray stone and rough, were, Margaret thought, steep for an old lady's feet, but Margaret went up effortlessly, though timidly. The stairway turned around and around, going up to the tower, and Margaret followed, setting her feet carefully upon one step after another, and holding her hands against the warm stone wall on either side, looking forward and up, expecting to be seen or spoken to before she reached the top; perhaps, she thought once, the walls of the tower were transparent and she was clearly, ridiculously visible from the outside, and Mrs. Montague and Carla, on the lawn—if indeed they ever looked upward to the tower—might watch her and turn to one another with smiles, saying, "There is Margaret, going up to the tower at last," and, smiling, nod to one another.

The stairway ended, as she had not expected it would, in a heavy wooden door, which made Margaret, standing on the step below to find room to raise her hand and knock, seem smaller, and even standing at the top of the tower she felt that she was not really tall.

"Come in," said the great-aunt's voice, when Margaret had knocked twice; the first knock had been received with an expectant silence, as though inside someone had said inaudibly, "Is that someone knocking at *this* door?" and then waited to be convinced by a second knock; and Margaret's knuckles hurt from the effort of knocking to be heard through a heavy wooden door. She opened the door awkwardly from below—how much easier this all would be, she thought, if I knew the way—went in, and said politely, before she looked around, "I'm Carla's friend. They said I might come up to the tower to see it, but of course if you would rather I went away I shall." She had planned to say this more gracefully, without such an implication that invitations to the tower were issued by the downstairs Montagues, but the long climb and her being out of breath forced her to say everything at once, and she had really no time for the sounding periods she had composed.

In any case the great-aunt said politely—she was sitting at the other side of the round room, against the window, and she was not very clearly visible—"I am amazed that they told you about me at all. However, since you are here I cannot pretend that I really object to having you; you may come in and sit down."

Margaret came obediently into the room and sat down on the stone bench which ran all the way around the tower room, under the windows which of course were on all sides and open to the winds, so that the movement of the air through the tower room was insistent and constant, making talk difficult and even distinguishing objects a matter of some effort.

As though it were necessary to establish her position in the house emphatically and immediately, the old lady said, with a gesture and a grin, "My tapestries," and waved at the windows. She seemed to be not older than a great-aunt, although perhaps too old for a mere aunt, but her voice was clearly able to carry through the sound of the wind in the tower room and she seemed compact and strong beside the window, not at all as though she might be dizzy from looking out, or tired from the stairs.

"May I look out the window?" Margaret asked, almost of the cat, which sat next to her and regarded her without friendship, but without, as yet, dislike.

"Certainly, said the great-aunt. "Look out the windows, by all means."

Margaret turned on the bench and leaned her arms on the wide stone ledge of the window, but she was disappointed. Although the tops of the trees did not reach halfway up the tower, she could see only branches and leaves below and no sign of the wide lawns or the roofs of the house or the curve of the river.

"I hoped I could see the way the river went, from here."

"The river doesn't *go* from here," said the old lady, and laughed.

"I mean," Margaret said, "they told me that the river went around in a curve, almost surrounding the house."

"Who told you?" said the old lady.

"Paul."

"I see," said the old lady. "*He's* back, is he?"

"He's been here for several days, but he's going away again soon."

"And what's *your* name?" asked the old lady, leaning forward.

"Margaret."

"I see," said the old lady again. "That's my name, too," she said.

Margaret thought that "How nice" would be an inappropriate reply to this, and something like "Is it?" or "Just imagine" or "What a coincidence" would certainly make her feel more foolish than she believed she really was, so she smiled uncertainly at the old lady and dismissed the notion of saying "What a lovely name."

"He should have come and gone sooner," the old lady went on, as though to herself. "Then we'd have it all behind us."

"Have all *what* behind us?" Margaret asked, although she felt that she was not really being included in the old lady's conversation with herself, a conversation that seemed—and probably was—part of a larger conversation which the old lady had with herself constantly and on larger subjects than the matter of Margaret's name, and which even Margaret, intruder as she was, and young, could not be allowed to interrupt for very long. "Have all *what* behind us?" Margaret asked insistently.

"I say," said the old lady, turning to look at Margaret, "he should have come and gone already, and we'd all be well out of it by now."

"I see," said Margaret. "Well, I don't think he's going to be here much longer. He's talking of going." In spite of herself, her voice trembled a little. In order to prove to the old lady that the trembling in her voice was imaginary, Margaret said almost defiantly, "It will be very lonely here after he has gone."

"We'll be well out of it, Margaret, you and I," the old lady said. "Stand away from the window, child, you'll be wet."

Margaret realized with this that the storm, which had—she knew now—been hanging over the house for long sunny days had broken, suddenly, and that the wind had grown louder and was bringing with it through the windows of the tower long stinging rain. There were drops on the cat's black fur, and Margaret felt the side of her face wet. "Do your windows close?" she asked. "If I could help you—?"

"*I* don't mind the rain," the old lady said. "It wouldn't be the first time it's rained around the tower."

"*I* don't mind it," Margaret said hastily, drawing away from the window. She realized that she was staring back at the cat, and added nervously, "Although, of course, getting wet is—" She hesitated and the cat stared back at her without expression. "I mean," she said apologetically, "some people don't *like* getting wet."

The cat deliberately turned its back on her and put its face closer to the window.

"What were you saying about Paul?" Margaret asked the old lady, feeling somehow that there might be a thin thread of reason tangling the old lady and the cat and the tower and the rain, and even, with abrupt clarity, defining Margaret herself and the strange hesitation which had caught at her here in the tower. "He's going away soon, you know."

"It would have been better if it were over with by now," the old lady said. "These things don't take really long, you know, and the sooner the better, I say."

"I suppose *that's* true," Margaret said intelligently.

"After all," said the old lady dreamily, with raindrops in her hair, "we don't always see ahead, into things that are going to happen."

Margaret was wondering how soon she might politely go back downstairs and dry herself off, and she meant to stay politely only so long as the old lady seemed to be talking, however remotely, about Paul. Also, the rain and the wind were coming through the window onto Margaret in great driving gusts, as though Margaret and the old lady and the books and the cat would be washed away, and the top of the tower cleaned of them.

"I *would* help you if I could," the old lady said earnestly to Margaret, raising her voice almost to a scream to be heard over the wind and the rain. She stood up to approach Margaret, and Margaret, thinking she was about to fall, reached out a hand to catch her. The cat stood up and spat, the rain came through the window in a great sweep, and Margaret, holding the old lady's hands, heard through the sounds of the wind the equal sounds of all the voices in the world, and they called to her saying, "Goodbye, goodbye," and "All is lost" and another voice saying, "I will always remember you," and still another called, "It is so dark." And, far away from the others, she could hear a voice calling, "Come back, come back." Then the old lady pulled her hands away from Margaret and the voices were gone. The cat shrank back and the old lady looked coldly at Margaret and said, "As I was saying, I would help you if I *could*."

"I'm so sorry," Margaret said weakly. "I thought you were going to fall."

"Goodbye," said the old lady.

III

At the ball Margaret wore a gown of thin blue lace that belonged to Carla, and yellow roses in her hair, and she carired one of the fans from the fan room, a daintily painted ivory thing which seemed indestructible, since she dropped it twice, and which had a tiny picture of the house painted on its ivory sticks, so that when the fan was closed the house was gone. Mrs. Montague had given it to her to carry, and had given Carla another, so that when Margaret and Carla passed one another dancing, or met by the punch bowl or in the halls, they said happily to one another, "Have you still got your fan? I gave mine to someone to hold for a minute; I showed mine to everyone. Are you still carrying your fan? I've got *mine*."

Margaret danced with strangers and with Paul, and when she danced with Paul they danced away from the others, up and down the long gallery hung with pictures, in and out between the pillars which led to the great hall opening into the room of the tiles. Near them danced ladies in scarlet silk, and green satin, and white velvet, and Mrs. Montague, in black with diamonds at her throat and on her hands, stood at the top of the room and smiled at the dancers, or went on Mr. Montague's arm to greet guests who came laughingly in between the pillars looking eagerly and already moving in time to the music as they walked. One lady wore white feathers in her hair, curling down against her shoulder; another had a pink scarf over her arms, and it floated behind her as she danced. Paul was in his haughty uniform, and Carla wore red roses in her hair and danced with the captain.

"Are you really going tomorrow?" Margaret asked Paul once during the evening; she knew that he was, but somehow asking the question—which she had done several times before—established a communication between them, of his right to go and her right to wonder, which was sadly sweet to her.

"I *said* you might meet the great-aunt," said Paul, as though in answer; Margaret followed his glance, and saw the old lady of the tower. She was dressed in yellow satin, and looked very regal and proud as she moved through the crowd of dancers, drawing her skirt aside if any of them came too close to her. She was coming toward Margaret and Paul where they sat on small chairs against the wall, and when she came close enough she smiled, looking at Paul, and said to him, holding out her hands, "I am very glad to see you, my dear."

Then she smiled at Margaret and Margaret smiled back, thankful that the old lady held out no hands to her.

"Margaret told me you were here," the old lady said to Paul, "and I came down to see you once more."

"I'm happy that you did," Paul said. "I wanted to see you so much that I almost came to the tower."

They both laughed and Margaret, looking from one to the other of them, wondered at the strong resemblance between them. Margaret sat very straight and stiff on her narrow chair, with her blue lace skirt falling charmingly around her and her hands folded neatly in her lap, and listened to their talk. Paul had found the old lady a chair and they sat with their heads near together, looking at one another as they talked, and smiling.

"You look very fit," the old lady said. "Very fit indeed." She sighed.

"You look wonderfully well," Paul said.

"Oh, well," said the old lady. "I've aged. I've aged, I know it."

"So have I," said Phil.

"Not noticeably," said the old lady, shaking her head and regarding him soberly for a minute. "*You* never will, I suppose."

At that moment the captain came up and bowed in front of Margaret, and Margaret, hoping that Paul might notice, got up to dance with him.

"I saw you sitting there alone," said the captain, "and I seized the precise opportunity I have been awaiting all evening."

"Excellent military tactics," said Margaret, wondering if these remarks had not been made a thousand times before, at a thousand different balls.

"I could be a splendid tactician," said the captain gallantly, as though carrying on his share of the echoing conversation, the words spoken under so many glittering chandeliers, "if my objective were always so agreeable to me."

"I saw you dancing with Carla," said Margaret.

"Carla," he said, and made a small gesture that somehow showed Carla as infinitely less than Margaret. Margaret knew that she had seen him make the same gesture to Carla, probably with reference to Margaret. She laughed.

"I forget what I'm supposed to say now," she told him.

"You're supposed to say," he told her seriously, "'And do you really leave us so soon?'"

"And do you really leave us so soon?" said Margaret obediently.

"The sooner to return," he said, and tightened his arm around her waist. Margaret said, it being her turn, "We shall miss you very much."

"*I* shall miss *you*," he said with a manly air of resignation.

They danced two waltzes, after which the captain escorted

her handsomely back to the chair from which he had taken her, next to which Paul and the old lady continued in conversation, laughing and gesturing. The captain bowed to Margaret deeply, clicking his heels.

"May I leave you alone for a minute or so?" he asked. "I believe Carla is looking for me."

"I'm perfectly all right here," Margaret said. As the captain hurried away she turned to hear what Paul and the old lady were saying.

"I remember, I remember," said the old lady laughing, and she tapped Paul on the wrist with her fan. "I never imagined there would be a time when I should find it funny."

"But it *was* funny," said Paul.

"We were so young," the old lady said. "I can hardly remember."

She stood up abruptly, bowed to Margaret, and started back across the room among the dancers. Paul followed her as far as the doorway and then left her to come back to Margaret. When he sat down next to her he said, "So you met the old lady?"

"I went to the tower," Margaret said.

"She told me," he said absently, looking down at his gloves. "Well," he said finally, looking up with an air of cheerfulness. "Are they *never* going to play a waltz?"

Shortly before the sun came up over the river the next morning they sat at breakfast, Mr. and Mrs. Montague at the ends of the table, Carla and the captain, Margaret and Paul. The red roses in Carla's hair had faded and been thrown away, as had Margaret's yellow roses, but both Carla and Margaret still wore their ball gowns, which they had been wearing for so long that the soft richness of them seemed natural, as though they were to wear nothing else for an eternity in the house, and the gay confusion of helping one another dress, and admiring one another, and straightening the last folds to hang more gracefully, seemed all to have happened longer ago than memory, to be perhaps a dream that might never have happened at all, as perhaps the figures in the tapestries on the walls of the dining room might remember, secretly, an imagined process of dressing themselves and coming with laughter and light voices to sit on the lawn where they were woven. Margaret, looking at Carla, thought that she had never seen Carla so familiarly as in this soft white gown, with her hair dressed high on her head—had it really been curled and pinned that way? Or had it always, forever, been so?—and the fan in her hand—had she not always had that fan, held just so?—and when Carla turned her head slightly on her long neck she captured the air of one of the portraits in the long gallery. Paul and the captain were still somehow trim in their uniforms; they were leaving at sunrise.

"Must you really leave this morning?" Margaret whispered to Paul.

"You are all kind to stay up and say goodbye," said the captain, and he leaned forward to look down the table at Margaret, as though it were particularly kind of her.

"Every time my son leaves me," said Mrs. Montague, "it is as though it were the first time."

Abruptly, the captain turned to Mrs. Montague and said, "I noticed this morning that there was a bare patch on the grass before the door. Can it be restored?"

"I had not known," Mrs. Montague said, and she looked nervously at Mr. Montague, who put his hand quietly on the table and said, "We hope to keep the house in good repair so long as we are able."

"But the broken statue by the lake?" said the captain. "And the tear in the tapestry behind your head?"

"It is wrong of you to notice these things," Mrs. Montague said, gently.

"What can I do?" he said to her. "It is impossible not to notice these things. The fish are dying, for instance. There are no grapes in the arbor this year. The carpet is worn to thread near your embroidery frame," he bowed to Mrs. Montague, "and in the house itself—" bowing to Mr. Montague, "—there is a noticeable crack over the window of the conservatory, a crack in the solid stone. Can you repair that?"

Mr. Montague said weakly, "It is very wrong of you to notice these things. Have you neglected the sun, and the bright perfection of the drawing room? Have you been recently to the gallery of portraits? Have you walked on the green portions of the lawn, or only watched for the bare places?"

"The drawing room is shabby," said the captain softly. "The green brocade sofa is torn a little near the arm. The carpet has lost its luster. The gilt is chipped on four of the small chairs in the gold room, the silver paint scratched in the silver room. A tile is missing from the face of Margaret, who died for love, and in the great gallery the paint has faded slightly on the portrait of—" bowing to Mr. Montague, "—your great-great-great-grandfather, sir."

Mr. Montague and Mrs. Montague looked at one another, and then Mrs. Montague said, "Surely it is not necessary to reproach *us* for these things?"

The captain reddened and shook his head.

"My embroidery is very nearly finished," Mrs. Montague said. "I have only to put the figures into the foreground."

"*I* shall mend the brocade sofa," said Carla.

The captain glanced once around the table, and sighed. "I must pack," he said. "We cannot delay our duties even though we have offended lovely women." Mrs. Montague, turning coldly away from him, rose and left the table, with Carla and Margaret following.

Margaret went quickly to the tile room, where the white face of Margaret who died for love stared eternally into the sky beyond the broad window. There was indeed a tile missing from the wide white cheek, and the broken spot looked like a tear, Margaret thought; she knelt down and touched the tile face quickly to be sure that it was not a tear.

Then she went slowly back through the lovely rooms, across the broad rose and white tiled hall, and into the drawing room, and stopped to close the tall doors behind her.

"There really is a tile missing," she said.

Paul turned and frowned; he was standing alone in the drawing room, tall and bright in his uniform, ready to leave. "You are mistaken," he said. "It is not possible that anything should be missing."

"I saw it."

"It is not *true*, you know," he said. He was walking quickly up and down the room, slapping his gloves on his wrist, glancing nervously, now and then, at the door, at the tall windows opening out onto the marble stairway. "The house is the same as ever," he said. "It does not change."

"But the worn carpet . . ." It was under his feet as he walked.

"Nonsense," he said violently. "Don't you think I'd know my own house? I care for it constantly, even when *they* forget; without this house I could not exist; do you think it would begin to crack while I am here?"

"How can you keep it from aging? Carpets *will* wear, you know, and unless they are replaced . . ."

"Replaced?" he stared as though she had said something evil. "What could replace anything in this house?" He touched Mrs. Montague's embroidery frame, softly. "All we can do is add to it."

There was a sound outside; it was the family coming down the great stairway to say goodbye. He turned quickly and listened, and it seemed to be the sound he had been expecting. "I will always remember you," he said to Margaret, hastily, and turned again toward the tall windows. "Goodbye."

"It is so dark," Margaret said, going beside him. "You will come back?"

"I will come back," he said sharply. "Goodbye." He stepped across the sill of the window onto the marble stairway outside; he was black for a moment against the white marble, and Margaret stood still at the window watching him go down the steps and away through the gardens. "Lost, lost," she heard faintly, and, from far away, "all is lost."

She turned back to the room, and, avoiding the worn spot in the carpet and moving widely around Mrs. Montague's embroidery frame, she went to the great doors and opened them. Outside, in the hall with the rose and white tiled floor, Mr. and Mrs. Montague and Carla were standing with the captain.

"Son," Mrs. Montague was saying. "When will you be back?"

"Don't *fuss* at me," the captain said. "I'll be back when I can."

Carla stood silently, a little away. "Please be careful," she said, and, "Here's Margaret, come to say goodbye to you, brother."

"Don't linger m'boy," said Mr. Montague. "Hard on the women."

"There are so many things Margaret and I planned for you while you were here," Carla said to her brother. "The time has been so short."

Margaret, standing beside Mrs. Montague, turned to Carla's brother (*and Paul; who was Paul?*) and said "Goodbye." He bowed to her and moved to go to the door with his father.

"It is hard to see him go," Mrs. Montague said. "And we do not know when he will come back." She put her hand gently on Margaret's shoulder. "We must show you more of the house," she said. "I saw you one day try the door of the ruined tower; have you seen the hall of flowers? Or the fountain room?"

"When my brother comes again," Carla said, "we shall have a musical evening, and perhaps he will take us boating on the river."

"And my visit?" said Margaret smiling. "Surely there will be an end to my visit?"

Mrs. Montague, with one last look at the door from which Mr. Montague and the captain had gone, dropped her hand from Margaret's shoulder and said, "I must go to my embroidery. I have neglected it while my son was with us."

"You will not leave us before my brother comes again?" Carla asked Margaret.

"I have only to put the figures into the foreground," Mrs. Montague said, hesitating on her way to the drawing room. "I shall have you exactly if you sit on the lawn near the river."

"We shall be models of stillness," said Carla, laughing. "Margaret, will you come and sit beside me on the lawn?"

Alice Perrin

(1867–1934)

ALICE PERRIN, born Alice Robinson, was the daughter of a major-general in the Bengal Cavalry, and though educated in England, spent several years in India, where she married Charles Perrin, an engineer, in 1886. She frequently accompanied him to remote places, where construction works were being monitored and she was usually the only woman in the area. To occupy her mind she turned to writing, selling brief articles and stories to *The Pioneer*, at the time when Rudyard Kipling was its sub-editor. When she and her husband returned to England, she continued to write, eventually having much success with a collection of stories, *East of Suez* (1901), some of which are strange and mystical. Most of her books explore aspects of the British in India, often with supernatural overtones, as in "The Footsteps in the Dust" from her second collection, *Red Records* (1906).

The Footsteps in the Dust

Here and there, mysteriously, in India exist Englishmen who seem to have been left behind on the strenuous march of British administration; who, from instability, misfortune, or wickedness, have sunk down, not entirely to the level of the loafer, but to a stage where they remain rooted in exile, apparently without home connections, correspondents, or interests, and who live and die in apathetic obscurity, while their histories, curious, pitiful, or unworthy, remain unrecorded and forgotten.

Captain Bogle was one of these derelicts. Being the oldest European inhabitant of Mynapur, he was accepted by the ever-changing officials of the district, who played cards and billiards with him in the little club, and whose wives occasionally asked him to dinner. He was an elderly man, and lived in a miserable little two-roomed bungalow opposite the great white stuccoed mansion owned by Gunga Pershad, the rich Hindoo "buniah," or merchant; but no one could say how long he had lived there, who he was, whence came his means of living, what had been his regiment, or why he voluntarily buried himself in a small civil station in Northern India. There had been rumours, of course: he had eloped with his Colonel's wife and been ruined over the damages; he had been dismissed from the army for embezzling mess funds; he was a Russian spy, a suspected murderer, the rightful heir to a great title, &c. &c. But nothing was ever proved, and Captain Bogle saw Collector, Joint Magistrate, Civil Surgeon, Police Officer, and Engineer, come and go, while his bungalow, and that of Gunga Pershad, remained the only dwellings in the station that still held their original occupants.

Captain Bogle and the buniah were apparently close friends, that is to say, the Englishman had the use of the native's horses, baskets of vegetables and fruit from the rambling garden, and they occasionally attended a race meeting down country together, when it was popularly supposed that if Captain Bogle lost, Gunga Pershad paid up—but not vice versâ. In the evenings the couple were frequently to be seen driving in Gunga Pershad's roomy old-fashioned landau drawn by a pair of big Australian horses, with a fat coachman in purple livery, and a tatterdemalion outrider clattering behind on a white stallion. Gunga Pershad, clad in a plum-coloured satin coat, with a yellow turban, his loose lips stained red with betel-nut juice, would loll in his seat deep in conversation with his companion whose appearance resembled that of a decayed Mephistopheles.

"It's a queer alliance," said the Civil Surgeon, who had lately been transferred to Mynapur, and had not yet assimilated the accepted customs of the place. "And it's my belief that Bogle gets far more out of Gunga Pershad than meets the naked eye."

"I have sometimes thought so myself lately," replied Petersham, the police officer, with whom the doctor had been dining, and the two were now seated in the verandah smoking their Bahadur cheroots. "And yet the fellow lives on like a half-caste in that little pig-sty of a bungalow, and his clothes would disgrace a rag-and-bone shop."

"You see he drinks," said the doctor.

"I've never seen him drunk, and I've been here six months—worse luck!"

"No, and I don't suppose you ever would. That chap's pickled with spirit from head to foot. He can stand any amount, I should say; but it must come to an end sooner or later. It's my belief that he's taught Gunga Pershad the same game—half brandy, half champagne is probably their usual drink. A native does that kind of thing pretty thoroughly when he once takes to it."

The police officer grew thoughtful. "I was here some years ago as assistant," he said recollectively, "and now I come to think of it, Gunga Pershad was then a very different being from what he is at present. He was a smart, healthy-looking fellow, always riding about, and ready for a chat whenever one met him, and now he's fat and bloated and never stirs out except in that old shandridan of his; and he can't look one in the face or answer civilly when he's spoken to. I see a great change in him for the worse."

"Natives go down hill fast when they start, and I fancy our friend the Captain gave him the first shove and keeps him going. My bearer declares that the pair of them sit up till four o'clock every morning drinking and gambling in Gunga Pershad's bungalow."

Then, since the hour was late, and he had to be up early on duty, the doctor said goodnight, and started home on foot, carrying his own lantern, for all the bungalows in Mynapur were fairly close together. His route led him past the large untidy compound, in the centre of which stood Gunga Pershad's mansion with the deep verandahs, pucca roof, and imposing porch. The long doors, reaching almost from ceiling to floor, stood wide open, for the night was hot and airless, and the lofty room facing the road was brightly illuminated with rows of wall lamps, while a great white punkah waved to and fro. Under the punkah stood a card table, and at it sat Gunga Pershad and the Captain, absorbed in their game, with long tumblers full of liquid at their elbows.

The doctor, fascinated by the curious picture, stood and gazed, and presently the native threw down his cards, and stood up gesticulating wildly. Captain Bogle leaned back in his chair, and proceeded to light a cheroot. Then the voice of Gunga Pershad rose in angry remonstrance, though to the watcher outside the words were not distinguishable; but they sounded threatening, beseeching, despairing by turns. The man dragged off his turban, tore his clothes, and beat his breast; he knelt in front of the Englishman, and laid his forehead on the stone floor, and throughout this piteous scene the Captain sat apparently unmoved, blowing clouds of smoke through his nostrils. The doctor turned away in disgust. The sight sickened him, it was sordid and revolting, and made him ashamed of his countryman. What did it all mean? That Bogle had been compassing the ruin of Gunga Pershad for some years past he felt convinced, and it now seemed as though a crisis had arrived. Something was going to happen.

And next morning came the news that Gunga Pershad had committed suicide by taking poison; moreover, it eventually transpired that the once rich merchant had died penniless, and that the big bungalow, the landau and horses, the mirrors, chandeliers, marble-topped tables, and all the rest of the garish possessions so dear to the heart of a native, together with savings, and investments, and valuable house property in the bazaar, had all been gambled away to Captain Bogle.

The question most discussed in the station was what the man would do with his evilly won fortune? That he was legally entitled to it all there was no disputing, but public opinion rose high against him, and though curiosity raged in every breast, Captain Bogle found himself ignored when he entered the little club, and apparently invisible when he met any one on the road.

This treatment at last caused him to avoid the club and his English neighbours, but he remained on in the shabby bungalow, and only took long solitary drives in the landau so lately the property of his victim. People wondered why he did not occupy the big white house now it was his own, or why he stayed on in Mynapur instead of going home, and old gossip and conjectures concerning him revived with additions and improvements.

Still he continued his curious existence, driving out in the evenings along the hard, dusty roads; and the doctor who met him often on his way back from the Government dispensary, expressed his opinion that the man was on the verge of delirium tremens.

"I saw him yesterday afternoon," he said to Petersham, "driving along jabbering like a monkey, just for all the world as if he had someone beside him! He seemed to be arguing and explaining till I felt quite uncanny. I could have sworn that old Gunga Pershad was sitting next him if I hadn't seen for myself that the seat was empty!"

"He was going on anyhow last night too," said Petersham. "I heard him when I was coming home from dining with the Dunnes. You know how close that little hovel of his is to the road; he was standing outside waving his hands and shouting in

Hindustani. I pulled up and asked him what was the matter, and he solemnly implored me to go over and tell Gunga Pershad to stop calling him, because nothing would induce him to go over to the bungalow and give the native his revenge at cards. I said, 'My dear chap, Gunga Pershad's dead, how can he call you, or play cards, or do anything else?' But he only looked at me like a screwed owl and said he knew Gunga Pershad was dead, well enough, and that was just why he didn't want to go over and play cards with him! We shall have trouble with that fellow, sooner or later."

"I think I'd better go and look him up today," said the doctor, who was a kind-hearted individual. But, owing to an unexpected press of work, it was not until after a late and hurried tiffin at a patient's house that he found himself free to visit Captain Bogle.

The little bungalow looked deserted when he drove up to the verandah, and it was some minutes before his shouts attracted the attention of the servants. He could hear them laughing, coughing, gossiping in the cook-house. At length a disreputable creature appeared who pronounced himself to be the Captain-sahib's bearer, as he hastily wound a dirty turban about his greasy black head.

"Where is the sahib?" inquired the doctor.

"Huzoor! He commanded the carriage but two hours since, and drove forth to eat the air. Whither he went thy slave knoweth not."

Rather relieved than otherwise the doctor turned his trap round; but as he drove down the road past the opposite compound he caught sight of the well-known landau standing under the porch of the big bungalow, and he drove in through the white gate-posts and up the ill-kept drive. The place had not been touched since Gunga Pershad's death, and the house had stood unlived in and neglected.

When he reached the porch he found the pair of horses standing in easy attitudes with drooping heads, while the coachman and groom were seated on the ground sharing a hookah and conversing in low tones. They had the patient apathetic air of natives, to whom time is no object, and one spot quite as satisfactory as another in which to smoke and discuss the price of food. They rose when they saw the doctor, and the fat coachman explained that the Captain-sahib was within the bungalow, and had been there for nearly two hours.

"It be the first time he hath entered the building since the death of Gunga Pershad," he added, as though to account for the length of the visit.

The utter silence of the neglected house struck the doctor with an odd sense of uneasiness. He descended from his trap and looked into the entrance hall. The dust lay thick on the matting, and in the dust, sharply imprinted, were the marks of Captain Bogle's boots. The doctor followed the footsteps, and they led him into the principal room where the dust covered everything. It soiled the satin upholstered chairs and couches, dimmed the mirrors, clung to the dingy punkah frill, and was deep on the floor. In the middle of the vast room was a little green-covered card table with two chairs, one of which had been pushed aside as though the occupant had risen abruptly. Cards were scattered over the table and a few lay on the floor with the remains of a broken tumbler. Evidently, thought the doctor, the room had never been touched since Gunga Pershad had played his last disastrous game.

He followed the fresh footmarks up to the table, noticed that the Captain must have first sat down in the chair that was turned aside, for it had been pushed back quite recently, and the footmarks about it were a little confused. He was vaguely conscious of something unnatural, and then realised suddenly that though the steps had led up to the table they were neither continued nor retraced. The dust lay undisturbed everywhere else—the fine grey Indian dust that gathers thickly even in a few hours if unopposed; and yet Captain Bogle was not present.

The doctor stood completely puzzled, gazing with attention at the tracks that were unmistakably in one direction only. Then he lifted up his voice and called the Captain by name again and again. His voice echoed through the lofty rooms; but there was no reply, except the scream of a frightened starling that had built its nest in a ventilator in the ceiling. He picked his way carefully back, stepping as far as possible in his own footmarks, and looked into the other rooms that led from the entrance hall. There was nothing but silence, emptiness, undisturbed dust.

Captain Bogle was not in the bungalow, and with a feeling of resentful bewilderment the doctor drove off to fetch Petersham, after giving the waiting servants orders that no one was to enter the house until his return. He brought the police officer back with him, and together they surveyed the single line of footsteps terminating at the table, the chair's position, the evidence of its occupant having sat down and risen hurriedly.

"The other chair hasn't been sat in," said Petersham, peering at it closely; "it's covered with dust, but those cards have only lately been dropped on the floor. Bogle came in here right enough, but how the devil did he get out again—unless he flew!"

Together the two men went over every room and every corner. They searched the roof, the garden, the stables, the outhouses; but Captain Bogle was nowhere to be found. He had disappeared completely and unaccountably, and the very last traces of him ever discovered were the footsteps in the dust that led up to the card table in the middle of the big room of Gunga Pershad's bungalow—and no farther.

Hildegarde Hawthorne
(1871–1952)

HILDEGARDE HAWTHORNE was the daughter of Julian Hawthorne and the granddaughter of Nathaniel Hawthorne. With such a pedigree, it is no surprise that she also became a full-time writer. What *is* a surprise is that she chose to write westerns and children's stories and wrote only a handful of ghost stories, most of which had been completely forgotten until Jessica Salmonson collected them together in *Faded Garden* (1985). She not only wrote, but was also a great traveler and enjoyed the outdoor life. Hildegarde was the eldest of nine children. When she was eighteen, her youngest sister, Perdita, died when just one day old. Six years later, Hildegarde immortalized the child's name in the story reprinted here, first published in *Harper's New Monthly Magazine* for March 1897.

Perdita

I. ALFALFA RANCH

Alfalfa Ranch, low, wide, with spreading verandas all over-grown by roses and woodbine, and commanding on all sides a wide view of the rolling alfalfa-fields, was a most bewitching place for a young couple to spend the first few months of their married life. So Jack and I were naturally much delighted when Aunt Agnes asked us to consider it our own for as long as we chose. The ranch, in spite of its distance from the nearest town, surrounded as it was by the prairies, and without a neighbor within a three-mile radius, was yet luxuriously fitted with all the modern conveniences. Aunt Agnes was a rich young widow, and had built the place after her husband's death, intending to live there with her child, to whom she transferred all the wealth of devotion she had lavished on her husband. The child, however, had died when only three years old, and Aunt Agnes, as soon as she recovered sufficient strength, had left Alfalfa Ranch, intending never to visit the place again. All this had happened nearly ten years ago, and the widow, relinquishing all the advantages her youth and beauty, quite as much as her wealth, could give her, had devoted herself to work amid the poor of New York.

At my wedding, which she heartily approved, and where to a greater extent than ever before she cast off the almost morbid quietness which had grown habitual with her, she seemed particularly anxious that Jack and I should accept the loan of Alfalfa Ranch, apparently having an old idea that the power of our happiness would somehow lift the cloud of sorrow which, in her mind, brooded over the place. I had not been strong, and Jack was overjoyed at such an opportunity of taking me into the country. High as our expectations were, the beauty of the place far exceeded them all. What color! What glorious sunsets! And the long rides we took, seeming to be utterly tireless in that fresh sweet air!

One afternoon I sat on the veranda at the western wing of the house. The veranda here was broader than elsewhere, and it was reached only by a flight of steps leading up from the lawn on one side, and by a door opposite these steps that opened into Jack's study. The rest of this veranda was enclosed by a high railing, and by wire nettings so thickly overgrown with vines that the place was always very shady. I sat near the steps, where I could watch the sweep of the great shadows thrown by the clouds that were sailing before the west wind. Jack was inside, writing, and now and then he would say something to me through the open window. As I sat, lost in delight at the beauty of the view and the sweetness of the flower-scented air, I marvelled that Aunt Agnes could ever have left so charming a spot. "She must still love it," I thought, getting up to move my chair to where I might see still further over the prairies, "and some time she will come back—" At this moment I happened to glance to the further end of the veranda, and there I saw, to my amazement, a little child seated on the floor, playing with the shifting shadows of the tangled creepers. It was a little girl in a daintily embroidered white dress, with golden curls around her baby head. As I still gazed, she suddenly turned, with a roguish toss of the yellow hair, and fixed her serious blue eyes on me.

"Baby!" I cried. "Where did you come from? Where's your mamma, darling?" And I took a step towards her.

"What's that, Silvia?" called Jack from within. I turned my head and saw him sitting at his desk.

"Come quick, Jack; there's the loveliest baby—" I turned back to the child, looked, blinked, and at this moment Jack stepped out beside me.

"Baby?" he inquired. "What on earth are you talking about, Silvia dearest?"

"Why, but—" I exclaimed. "There *was* one! How did she get away? She was sitting right there when I called."

"A *baby!*" repeated my husband. "My dear, babies don't appear and disappear like East-Indian magicians. You have been napping, and are trying to conceal the shameful fact."

"Jack," I said, decisively, "don't you suppose I know a baby when I see one? She was sitting right there, playing with the shadows, and I—It's certainly very queer!"

Jack grinned. "Go and put on your habit," he replied; "the horses will be here in ten minutes. And remember that when you have accounted for her disappearance, her presence still remains to be explained. Or perhaps you think Wah Sing produced her from his sleeve?"

I laughed. Wah Sing was our Chinese cook, and more apt, I thought, to put something up his sleeve than to take anything out.

"I suppose I *was* dreaming," I said, "though I could almost as well believe I had only dreamed our marriage."

"Or rather," observed Jack, "that our marriage had only dreamed us."

II. SHADOWS

About a week later I received a letter from Aunt Agnes. Among other things, chiefly relating to New York's slums, she said:

"I am in need of rest, and if you and Jack could put up with me for a few days, I believe I should like to get back to the old place. As you know, I have always dreaded a return there, but lately I seem somehow to have lost that dread. I feel that the time has come for me to be there again, and I am sure you will not mind me."

Most assuredly we would not mind her. We sat in the moonlight that night on the veranda, Jack swinging my hammock slowly, and talked of Aunt Agnes. The moon silvered the waving alfalfa, and sifted through the twisted vines that fenced us in, throwing intricate and ever-changing patterns on the smooth flooring. There was a hum of insects in the air, and the soft wind ever and anon blew a fleecy cloud over the moon, dimming for a moment her serene splendor.

"Who knows?" said Jack, lighting another cigar. "This may be a turning-point in Aunt Agnes's life, and she may once more be something like the sunny, happy girl your mother describes. She is beautiful, and she is yet young. It may mean the beginning of a new life for her."

"Yes," I answered. "It isn't right that her life should always be shadowed by that early sorrow. She is so lovely, and could be so happy. Now that she has taken the first step, there is no reason why she shouldn't go on."

"We'll do what we can to help her," responded my husband. "Let me fix your cushions, darling; they have slipped." He rose to do so, and suddenly stood still, facing the further end of the veranda. His expression was so peculiar that I turned, following the direction of his eyes, even before his smothered exclamation of "Silvia, look there!" reached me.

Standing in the fluttering moonlight and shadows was the same little girl I had seen already. She still wore white, and her tangled curls floated shining around her head. She seemed to be smiling, and slightly shook her head at us.

"What does it mean, Jack?" I whispered, slipping out of the hammock.

"How did she get there? Come!" said he, and we walked hastily towards the little thing, who again shook her head. Just at this moment another cloud obscured the moon for a few seconds, and though in the uncertain twilight I fancied I still saw her, yet when the cloud passed she was not to be found.

III. PERDITA

Aunt Agnes certainly did look as though she needed rest. She seemed very frail, and the color had entirely left her face. But her curling hair was as golden as ever, and her figure as girlish and graceful. She kissed me tenderly, and kept my hand in hers as she wandered over the house and took long looks across the prairie.

"Isn't it beautiful?" she asked, softly. "Just the place to be happy in! I've always had a strange fancy that I should be happy here again some day, and now I feel as though that day had almost come. You are happy, aren't you, dear?"

I looked at Jack, and felt the tears coming to my eyes. "Yes, I am happy. I did not know one could be so happy," I answered, after a moment.

Aunt Agnes smiled her sweet smile and kissed me again. "God bless you and your Jack! You almost make me feel young again."

"As though you could possibly feel anything else," I retorted, laughing. "You little humbug, to pretend you are old!" and slipping my arm round her waist, for we had always been dear friends, I walked off to chat with her in her room.

We took a ride that afternoon, for Aunt Agnes wanted another gallop over that glorious prairie. The exercise and the perfect afternoon brought back the color to her cheeks.

"I think I shall be much better tomorrow," she observed, as we trotted home. "What a country this is, and what horses!" slipping her hand down her mount's glossy neck. "I did right to come back here. I do not believe I will go away again." And she smiled on Jack and me, who laughed, and said she would find it a difficult thing to attempt.

We all three came out on the veranda to see the sunset. It was always a glorious sight, but this evening it was more than usually magnificent. Immense rays of pale blue and pink spread over the sky, and the clouds, which stretched in horizontal masses, glowed rose and golden. The whole sky was luminous and tender, and seemed to tremble with light.

We sat silent, looking at the sky and at the shadowy grass that seemed to meet it. Slowly the color deepened and faded.

"There can never be a lovelier evening," said Aunt Agnes, with a sigh.

"Don't say that," replied Jack. "It is only the beginning of even more perfect ones."

Aunt Agnes rose with a slight shiver, "It grows chilly when the sun goes," she murmured, and turned lingeringly to enter the house. Suddenly she gave a startled exclamation. Jack and I jumped up and looked at her. She stood with both hands pressed to her heart, looking—

"The child again," said Jack, in a low voice, laying his hand on my arm.

He was right. There in the gathering shadow stood the little girl in the white dress. Her hands were stretched towards us, and her lips parted in a smile. A belated gleam of sunlight seemed to linger in her hair.

"Perdita!" cried Aunt Agnes, in a voice that shook with a kind of terrible joy. Then, with a stifled sob, she ran forward and sank before the baby, throwing her arms about her. The little girl leaned back her golden head and looked at Aunt Agnes with her great, serious eyes. Then she flung both baby arms round her neck, and lifted her sweet mouth—

Jack and I turned away, looking at each other with tears in our eyes. A slight sound made us turn back. Aunt Agnes had fallen forward to the floor, and the child was nowhere to be seen.

We rushed up, and Jack raised my aunt in his arms and carried her into the house. But she was quite dead. The little child we never saw again.

Charlotte Riddell

(1832–1906)

CHARLOTTE RIDDELL was born Charlotte Cowan, but usually published as Mrs. J. H. Riddell after her marriage to Joseph Riddell, a civil engineer, in 1857. Regarded by many as the preeminent Victorian woman writer of ghost stories, she was born in Carrickfergus in Northern Ireland, where her father was High Sheriff of County Antrim. After her father's death in 1854, she and her mother traveled to London, where Charlotte hoped to establish herself as a writer. Her mother died soon after, and Charlotte succeeded in supporting herself through her writing; she later provided for her husband as well, after his financial failure. She wrote over fifty books, most of them non-supernatural, frequently considering the many pitfalls for the unwary in society. She also established herself as a writer of highly atmospheric ghost stories and became a regular contributor to the popular Christmas annuals, which ran such novellas as "The Uninhabited House" (1875) and "The Haunted River" (1877). Most of her short ghost stories were collected in the hard-to-find *Frank Sinclair's Wife* (1874), *Weird Stories* (1882), and *Idle Tales* (1887). The only modern volume of her short stories is *The Collected Ghost Stories* (1977), compiled by E. F. Bleiler, while her longer work has been assembled by Richard Dalby as *The Haunted River and Three Other Ghostly Novellas* (2001). "The Open Door" is taken from *Weird Stories*.

The Open Door

S ome people do not believe in ghosts. For that matter, some
people do not believe in anything. There are persons who
even affect incredulity concerning that open door at Ladlow
Hall. They say it did not stand wide open—that they could have
shut it; that the whole affair was a delusion; that they are sure it
must have been a conspiracy; that they are doubtful whether
there is such a place as Ladlow on the face of the earth; that the
first time they are in Meadowshire they will look it up.

That is the manner in which this story, hitherto unpublished,
has been greeted by my acquaintances. How it will be received
by strangers is quite another matter. I am going to tell what happened to me exactly as it happened, and readers can credit or
scoff at the tale as it pleases them. It is not necessary for me to
find faith and comprehension in addition to a ghost story, for the
world at large. If such were the case, I should lay down my pen.

Perhaps, before going further, I ought to premise there was a
time when I did not believe in ghosts either. If you had asked
me one summer's morning years ago when you met me on
London Bridge if I held such appearances to be probable or
possible, you would have received an emphatic "No" for
answer.

But, at this rate, the story of the Open Door will never be
told; so we will, with your permission, plunge into it
immediately.

"Sandy!"

"What do you want?"

"Should you like to earn a sovereign?"

"Of course I should."

A somewhat curt dialogue, but we were given to curtness in the office of Messrs. Frimpton, Frampton and Fryer, auctioneers and estate agents, St. Benet's Hill, City.

(My name is not Sandy or anything like it, but the other clerks so styled me because of a real or fancied likeness to some character, an ill-looking Scotchman, they had seen at the theatre. From this it may be inferred I was not handsome. Far from it. The only ugly specimen in my family, I knew I was very plain; and it chanced to be no secret to me either that I felt grievously discontented with my lot.

I did not like the occupation of clerk in an auctioneer's office, and I did not like my employers.

We are all of us inconsistent, I suppose, for it was a shock to me to find they entertained a most cordial antipathy to me.)

"Because," went on Parton, a fellow, my senior by many years—a fellow who delighted in chaffing me, "I can tell you how to lay hands on one."

"How?" I asked, sulkily enough, for I felt he was having what he called his fun.

"You know that place we let to Carrison, the tea-dealer?"

Carrison was a merchant in the China trade, possessed of fleets of vessels and towns of warehouses; but I did not correct Parton's expression, I simply nodded.

"He took it on a long lease, and he can't live in it; and our governor said this morning he wouldn't mind giving anybody who could find out what the deuce is the matter, a couple of sovereigns and his travelling expenses."

"Where is the place?" I asked, without turning my head; for the convenience of listening I had put my elbows on the desk and propped up my face with both hands.

"Away down in Meadowshire, in the heart of the grazing country."

"And what *is* the matter?" I further inquired.

"A door that won't keep shut."

"What?"

"A door that will keep open, if you prefer that way of putting it," said Parton.

"You are jesting."

"If I am, Carrison is not, or Fryer either. Carrison came here in a nice passion, and Fryer was in a fine rage; I could see he was, though he kept his temper outwardly. They have had an active correspondence it appears, and Carrison went away to talk to his lawyer. Won't make much by that move, I fancy."

"But tell me," I intreated, "why the door won't keep shut?"

"They say the place is haunted."

"What nonsense!" I exclaimed.

"Then you are just the person to take the ghost in hand. I thought so while old Fryer was speaking."

"If the door won't keep shut," I remarked, pursuing my own train of thought, "why can't they let it stay open?"

"I have not the slightest idea. I only know there are two sovereigns to be made, and that I give you a present of the information."

And having thus spoken, Parton took down his hat and went out, either upon his own business or that of his employers.

There was one thing I can truly say about our office, we were never serious in it. I fancy that is the case in most offices nowadays; at all events, it was the case in ours. We were always chaffing each other, playing practical jokes, telling stupid stories, scamping our work, looking at the clock, counting the weeks to next St. Lubbock's Day, counting the hours to Saturday.

For all that we were all very earnest in our desire to have our salaries raised, and unanimous in the opinion no fellows ever before received such wretched pay. I had twenty pounds a year, which I was aware did not half provide for what I ate at home. My mother and sisters left me in no doubt on the point, and when new clothes were wanted I always hated to mention the fact to my poor worried father.

We had been better off once, I believe, though I never remember the time. My father owned a small property in the country, but owing to the failure of some bank, I never could understand what bank, it had to be mortgaged; then the interest was not paid, and the mortgages foreclosed, and we had nothing left save the half-pay of a major, and about a hundred a year which my mother brought to the common fund.

We might have managed on our income, I think, if we had not been so painfully genteel; but we were always trying to do something quite beyond our means, and consequently debts accumulated, and creditors ruled us with rods of iron.

Before the final smash came, one of my sisters married the younger son of a distinguished family, and even if they had been disposed to live comfortably and sensibly she would have kept her sisters up to the mark. My only brother, too, was an officer, and of course the family thought it necessary he should see we preserved appearances.

It was all a great trial to my father, I think, who had to bear the brunt of the dunning and harass, and eternal shortness of money; and it would have driven me crazy if I had not found a happy refuge when matters were going wrong at home at my aunt's. She was my father's sister, and had married so "dreadfully below her" that my mother refused to acknowledge the relationship at all.

For these reasons and others, Parton's careless words about the two sovereigns stayed in my memory.

I wanted money badly—I may say I never had sixpence in the world of my own—and I thought if I could earn two sovereigns I might buy some trifles I needed for myself, and present my father with a new umbrella. Fancy is a dangerous little jade to flirt with, as I soon discovered.

She led me on and on. First I thought of the two sovereigns; then I recalled the amount of the rent Mr. Carrison agreed to pay for Ladlow Hall; then I decided he would gladly give more than two sovereigns if he could only have the ghost turned out of possession. I fancied I might get ten pounds—twenty pounds. I considered the matter all day, and I dreamed of it all night, and when I dressed myself next morning I was determined to speak to Mr. Fryer on the subject.

I did so—I told that gentleman Parton had mentioned the matter to me, and that if Mr. Fryer had no objection, I should like to try whether I could not solve the mystery. I told him I had been accustomed to lonely houses, and that I should not feel at all nervous; that I did not believe in ghosts, and as for burglars, I was not afraid of them.

"I don't mind your trying," he said at last. "Of course you understand it is no cure, no pay. Stay in the house for a week; if at the end of that time you can keep the door shut, locked, bolted, or nailed up, telegraph for me, and I will go down—if not, come back. If you like to take a companion there is no objection."

I thanked him, but said I would rather not have a companion.

"There is only one thing, sir, I should like," I ventured.

"And that—?" he interrupted.

"Is a little more money. If I lay the ghost, or find out the ghost, I think I ought to have more than two sovereigns."

"How much more do you think you ought to have?" he asked.

His tone quite threw me off my guard, it was so civil and conciliatory, and I answered boldly:

"Well, if Mr. Carrison cannot now live in the place perhaps he wouldn't mind giving me a ten-pound note."

Mr. Fryer turned, and opened one of the books lying on his desk. He did not look at or refer to it in any way—I saw that.

"You have been with us how long, Edlyd?" he said.

"Eleven months tomorrow," I replied.

"And our arrangement was, I think, quarterly payments, and one month's notice on either side?"

"Yes, sir." I heard my voice tremble, though I could not have said what frightened me.

"Then you will please to take your notice now. Come in before you leave this evening, and I'll pay you three months' salary, and then we shall be quits."

"I don't think I quite understand," I was beginning, when he broke in:

"But I understand, and that's enough. I have had enough of you and your airs, and your indifference, and your insolence here. I never had a clerk I disliked as I do you. Coming and dictating terms, forsooth! No, you shan't go to Ladlow. Many a poor chap"—(he said "devil")—"would have been glad to earn half a guinea, let alone two sovereigns; and perhaps you may be before you are much older."

"Do you mean that you won't keep me here any longer, sir?" I asked in despair. "I had no intention of offending you. I——" "Now you need not say another word," he interrupted, "for I won't bandy words with you. Since you have been in this place you have never known your position, and you don't seem able to realize it. When I was foolish enough to take you, I did it on the strength of your connections, but your connections have done nothing for me. I have never had a penny out of any one of your friends—if you have any. You'll not do any good in business for yourself or anybody else, and the sooner you go to Australia"— (here he was very emphatic)—"and get off these premises, the better I shall be pleased."

I did not answer him—I could not. He had worked himself to a white heat by this time, and evidently intended I should leave his premises then and there. He counted five pounds out of his cash-box, and, writing a receipt, pushed it and the money across the table, and bade me sign and be off at once.

My hand trembled so I could scarcely hold the pen, but I had presence of mind enough left to return one pound ten in gold, and three shillings and fourpence I had, quite by the merest good fortune, in my waistcoat pocket.

"I can't take wages for work I haven't done," I said, as well as sorrow and passion would let me. "Good-morning," and I left his office and passed out among the clerks.

I took from my desk the few articles belonging to me, left the papers it contained in order, and then, locking it, asked Parton if he would be so good as to give the key to Mr. Fryer.

"What's up?" he asked "Are you going?"

I said, "Yes, I am going."

"Got the sack?"

"That is exactly what has happened."

"Well, I'm——!" exclaimed Mr. Parton.

I did not stop to hear any further commentary on the matter, but bidding my fellow-clerks goodbye, shook the dust of Frimpton's Estate and Agency Office from off my feet.

I did not like to go home and say I was discharged, so I walked about aimlessly, and at length found myself in Regent Street. There I met my father, looking more worried than usual.

"Do you think, Phil," he said (my name is Theophilus), "you could get two or three pounds from your employers?"

Maintaining a discreet silence regarding what had passed, I answered:

"No doubt I could."

"I shall be glad if you will then, my boy," he went on, "for we are badly in want of it."

I did not ask him what was the special trouble. Where would have been the use? There was always something—gas, or water, or poor-rates, or the butcher, or the baker, or the bootmaker. Well, it did not much matter, for we were well accustomed to the life; but, I thought, "if ever I marry, we will keep within our means." And then there rose up before me a vision of Patty, my cousin—the blithest, prettiest, most useful, most sensible girl that ever made sunshine in a poor man's house.

My father and I had parted by this time, and I was still walking aimlessly on, when all at once an idea occurred to me. Mr. Fryer had not treated me well or fairly. I would hoist him on his own petard. I would go to headquarters, and try to make terms with Mr. Carrison direct.

No sooner thought than done. I hailed a passing omnibus, and was ere long in the heart of the city. Like other great men, Mr. Carrison was difficult of access—indeed, so difficult of access, that the clerk to whom I applied for an audience told me plainly I could not see him at all. I might send in my message if I liked, he was good enough to add, and no doubt it would be attended to. I said I should not send in a message, and was then asked what I would do. My answer was simple. I meant to wait till I did see him. I was told they could not have people waiting about the office in this way.

I said I supposed I might stay in the street. "Carrison didn't own that," I suggested.

The clerk advised me not to try that game, or I might get locked up.

I said I would take my chance of it.

After that we went on arguing the question at some length, and we were in the middle of a heated argument, in which several of Carrison's "young gentlemen," as they called themselves, were good enough to join, when we were all suddenly silenced by a grave-looking individual, who authoritatively inquired:

"What is all this noise about?"

Before anyone could answer I spoke up:

"I want to see Mr. Carrison, and they won't let me."

"What do you want with Mr. Carrison?"

"I will tell that to himself only."

"Very well, say on—I am Mr. Carrison."

For a moment I felt abashed and almost ashamed of my persistency; next instant, however, what Mr. Fryer would have called my "native audacity" came to the rescue, and I said, drawing a step or two nearer to him, and taking off my hat:

"I wanted to speak to you about Ladlow Hall, if you please, sir."

In an instant the fashion of his face changed, a look of irritation succeeded to that of immobility; an angry contraction of the eyebrows disfigured the expression of his countenance.

"Ladlow Hall!" he repeated; "and what have you got to say about Ladlow Hall?"

"That is what I wanted to tell you, sir," I answered, and a dead hush seemed to fall on the office as I spoke.

The silence seemed to attract his attention, for he looked sternly at the clerks, who were not using a pen or moving a finger.

"Come this way, then," he said abruptly; and next minute I was in his private office.

"Now, what is it?" he asked, flinging himself into a chair, and addressing me, who stood hat in hand beside the great table in the middle of the room.

I began—I will say he was a patient listener—at the very beginning, and told my story straight through. I concealed nothing. I enlarged on nothing. A discharged clerk I stood before him, and in the capacity of a discharged clerk I said what I had to say. He heard me to the end, then he sat silent, thinking.

At last he spoke.

"You have heard a great deal of conversation about Ladlow, I suppose?" he remarked.

"No sir; I have heard nothing except what I have told you."

"And why do you desire to strive to solve such a mystery?"

"If there is any money to be made, I should like to make it, sir."

"How old are you?"

"Two-and-twenty last January."

"And how much salary had you at Frimpton's?"

"Twenty pounds a year."

"Humph! More than you are worth, I should say."

"Mr. Fryer seemed to imagine so, sir, at any rate," I agreed, sorrowfully.

"But what do you think?" he asked, smiling in spite of himself.

"I think I did quite as much work as the other clerks," I answered.

"That is not saying much, perhaps," he observed. I was of his opinion, but I held my peace.

"You will never make much of a clerk, I am afraid," Mr. Carrison proceeded, fitting his disparaging remarks upon me as he might on a lay figure. "You don't like desk work?"

"Not much, sir."

"I should judge the best thing you could do would be to emigrate," he went on, eyeing me critically.

"Mr. Fryer said I had better go to Australia or——" I stopped, remembering the alternative that gentleman had presented.

"Or where?" asked Mr. Carrison.

"The ——, sir," I explained, softly and apologetically.

He laughed—he lay back in his chair and laughed—and I laughed myself, though ruefully.

After all, twenty pounds was twenty pounds, though I had not thought much of the salary till I lost it.

We went on talking for a long time after that; he asked me all about my father and my early life, and how we lived, and where we lived, and the people we knew; and, in fact, put more questions than I can well remember.

"It seems a crazy thing to do," he said at last; "and yet I feel disposed to trust you. The house is standing perfectly empty. I can't live in it, and I can't get rid of it; all my own furniture I have removed, and there is nothing in the place except a few old-fashioned articles belonging to Lord Ladlow. The place is a loss to me. It is of no use trying to let it, and thus, in fact, matters are at a deadlock. You won't be able to find out anything, I know, because, of course, others have tried to solve the mystery ere now; still, if you like to try you may. I will make this bargain with you. If you like to go down, I will pay your reasonable expenses for a fortnight; and if you do any good for me, I will give you a ten-pound note for yourself. Of course I must be satisfied that what you have told me is true and that you are what you represent. Do you know anybody in the city who would speak for you?"

I could think of no one but my uncle. I hinted to Mr. Carrison he was not grand enough or rich enough, perhaps, but I knew nobody else to whom I could refer him.

"What!" he said, "Robert Dorland, of Cullum Street. He does business with us. If he will go bail for your good behaviour I shan't want any further guarantee. Come along." And to my intense amazement, he rose, put on his hat, walked me across the outer office and along the pavements till we came to Cullum Street.

"Do you know this youth, Mr. Dorland?" he said, standing in front of my uncle's desk, and laying a hand on my shoulder.

"Of course I do, Mr. Carrison," answered my uncle, a little apprehensively; for, as he told me afterwards, he could not imagine what mischief I had been up to. "He is my nephew."

"And what is your opinion of him—do you think he is a young fellow I may safely trust?"

My uncle smiled, and answered, "That depends on what you wish to trust him with."

"A long column of addition, for instance."

"It would be safer to give that task to somebody else."

"Oh, uncle!" I remonstrated; for I had really striven to conquer my natural antipathy to figures—worked hard, and every bit of it against the collar.

My uncle got off his stool, and said, standing with his back to the empty fire-grate:

"Tell me what you wish the boy to do, Mr. Carrison, and I will tell you whether he will suit your purpose or not. I know him, I believe, better than he knows himself."

In an easy, affable way, for so rich a man, Mr. Carrison took possession of the vacant stool, and nursing his right leg over his left knee, answered:

"He wants to go and shut the open door at Ladlow for me. Do you think he can do that?"

My uncle looked steadily back at the speaker, and said, "I thought, Mr. Carrison, it was quite settled no one could shut it?"

Mr. Carrison shifted a little uneasily on his seat, and replied: "*I* did not set your nephew the task he fancies he would like to undertake."

"Have nothing to do with it, Phil," advised my uncle, shortly.

"You don't believe in ghosts, do you, Mr. Dorland?" asked Mr. Carrison, with a slight sneer.

"Don't you, Mr. Carrison?" retorted my uncle.

There was a pause—an uncomfortable pause—during the course of which I felt the ten pounds, which, in imagination, I had really spent, trembling in the scale. I was not afraid. For ten pounds, or half the money, I would have faced all the inhabitants of spirit land. I longed to tell them so; but something in the way those two men looked at each other stayed my tongue.

"If you ask me the question here in the heart of the city, Mr. Dorland," said Mr. Carrison, at length, slowly and carefully, "I answer 'No'; but if you were to put it to me on a dark night at Ladlow, I should beg time to consider. I do not believe in supernatural phenomena myself, and yet—the door at Ladlow is as much beyond my comprehension as the ebbing and flowing of the sea."

"And you can't live at Ladlow?" remarked my uncle.

"I can't live at Ladlow, and what is more, I can't get anyone else to live at Ladlow."

"And you want to get rid of your lease?"

"I want so much to get rid of my lease that I told Fryer I would give him a handsome sum if he could induce anyone to solve the mystery. Is there any other information you desire, Mr. Dorland? Because if there is, you have only to ask and have. I feel I am not here in a prosaic office in the city of London, but in the Palace of Truth."

My uncle took no notice of the implied compliment. When wine is good it needs no bush. If a man is habitually honest in his speech and in his thoughts, he desires no recognition of the fact.

"I don't think so," he answered; "it is for the boy to say what he will do. If he be advised by me he will stick to his ordinary work in his employers' office, and leave ghost-hunting and spirit-laying alone."

Mr. Carrison shot a rapid glance in my direction, a glance which, implying a secret understanding, might have influenced my uncle could I have stooped to deceive my uncle.

"I can't stick to my work there any longer," I said. "I got my marching orders today."

"What *had* you been doing, Phil?" asked my uncle.

"I wanted ten pounds to go and lay the ghost!" I answered, so dejectedly, that both Mr. Carrison and my uncle broke out laughing.

"Ten pounds!" cried my uncle, almost between laughing and crying. "Why, Phil boy, I had rather, poor man though I am, have given thee ten pounds than that thou should'st go ghost-hunting or ghost-laying."

When he was very much in earnest my uncle went back to thee and thou of his native dialect. I liked the vulgarism, as my mother called it, and I knew my aunt loved to hear him use the caressing words to her. He had risen, not quite from the ranks it is true, but if ever a gentleman came ready born into the world it was Robert Dorland, upon whom at our home everyone seemed to look down.

"What will you do, Edlyd?" asked Mr. Carrison; "you hear what your uncle says, 'Give up the enterprise,' and what I say; I do not want either to bribe or force your inclinations."

"I will go, sir," I answered quite steadily. "I am not afraid, and I should like to show you——" I stopped. I had been going to say, "I should like to show you I am not such a fool as you all take me for," but I felt such an address would be too familiar, and refrained.

Mr. Carrison looked at me curiously. I think he supplied the end of the sentence for himself, but he only answered:

"I should like you to show me that door fast shut; at any rate, if you can stay in the place alone for a fortnight, you shall have your money."

"I don't like it, Phil," said my uncle: "I don't like this freak at all."

"I am sorry for that, uncle," I answered, "for I mean to go."

"When?" asked Mr. Carrison.

"Tomorrow morning," I replied.

"Give him five pounds, Dorland, please, and I will send you my cheque. You will account to me for that sum, you understand," added Mr. Carrison, turning to where I stood.

"A sovereign will be quite enough," I said.

"You will take five pounds, and account to me for it," repeated Mr. Carrison, firmly; "also, you will write to me every day, to my private address, and if at any moment you feel the thing too much for you, throw it up. Good afternoon," and without more formal leave-taking he departed.

"It is of no use talking to you, Phil, I suppose?" said my uncle.

"I don't think it is," I replied; "you won't say anything to them at home, will you?"

"I am not very likely to meet any of them, am I?" he answered, without a shade of bitterness—merely stating a fact.

"I suppose I shall not see you again before I start," I said, "so I will bid you goodbye now."

"Goodbye, my lad; I wish I could see you a bit wiser and steadier."

I did not answer him; my heart was very full, and my eyes too. I had tried, but office-work was not in me, and I felt it was just as vain to ask me to sit on a stool and pore over writing and figures as to think a person born destitute of musical ability could compose an opera.

Of course I went straight to Patty; though we were not then married, though sometimes it seemed to me as if we never should be married, she was my better half then as she is my better half now.

She did not throw cold water on the project; she did not discourage me. What she said, with her dear face aglow with excitement, was, "I only wish, Phil, I was going with you." Heaven knows, so did I.

Next morning I was up before the milkman. I had told my people overnight I should be going out of town on business. Patty and I settled the whole plan in detail. I was to breakfast and dress there, for I meant to go down to Ladlow in my volunteer garments. That was a subject upon which my poor father and I never could agree; he called volunteering child's play, and other things equally hard to bear; whilst my brother, a very carpet warrior to my mind, was never weary of ridiculing the force, and chaffing me for imagining I was "a soldier."

Patty and I had talked matters over, and settled, as I have said, that I should dress at her father's.

A young fellow I knew had won a revolver at a raffle, and willingly lent it to me. With that and my rifle I felt I could conquer an army.

It was a lovely afternoon when I found myself walking through leafy lanes in the heart of Meadowshire. With every vein of my heart I loved the country, and the country was looking its best just then: grass ripe for the mower, grain forming in the ear, rippling streams, dreamy rivers, old orchards, quaint cottages.

"Oh that I had never to go back to London," I thought, for I am one of the few people left on earth who love the country and hate cities. I walked on, I walked a long way, and being uncertain as to my road, asked a gentleman who was slowly riding a powerful roan horse under arching trees—a gentleman accompanied by a young lady mounted on a stiff white pony—my way to Ladlow Hall.

"That is Ladlow Hall," he answered, pointing with his whip over the fence to my left hand. I thanked him and was going on, when he said:

"No one is living there now."

"I am aware of that," I answered.

He did not say anything more, only courteously bade me good-day, and rode off. The young lady inclined her head in acknowledgement of my uplifted cap, and smiled kindly. Altogether I felt pleased, little things always did please me. It was a good beginning—half-way to a good ending!

When I got to the Lodge I showed Mr. Carrison's letter to the woman, and received the key.

"You are not going to stop up at the Hall alone, are you, sir?" she asked.

"Yes, I am," I answered, uncompromisingly, so uncompromisingly that she said no more.

The avenue led straight to the house; it was uphill all the way, and bordered by rows of the most magnificent limes I ever beheld. A light iron fence divided the avenue from the park, and between the trunks of the trees I could see the deer browsing and cattle grazing. Ever and anon there came likewise to my ear the sound of a sheep-bell.

It was a long avenue, but at length I stood in front of the Hall—a square, solid-looking, old-fashioned house, three stories high, with no basement; a flight of steps up to the principal entrance; four windows to the right of the door, four windows to the left; the whole building flanked and backed with trees; all the blinds pulled down, a dead silence brooding over the place: the sun westering behind the great trees studding the park. I took all this in as I approached, and afterwards as I stood for a moment under the ample porch; then, remembering the business which had brought me so far, I fitted the great key in the lock, turned the handle, and entered Ladlow Hall.

For a minute—stepping out of the bright sunlight—the place looked to me so dark that I could scarcely distinguish the objects by which I was surrounded; but my eyes soon grew accustomed to the comparative darkness, and I found I was in an immense hall, lighted from the roof, a magnificent old oak staircase conducted to the upper rooms.

The floor was of black and white marble. There were two fireplaces, fitted with dogs for burning wood; around the walls hung pictures, antlers, and horns, and in odd niches and corners stood groups of statues, and the figures of men in complete suits of armour.

To look at the place outside, no one would have expected to find such a hall. I stood lost in amazement and admiration, and then I began to glance more particularly around.

Mr. Carrison had not given me any instructions by which to

identify the ghostly chamber—which I concluded would most probably be found on the first floor.

I knew nothing of the story connected with it—if there were a story. On that point I had left London as badly provided with mental as with actual luggage—worse provided, indeed, for a hamper, packed by Patty, and a small bag were coming over from the station; but regarding the mystery I was perfectly unencumbered. I had not the faintest idea in which apartment it resided. Well, I should discover that, no doubt, for myself ere long.

I looked around me—doors—doors—doors. I had never before seen so many doors together all at once. Two of them stood open—one wide, the other slightly ajar.

"I'll just shut them as a beginning," I thought, "before I go upstairs."

The doors were of oak, heavy, well-fitting, furnished with good locks and sound handles. After I had closed I tried them. Yes, they were quite secure. I ascended the great staircase feeling curiously like an intruder, paced the corridors, entered the many bed-chambers—some quite bare of furniture, others containing articles of an ancient fashion, and no doubt of considerable value—chairs, antique dressing-tables, curious wardrobes, and such like. For the most part the doors were closed, and I shut those that stood open before making my way into the attics.

I was greatly delighted with the attics. The windows lighting them did not, as a rule, overlook the front of the Hall, but commanded wide views over wood, and valley, and meadow. Leaning out of one, I could see, that to the right of the Hall the ground, thickly planted, shelved down to a stream, which came out into the daylight a little distance beyond the plantation, and meandered through the deer park. At the back of the Hall the windows looked out on nothing save a dense wood and a portion of the stable-yard, whilst on the side nearest the point from whence I had come there were spreading gardens surrounded by thick yew hedges, and kitchen-gardens protected by high walls; and further on a farmyard, where I could perceive cows and oxen, and, further still, luxuriant meadows, and fields glad with waving corn.

"What a beautiful place!" I said. "Carrison must have been a duffer to leave it." And then I thought what a great ramshackle house it was for anyone to be in all alone.

Getting heated with my long walk, I suppose, made me feel chilly, for I shivered as I drew my head in from the last dormer window, and prepared to go downstairs again.

In the attics, as in the other parts of the house I had as yet explored, I closed the doors, when there were keys locking them; when there were not, trying them, and in all cases, leaving them securely fastened.

When I reached the ground floor the evening was drawing on apace, and I felt that if I wanted to explore the whole house before dusk I must hurry my proceedings.

"I'll take the kitchens next," I decided, and so made my way to a wilderness of domestic offices lying to the rear of the great hall. Stone passages, great kitchens, an immense servants'-hall, larders, pantries, coal-cellars, beer-cellars, laundries, brew-houses, housekeeper's room—it was not of any use lingering over these details. The mystery that troubled Mr. Carrison could scarcely lodge amongst cinders and empty bottles, and there did not seem much else left in this part of the building.

I would go through the living-rooms, and then decide as to the apartments I should occupy myself.

The evening shadows were drawing on apace, so I hurried back into the hall, feeling it was a weird position to be there all alone with those ghostly hollow figures of men in armour, and the statues on which the moon's beams must fall so coldly. I would just look through the lower apartments and then kindle a fire. I had seen quantities of wood in a cupboard close at hand, and felt that beside a blazing hearth, and after a good cup of tea, I should not feel the solitary sensation which was oppressing me.

The sun had sunk below the horizon by this time, for to reach Ladlow I had been obliged to travel by cross lines of railway, and wait besides for such trains as condescended to carry third-class passengers; but there was still light enough in the hall to see all objects distinctly. With my own eyes I saw that one of the doors I had shut with my own hands was standing wide!

I turned to the door on the other side of the hall. It was as I had left it—closed. *This, then, was the room—this with the open door.* For a second I stood appalled; I think I was fairly frightened.

That did not last long, however. There lay the work I had desired to undertake, the foe I had offered to fight; so without more ado I shut the door and tried it.

"Now I will walk to the end of the hall and see what happens," I considered. I did so. I walked to the foot of the grand staircase and back again, and looked.

The door stood wide open.

I went into the room, after just a spasm of irresolution—went in and pulled up the blinds: a good-sized room, twenty by twenty (I knew, because I paced it afterwards), lighted by two long windows.

The floor, of polished oak, was partially covered with a Turkey carpet. There were two recesses beside the fireplace, one fitted up as a bookcase, the other with an old and elaborately carved cabinet. I was astonished also to find a bedstead in an apartment so little retired from the traffic of the house; and there were also some chairs of an obsolete make, covered, so far as I could make out, with faded tapestry. Beside the bedstead, which stood against the wall opposite to the door, I perceived another door. It was fast locked, the only locked door I had as yet met with in the interior of the house. It was a dreary, gloomy room: the dark panelled walls; the black, shining floor; the windows high from the ground; the antique furniture; the dull four-poster bedstead, with dingy velvet curtains; the gaping chimney; the silk counterpane that looked like a pall.

"Any crime might have been committed in such a room," I thought pettishly; and then I looked at the door critically.

Someone had been at the trouble of fitting bolts upon it, for when I passed out I not merely shut the door securely, but bolted it as well.

"I will go and get some wood, and then look at it again," I soliloquized. When I came back it stood wide open once more.

"Stay open, then!" I cried in a fury. "I won't trouble myself any more with you tonight!"

Almost as I spoke the words, there came a ring at the front door. Echoing through the desolate house, the peal in the then state of my nerves startled me beyond expression.

It was only the man who had agreed to bring over my traps. I bade him lay them down in the hall, and, while looking out some small silver, asked where the nearest post-office was to be found. Not far from the park gates, he said; if I wanted any letter sent, he would drop it in the box for me; the mail-cart picked up the bag at ten o'clock.

I had nothing ready to post then, and told him so. Perhaps the money I gave was more than he expected, or perhaps the dreariness of my position impressed him as it had impressed me, for he paused with his hand on the lock, and asked:

"Are you going to stop here all alone, master?"

"All alone," I answered, with such cheerfulness as was possible under the circumstances.

"That's the room, you know," he said, nodding in the direction of the open door, and dropping his voice to a whisper.

"Yes, I know," I replied.

"What, you've been trying to shut it already, have you? Well, you are a game one!" And with this complimentary if not very respectful comment he hastened out of the house. Evidently he had no intention of proffering his services towards the solution of the mystery.

I cast one glance at the door—it stood wide open. Through the windows I had left bare to the night, moonlight was beginning to stream cold and silvery. Before I did aught else I felt I must write to Mr. Carrison and Patty, so straightway I hurried to one of the great tables in the hall, and lighting a candle my thoughtful little girl had provided, with many other things, sat down and dashed off the two epistles.

Then down the long avenue, with its mysterious lights and shades, with the moonbeams glinting here and there, playing at hide-and-seek round the boles of the trees and through the tracery of quivering leaf and stem, I walked as fast as if I were doing a match against time.

It was delicious, the scent of the summer odours, the smell of the earth; if it had not been for the door I should have felt too happy. As it was——

"Look here, Phil," I said, all of a sudden; "life's not child's play, as uncle truly remarks. That door is just the trouble you have now to face, and you must face it! But for that door you would never have been here. I hope you are not going to turn coward the very first night. Courage!—that is your enemy—conquer it."

"I will try," my other self answered back. "I can but try. I can but fail."

The post-office was at Ladlow Hollow, a little hamlet through which the stream I had remarked dawdling on its way across the park flowed swiftly, spanned by an ancient bridge.

As I stood by the door of the little shop, asking some questions of the postmistress, the same gentleman I had met in the afternoon mounted on his roan horse, passed on foot. He wished me goodnight as he went by, and nodded familiarly to my companion, who curtseyed her acknowledgments.

"His lordship ages fast," she remarked, following the retreating figure with her eyes.

"His lordship," I repeated. "Of whom are you speaking?"

"Of Lord Ladlow," she said.

"Oh! I have never seen him," I answered, puzzled.

"Why, *that* was Lord Ladlow!" she exclaimed.

You may be sure I had something to think about as I walked back to the Hall—something beside the moonlight and the sweet night-scents, and the rustle of beast and bird and leaf, that make silence seem more eloquent than noise away down in the heart of the country.

Lord Ladlow! my word, I thought he was hundreds, thousands of miles away; and here I find him—he walking in the opposite direction from his own home—I an inmate of his desolate abode. Hi!—what was that? I heard a noise in a shrubbery close at hand, and in an instant I was in the thick of the underwood. Something shot out and darted into the cover of the further plantation. I followed, but I could catch never a glimpse of it. I did not know the lie of the ground sufficiently to course with success, and I had at length to give up the hunt—heated, baffled, and annoyed.

When I got into the house the moon's beams were streaming down upon the hall; I could see every statue, every square of marble, every piece of armour. For all the world it seemed to me like something in a dream; but I was tired and sleepy, and decided I would not trouble about fire or food, or the open door, till the next morning: I would go to sleep.

With this intention I picked up some of my traps and carried them to a room on the first floor I had selected as small and habitable. I went down for the rest, and this time chanced to lay my hand on my rifle.

It was wet. I touched the floor—it was wet likewise.

I never felt anything like the thrill of delight which shot through me. I had to deal with flesh and blood, and I would deal with it, heaven helping me.

The next morning broke clear and bright. I was up with the lark—had washed, dressed, breakfasted, explored the house before the postman came with my letters.

One from Mr. Carrison, one from Patty, and one from my uncle: I gave the man half a crown, I was so delighted, and said I was afraid my being at the Hall would cause him some additional trouble.

"No, sir," he answered, profuse in his expressions of gratitude; "I pass here every morning on my way to her ladyship's."

"Who is her ladyship?" I asked.

"The Dowager Lady Ladlow," he answered—"the old lord's widow."

"And where is her place?" I persisted.

"If you keep on through the shrubbery and across the waterfall, you come to the house about a quarter of a mile further up the stream."

He departed, after telling me there was only one post a day; and I hurried back to the room in which I had breakfasted, carrying my letters with me.

I opened Mr. Carrison's first. The gist of it was, "Spare no expense; if you run short of money telegraph for it."

I opened my uncle's next. He implored me to return; he had

always thought me hair-brained, but he felt a deep interest in and affection for me, and thought he could get me a good berth if I would only try to settle down and promise to stick to my work. The last was from Patty. O Patty, God bless you! Such women, I fancy, the men who fight best in battle, who stick last to a sinking ship, who are firm in life's struggles, who are brave to resist temptation, must have known and loved. I can't tell you more about the letter, except that it gave me strength to go on to the end.

I spent the forenoon considering that door. I looked at it from within and from without. I eyed it critically. I tried whether there was any reason why it should fly open, and I found that so long as I remained on the threshold it remained closed; if I walked even so far away as the opposite side of the hall, it swung wide.

Do what I would, it burst from latch and bolt. I could not lock it because there was no key. Well, before two o'clock I confess I was baffled.

At two there came a visitor—none other than Lord Ladlow himself. Sorely I wanted to take his horse round to the stables, but he would not hear of it.

"Walk beside me across the park, if you will be so kind," he said; "I want to speak to you."

We went together across the park, and before we parted I felt I could have gone through fire and water for this simple-spoken nobleman.

"You must not stay here ignorant of the rumours which are afloat," he said. "Of course, when I let the place to Mr. Carrison I knew nothing of the open door."

"Did you not, sir?—my lord, I mean," I stammered.

He smiled. "Do not trouble yourself about my title, which, indeed, carries a very empty state with it, but talk to me as you might to a friend. I had no idea there was any ghost story connected with the Hall, or I should have kept the place empty."

I did not exactly know what to answer, so I remained silent.

"How did you chance to be sent here?" he asked, after a pause.

I told him. When the first shock was over, a lord did not seem very different from anybody else. If an emperor had taken a morning canter across the park, I might, supposing him equally affable, have spoken as familiarly to him as to Lord Ladlow. My mother always said I entirely lacked the bump of veneration!

Beginning at the beginning, I repeated the whole story, from Parton's remark about the sovereign to Mr. Carrison's conversation with my uncle. When I had left London behind in the narrative, however, and arrived at the Hall, I became somewhat more reticent. After all, it was *his* Hall people could not live in—*his* door that would not keep shut; and it seemed to me these were facts he might dislike being forced upon his attention.

But he would have it. What had *I* seen? What did *I* think of the matter? Very honestly I told him I did not know what to say. The door certainly would not remain shut, and there seemed no human agency to account for its persistent opening; but then, on the other hand, ghosts generally did not tamper with fire-arms, and my rifle, though not loaded, had been tampered with—I was sure of that.

My companion listened attentively. "You are not frightened, are you?" he inquired at length.

"Not now," I answered. "The door did give me a start last evening, but I am not afraid of that since I find someone else is afraid of a bullet."

He did not answer for a minute; then he said:

"The theory people have set up about the open door is this: As in that room my uncle was murdered, they say the door will never remain shut till the murderer is discovered."

"Murdered!" I did not like the word at all; it made me feel chill and uncomfortable.

"Yes—he was murdered sitting in his chair, and the assassin has never been discovered. At first many persons inclined to the belief that I killed him; indeed, many are of that opinion still."

"But you did not, sir—there is not a word of truth in that story, is there?"

He laid his hand on my shoulder as he said:

"No, my lad; not a word. I loved the old man tenderly. Even when he disinherited me for the sake of his young wife, I was sorry, but not angry; and when he sent for me and assured me he had resolved to repair that wrong, I tried to induce him to leave the lady a handsome sum in addition to her jointure. "If you do not, people may think she has not been the source of happiness you expected," I added.

"Thank you, Hal," he said. "You are a good fellow; we will talk further about this tomorrow." And then he bade me good-night.

"Before morning broke—it was in the summer two years ago—the household was aroused by a fearful scream. It was his death-cry. He had been stabbed from behind in the neck. He was seated in his chair writing—writing a letter to me. But for that I might have found it harder to clear myself than was in the case; for his solicitors came forward and said he had signed a will leaving all his personalty to me—he was very rich—uncon-ditionally, only three days previously. That, of course, supplied the motive, as my lady's lawyer put it. She was very vindictive, spared no expense in trying to prove my guilt, and said openly she would never rest till she saw justice done, if it cost her the whole of her fortune. The letter lying before the dead man, over which blood had spurted, she declared must have been placed on his table by me; but the coroner saw there was an animus in this, for the few opening lines stated my uncle's desire to confide in me his reasons for changing his will—rea-sons, he said, that involved his honour, as they had destroyed his peace. 'In the statement you will find sealed up with my will in——' At that point he was dealt his death-blow. The papers were never found, and the will was never proved. My lady put in the former will, leaving her everything. Ill as I could afford to go to law, I was obliged to dispute the matter, and the law-yers are at it still, and very likely will continue at it for years. When I lost my good name, I lost my good health, and had to go abroad; and while I was away Mr. Carrison took the Hall. Till I returned, I never heard a word about the open door. My solicitor said Mr. Carrison was behaving badly; but I think now I must see them or him, and consider what can be done in the affair. As for yourself, it is of vital importance to me that this mystery should be cleared up, and if you are really not timid, stay on. I am too poor to make rash promises, but you won't find me ungrateful."

"Oh, my lord!" I cried—the address slipped quite easily and naturally off my tongue—"I don't want any more money or anything, if I can only show Patty's father I am good for something——"

"Who is Patty?" he asked.

He read the answer in my face, for he said no more.

"Should you like to have a good dog for company?" he inquired after a pause.

I hesitated; then I said:

"No, thank you. I would rather watch and hunt for myself."

And as I spoke, the remembrance of that "something" in the shrubbery recurred to me, and I told him I thought there had been someone about the place the previous evening.

"Poachers," he suggested; but I shook my head.

"A girl or a woman I imagine. However, I think a dog might hamper me."

He went away, and I returned to the house. I never left it all day. I did not go into the garden, or the stable-yard, or the shrubbery, or anywhere; I devoted myself solely and exclusively to that door.

If I shut it once, I shut it a hundred times, and always with the same result. Do what I would, it swung wide. Never, however, when I was looking at it. So long as I could endure to remain, it stayed shut—the instant I turned my back, it stood open.

About four o'clock I had another visitor; no other than Lord Ladlow's daughter—the Honourable Beatrice, riding her funny little white pony.

She was a beautiful girl of fifteen or thereabouts, and she had the sweetest smile you ever saw.

"Papa sent me with this," she said; "he would not trust any other messenger," and she put a piece of paper in my hand.

"Keep your food under lock and key; buy what you require yourself. Get your water from the pump in the stable-yard. I am going from home; but if you want anything, go or send to my daughter."

"Any answer?" she asked, patting her pony's neck.

"Tell his lordship, if you please, I will 'keep my powder dry'!" I replied.

"You have made papa look so happy," she said, still patting that fortunate pony.

"If it is in my power, I will make him look happier still, Miss——" and I hesitated, not knowing how to address her.

"Call me Beatrice," she said, with an enchanting grace; then added, slily, "Papa promises me I shall be introduced to Patty ere long," and before I could recover from my astonishment, she had tightened the bit and was turning across the park.

"One moment, please," I cried. "You can do something for me."

"What is it?" and she came back, trotting over the great sweep in front of the house.

"Lend me your pony for a minute."

She was off before I could even offer to help her alight—off, and gathering up her habit dexterously with one hand, led the docile old sheep forward with the other.

I took the bridle—when I was with horses I felt amongst my own kind—stroked the pony, pulled his ears, and let him thrust his nose into my hand.

Miss Beatrice is a countess now, and a happy wife and mother; but I sometimes see her, and the other night she took me carefully into a conservatory and asked:

"Do you remember Toddy, Mr. Edlyd?"

"Remember him!" I exclaimed; "I can never forget him!"

"He is dead!" she told me, and there were tears in her beautiful eyes as she spoke the words. "Mr. Edlyd, *I loved Toddy!*"

Well, I took Toddy up to the house, and under the third window to the right hand. He was a docile creature, and let me stand on the saddle while I looked into the only room in Ladlow Hall I had been unable to enter.

It was perfectly bare of furniture, there was not a thing in it—not a chair or table, not a picture on the walls, or ornament on the chimney-piece.

"That is where my grand-uncle's valet slept," said Miss Beatrice. "It was he who first ran in to help him the night he was murdered."

"Where is the valet?" I asked.

"Dead," she answered. "The shock killed him. He loved his master more than he loved himself."

I had seen all I wished, so I jumped off the saddle, which I had carefully dusted with a branch plucked from a lilac tree; between jest and earnest pressed the hem of Miss Beatrice's habit to my lips as I arranged its folds; saw her wave her hand as she went at a hand-gallop across the park; and then turned back once again into the lonely house, with the determination to solve the mystery attached to it or die in the attempt.

Why, I cannot explain, but before I went to bed that night I drove a gimlet I found in the stables hard into the floor, and said to the door:

"Now *I* am keeping you open."

When I went down in the morning the door was close shut, and the handle of the gimlet, broken off short, lying in the hall.

I put my hand to wipe my forehead; it was dripping with per-spiration. I did not know what to make of the place at all! I went out into the open air for a few minutes; when I returned the door again stood wide.

If I were to pursue in detail the days and nights that followed, I should weary my readers. I can only say they changed my life. The solitude, the solemnity, the mystery, produced an effect I do not profess to understand, but that I cannot regret.

I have hesitated about writing of the end, but it must come, so let me hasten to it.

Though feeling convinced that no human agency did or could keep the door open, I was certain that some living person had means of access to the house which I could not discover. This was made apparent in trifles which might well have escaped unnoticed had several, or even two people occupied the man-sion, but that in my solitary position it was impossible to over-look. A chair would be misplaced, for instance; a path would be visible over a dusty floor; my papers I found were moved; my clothes touched—letters I carried about with me, and kept under my pillow at night; still, the fact remained that when I went to the post-office, and while I was asleep, someone did wander over the house. On Lord Ladlow's return I meant to ask him for some further particulars of his uncle's death, and I was about to write to Mr. Carrison and beg permission to have the door where the valet had slept broken open, when one morning, very early indeed, I spied a hairpin lying close beside it.

What an idiot I had been! If I wanted to solve the mystery of the open door, of course I must keep watch in the room itself. The door would not stay wide unless there was a reason for it, and most certainly a hairpin could not have got into the house without assistance.

I made up my mind what I should do—that I would go to the post early, and take up my position about the hour I had hitherto started for Ladlow Hollow. I felt on the eve of a discovery, and longed for the day to pass, that the night might come.

It was a lovely morning; the weather had been exquisite during the whole week, and I flung the hall-door wide to let in the sunshine and the breeze. As I did so, I saw there was a basket on the top step—a basket filled with rare and beautiful fruit and flowers.

Mr. Carrison had let off the gardens attached to Ladlow Hall for the season—he thought he might as well save something out of the fire, he said, so my fare had not been varied with delicacies of that kind. I was very fond of fruit in those days, and seeing a card addressed to me, I instantly selected a tempting peach, and ate it a little greedily perhaps.

I might say I had barely swallowed the last morsel, when Lord Ladlow's caution recurred to me. The fruit had a curious flavour—there was a strange taste hanging about my palate. For a moment, sky, trees and park swam before my eyes; then I made up my mind what to do.

I smelt the fruit—it had all the same faint odour; then I put some in my pocket—took the basket and locked it away—walked round to the farmyard—asked for the loan of a horse that was generally driven in a light cart, and in less than half an hour was asking Ladlow to be directed to a doctor.

Rather cross at being disturbed so early, he was at first inclined to pooh-pooh my idea; but I made him cut open a pear and satisfy himself the fruit had been tampered with.

"It is fortunate you stopped at the first peach," he remarked, after giving me a draught, and some medicine to take back, and advising me to keep in the open air as much as possible. "I should like to retain this fruit and see you again tomorrow."

We did not think then on how many morrows we should see each other!

Riding across to Ladlow, the postman had given me three letters, but I did not read them till I was seated under a great tree in the park, with a basin of milk and a piece of bread beside me.

Hitherto, there had been nothing exciting in my correspondence. Patty's epistles were always delightful, but they could not be regarded as sensational; and about Mr. Carrison's there was a monotony I had begun to find tedious. On this occasion, however, no fault could be found on that score. The contents of his letter greatly surprised me. He said Lord Ladlow had released him from his bargain—that I could, therefore, leave the Hall at once. He enclosed me ten pounds, and said he would consider how he could best advance my interests; and that I had better call upon him at his private house when I returned to London.

"I do not think I shall leave Ladlow yet awhile," I considered, as I replaced his letter in its envelope. "Before I go I should like to make it hot for whoever sent me that fruit; so unless Lord Ladlow turns me out I'll stay a little longer."

Lord Ladlow did not wish me to leave. The third letter was from him.

"I shall return home tomorrow night," he wrote, "and see you on Wednesday. I have arranged satisfactorily with Mr. Carrison, and as the Hall is my own again, I mean to try to solve the mystery it contains myself. If you choose to stop and help me to do so, you would confer a favour, and I will try to make it worth your while."

"I will keep watch tonight, and see if I cannot give you some news tomorrow," I thought. And then I opened Patty's letter— the best, dearest, sweetest letter any postman in all the world could have brought me.

If it had not been for what Lord Ladlow said about his sharing my undertaking, I should not have chosen that night for my vigil. I felt ill and languid—fancy, no doubt, to a great degree inducing these sensations. I had lost energy in a most unaccountable manner. The long, lonely days had told upon my spirits—the fidgety feeling which took me a hundred times in the twelve hours to look upon the open door, to close it, and to count how many steps I could take before it opened again, had tried my mental strength as a perpetual blister might have worn away my physical. In no sense was I fit for the task I had set myself, and yet I determined to go through with it. Why had I never before decided to watch in that mysterious chamber? Had I been at the bottom of my heart afraid? In the bravest of us there are depths of cowardice that lurk unsuspected till they engulf our courage.

The day wore on—the long, dreary day; evening approached—the night shadows closed over the Hall. The moon would not rise for a couple of hours more. Everything was still as death. The house had never before seemed to me so silent and so deserted.

I took a light, and went up to my accustomed room, moving about for a time as though preparing for bed; then I extinguished the candle, softly opened the door, turned the key, and put it in my pocket, slipped softly downstairs, across the hall, through the open door. Then I knew I had been afraid, for I felt a thrill of terror as in the dark I stepped over the threshold. I paused and listened—there was not a sound—the night was still and sultry, as though a storm were brewing. Not a leaf seemed moving—the very mice remained in their holes! Noiselessly I made my way to the other side of the room. There was an old-fashioned easy-chair between the bookshelves and the bed; I sat down in it, shrouded by the heavy curtain.

The hours passed—were ever hours so long? The moon rose, came and looked in at the windows, and then sailed away to the west; but not a sound, no, not even the cry of a bird. I seemed to myself a mere collection of nerves. Every part of my body appeared twitching. It was agony to remain still; the desire to move became a form of torture. Ah! a streak in the sky; morning at last, Heaven be praised! Had ever anyone before so welcomed the dawn? A thrush began to sing—was there ever heard such delightful music? It was the morning twilight, soon the sun would rise; soon that awful vigil would be over, and yet I was no nearer the mystery than before. Hush! what was that? It had *come*. After the hours of watching and waiting; after the long night and the long suspense, it came in a moment.

The locked door opened—so suddenly, so silently, that I had barely time to draw back behind the curtain, before I saw a woman in the room. She went straight across to the other door and closed it, securing it as I saw with bolt and lock. Then just glancing around, she made her way to the cabinet, and with a key she produced shot back the wards. I did not stir, I scarcely breathed, and yet she seemed uneasy. Whatever she wanted to do she evidently was in haste to finish, for she took out the drawers one by one, and placed them on the floor; then, as the light grew better, I saw her first kneel on the floor, and peer into every aperture, and subsequently repeat the same process, standing on a chair she drew forward for the purpose. A slight, lithe woman, not a lady, clad all in black—not a bit of white about her. What on earth could she want? In a moment it flashed upon me—THE WILL AND THE LETTER! SHE IS SEARCHING FOR THEM.

I sprang from my concealment—I had her in my grasp; but she tore herself out of my hands, fighting like a wild-cat: she hit, scratched, kicked, shifting her body as though she had not a bone in it, and at last slipped herself free, and ran wildly towards the door by which she had entered.

If she reached it, she would escape me. I rushed across the room and just caught her dress as she was on the threshold. My blood was up, and I dragged her back: she had the strength of twenty devils, I think, and struggled as surely no woman ever did before.

"I do not want to kill you," I managed to say in gasps, "but I will if you do not keep quiet."

"Bah!" she cried; and before I knew what she was doing she had the revolver out of my pocket and fired.

She missed: the ball just glanced off my sleeve. I fell upon her—I can use no other expression, for it had become a fight for life, and no man can tell the ferocity there is in him till he is placed as I was then—fell upon her, and seized the weapon. She would not let it go, but I held her so tight she could not use it. She bit my face; with her disengaged hand she tore my hair. She turned and twisted and slipped about like a snake, but I did not feel pain or anything except a deadly horror lest my strength should give out.

Could I hold out much longer? She made one desperate plunge, I felt the grasp with which I held her slackening; she felt it too, and seizing her advantage tore herself free, and at the same instant fired again blindly, and again missed.

Suddenly there came a look of horror into her eyes—a frozen expression of fear.

"See!" she cried; and flinging the revolver at me, fled.

I saw, as in a momentary flash, that the door I had beheld locked stood wide—that there stood beside the table an awful figure, with uplifted hand—and then I saw no more. I was struck at last; as she threw the revolver at me she must have pulled the trigger, for I felt something like red-hot iron enter my shoulder, and I could but rush from the room before I fell senseless on the marble pavement of the hall.

When the postman came that morning, finding no one stirring, he looked through one of the long windows that flanked the door; then he ran to the farmyard and called for help.

"There is something wrong inside," he cried. "That young gentleman is lying on the floor in a pool of blood."

As they rushed round to the front of the house they saw Lord Ladlow riding up the avenue, and breathlessly told him what had happened.

"Smash in one of the windows," he said; "and go instantly for a doctor."

They laid me on the bed in that terrible room, and telegraphed for my father. For long I hovered between life and death, but at length I recovered sufficiently to be removed to the house Lord Ladlow owned on the other side of the Hollow.

Before that time I had told him all I knew, and begged him to make instant search for the will.

"Break up the cabinet if necessary," I entreated, "I am sure the papers are there."

And they were. His lordship got his own, and as to the scandal and the crime, one was hushed up and the other remained unpunished. The dowager and her maid went abroad the very morning I lay on the marble pavement at Ladlow Hall—they never returned.

My lord made that one condition of his silence.

Not in Meadowshire, but in a fairer county still, I have a farm which I manage, and make both ends meet comfortably.

Patty is the best wife any man ever possessed—and I—well, I am just as happy if a trifle more serious than of old; but there are times when a great horror of darkness seems to fall upon me, and at such periods I cannot endure to be left alone.

Joyce Carol Oates
(b. 1938)

JOYCE CAROL OATES is America's preeminent lady of letters, a formidable and prolific talent who has been on the top of her form for over forty years. She has won many awards, including the National Book Award for *Them* (1969), the Rea Award (1990) for her contribution to the short story medium, and the Bram Stoker Award from the Horror Writers of America for *Zombie* (1995). The supernatural permeates through much of her work though it is seldom overt. The events are rather dreamlike and surreal, as likely to stem from a psychological aberration as anything genuinely spectral. Writing in her collection, *Haunted* (1994), subtitled "Tales of the Grotesque," Oates said: "I take as the most profound mystery of our human experience the fact that though we each exist subjectively, and know the world only through the prism of self, this 'subjectivity' is inaccessible, thus unreal and mysterious to others." Thus all our activities may invoke an overwhelming sense of strangeness, like a waking nightmare, just as in this story, "An Urban Paradox," from *Witness* (1994).

An Urban Paradox

For some months there has been a heated public debate in our city, at least among intellectuals and persons of civic responsibility. *Where are these people coming from? This seemingly inexhaustible supply of humanity?* As a scholar, and a translator, I have tried to retain a morally neutral perspective, free of all prejudice and bias. Therefore I have taken no sides.

However, it is clear that, during the past decade, our aging city has become one of the most densely populated cities in North America. Of course, it is a principle that, in the right circumstances, human beings engender human beings; yet that cannot explain the influx of mature men and women into our city, and most visibly onto our already traffic-clogged streets. As I say, I offer no opinion, still less do I offer any remedy. I keep assiduously to myself, spending most of my time in the Institute library, when I am not safely at home a few blocks away. (As a University appointee with tenure, I am privileged to live in the historic district of the city. My life's work, which in no way touches upon these speculations, involves the translation of fifteenth-century Italian theological texts into English, complete with exegeses, footnotes, bibliographies, et al. A challenging task which has required twelve years' intense concentration thus far, begun when I was a graduate student, and nowhere near completion!)

Yet it has happened, and I scarcely understand how, that certain (unmarked) municipal vehicles have begun to seriously distract me from my scholarly routine. These vans are a steely metallic-gray, with dark-tinted windows in front and no windows at all in the rear; they resemble delivery trucks, but there are no visible markings to identify them. Nor are there manufacturers' logos to identify their makers. The vans move unobtrusively about the city, even into the University district, at any hour of the day or night; I assume that they are concentrated in the more populous and crime-ridden urban areas, but they are likely to turn up one of our narrow cobblestone residential streets as well. Rarely do they call attention to themselves by speeding, or making abrupt U-turns in traffic, or driving up onto the sidewalk to bypass traffic, like police vehicles; nor are they equipped with sirens, emergency horns, or flashing lights. They are equipped, evidently, with hoses—but they are not firefighting vehicles. The windows are so darkly tinted that one cannot even see one's reflection in them—or so it is said. (I mean, so I have overheard. Occasionally I hear University students, or the younger members of the faculty, discussing such matters a bit recklessly.) One certainly cannot, and would not want to, peer inside to see who, or what, is behind the wheel!

When I first began seeing these (unmarked) municipal vehicles, of course I could not have considered them in the plural— *vehicles;* I probably surmised, without giving much thought to the subject, for indeed it had not seemed at the time to warrant much thought, still less concern, that I'd happened by chance, in my absentminded way, to be seeing the same single *vehicle* repeatedly. But then, with the passage of time, I began to realize that there must be more than one of the metallic-gray vans since, by degrees, I had begun to see so many of them.

Of course, I haven't made a count. I would never record, on paper, even in code, actual *notations.*

Several weeks ago, for instance. Shortly after nine o'clock of a weekday evening, hardly a late hour in a city so cosmopolitan as ours. I was returning home from my office at the Institute, taking my usual route past the handsome weathered Gothic stone buildings that have shaped my life, when I saw, or seemed to see, a confused dreamlike scene in the northeast corner of University Memorial Park. A child naked from the waist down, its hair lifting in greenish flames, ran out of the shadows of the plane trees and toward the street, shrieking for help, as if having sighted me (?). (At least, I assume the poor creature was shrieking for help. I could not comprehend a word of its harsh, guttural language, which bore no resemblance to the half-dozen European languages with which I am familiar.) I stood rooted to the spot, not knowing what to do. I am not a man of instinct, still less of impulsive acts. And this was all happening so swiftly! (There were relatively few people on the street, and those who were continued on their way not glancing left or right.) The child shrieked again, now at the edge of the park—but was suddenly hidden from my view by the appearance of one of the (unmarked) vans which drove up, braked to a jarring halt, and, after no more than fifteen seconds, drove on again, and disappeared around a corner.

The child with the flaming hair had vanished as if it had never been!

Which is why I characterize the episode as confused and dreamlike. One of those myriad episodes, or impressions of episodes, we are apt to experience in the course of a day, especially in public places in which we are not in *control,* still less in *anticipation,* of what is happening.

(Except I saw, I believe—in some sense "saw"—or was left with the optical residue of "seeing"—a glisten of frothy water on the pavement and on the trampled grass where the child had been; I was left with the fleeting, unverifiable impression that a hose (?) had been used—but by whom, I had not seen. Or could not remember seeing.)

After all, such episodes, in public places, are over so quickly!

One no more adjusts one's eyes to seeing what, a moment before, could not possibly have been there, than the vision is gone, irretrievable.

Nor are fellow witnesses helpful. After the child with the flaming hair appeared, and almost immediately disappeared, I hurried to catch up with a fellow pedestrian, a middle-aged man associated with the Institute, his face and name known to me as mine are known to him, and I asked, Excuse me! Did you see—? and my colleague frowned and said, annoyed, Excuse *me!* I'm really in a bit of a hurry.

He walked quickly off, and I followed, somewhat dazedly, and did not look back.

What is wanted, I thought, is a theory—!

In the weeks following, there have been, quite without my seeking them out, similar mysterious sightings. Here in the historic district where one would not expect (would one?) any disruption of the commonweal. Whether these sightings have been by me alone or by me amid others, I am in no position to say. For the mere presence of others does not mean that others *see*. (At the Institute, where privacy is respected at all costs, and where resident scholars can go for weeks, or even years, without speaking to one another beyond courteous hellos, naturally there has been no discussion of the metallic-gray vans and their activities.) I have learned in fact that the presence of others, ostensibly "witnesses," may mean in fact that these others do *not* *see*.

At the same time, I should say that, since each sighting has been both like and unlike the others, I have no legitimate way of knowing that one sighting is related to the others, or even to one other. I have no legitimate way of knowing that something "seen" by me is in fact "seen" by me and not hallucinated. And since I am not keeping a formal record, not even making a systematic attempt to remember, it is possible (isn't it?) that I am unconsciously exaggerating. Or even inventing.

As I've said, what is wanted, so very badly, is a theory to encompass these mysterious phenomena. Ah, a theory!

This most recent sighting, for instance. It has left me quite dazed. It has left me quite breathless, and suffused with anxiety. *And this is not my nature, but an alien nature.* Very early this morning, at dawn of what would be a hard bright windswept March day, a babble of voices—shouts, cries, accusations, pleas, lamentations—woke me from a deep stuporous sleep; and drew me to my bedroom window where I peered cautiously through the slats of my venetian blinds to see what was happening in the street. (I have lived for the past twelve years in this apartment on the sixth floor of an old, venerable building owned by the University. Yes, I have been happy here! I cannot conceive of living elsewhere, any more than I can conceive of doing work other than the work I was born to do.) Blinking in amazement, I saw a hellish sight: a gathering of shabby, stunted figures, both male and female, pathetic as animated scarecrows, lurching on diseased legs, or stumps of legs, struggling together over scraps of garbage from an overturned trash can. It was hideous—repugnant! I had never witnessed anything like it, so close to *my* home. Subhuman faces contorted in greed, rapacity, anguish—fury gleaming in a man's eyes—a hunchbacked female scrambling to seize a smashed, rotted melon someone had kicked along the sidewalk—another, younger dark-skinned woman on her knees clawing at something that appeared to be alive, and frantic to escape—a cat? a rat? a small mongrel dog? I was revolted, yet I could not bring myself to turn away. *Who are these creatures, where have they come from?*

Almost at once, as if summoned by my horror, one of the (unmarked) municipal vehicles drew up at the curb below, braked to a stop, and obscured my vision of the struggle. What a relief! And then another van drew up, and still a third. The most I'd ever seen together at one time.

Again, the vans paused only briefly before moving on. Their efficiency, coupled with their eerie silence, was remarkable. There was a confused impression of a flurry of activity—the vans' rear doors being opened, uniformed figures rushing out—but it occurred too rapidly for me to see, still less comprehend, like a film run at several times its normal speed. And once the vans were gone, driving off unobtrusively, the street below was empty as one might expect at this hour of the day—except for puddles of water with an odd reddish glisten.

The struggling figures had vanished as if they had never been!

All this fierce bright windswept March morning I have crouched by my window, tormented by thought.

The street six storeys below is narrow even for the University district, the perspective from my window steep and vertiginous. I do not want to dwell upon it yet, seemingly, being human, and gripped by the human instinct to comprehend, I cannot resist.

Leaning weakly against the windowsill and peering through dusty blind slats down at the vacant pavement where the figures (?) had been, and now nothing (?) is.

Trying to grasp the principle that, having seen what had possibly not been there, I can ever bring myself to see what *is* there—or anywhere.

For once you begin to doubt the evidence of your senses, there is no logical end to your doubting.

At the same time reminding myself that there is no inevitable reason to conclude that the hellish scene that was *not* there after the (unmarked) vans' departure—indeed, *is not* there now—had ever in fact been there. Even in theory. For perhaps I had not been awakened from my sleep, but had merely dreamt the entire episode. What responsibility, then, rests with me?

In certain of the theological tracts I am translating at the present time, it is argued that human beings cannot be held responsible for dreams or dream-visions, no matter how sinful; for some of these may be the work of the Devil, and where we do not consciously choose, direct, and control, we must be absolved of blame. The ancient, primitive world adhered to a different kind of justice, for repeatedly in the old Greek and Roman tales of gods, demi-gods, and hapless mortals, mortals were held culpable for actions that had in fact been dictated by gods; their "destinies" were not their own, but the fruit of cruel, childlike gods in perpetual feuds with one another. In the enlightened centuries that followed, and into the present time, it is understood that human beings must be judged only if they are free agents. They must be forgiven for that which is no one's fault!—whether dreams, hallucinations, or utterly mysterious and unknowable events that resist all classification.

Can what is (unmarked) be (marked)?

And so I have worked out a theory of the (unmarked) municipal vehicles. At least to my personal satisfaction. Others may attack it, but others will know nothing of it; I have not committed it to writing, nor shall I do so. The most pure of intellectual exercises is that which is wholly private.

My theory is, simply: the (unmarked) municipal vehicles do not, in the strictest sense of the term, "exist"; just as the laws they apparently enforce do not "exist." *That which is not imagined as existing, cannot exist.*

Which is to say: the (hypothetical) reality beyond the flood of surface impressions we receive by way of the brain's intricate (but necessarily restricted) neurological apparatus is but one factor in the immense field of sensory information available to the brain. No part of it can be deemed *more real* than any other; and when it disappears, if it disappears, the fact of its disappearance—its transience—argues for its *irreality*.

What is not here now, was never here at all. For how to prove it?

What is (unmarked) is (unmarked).

Beyond that, it's a matter of hurrying home well before dark, and shutting one's window and blinds tight against the day.

Francis Stevens

(1884–1948)

FRANCIS STEVENS was the male pseudonym adopted by
Minneapolis-born Gertrude Barrows Bennett. She had sold a
story to *Argosy* while still in her teens, "The Curious Experience
of Thomas Dunbar" (March 1904), but she seems to have written nothing else for over ten years. She married in 1909 and
moved to Pennsylvania, but her husband died on a treasure-
hunting expedition the following year and Gertrude was left to
raise their young child alone. She undertook various secretarial
duties at the University of Pennsylvania, but found she could
earn more by selling her stories to the pulp magazines and
reverted to writing in order to support her widowed mother as
well as her daughter. She now concocted her male alias for her
first new story, "The Nightmare," published in *Argosy* in 1917.
She published prolifically over the next six years and then seems
to have stopped as abruptly as she started, after her mother's
death. None of her material was published in book form during
her lifetime, but her reputation was rekindled after the Second
World War, with the reprinting in 1952 of her 1919 serial *The
Heads of Cerberus*, set in a despotic Philadelphia. Her short
supernatural novel, *Claimed*, from 1920 was reprinted in 1966,
and her dramatic 1918 lost-race novel, *The Citadel of Fear*, possibly inspired by her husband's adventures, was eventually
reprinted in 1970. It was not until 2004 that most of her remaining strange tales were collected by Gary Hoppenstand as *The
Nightmare and Other Tales of Dark Fantasy*. "Unseen—
Unfeared," first published in *The People's Favorite Magazine*
for 10 February 1919, seeks to provide a scientific basis to our
base fears.

Unseen—Unfeared

I

I had been dining with my ever-interesting friend, Mark Jenkins, at a little Italian restaurant near South Street. It was a chance meeting. Jenkins is too busy, usually, to make dinner engagements. Over our highly seasoned food and sour, thin, red wine, he spoke of little odd incidents and adventures of his profession. Nothing very vital or important, of course. Jenkins is not the sort of detective who first detects and then pours the egotistical and revealing details of achievement in the ears of every acquaintance, however appreciative.

But when I spoke of something I had seen in the morning papers, he laughed. "Poor old 'Doc' Holt! Fascinating old codger, to anyone who really knows him. I've had his friendship for years—since I was first on the city force and saved a young assistant of his from jail on a false charge. And they had to drag him into the poisoning of this young sport, Ralph Peeler!"

"Why are you so sure he couldn't have been implicated?" I asked.

But Jenkins only shook his head, with a quiet smile. "I have reasons for believing otherwise," was all I could get out of him on that score, "But," he added, "the only reason he was suspected at all is the superstitious dread of these ignorant people around him. Can't see why he lives in such a place. I know for a fact he doesn't have to. Doc's got money of his own. He's an amateur chemist and dabbler in different sorts of research work, and I suspect he's been guilty of 'showing off.' Result, they all swear he has the evil eye and holds forbidden communion with invisible powers. Smoke?"

Jenkins offered me one of his invariably good cigars, which I accepted, saying thoughtfully: "A man has no right to trifle with the superstitions of ignorant people. Sooner or later, it spells trouble."

"Did in his case. They swore up and down that he sold love charms openly and poisons secretly, and that, together with his living so near to—somebody else—got him temporarily suspected. But my tongue's running away with me, as usual!"

"As usual," I retorted impatiently, "you open up with all the frankness of a Chinese diplomat."

He beamed upon me engagingly and rose from the table, with a glance at his watch. "Sorry to leave you, Blaisdell, but I have to meet Jimmy Brennan in ten minutes."

He so clearly did not invite my further company that I remained seated for a little while after his departure; then took my own way homeward. Those streets always held for me a certain fascination, particularly at night. They are so unlike the rest of the city, so foreign in appearance, with their little shabby stores, always open until late evening, their unbelievably cheap goods, displayed as much outside the shops as in them, hung on the fronts and laid out on tables by the curb and in the street itself. Tonight, however, neither people nor stores in any sense appealed to me. The mixture of Italians, Jews and a few Negroes, mostly bareheaded, unkempt and generally unhygienic in appearance, struck me as merely revolting. They were all humans, and I, too, was human. Some way I did not like the idea.

Puzzled a trifle, for I am more inclined to sympathize with poverty than accuse it, I watched the faces that I passed. Never before had I observed how bestial, how brutal were the countenances of the dwellers in this region. I actually shuddered when an old-clothes man, a gray-bearded Hebrew, brushed me as he toiled past with his barrow.

There was a sense of evil in the air, a warning of things which it is wise for a clean man to shun and keep clear of. The impression became so strong that before I had walked two squares I began to feel physically ill. Then it occurred to me that the one glass of cheap Chianti I had drunk might have something to do with the feeling. Who knew how that stuff had been manufactured, or whether the juice of the grape entered at all into its ill-flavored composition? Yet I doubted if that were the real cause of my discomfort.

By nature I am rather a sensitive, impressionable sort of chap. In some way tonight this neighborhood, with its sordid sights and smells, had struck me wrong.

My sense of impending evil was merging into actual fear. This would never do. There is only one way to deal with an imaginative temperament like mine—conquer its vagaries. If I left South Street with this nameless dread upon me, I could never pass down it again without a recurrence of the feeling. I should simply have to stay here until I got the better of it—that was all.

I paused on a corner before a shabby but brightly lighted little drug store. Its gleaming windows and the luminous green of its conventional glass show jars made the brightest spot on the block. I realized that I was tired, but hardly wanted to go in there and rest. I knew what the company would be like at its shabby, sticky soda fountain. As I stood there, my eyes fell on a long white canvas sign across from me, and its black-and-red lettering caught my attention.

SEE THE GREAT UNSEEN!
Come in! This Means You!
FREE TO ALL!

A museum of fakes, I thought, but also reflected that if it were a show of some kind I could sit down for a while, rest, and fight off this increasing obsession of nonexistent evil. That side of the street was almost deserted, and the place itself might well be nearly empty.

II

I walked over, but with every step my sense of dread increased. Dread of I knew not what. Bodiless, inexplicable horror had me as in a net, whose strands, being intangible, without reason for existence, I could by no means throw off. It was not the people now. None of them were about me. There, in the open, lighted street, with no sight nor sound of terror to assail me, I was the shivering victim of such fear as I had never known was possible. Yet still I would not yield.

Setting my teeth, and fighting with myself as with some pet animal gone mad, I forced my steps to slowness and walked along the sidewalk, seeking entrance. Just here there were no shops, but several doors reached in each case by means of a few iron-railed stone steps. I chose the one in the middle beneath the sign. In that neighborhood there are museums, shops and other commercial enterprises conducted in many shabby old residences, such as were these. Behind the glazing of the door I had chosen I could see a dim, pinkish light, but on either side the windows were quite dark.

Trying the door, I found it unlocked. As I opened it a party of Italians passed on the pavement below and I looked back at them over my shoulder. They were gayly dressed, men, women and children, laughing and chattering to one another; probably on their way to some wedding or other festivity.

In passing, one of the men glanced up at me and involuntarily I shuddered back against the door. He was a young man, handsome after the swarthy manner of his race, but never in my life had I seen a face so expressive of pure, malicious cruelty, naked and unashamed. Our eyes met and his seemed to light up with a vile gleaming, as if all the wickedness of his nature had come to a focus in the look of concentrated hate he gave me.

They went by, but for some distance I could see him watching me, chin on shoulder, till he and his party were swallowed up in the crowd of marketers farther down the street.

Sick and trembling from that encounter, merely of eyes though it had been, I threw aside my partly smoked cigar and entered. Within there was a small vestibule, whose ancient tesselated floor was grimy with the passing of many feet. I could feel the grit of dirt under my shoes, and it rasped on my rawly quivering nerves. The inner door stood partly open, and going on I found myself in a bare, dirty hallway, and was greeted by the sour, musty, poverty-stricken smell common to dwellings of the very ill-to-do. Beyond there was a stairway, carpeted with ragged grass matting. A gas jet, turned low inside a very dusty pink globe, was the light I had seen from without.

Listening, the house seemed entirely silent. Surely, this was no place of public amusement of any kind whatever. More likely it was a rooming house, and I had, after all, mistaken the entrance.

To my intense relief, since coming inside, the worst agony of my unreasonable terror had passed away. If I could only get in some place where I could sit down and be quiet, probably I should be rid of it for good. Determining to try another entrance, I was about to leave the bare hallway when one of several doors along the side of it suddenly opened and a man stepped out into the hall.

"Well?" he said, looking at me keenly, but with not the least show of surprise at my presence.

"I beg your pardon," I replied. "The door was unlocked and I came in here, thinking it was the entrance to the exhibit—what do they call it? the 'Great Unseen.' The one that is mentioned on that long white sign. Can you tell me which door is the right one?"

"I can."

With that brief answer he stopped and stared at me again. He was a tall, lean man, somewhat stooped, but possessing considerable dignity of bearing. For that neighborhood, he appeared uncommonly well dressed, and his long, smooth-shaven face was noticeable because, while his complexion was dark and his eyes coal-black, above them the heavy brows and his hair were almost silvery-white. His age might have been anything over the threescore mark.

I grew tired of being stared at. "If you can and—won't, then never mind," I observed a trifle irritably, and turned to go. But his sharp exclamation halted me.

"No!" he said. "No—no! Forgive me for pausing—it was not hesitation, I assure you. To think that one—one, even, has come! All day they pass my sign up there—pass and fear to enter. But you are different. *You* are not of these timorous, ignorant foreign peasants. You ask me to tell you the right door? Here it is! Here!"

And he struck the panel of the door, which he had closed behind him, so that the sharp yet hollow sound of it echoed up through the silent house.

Now it may be thought that after all my senseless terror in the open street, so strange a welcome from so odd a showman would have brought the feeling back, full force. But there is an emotion stronger, to a certain point, than fear. This queer old fellow aroused my curiosity. What kind of museum could it be that he accused the passing public of fearing to enter? Nothing really terrible, surely, or it would have been closed by the police. And normally I am not an unduly timorous person. "So it's in there, is it?" I asked, coming toward him. "And I'm to be sole audience? Come, that will be an interesting experience." I was half laughing now.

"The most interesting in the world," said the old man, with a solemnity which rebuked my lightness.

With that he opened the door, passed inward and closed it again—in my very face. I stood staring at it blankly. The panels, I remember, had been originally painted white, but now the paint was flaked and blistered, gray with dirt and dirty finger marks. Suddenly it occurred to me that I had no wish to enter there. Whatever was behind it could be scarcely worth seeing, or he would not choose such a place for its exhibition. With the old man's vanishing my curiosity had cooled, but just as I again turned to leave, the door opened and this singular showman stuck his white-eyebrowed face through the aperture. He was frowning impatiently. "Come in—come in!" he snapped, and promptly withdrawing his head, once more closed the door.

"He has something there he doesn't want should get out," was the very natural conclusion which I drew. "Well, since it can hardly be anything dangerous, and he's so anxious I should see it—here goes!"

With that I turned the soiled white porcelain handle, and entered.

The room I came into was neither very large nor very brightly lighted. In no way did it resemble a museum or lecture room.

On the contrary, it seemed to have been fitted up as a quite well-appointed laboratory. The floor was linoleum-covered, there were glass cases along the walls whose shelves were filled with bottles, specimen jars, graduates, and the like. A large table in one corner bore what looked like some odd sort of camera, and a larger one in the middle of the room was fitted with a long rack filled with bottles and test tubes, and was besides littered with papers, glass slides, and various paraphernalia which my ignorance failed to identify. There were several cases of books, a few plain wooden chairs, and in the corner a large iron sink with running water.

My host of the white hair and black eyes was awaiting me, standing near the larger table. He indicated one of the wooden chairs with a thin forefinger that shook a little, either from age or eagerness. "Sit down—sit down! Have no fear but that you will be interested, my friend. Have no fear at all—of anything!"

As he said it he fixed his dark eyes upon me and stared harder than ever. But the effect of his words was the opposite of their meaning. I did sit down, because my knees gave under me, but if in the outer hall I had lost my terror, it now returned twofold upon me. Out there the light had been faint, dingily roseate, indefinite. By it I had not perceived how this old man's face was a mask of living malice—of cruelty, hate and a certain masterful contempt. Now I knew the meaning of my fear, whose warning I would not heed. Now I knew that I had walked into the very trap from which my abnormal sensitiveness had striven in vain to save me.

III

Again I struggled within me, bit at my lip till I tasted blood, and presently the blind paroxysm passed. It must have been longer in going than I thought, and the old man must have all that time been speaking, for when I could once more control my attention, hear and see him, he had taken up a position near the sink, about ten feet away, and was addressing me with a sort of "platform" manner, as if I had been the large audience whose absence he had deplored.

"And so," he was saying, "I was forced to make these plates very carefully, to truly represent the characteristic hues of each separate organism. Now, in color work of every kind the film is necessarily extremely sensitive. Doubtless you are familiar in a general way with the exquisite transparencies produced by color photography of the single-plate type."

He paused, and trying to act like a normal human being, I observed: "I saw some nice landscapes done in that way—last week at an illustrated lecture in Franklin Hall."

He scowled, and made an impatient gesture at me with his hand. "I can proceed better without interruptions," he said. "My pause was purely oratorical."

I meekly subsided, and he went on in his original loud, clear voice. He would have made an excellent lecturer before a much larger audience—if only his voice could have lost that eerie, ringing note. Thinking of that I must have missed some more, and when I caught it again he was saying:

"As I have indicated, the original plate is the final picture. Now, many of these organisms are extremely hard to photograph, and microphotography in color is particularly difficult. In consequence, to spoil a plate tries the patience of the photographer. They are so sensitive that the ordinary darkroom ruby lamp would instantly ruin them, and they must therefore be developed either in darkness or by a special light produced by interposing thin sheets of tissue of a particular shade of green and of yellow between lamp and plate, and even that will often cause ruinous fog. Now I, finding it hard to handle them so, made numerous experiments with a view of discovering some glass or fabric of a color which should add to the safety of the green, without robbing it of all efficiency. All proved equally useless, but intermittently I persevered—until last week."

His voice dropped to an almost confidential tone, and he leaned slightly toward me. I was cold from my neck to my feet, though my head was burning, but I tried to force an appreciative smile.

"Last week," he continued impressively, "I had a prescription filled at the corner drug store. The bottle was sent home to me wrapped in a piece of what I first took to be whitish, slightly opalescent paper. Later I decided that it was some kind of membrane. When I questioned the druggist, seeking its source, he said it was a sheet of 'paper' that was around a bundle of herbs from South America. That he had no more, and doubted if I could trace it. He had wrapped my bottle so, because he was in haste and the sheet was handy.

"I can hardly tell you what first inspired me to try that membrane in my photographic work. It was merely dull white with a faint hint of opalescence, except when held against the light. Then it became quite translucent and quite brightly prismatic. For some reason it occurred to me that this refractive effect might help in breaking up the actinic rays—the rays which affect the sensitive emulsion. So that night I inserted it behind the sheets of green and yellow tissue, next the lamp prepared my trays and chemicals laid my plate holders to hand, turned off the white light and—turned on the green!

There was nothing in his words to inspire fear. It was a wearisomely detailed account of his struggles with photography. Yet, as he again paused impressively, I wished that he might never speak again. I was desperately, contemptibly in dread of the thing he might say next.

Suddenly, he drew himself erect, the stoop went out of his shoulders, he threw back his head and laughed. It was a hollow sound, as if he laughed into a trumpet. "I won't tell you what I saw! Why should I? Your own eyes shall bear witness. But this much I'll say, so that you may better understand—later. When our poor, faultily sensitive vision can perceive a thing, we say that it is visible. When the nerves of touch can feel it, we say that it is tangible. Yet I tell you there are beings intangible to our physical sense, yet whose presence is felt by the spirit, and invisible to our eyes merely because those organs are not attuned to the light as reflected from their bodies. But light passed through the screen, which we are about to use has a wave length novel to the scientific world, and by it you shall see with the eyes of the flesh that which has been invisible since life began. Have no fear!"

He stopped to laugh again, and his mirth was yellow-toothed—menacing.

"*Have no fear!*" he reiterated, and with that stretched his hand toward the wall, there came a click and we were in black, impenetrable darkness. I wanted to spring up, to seek the door by which I had entered and rush out of it, but the paralysis of unreasoning terror held me fast.

I could hear him moving about in the darkness, and a moment later a faint green glimmer sprang up in the room. Its source was over the large sink, where I suppose he developed his precious "color plates."

Every instant, as my eyes became accustomed to the dimness, I could see more clearly. Green light is peculiar. It may be far fainter than red, and at the same time far more illuminating. The old man was standing beneath it, and his face by that ghastly radiance had the exact look of a dead man's. Besides this, however, I could observe nothing appalling.

"That," continued the man, "is the simple developing light of which I have spoken—now watch, for what you are about to behold no mortal man but myself has ever seen before."

For a moment he fussed with the green lamp over the sink. It was so constructed that all the direct rays struck downward. He opened a flap at the side, for a moment there was a streak of comforting white luminance from within, then he inserted something, slid it slowly in—and closed the flap.

The thing he put in—that South American "membrane" it must have been—instead of decreasing the light increased it—amazingly. The hue was changed from green to greenish-gray, and the whole room sprang into view, a livid, ghastly chamber, filled with—overcrawled by—what?

My eyes fixed themselves, fascinated, on something that moved by the old man's feet. It writhed there on the floor like a huge, repulsive starfish, an immense, armed, legged thing, that twisted convulsively. It was smooth, as if made of rubber, was whitish-green in color; and presently raised its great round blob of a body on tottering tentacles, crept toward my host and writhed upward—yes, climbed up his legs, his body. And he stood there, erect, arms folded, and stared sternly down at the thing which climbed.

But the room—the whole room was alive with other creatures than that. Everywhere I looked they were—centipedish things, with yard-long bodies, detestable, furry spiders that lurked in shadows, and sausage-shaped translucent horrors that moved—and floated through the air. They dived—here and there between me and the light, and I could see its bright greenness through their greenish bodies.

Worse, though; far worse than these were the *things with human faces.* Mask-like, monstrous, huge gaping mouths and slitlike eyes—I find I cannot write of them. There was that about them which makes their memory even now intolerable.

The old man was speaking again, and every word echoed in my brain like the ringing of a gong. "Fear nothing! Among such as these do you move every hour of the day and night. Only you and I have seen, for God is merciful and has spared our race from sight. But I am not merciful! I loathe the race which gave these creatures birth—the race which might be so surrounded by invisible, unguessed but blessed beings—and chooses these for its companions! All the world shall see and know. One by one shall they come here, learn the truth, and perish. For who can survive the ultimate of terror? Then I, too, shall find peace, and leave the earth to its heritage of man-created horrors. Do you know what these are—whence they come?"

This voice boomed now like a cathedral bell. I could not answer, him, but he waited for no reply. "Out of the ether—out of the omnipresent ether from whose intangible substance the mind of God made the planets, all living things, and man—man has made these! By his evil thoughts, by his selfish panics, by his lusts and his interminable, never-ending hate he has made them, and they are everywhere! Fear nothing—but see where there comes to you, its creator, the shape and the body of your FEAR!"

And as he said it I perceived a great Thing coming toward me—a Thing—but consciousness could endure no more. The ringing, threatening voice merged in a roar within my ears, there came a merciful dimming of the terrible, lurid vision, and blank nothingness succeeded upon horror too great for bearing.

IV

There was a dull, heavy pain above my eyes. I knew that they were closed, that I was dreaming, and that the rack full of colored bottles which I seemed to see so clearly was no more than a part of the dream. There was some vague but imperative reason why I should rouse myself. I wanted to awaken, and thought that by staring very hard indeed I could dissolve this foolish vision of blue and yellow-brown bottles. But instead of dissolving they grew clearer, more solid and substantial of appearance, until suddenly the rest of my senses rushed to the support of sight, and I became aware that my eyes were open, the bottles were quite real, and that I was sitting in a chair, fallen sideways so that my cheek rested most uncomfortably on the table which held the rack.

I straightened up slowly and with difficulty, groping in my dulled brain for some clue to my presence in this unfamiliar place, this laboratory that was lighted only by the rays of an arc light in the street outside its three large windows. Here I sat, alone, and if the aching of cramped limbs meant anything, here I had sat for more than a little time.

Then, with the painful shock which accompanies awakening to the knowledge of some great catastrophe, came memory. It was this very room, shown by the street lamp's rays to be empty of life, which I had seen thronged with creatures too loathsome for description. I staggered to my feet, staring fearfully about. There were the glass-floored cases, the bookshelves, the two tables with their burdens, and the long iron sink above which, now only a dark blotch of shadow, hung the lamp from which had emanated that livid, terrifically revealing illumination. Then the experience had been no dream, but a frightful reality. I was alone here now. With callous indifference my strange host had allowed me to remain for hours unconscious, with not the least effort to aid or revive me. Perhaps, hating me so, he had hoped that I would die there.

At first I made no effort to leave the place. Its appearance filled me with reminiscent loathing. I longed to go, but as yet felt too weak and ill for the effort. Both mentally and physically my condition was deplorable, and for the first time I realized that a shock to the mind may react upon the body as vilely as any debauch of self-indulgence.

Quivering in every nerve and muscle, dizzy with headache and nausea, I dropped back into the chair, hoping that before the old man returned I might recover sufficient self-control to escape him. I knew that he hated me, and why. As I waited, sick, miserable, I understood the man. Shuddering, I recalled the loathsome horrors he had shown me. If the mere desires and emotions of mankind were daily carnified in such forms as those, no wonder that he viewed his fellow beings with detestation and longed only to destroy them.

I thought, too, of the cruel, sensuous faces I had seen in the streets outside—seen for the first time, as if a veil had been withdrawn from eyes hitherto blinded by self-delusion. Fatuously trustful as a month-old puppy, I had lived in a grim, evil world, where goodness is a word and crude selfishness the only actuality. Drearily my thoughts drifted back through my own life, its futile purposes, mistakes and activities. All of evil that I knew returned to overwhelm me. Our gropings toward divinity were a sham, a writhing sunward of slime-covered beasts who claimed sunlight as their heritage, but in their hearts preferred the foul and easy depths.

Even now, though I could neither see nor feel them, this room, the entire world, was acrawl with the beings created by our real natures. I recalled the cringing, contemptible fear to which my spirit had so readily yielded, and the faceless Thing to which the emotion had given birth.

Then abruptly, shockingly, I remembered that every moment I was adding to the horde. Since my mind could conceive only repulsive incubi, and since while I lived I must think, feel, and so continue to shape them, was there no way to check so abominable a succession? My eyes fell on the long shelves with their many-colored bottles. In the chemistry of photography there are deadly poisons—I knew that. Now was the time to end it—now! Let him return and find his desire accomplished. One good thing I could do, if one only. I could abolish my monster-creating self.

V

My friend Mark Jenkins is an intelligent and usually a very careful man. When he took from "Smiler" Callahan a cigar which had every appearance of being excellent, innocent Havana, the act denoted both intelligence and caution. By very clever work he had traced the poisoning of young Ralph Peeler to Mr. Callahan's door, and he believed this particular cigar to be the mate of one smoked by Peeler just previous to his demise. And if, upon arresting Callahan, he had not confiscated this bit of evidence, it would have doubtless been destroyed by its regrettably unconscientious owner.

But when Jenkins shortly afterward gave me that cigar, as one of his own, he committed one of those almost inconceivable blunders which, I think, are occasionally forced upon clever men to keep them from overweening vanity. Discovering his slight mistake, my detective friend spent the night searching for his unintended victim, myself; and that his search was successful was due to Pietro Marini, a young Italian of Jenkins' acquaintance, whom he met about the hour of 2:00 AM returning from a dance.

Now, Marini had seen me standing on the steps of the house where Doctor Frederick Holt had his laboratory and living rooms, and he had stared at me, not with any ill intent, but because he thought I was the sickest-looking, most ghastly specimen of humanity that he had ever beheld. And, sharing the superstition of his South Street neighbors, he wondered if the worthy doctor had poisoned me as well as Peeler. This suspicion he imparted to Jenkins, who, however, had the best of reasons for believing otherwise. Moreover, as he informed Marini, Holt was dead, having drowned himself late the previous afternoon. An hour or so after our talk in the restaurant, news of his suicide reached Jenkins.

It seemed wise to search any place where a very sick-looking young man had been seen to enter, so Jenkins came straight to the laboratory. Across the fronts of those houses was the long sign with its mysterious inscription, "See the Great Unseen," not at all mysterious to the detective. He knew that next door to Doctor Holt's the second floor had been thrown together into a lecture room, where at certain hours a young man employed by settlement workers displayed upon a screen stereopticon views of various deadly bacilli, the germs of diseases appropriate to dirt and indifference. He knew, too, that Doctor Holt himself had helped the educational effort along by providing some really wonderful lantern slides, done by micro-color photography.

On the pavement outside, Jenkins found the two-thirds remnant of a cigar, which he gathered in and came up the steps, a very miserable and self-reproachful detective. Neither outer nor inner door was locked, and in the laboratory he found me, alive, but on the verge of death by another means that he had feared.

In the extreme physical depression following my awakening from drugged sleep, and knowing nothing of its cause, I believed my adventure fact in its entirety. My mentality was at too low an ebb to resist its dreadful suggestion. I was searching among Holt's various bottles when Jenkins burst in. At first I was merely annoyed at the interruption of my purpose, but before the anticlimax of his explanation the mists of obsession drifted away and left me still sick in body, but in spirit happy as any man may well be who has suffered a delusion that the world is wholly bad—and learned that its badness springs from his own poisoned brain.

The malice which I had observed in every face, including young Marini's, existed only in my drug-affected vision. Last week's "popular-science" lecture had been recalled to my subconscious mind—the mind that rules dreams and delirium—by the photographic apparatus in Holt's workroom. "See the Great

Unseen" assisted materially, and even the corner drug store
before which I had paused, with its green-lit show vases, had
doubtless played a part. But presently, following something
Jenkins told me, I was driven to one protest. "If Holt was not
here," I demanded, "if Holt is dead, as you say, how do you
account for the fact that I, who have never seen the man, was
able to give you an accurate description which you admit to be
that of Doctor Frederick Holt?"

He pointed across the room. "See that?" It was a life-size bust
portrait, in crayons, the picture of a white-haired man with
bushy eyebrows and the most piercing black eyes I had ever
seen—until the previous evening. It hung facing the door and
near the windows, and the features stood out with a strangely
lifelike appearance in the white rays of the arc lamp just outside.
"Upon entering," continued Jenkins, "the first thing you saw was
that portrait, and from it your delirium built a living, speaking
man. So, there are your white-haired showman, your unnatural
fear, your color photography and your pretty green golliwogs all
nicely explained for you, Blaisdell, and thank God you're alive to
hear the explanation. If you had smoked the whole of that
cigar—well, never mind. You didn't. And now, my very dear
friend, I think it's high time that you interviewed a real, flesh-
and-blood doctor. I'll phone for a taxi."

"Don't," I said. "A walk in the fresh air will do me more good
than fifty doctors."

"Fresh air! There's no fresh air on South Street in July," complained Jenkins, but reluctantly yielded.

I had a reason for my preference. I wished to see people, to
meet face to face even such stray prowlers as might be about at
this hour, nearer sunrise than midnight, and rejoice in the goodness and kindliness of the human countenance—particularly as
found in the lower classes.

But even as we were leaving there occurred to me a curious
inconsistency.

"Jenkins," I said, "you claim that the reason Holt, when I first
met him in the hall, appeared to twice close the door in my face,
was because the door never opened until I myself unlatched
it."

"Yes," confirmed Jenkins, but he frowned, foreseeing my next question.

"Then why, if it was from that picture that I built so solid, so convincing a vision of the man, did I see Holt in the hall before the door was open?"

"You confuse your memories," retorted Jenkins rather shortly.

"Do I? Holt was dead at that hour, but—*I tell you I saw Holt outside the door!* And what was his reason for committing suicide?"

Before my friend could reply I was across the room, fumbling in the dusk there at the electric lamp above the sink. I got the tin flap open and pulled out the sliding screen, which consisted of two sheets of glass with fabric between, dark on one side, yellow on the other. With it came the very thing I dreaded—a sheet of whitish, parchment-like, slightly opalescent stuff.

Jenkins was beside me as I held it at arm's length toward the windows. Through it the light of the arc lamp fell—divided into the most astonishingly brilliant rainbow hues. And instead of diminishing the light, it was perceptibly increased in the oddest way. Almost one thought that the sheet itself was luminous, and yet when held in shadow it gave off no light at all.

"Shall we—put it in the lamp again—and try it?" asked Jenkins slowly, and in his voice there was no hint of mockery.

I looked him straight in the eyes. "No," I said, "we won't. I was drugged. Perhaps in that condition I received a merciless revelation of the discovery that caused Holt's suicide, but I don't believe it. Ghost or no ghost, I refuse to ever again believe in the depravity of the human race. If the air and the earth are teeming with invisible horrors, they are *not* of our making, and—the study of demonology is better let alone. Shall we burn this thing, or tear it up?"

"We have no right to do either," returned Jenkins thoughtfully, "but you know, Blaisdell, there's a little too darn much realism about some parts of your 'dream.' I haven't been smoking any doped cigars; but when you held that up to the light, I'll swear I saw—well, never mind. Burn it—send it back to the place it came from."

"South America?" said I.

"A hotter place than that. Burn it."

So he struck a match and we did. It was gone in one great white flash.

A large place was given by morning papers to the suicide of Doctor Frederick Holt, caused, it was surmised, by mental derangement brought about by his unjust implication in the Peeler murder. It seemed an inadequate reason, since he had never been arrested, but no other was ever discovered.

Of course, our action in destroying that "membrane" was illegal and rather precipitate, but, though he won't talk about it, I know that Jenkins agrees with me—doubt is sometimes better than certainty, and there are marvels better left unproved. Those, for instance, which concern the Powers of Evil.

Greye La Spina
(1880–1969)

FANNY GREYE BRAGG, who became Baroness La Spina after her second marriage in 1910 to Robert La Spina, Barone di Savuto, was born in Wakefield, Massachusetts, but lived for many years in Pennsylvania. When she later moved to New York as possibly the first woman newspaper photographer, she found it difficult to sleep unless she played a tape of the sound of crickets to remind her of home. She was also a master weaver and won prizes for her rugs and tapestries. In the 1920s, she became a regular contributor to the legendary pulp magazine, *Weird Tales*, which serialized her novels, *Invaders from the Dark* (1925) and *Fettered* (1926). Her first sales were to the now-very-rare adventure pulp, *The Thrill Book*, which ran for just sixteen issues during 1919. "The Wax Doll," which appeared under the pseudonym Ezra Putnam in the issue for 1 August, is another moving story of child abuse and reads as powerfully today as it did eighty years ago.

The Wax Doll

"Anice Butterworth, beloved and only child of Worthy and Zebedee Butterworth. Aged nine years and three weeks. Requiescat in pace."

That is the inscription. As for the first part, it is plain enough; he who runs may read. But for the Latin inscription, there are those in Ellersville who assert that it has not always been true.

While there is nothing *outré* about the tiny marker with its sculptured words, nothing out of the ordinary about the softly sloping mound, covered with living green by the English ivy that has grown closely over it, yet there is something strange about that grave that draws a stranger's attention as would a lodestone and holds it until the story of little Anice Butterworth and the wax doll has transformed idle curiosity into deep wonder and aching pity.

About her grave lie children's toys, some of them quite new and shiny. And chief among them all is a great, weather-beaten wax doll that sits against the headstone gazing vacantly across the burial ground from her post of vantage. Any Ellersville child will tell you they are there for Anice to play with.

Poor little Anice! She has her share of toys now. God only knows with what agony of longing and remorse her bereaved parents put them there for her eyes to gloat upon, for her unseen fingers to caress. If it be true that our every action brings with it the appropriate reward or castigation, then how terribly have Worthy and Zebedee Butterworth been punished for their blind, willful ignorance of the heart of a little child!

They had their own ideas about bringing up children, did

Worthy and Zebedee. Her people had been the kind that never smiled on the Sabbath day for fear God might be offended at their sinful levity. Zebedee's had been the kind that wept over every penny spent and—figuratively speaking—killed the fatted calf over each dollar that came in. The combination of temperaments proved an unfortunate one for the innocent victim of their solicitous love.

From the time she was old enough to take notice, Anice Butterworth had been an object of deep commiseration to Ellersville. She was never seen playing as other children play. She was never permitted a toy. Toys cost good money, her father said. Her mother's reason was deeper laid; if we miserable sinners expect to attain heaven eventually, we must offer unto God the sacrifice of a broken and contrite spirit, she asserted. This was interpreted as a sacrifice of every joy-inspiring emotion of the human heart. Between the two of them, they gave their only child a fine babyhood and little-girlhood!"

They loved her, her father and mother. They loved her with an affection that almost terrified them by its strength. But the more they realized its depth, the more they felt assured that it was an idolatrous passion that must be strangled at its birth. The Eastern mother's superstitious terror that her babe's beauty will bring upon it the curse of the Evil Eye was as nothing to the fear of these Christian parents that God would punish their presumption in loving so deeply and tenderly what was, after all, only a thing of the flesh. So, they crucified Anice to save her from the wrath of God; crucified her on the cross of their own terrors, and gloated over her misery in a vain belief that they were propitiating the Almighty in her behalf.

Ellersville looked on indignantly but impotently to see the loving little creature crushed slowly and systematically under the Juggernaut created by her parents. She was deprived conscientiously of everything that promised to give her pleasure. Her father repeatedly told her that playthings cost too much, which was his own way of refusing her what he felt was harmful to her spiritual welfare. Her mother taught her that God loves those who *fear* Him, and carefully guided those tiny faltering feet into paths of darkness and terror that the Heavenly Father surely never meant for her tender youth to travel. Anice became an old little thing at six years of age, age measured by standards of time, at nine, she was older than the oldest inhabitant of Ellersville, if one judged her age by the gleam of her crushed soul out of inexpressibly pathetic eyes.

It was only natural that people should try to soften the harsh rules the Butterworths had laid down for the little girl, by giving her playthings from time to time. Not that it did much good. Either the toys were returned with frigid courtesy or they disappeared entirely from the face of the earth so far as Anice was concerned. Worthy Butterworth filled every moment of Anice's time with doleful readings from some fearfully pious book of ancient sermons or with plain sewing, that bane of the life of little girls. Very early Anice had learned to give up attempts to play make-believe by herself; her mother soon learned of this wayward tendency and enforced her ideas upon the child by keeping the poor little creature constantly at her side, busied with her morbid reading or with endless patchwork.

On Anice's ninth birthday, nevertheless, Ellersville people plucked up sufficient courage to dare cross the path of the Juggernaut. They got together and bought a special gift for Anice, a wonderfully beautiful great wax doll, dressed marvellously in silk and laces; a doll to have warmed the heart of even the most pampered little girl. The ladies' sewing circle of the Methodist church collected the money for this present with great privacy and then went in a body to the Butterworth home on Anice's birthday, to present her boldly with the doll.

Worthy could hardly have refused the gift. Her husband had recently given the church a donation, generous for him, toward new pews, and she felt that the doll was by way of being appreciative recognition on the part of the sewing circle. Zebedee could not have refused it if he would; there was something in the attitude of the ladies who presented it that prevented his saying a word of protest. Moreover, it had cost a pretty penny and he knew it. He figured it could be put away against the day when Anice would no longer be tempted by such worldly toys. Yet both the Butterworths were inwardly certain that the possession of this doll would be the complete ruination of their little precious daughter.

During the hours that the members of the sewing circle remained in the house, Anice Butterworth sat in their midst, the marvellous doll in her arms, enjoying such an ecstasy of exaltation as the poor little creature had never experienced in her entire short life. On a low hassock she sat, her feet straight before her on the floor; her little petticoats, painfully sewed, washed and ironed by her own busy child hands, stiffly refusing to be smoothed down decorously enough to give the wonderful doll a comfortable seat. Not that she noticed this objectively; she was too completely wrapped up in the exquisite joy of holding in her own arms, against her thumping little heart, such a plaything as she had never, in her wildest imaginings, dreamed might be hers. To hold it unrebuked—what bliss! What unutterable felicity!

She clung to it, hardly daring a close examination, lest she draw upon herself the disapprobation of her troubled parents. Occasionally she stole a downward glance into the smiling waxen face with an expression of such tender adoration on her own that some of the ladies declared afterward that it was enough to bring tears to one's eyes. One hand stroked the silken skirts caressingly with slow motions of luxurious enjoyment; the other gripped the doll feverishly. For an hour, one excruciatingly beautiful hour, Anice lived such emotions as other children spread over years of childhood experience.

The ladies rose to go. One of them asked her: "What will you name your doll, Anice?"

Without hesitation, but as if she had already cogitated long and seriously upon this difficult subject and had arrived at a firm decision, Anice had replied with a world of affection in her tones:

"Beloved!"

And amid the cautiously exchanged glances, she buried her face deeply, with a sigh of utter contentment, in the silken attire of her treasure.

Anice's ninth birthday became an event of much speculation in Ellersville, as might be surmised. It was for a time believed that the Ladies' Sewing Circle had managed by their gift to alter the attitude of the Butterworths toward the poor little one. Everywhere the wish was expressed that Anice might from then on enjoy some of the innocent pleasures and happinesses of life that other children had so freely as their just portion. But the villagers were yet to learn that they had reckoned without their Butterworths.

Out of deference to the opinions of the ladies who had just left the house, Worthy did not immediately exile the wax doll; she took it firmly from Anice's arms and set it high out of reach upon a mantel. This simple act was not accomplished with ease. For once in her life the little girl resented from the very depths of her being the wrong that she instinctively felt was put upon her. She clung to the beautiful plaything with fierce strength; she actually kicked at her mother with stoutly clad little feet. She screamed and gritted her teeth in mad determination not to be parted from her first and only love. Worthy actually found it necessary to pry the clinging fingers from the silken garments of that disturber of family peace by main force.

The worse Anice behaved, the more strongly was Worthy convinced that in keeping playthings from the child she had acted wisely. If a single hour's association with a mere wax doll could affect Anice so terribly after nine years of careful training, how would she have been behaving, Worthy wondered, had she always been permitted toys? Zebedee agreed fully with his wife in her action and in her conclusions. He went a little further; he took the doll from the mantel, his face dark with a disapproving scowl, and hid it in the garret.

Anice's sad fall from grace was meted out severe punishment, in allotting which Worthy showed her ingenuity. The child had to read aloud, page after page of Fox's *Martyrs* for days, while her mother passed in and out of the room to which the child had been banished for a week. She was also condemned to rip out and make over an entire patchwork quilt which she had recently finished with innocent pride and satisfaction, as well as infinite labor.

The childish mind rebelled, God knows how bitterly, but in silence. She sat quietly in her high-backed chair and read in toneless monotony the horrors of the early martyrs' sufferings, or bent dull eyes upon the bits of colored cloth which she had ripped apart and must sew together again at her mother's behest.

When the week's punishment was over, her parents missed her one night from her bed, after hearing soft footsteps stealing down the hall. Zebedee intuitively went at once to the garret, the lines of his mouth tightening ominously. He found her there, the small face raised up to his, smiling and contented; the little arms clasped warmly about the bone of contention which lay against her yearning heart. He stood looking down at her with strange expressions chasing each other across his stern countenance. He returned to bed with the simple observation that she must have walked in her sleep to the garret and that he had tucked a blanket about her and left her there; it would be time enough in the morning, he said, to settle with her. Worthy knew only too well what had taken the child to the garret, but she gave no outward sign of her knowledge; she acquiesced with her husband's decision.

In the morning Anice was parted again from the doll, although she showed herself yet more obstreperous and determined, refusing to be separated from her beloved. The tears, the cries, the pleading, all fell upon unseeing eyes and deaf ears. Such was the love of those two for her future salvation that they damned her earthly happiness completely. By degrees the child became calmer but her expression was one that almost terrified her parents by its unearthly resolution.

"I shall always find my Beloved," she declared, rebellious eyes and compressed lips defying them. "You cannot keep her away from me. We cannot be separated, because she loves me as I love her."

That was in late autumn. Winter came on as it sometimes does, in a sudden, unexpected storm of biting cold, bitter winds, and driving snow. From November soddenness of skies emerged the bleak December weather.

During the days that followed Anice made no further outward signs of the rebellion she had so passionately declared. She sewed her wrinkled little patches together again; she read the horrors of the early martyrs with dull indifference. No word, no sign, escaped her that was connected with the wax doll. Her parents congratulated themselves that she had at last entirely forgotten it. It was not so, however, and they were soon to learn how tragically deep had grown Anice's love for her Beloved.

Zebedee had put the doll in the woodshed, locking it in without further precautions of concealment from the child, whose great dark eyes followed his every movement the day he carried her Beloved away. He remarked to Worthy, almost contemptuously, that he guessed he'd settled that matter for good and all. He was to recall his words afterward with an agony of remorse.

Ellersville can never forget the blizzard that raged for three days that winter, covering the entire countryside with deep drifts. The third night of the storm Worthy Butterworth roused from her sleep and grasped at her husband's shoulder, shaking him to alertness. She thought she had heard a strange noise. Zebedee sat up and listened intently.

It was Anice sobbing in her sleep. She was calling in heart-rending tones: "Beloved! Beloved!"

The mother's heart ached within her but her thoughts of an angry and jealous God restrained and hardened her.

She did go so far as to whisper to her husband, "Do you suppose we can have been wrong about that doll?"

He shook his head emphatically. But even as he denied the possibility of an error in their combined judgment, he felt that weakening toward the sobbing, dreaming child which proves to us what playthings we ourselves are in the force of our emotions.

They composed themselves to sleep again but their dreams were troubled. So troubled that, although she could not remember what hers had been about, Worthy rose with the first dim light of a white day that broke in through the swirling snow that beat and tore with pale, malevolent fingers at the windows, and went into Anice's room to assure herself that the child was sleeping quietly. Her wild screams brought Zebedee to her side in a flash.

"My baby! Where is my baby?" she shrieked, sudden terror

clutching at her heart. "Something is wrong! Something has happened to Anice! Where can she be?"

For the bed was empty of its small occupant.

Her husband strove to quiet her.

"She is probably hiding in the garret again," he assured her, but he knew his words were foolish. The wax doll was not in the garret.

He began to tremble with the vehemence of the emotion that shook Worthy, whose trembling body he was supporting. She looked from the window with dazed, vacant eyes, as though she would pierce by sheer strength of will those blinding flurries of snow.

"God forgive us!" she screamed out suddenly. "She is there!"

She fell, a limp weight, against her husband's breast.

He laid her on Anice's bed. He did not dare take time to bring her back to merciless consciousness, for now something pulled at him with invisible fingers that would not be denied. He let himself be led.

Out of the kitchen door into the shrieking, howling storm he went, the bitter cold penetrating his very heart, chilling it so that it beat slowly and sluggishly as though some power from without were striving to stop its beating. Down the pathway he plunged blindly, fighting for every step against the surging of that mighty wind, terrified apprehensions growing upon him with every forward step. His leaden feet dragged him back when he tried to pull them through the deep drifts that in three days and nights had changed the entire aspect of the countryside. On he went, to the woodshed where, but a short two weeks ago he had hidden the wax doll away from the longing child heart that had loved it so tenderly, from the gentle hands that would have caressed it so lovingly.

It was there he found his child, as he knew he would. White as the snow that clung in frozen clods to her thin little nightdress; pale as the pallor of that dead morning, she half reclined, half knelt as if in supplication, against the door that kept her away from her Beloved. Upon the childish face was a frozen appeal; in the wide-open staring eyes an entreaty. They were the more pathetic and heartrending because Zebedee knew their meaning well, and knew that it had gone unanswered.

The father gathered up that poor little body and held it tightly to him as though to cool the fires of burning grief that consumed him. He fought his way grimly back to the house.

Worthy stood at the door to receive him. Mercifully had the knowledge come to her of the tragic death of her child. It did not stagger her now as with a sudden blow; she knew well what had befallen. She stood there, dumbly holding out her arms for that precious little body.

It was natural and inevitable that they should have tried everything their brains could devise, in mad and hopeless attempts to call back the spirit of their only child to its deserted habitation. All was vain. They knew it even while they worked over the cold, lifeless body. But their unutterable grief, hoping against the evidence of their senses, drove them on until they reached the moment when they had to admit to each other with despairing glances that their efforts were futile. Anice had slipped quietly away from them in the terror of that surging storm of howling wind and driving snow, never to return.

Their grief was terrible, but they repressed it as they had always forced themselves to repress the tenderer emotions of their hearts. The Lord had given. The Lord had taken away. Blessed be the name of the Lord. Of their own instrumentality in this taking away, did they ever think at all? Who knows?

Dumbly, numbly, they went about their daily tasks. Then Zebedee hitched up and went for the undertaker through the wild gusts of wind that whipped him as he drove, while the mother sat dry-eyed by the body of her only child.

The storm had died down when the day of Anice's funeral came, so that the morning dawned shining upon a spotlessly beautiful world, in harmony with the pure soul that had taken flight. They made her grave where you can see it now, and a few days afterwards the headstone, so pitiful in its pathetic brevity and the condensed tragedy of its inscription, marked her resting place. They left her then, to repose in peace. But did she? Opinion even in Ellersville is divided on that point.

Zebedee did not go near the woodshed until actually forced by the necessity for firewood. Then he unlocked the door. He dared not face the silent reproach in the fixed smile of the wax doll, reminding him of the loved child who had gone from him forever. When he came out with an armful of wood, a strange expression was etched on his face, an expression of mingled incredulity and horror and dismay. He said nothing to Worthy at the time.

"I'm imagining things," he muttered to himself.

But the next time wood was needed, he managed to be beyond his wife's call, so that she had to go for it herself. When she returned, he said to her with an air of repressed excitement:

"Where—where was the doll?"

"On the shelf," she replied, wonderingly, looking at him with query in her sad eyes.

"Were there—were there boxes—piled under the shelf—as if—someone small had tried to climb up—to the doll?" he faltered shamefacedly, his eyes avoiding hers.

She stopped short on her way to the wood-box near the stove to regard him with searching face.

"Just what do you mean?" she demanded nervously.

"Nothing! Nothing!" he cried quickly, as if denying an allegation made.

She withdrew her eyes but stood for a long moment with knit brows before she proceeded disheartenedly with her work.

The following day it was Worthy who went first, early in the morning, to get stovewood. She had gone with a purpose, because she had lain awake all night hearing—perhaps she had been fanciful, morbid, in her thoughts—the sound as of a child's voice crooning. It even seemed to her that she had distinguished words.

"Beloved! Beloved!" the voice seemed murmuring plaintively.

She told herself that she must check her vain imaginings, born of brooding over Anice's tragic death. She realized that the event of that last night of the blizzard had wrought up her nerves to finest tension. But she felt she must satisfy herself once for all that her fancies were absolutely unfounded, so that her reason could in future rebuke her wandering imagination.

Therefore she went with faltering but determined step to the woodshed and opened the door, the key to which she had herself retained since the preceding day. Yesterday she had removed a number of wooden boxes from under the shelf where the doll lay, and pushed them to the other side of the shed. This morning, as she peered into the semi-darkness, she saw distinctly that *the boxes were back under the shelf, piled one upon the other, as a child might place them who desired to reach the shelf above. And further, the wax doll which yesterday her own eyes had seen lying on the shelf, was now sitting against the wall on the floor of the shed at the foot of the boxes.*

Worthy did not advance a foot across the threshold. She stood without, stupefied. Strange and dreadful thoughts assailed her and beat down upon her. She could not bear it, all at once, and fled back into the house. She made Zebedee go for the wood without telling him why she had failed to bring it. Then she went into the rarely used front room, shut the door, and remained alone there the rest of the morning.

Her husband did not disturb her. Too well he knew why she had gone away by herself. He, too, had seen the pile of boxes under the shelf, put there by other hands than his or hers; put there as if a child had piled them up to reach the shelf where had lain the forbidden plaything. He brought back wood but when he came into the kitchen again he was paler than he had ever been in his life and was trembling in every limb. The wood fell unheeded from his nerveless hands upon the floor, and he sank weakly into a chair, struggling with difficulty to compose his distressful thoughts.

Winter passed on with chill and dragging tread. Late spring found the Butterworths grayer, more worn, more wan, than even the loss of a beloved child would seem to indicate. The uncanny secret that had become a part of their lives was pulling them down both mentally and physically. By May, Worthy had grown so weak that Zebedee hitched up one morning and hurriedly drove to get the doctor.

Serena Lovejoy saw him pass and surmised his errand, for her farm adjoined the Butterworth place. She ran across the private road between the two farms and made an unexpected visit to Worthy. At first glance Serena divined that here was no malady of body but the gnawing canker of mental sickness. Halfway measures never suited her, so she abruptly opened the subject to her hostess.

"Better tell me about it, Worthy," she said with direct simplicity. "I half believe I know, already, what is troubling you. Perhaps I can find the way out."

Worthy looked long and deeply into the gravely tender eyes of her neighbor.

"Perhaps you can," she considered. Then with sudden sharp pain wracking her soul: "Serena, she is not at rest in her grave! My poor little baby comes back every night, to play with her wax doll!"

"Poor baby!" murmured Serena understandingly. She was credited in Ellersville with being a seeress. "Go on, poor soul. Tell me the rest."

"I cannot bear it," wailed the wretched Worthy, her hands pressed agonizedly to her temples. "There is no night that I can sleep. Always I hear her voice calling 'Beloved!' What can I do—what can I do—to give peace to my baby's soul?"

She broke down, sobbing into her hands hysterically.

Serena regarded her with mingled pity and reproach. She shook her head slowly. Then she put a gentle hand on the weeping mother's shoulder.

"Stop crying and listen to me," she commanded. "Give me the key to the woodshed. I promise you, Worthy, you will hear no crying tonight."

It was as she said. That night the bereaved parents slept as they had not slept for months. Worthy went across the road the next morning to ask Serena how such peace had been wrought.

"Go down to the burial ground, to Anice's grace," Serena responded quietly. "I think then you will understand."

And so it was that Worthy Butterworth received the bitterest lesson of all her repressed life.

Sitting against the little headstone that marked the grave of

"Anice Butterworth, aged nine years and three weeks," was the gaily dressed plaything that had been the innocent cause of the tragedy. Smiling fixedly, blue glass eyes meaningless under fringed lids, the wax doll waited patiently for night to bring its playmate back. Anice had not far to go to find her Beloved, any more.

As the graves of Indian chiefs are loaded with the good things of life that their spirits may attend upon the phantom of the dead, so today the grave of Anice is never without a new toy, reverently and with bitter remorse left there by the hands of her parents.

And the Christmas tree with its wonderful adornments, that each Yule-tide presides over the Sunday School room of the Methodist Church, is the annual gift of Zebedee and Worthy Butterworth in the name of Anice, to the children of Ellersville.

And Anice *Requiescat in pace.*

Gwendolyn Ranger Wormser
(1893–1953)

GWENDOLYN RANGER WORMSER was born in New York, the daughter of the banker Maurice Wormser. Gwendolyn started writing in her late teens, soon after her father's death in 1909, but little of her early work is known, and only two stories have been identified prior to the publication of her first and only collection, *The Scarecrow and Other Stories* (1918). She continued to sell stories over the next few years but then channeled her energies into writing plays and movie scenarios, though little seems to have come of this. She married Harry Guggenheimer, the brother of the noted philanthropist, in 1919. She published only one more book, a limited-edition short story, *Abraham Goode*, in 1924. Her work would have been forgotten but for Douglas Anderson who, in 2001, assembled all her strange tales as *The Scarecrow and Other Stories*. The title story is a singular psychological study with perhaps a hint of the supernatural.

The Scarecrow

"**B**en—"

The woman stood in the doorway of the ramshackle, tumble-down shanty. Her hands were cupped at her mouth. The wind blew loose, whitish blond wisps of hair around her face and slashed the faded blue dress into the uncorseted bulk of her body.

"Benny—oh, Benny—"

Her call echoed through the still evening.

Her eyes staring straight before her down the slope in front of the house caught sight of something blue and antiquatedly military standing waist deep and rigid in the corn field.

"That ole scarecrow," she muttered to herself, "that there old scarecrow with that there ole uniform onto him, too!"

The sun was going slowly just beyond the farthest hill. The unreal light of the skies' reflected colors held over the yellow, waving tips of the corn field.

"Benny—," she called again. "Oh—Benny!"

And then she saw him coming toward her trudging up the hill.

She waited until he stood in front of her.

"Supper, Ben," she said. "Was you down in the south meadow where you couldn't hear me call?"

"Naw."

He was young and slight. He had thick hair and a thin face. His features were small. There was nothing unusual about them. His eyes were deep-set and long, with the lids that were heavily fringed.

"You heard me calling you?"

"Yes, maw."

He stood there straight and still. His eyelids were lowered.

"Why ain't you come along then? What ails you, Benny, letting me shout and shout that way?"

"Nothing—maw."

"Where was you?"

He hesitated a second before answering her.

"I was to the bottom of the hill."

"And what was you doing down there to the bottom of the hill? What was you doing down there, Benny?"

Her voice had a hushed tenseness to it.

"I was watching, maw."

"Watching, Benny?"

"That's what I was doing."

His tone held a guarded sullenness.

"'Tain't no such a pretty sunset, Benny."

"Warn't watching no sunset."

"Benny—!"

"Well." He spoke quickly. "What d'you want to put it there for? What d'you want to do that for in the first place?"

"There was birds, Benny. You know there was birds."

"That ain't what I mean. What for d'you put on that there uniform?"

"I ain't had nothing else. There warn't nothing but your grand-dad's ole uniform. It's fair in rags, Benny. It's all I had to put on to it."

"Well, you done it yourself."

"Naw, Benny, naw! 'Tain't nothing but an ole uniform with a stick into it. Just to frighten off them birds. 'Tain't nothing else. Honest, 'tain't, Benny."

He looked up at her out of the corners of his eyes.

"It was waving its arms."

"That's the wind."

"Naw, maw. Waving its arms before the wind it come up."

"Sush, Benny! 'Tain't likely. 'Tain't."

"I was watching, maw. I seen it wave and wave. S'pose it should beckon—, s'pose it should beckon to me. I'd be going, then, maw."

"Sush, Benny."

"I'd fair have to go, maw."

"Leave your mammy? Naw, Ben; naw. You couldn't never go off and leave your mammy. Even if you ain't able to bear this here farm you couldn't go off from your mammy. You couldn't! Not—your—maw—Benny!"

She could see his mouth twitch. She saw him catch his lower lip in under his teeth.

"Aw—"

"Say you couldn't leave, Benny; say it!"

"I—I fair hate this here farm!" He mumbled. "Morning and night;—and morning and night. Nothing but chores and earth. And then some more of them chores. And always that there way. So it is! Always! And the stillness! Nothing alive, nothing! Sometimes I ain't able to stand it nohow. Sometimes—!"

"You'll get to like it—; later, mebbe—"

"Naw! naw, maw!"

"You will, Benny. Sure you will."

"I won't never. I ain't able to help fretting. It's all closed up tight inside of me. Eating and eating. It makes me feel sick."

She put out a hand and laid it heavily on his shoulder.

"Likely it's a touch of fever in the blood, Benny."

"Aw—! I ain't got no fever!"

"You'll be feeling better in the morning, Ben."

"I'll be feeling the same, maw. That's just it. Alway the same. Nothing but the stillness. Nothing alive. And down there in the corn field—"

"That ain't alive, Benny!"

"Ain't it, maw?"

"Don't say that, Benny. Don't!"

He shook her hand off of him.

"I was watching," he said doggedly. "I seen it wave and wave."

She turned into the house.

"That ole scarecrow!" She muttered to herself. "That there ole scarecrow!"

She led the way into the kitchen. The boy followed at her heels.

A lamp was lighted on the center table. The one window was uncurtained. Through the naked spot of it the evening glow poured shimmeringly into the room.

Inside the doorway they both paused.

"You set down, Benny."

He pulled a chair up to the table.

She took a steaming pot from the stove and emptying it into a plate, placed the dish before him.

He fell to eating silently.

She came and sat opposite him. She watched him cautiously. She did not want him to know that she was watching him. Whenever he glanced up she hurried her eyes away from his face. In the stillness the only live things were those two pair of eyes darting away from each other.

"Benny—!" She could not stand it any longer.

"Benny—just—you—just—you—"

He gulped down a mouthful of food.

"Aw, maw—don't you start nothing. Not no more to-night, maw."

She half rose from her chair. For a second she leaned stiffly against the table. Then she slipped back into her seat, her whole body limp and relaxed.

"I ain't going to start nothing, Benny. I ain't even going to talk about this here farm. Honest—I ain't."

"Aw—this—here—farm—!"

"I've gave the best years of my life to it."

She spoke the words defiantly.

"You said that all afore, maw."

"It's true," she murmured. "Terrible true. And I done it for you, Benny. I wanted to be giving you something. It's all I'd got to give you, Benny. There's many a man, Ben, that's glad of his farm. And grateful, too. There's many that makes it pay."

"And what'll I do if it does pay, maw? What'll I do then?"

"I—I—don't know, Benny. It's only just beginning, now."

"But if it does pay, maw? What'll I do? Go away from here?"

"Naw, Benny—. Not—away—. What'd you go away for, when it pays? After all them years I gave to it?"

His spoon clattered noisily to his plate. He pushed his chair

back from the table. The legs of it rasped loudly along the
uncarpeted floor. He got to his feet.

"Let's go on outside," he said. "There ain't no sense to this
here talking—and talking."

She glanced up at him. Her eyes were narrow and hard.

"All right, Benny. I'll clear up. I'll be along in a minute. All
right, Benny."

He slouched heavily out of the room.

She sat where she was, the set look pressed on her face.
Automatically her hands reached out among the dishes, pulling
them toward her.

Outside the boy sank down on the step.

It was getting dark. There were shadows along the ground.
Blue shadows. In the graying skies one star shone brilliantly.
Beyond the mist-slurred summit of a hill the full moon grew
yellow.

In front of him was the slope of wind-moved corn field, and
in the center of it the dim, military figure standing waist deep in
the corn.

His eyes fixed themselves to it.

"Ole—uniform—with—a—stick—into—it."

He whispered the words very low.

Still—standing there—still. The same wooden attitude of it.
His same, cunning watching of it.

There was a wind. He knew it was going over his face. He
could feel the cool of the wind across his moistened lips.

He took a deep breath.

Down there in the shivering corn field, standing in the dark,
blue shadows, the dim figure had quivered.

An arm moved—swaying to and fro. The other arm began
swaying—swaying—swaying. A tremor ran through it. Once it
pivoted. The head shook slowly from side to side. The arms rose
and fell—and rose again. The head came up and down and
rocked a bit to either side.

"I'm here—" he muttered involuntarily. "Here."

The arms were tossing and stretching.

He thought the head faced in his direction.

The wind had died out.

The arms went down and came up and reached.

"Benny—"

The woman seated herself on the step at his side.

"Look!" He mumbled. "Look!"

He pointed his hand at the dim figure shifting restlessly in the quiet, shadow-saturated corn field.

Her eyes followed after his.

"Oh—Benny—"

"Well—" His voice was hoarse. "It's moving, ain't it? You can see it moving for yourself, can't you? You ain't able to say you don't see it, are you?"

"The—wind—" She stammered.

"Where's the wind?"

"Down—there."

"D'you feel a wind? Say, d'you feel a wind?"

"Mebbe—down—there."

"There ain't no wind. Not now—there ain't! And it's moving, ain't it? Say, it's moving, ain't it?"

"It looks like it was dancing. So it does. Like as if it was—making—itself—dance—"

His eyes were still riveted on those arms that came up and down—; up and down—; and reached.

"It'll stop soon now." He stuttered it more to himself than to her. "Then it'll be still. I've watched it mighty often. Mebbe it knows I watch it. Mebbe that's why—it—moves—"

"Aw—Benny—"

"Well, you see it, don't you? You thought there was something the matter with me when I come and told you how it waves—and waves. But you seen it waving, ain't you?"

"It's nothing, Ben. Look, Benny. It's stopped!"

The two of them stared down the slope at the dim, military figure standing rigid and waist deep in the corn field.

The woman gave a quick sigh of relief.

For several moments they were silent.

From somewhere in the distance came the harsh, discordant sound of bull frogs croaking. Out in the night a dog bayed at the golden, full moon climbing up over the hills. A bird circled between sky and earth hovering above the corn field. They saw its slow descent, and then for a second they caught the startled whir of its wings, as it flew blindly into the night.

"That ole scarecrow!" She muttered.

"S'pose—" He whispered. "S'pose when it starts its moving like that; —s'pose some day it walks out of that there corn field! Just naturally walks out here to me. What then, if it walks out?"

"Benny—"

"That's what I'm thinking of all the time. If it takes it into its head to just naturally walk out here. What's going to stop it, if it wants to walk out after me; once it starts moving that way? What?"

"Benny—! It couldn't do that! It couldn't!"

"Mebbe it won't. Mebbe it'll just beckon first. Mebbe it won't come after me. Not if I go when it beckons. I kind of figure it'll beckon when it wants me. I couldn't stand the other. I couldn't wait for it to come out here after me. I kind of feel it'll beckon. When it beckons, I'll be going."

"Benny, there's sickness coming on you."

"'Tain't no sickness."

The woman's hands were clinched together in her lap.

"I wish to Gawd—" She said— "I wish I ain't never seen the day when I put that there thing up in that there corn field. But I ain't thought nothing like this could never happen. I wish to Gawd I ain't never seen the day—"

"'Tain't got nothing to do with you."

His voice was very low.

"It's got everything to do with me. So it has! You said that afore yourself; and you was right. Ain't I put it up? Ain't I looked high and low the house through? Ain't that ole uniform of your grand-dad's been the only rag I could lay my hands on? Was there anything else I could use? Was there?"

"Aw—maw—!"

"Ain't we needed a scarecrow down there? With them birds so awful bad? Pecking away at the corn; and pecking."

"'Tain't your fault, maw."

"There warn't nothing else but that there ole uniform. I wouldn't have took it, otherwise. Poor ole Pa so desperate proud of it as he was. Him fighting for his country in it. Always saying that he was. He couldn't be doing enough for his country. And that there ole uniform meaning so much to him. Like a part of him I used to think it,—and—. You wanting to say something, Ben?"

"He wouldn't even let us be burying him in it. 'Put my country's flag next my skin'; he told us. 'When I die keep the ole uniform.' Just like a part of him, he thought it. Wouldn't I have kept it, falling to pieces as it is, if there'd have been anything else to put up there in that there corn field?"

She felt the boy stiffen suddenly.

"And with him a soldier—"

He broke off abruptly.

She sensed what he was about to say.

"Aw, Benny—. That was different. Honest, it was. He warn't the only one in his family. There was two brothers."

The boy got to his feet.

"Why won't you let me go?" He asked it passionately. "Why d'you keep me here? You know I ain't happy! You know all the men've gone from these here parts. You know I ain't happy! Ain't you going to see how much I want to go ? Ain't you able to know that I want to fight for my country? The way he did his fighting?"

The boy jerked his head in the direction of the figure standing waist deep in the corn field; standing rigidly and faintly outlined beneath the haunting flood of moonlight.

"Naw, Benny. You can't go. Naw—!"

"Why, maw? Why d'you keep saying that and saying it?"

"I'm all alone, Benny. I've gave all my best years to make the farm pay for you. You got to stay, Benny. You got to stay on here with me. You just plain got—to! You'll be glad some day, Benny. Later—on. You'll be right glad."

She saw him thrust his hands hastily into his trouser pockets.

"Glad?" His voice sounded tired. "I'll be shamed. That's what I'll be. Nothing, d' you hear, nothing—but shamed!"

She started to her feet.

"Benny—" A note of fear shook through the words. "You wouldn't—wouldn't—go?"

He waited a moment before he answered her.

"If you ain't wanting me to go—; I'll stay. Gawd! I guess I plain got to—stay."

"That's a good boy, Benny. You won't never be sorry— nohow—I promise you!—I'll be making it up to you. Honest, I will!—There's lots of ways—I'll—!"

He interrupted her.

"Only, maw—; I won't let it come after me. If it beckons I—got—to—go—!"

She gave a sudden laugh that trailed off uncertainly.

"'Tain't going to beckon, Benny."

"If it beckons, maw—"

"'Tain't going to, Benny. 'Tain't nothing but the wind that moves it. It's just the wind, sure. Mebbe you got a touch of fever. Mebbe you better go on to bed. You'll be all right in the morning. Just you wait and see. You're a good boy, Benny. You'll never go off and leave your maw and the farm. You're a fine lad, Benny."

"If—it—beckons—" He repeated in weary monotone.

"'Tain't, Benny!"

"I'll be going to bed," he said.

"That's it, Benny. Good night."

"Good night, maw."

She stood there listening to his feet thudding up the stairs. She heard him knocking about in the room overhead. A door banged. She stood quite still. There were footsteps moving slowly. A window was thrown open.

She looked up to see him leaning far out over the sill.

Her eyes went down the slope of the moonlight-bathed corn field.

Her right hand curled itself into a fist.

"Ole—scarecrow—!"

She half laughed.

She waited there until she saw the boy draw away from the window. She went into the house and bolted the door behind her. Then she went up the narrow steps.

That night she lay awake for a long time. The heat had grown intense. She found herself tossing from side to side of the small bed.

The window shade had stuck at the top of the window.

The moonlight trickled into the room. She could see the window-framed, star-speckled patch of the skies. When she sat up she saw the round, reddish-yellow ball of the moon.

She must have dozed, because she woke with a start. She felt that she had had a fearful, evil dream. The horror of it clung to her.

The room was like an oven.

She thought the walls were coming together and the ceiling pressing down.

Her body was covered with sweat.

She forced herself wide awake. She made herself get out of the bed. She stood for a second uncertain. Then she went to the window.

Not a breath of air stirring.

The moon was high in the sky.

She looked out across the hills.

Down there to the left the acres of potatoes. Potatoes were paying. She counted on a big harvest. To the right the wheat. Only the second year for those five fields. She knew that she had done well with them.

She thought, with a smile running over her lips, back to the time when less than half of the place had been under cultivation. She remembered her dream of getting the whole of her farm in work. She and the boy had made good. She thought of that with savage complacency. It had been a struggle; a bitter, hard fight from the beginning. But she had made good with her farm.

And there down the slope, just in front of the house, the corn field. And in the center of it, standing waist deep in the corn, the antiquated, military figure.

The smile slid from her mouth.

The suffocating heat was terrific.

Not a breath of air.

Suddenly she began to shake from head to foot.

Her eyes wide and staring, were fixed on the moonlight-whitened corn field; her eyes were held to the moonlight-streaked figure standing in the ghostly corn.

Moving—

An arm swayed—swayed to and fro. Backwards and for-wards—backwards— The other arm—swaying— A tremor ran through it. Once it pivoted. The head shook slowly from side to side. The arms rose and fell—; and rose again. The head came up and down, and rocked a bit to either side.

"Dancing—" She whispered stupidly. "Dancing—"

She thought she could not breathe.

She had never felt such oppressive heat.

The arms were tossing and stretching.

She could not take her eyes from it.

And then she saw both arms reach out, and slowly, very slowly, she saw the hands of them, beckoning.

In the stillness of the room next to her she thought she heard a crash.

She listened intently, her eyes stuck to those reaching arms, and the hands of them that beckoned and beckoned.

"Benny—" She murmured—"Benny—"

Silence.

She could not think.

It was his talk that had done this—Benny's talk—He had said something about it—walking out—If it should come—out—! Moving all over like that— If its feet should start—! If they should of a sudden begin to shuffle—; shuffle out of the corn field—!

But Benny wasn't awake. He—couldn't—see—it. Thank Gawd! If only something—would—hold—it! If—only—it—would—stop—; Gawd!

Nothing stirring out there in the haunting moonlighted night. Nothing moving. Nothing but the figure standing waist deep in the corn field. And even as she looked, the rigid, military figure grew still. Still, now, but for those slow, beckoning hands.

A tremendous dizziness came over her.

She closed her eyes for a second and then she stumbled back to the bed.

She lay there panting. She pulled the sheets up across her face; her shaking fingers working the tops of them into a hard ball. She stuffed it between her chattering teeth.

Whatever happened, Benny mustn't hear her. She mustn't waken, Benny. Thank Heaven, Benny was asleep. Benny must never know how, out there in the whitened night, the hands of the figure slowly and unceasingly beckoned and beckoned.

The sight of those reaching arms stayed before her. When, hours later, she fell asleep, she still saw the slow-moving, motioning hands.

It was morning when she wakened.

The sun streamed into the room.

She went to the door and opened it.

"Benny—" She called. "Oh, Benny."

There was no answer.

"Benny—" She called again. "Get on up. It's late, Benny!"

The house was quiet.

She half dressed herself and went into his room.

The bed had been slept in. She saw that at a glance. His clothes were not there, Down—in—the—field—because—she'd—forgotten—to—wake—him—.

In a sudden stunning flash she remembered the crash she had heard.

It took her a long while to get to the little closet behind the bed. Before she opened it she knew it would be empty.

The door creaked open.

His one hat and coat were gone.

She had known that.

He had seen those two reaching arms! He had seen those two hands that had slowly, very slowly, beckoned!

She went to the window.

Her eyes staring straight before her, down the slope in front of the house, caught sight of something blue and antiquatedly military standing waist deep and rigid in the corn field.

"You ole scarecrow—!" She whimpered. "Why're you standing there?" She sobbed. "What're you standing still for—*now*?"

Gertrude Atherton
(1857–1948)

GERTRUDE ATHERTON was one of California's best-selling novelists with a career that spanned sixty-five years. She was born Gertrude Horn in San Francisco, the great-grandniece of Benjamin Franklin, but her family, though wealthy, was one of fading grandeur and her parents separated when she was two years old. Her mother kept the family together and Gertrude seems to have inherited her strong will and determination. When only eighteen she eloped with George Atherton, who had visited the family to court her mother. Gertrude moved into the Atherton Mansion in San Francisco along with George's equally strong-willed mother, Dominga. Wife and mother-in-law got on well together and George was sidelined, so he decided to travel abroad to prove himself. Unfortunately he died on board ship in 1887 and his body was preserved in a barrel of rum until it could be brought back home. George's spirit was supposed to have haunted Atherton Mansion ever after. Gertrude had already turned to writing as her primary pursuit, despite George's objections, and caused considerable controversy with her first novel, *The Randolphs of Redwoods*, originally serialized anonymously in 1882. It was based on a local family scandal and included what was then regarded as some daring sex scenes. She became a prolific writer, her most successful books including *Patience Sparhawk and Her Times* (1897), *The Californians* (1898), and *The Conqueror* (1902), a fictionalized biography of Alexander Hamilton. The supernatural was featured in her early novel about reincarnation, *What Dreams May Come* (1888), but the best of her strange tales appeared as short stories, collected in *The Bell in the Fog* (1905) and *The Foghorn* (1934). She also dabbled with experiments in rejuvenation with the use of radiation to stimulate the ovaries, and used her experiences as the basis for *Black Oxen* (1923), which was subsequently filmed. "The Striding Place," first published in *The Speaker* for 20 June 1896, is perhaps her most powerful ghost story and is set in a real place in Yorkshire, England.

The Striding Place

Weigall, continental and detached, tired early of grouse-shooting. To stand propped against a sod fence while his host's workmen routed up the birds with long poles and drove them towards the waiting guns, made him feel himself a parody on the ancestors who had roamed the moors and forests of this West Riding of Yorkshire in hot pursuit of game worth the killing. But when in England in August he always accepted whatever proffered for the season, and invited his host to shoot pheasants on his estates in the South. The amusements of life, he argued, should be accepted with the same philosophy as its ills.

It had been a bad day. A heavy rain had made the moor so spongy that it fairly sprang beneath the feet. Whether or not the grouse had haunts of their own, wherein they were immune from rheumatism, the bag had been small. The women, too, were an unusually dull lot, with the exception of a new-minded *débutante* who bothered Weigall at dinner by demanding the verbal restoration of the vague paintings on the vaulted roof above them.

But it was no one of these things that sat on Weigall's mind as, when the other men went up to bed, he let himself out of the castle and sauntered down to the river. His intimate friend, the companion of his boyhood, the chum of his college days, his fellow-traveller in many lands, the man for whom he possessed stronger affection than for all men, had mysteriously disappeared two days ago, and his track might have sprung to the upper air for all trace he had left behind him. He had been a guest on the adjoining estate during the past week, shooting with the fervor of the true sportsman, making love in the intervals to Adeline Cavan, and apparently in the best of spirits. As far as was known there was nothing to lower his mental mercury, for his rent-roll was a large one, Miss Cavan blushed whenever he looked at her, and, being one of the best shots in England, he was never happier than in August. The suicide theory was preposterous, all agreed, and there was as little reason to believe him murdered. Nevertheless, he had walked out of March Abbey two nights ago without hat or overcoat, and had not been seen since.

The country was being patrolled night and day. A hundred keepers and workmen were beating the woods and poking the bogs on the moors, but as yet not so much as a handkerchief had been found.

Weigall did not believe for a moment that Wyatt Gifford was dead, and although it was impossible not to be affected by the general uneasiness, he was disposed to be more angry than frightened. At Cambridge Gifford had been an incorrigible practical joker, and by no means had outgrown the habit; it would be like him to cut across the country in his evening clothes, board a cattle-train, and amuse himself touching up the picture of the sensation in West Riding.

However, Weigall's affection for his friend was too deep to companion with tranquillity in the present state of doubt, and, instead of going to bed early with the other men, he determined to walk until ready for sleep. He went down to the river and followed the path through the woods. There was no moon, but the stars sprinkled their cold light upon the pretty belt of water flowing placidly past wood and ruin, between green masses of overhanging rocks or sloping banks tangled with tree and shrub, leaping occasionally over stones with the harsh notes of an angry scold, to recover its equanimity the moment the way was clear again.

It was very dark in the depths where Weigall trod. He smiled as he recalled a remark of Gifford's: "An English wood is like a good many other things in life—very promising at a distance, but a hollow mockery when you get within. You see daylight on both sides, and the sun freckles the very bracken. Our woods need the night to make them seem what they ought to be—what they once were, before our ancestors' descendants demanded so much more money, in these so much more various days."

Weigall strolled along, smoking, and thinking of his friend, his pranks—many of which had done more credit to his imagination than this—and recalling conversations that had lasted the night through. Just before the end of the London season they had walked the streets one hot night after a party, discussing the various theories of the soul's destiny. That afternoon they had met at the coffin of a college friend whose mind had been a blank for the past three years. Some months previously they had called at the asylum to see him. His expression had been senile, his face imprinted with the record of debauchery. In death the face was placid, intelligent, without ignoble lineation—the face of the man they had known at college. Weigall and Gifford had had no time to comment there, and the afternoon and evening were full; but, coming forth from the house of festivity together, they had reverted almost at once to the topic.

"I cherish the theory," Gifford had said, "that the soul some-times lingers in the body after death. During madness, of course, it is an impotent prisoner, albeit a conscious one. Fancy its agony, and its horror! What more natural than that, when the life-spark goes out, the tortured soul should take possession of the vacant skull and triumph once more for a few hours while old friends look their last? It has had time to repent while com-pelled to crouch and behold the result of its work, and it has shrived itself into a state of comparative purity. If I had my way, I should stay inside my bones until the coffin had gone into its niche, that I might obviate for my poor old comrade the tragic impersonality of death. And I should like to see justice done to it, as it were—to see it lowered among its ancestors with the ceremony and solemnity that are its due. I am afraid that if I dissevered myself too quickly, I should yield to curiosity and hasten to investigate the mysteries of space."

"You believe in the soul as an independent entity, then—that it and the vital principle are not one and the same?"

"Absolutely. The body and soul are twins, life comrades—

sometimes friends, sometimes enemies, but always loyal in the last instance. Some day, when I am tired of the world, I shall go to India and become a mahatma, solely for the pleasure of receiving proof during life of this independent relationship."

"Suppose you were not sealed up properly, and returned after one of your astral flights to find your earthly part unfit for habitation? It is an experiment I don't think I should care to try, unless even juggling with soul and flesh had palled."

"That would not be an uninteresting predicament. I should rather enjoy experimenting with broken machinery."

The high wild roar of water smote suddenly upon Weigall's ear and checked his memories. He left the wood and walked out on the huge slippery stones which nearly close the River Wharfe at this point, and watched the waters boil down into the narrow pass with their furious untiring energy. The black quiet of the woods rose high on either side. The stars seemed colder and whiter just above. On either hand the perspective of the river might have run into a rayless cavern. There was no lonelier spot in England, nor one which had the right to claim so many ghosts, if ghosts there were.

Weigall was not a coward, but he recalled uncomfortably the tales of those that had been done to death in the Strid.[1] Wordsworth's Boy of Egremond had been disposed of by the practical Whitaker; but countless others, more venturesome than wise, had gone down into that narrow boiling course, never to appear in the still pool a few yards beyond. Below the great rocks which form the walls of the Strid was believed to be a natural vault, on to whose shelves the dead were drawn. The spot had an ugly fascination. Weigall stood, visioning skeletons, uncoffined and green, the home of the eyeless things which had devoured all that had covered and filled that rattling symbol of man's mortality; then fell to wondering if any one had attempted to leap the Strid of late. It was covered with slime; he had never seen it look so treacherous.

---

[1] "This striding place is called the 'Strid,'
　　 A name which it took of yore;
　 A thousand years hath it borne the name,
　　 And it shall a thousand more."

He shuddered and turned away, impelled, despite his man-hood, to flee the spot. As he did so, something tossing in the foam below the fall—something as white, yet independent of it—caught his eye and arrested his step. Then he saw that it was describing a contrary motion to the rushing water—an upward backward motion. Weigall stood rigid, breathless; he fancied he heard the crackling of his hair. Was that a hand? It thrust itself still higher above the boiling foam, turned sidewise, and four frantic fingers were distinctly visible against the black rock beyond.

Weigall's superstitious terror left him. A man was there, struggling to free himself from the suction beneath the Strid, swept down, doubtless, but a moment before his arrival, per-haps as he stood with his back to the current.

He stepped as close to the edge as he dared. The hand dou-bled as if in imprecation, shaking savagely in the face of that force which leaves its creatures to immutable law; then spread wide again, clutching, expanding, crying for help as audibly as the human voice.

Weigall dashed to the nearest tree, dragged and twisted off a branch with his strong arms, and returned as swiftly to the Strid. The hand was in the same place, still gesticulating as wildly; the body was undoubtedly caught in the rocks below, perhaps already half-way along one of those hideous shelves. Weigall let himself down upon a lower rock, braced his shoulder against the mass beside him, then, leaning out over the water, thrust the branch into the hand. The fingers clutched it convulsively. Weigall tugged powerfully, his own feet dragged perilously near the edge. For a moment he produced no impression, then an arm shot above the waters.

The blood sprang to Weigall's head; he was choked with the impression that the Strid had him in her roaring hold, and he saw nothing. Then the mist cleared. The hand and arm were nearer, although the rest of the body was still concealed by the foam. Weigall peered out with distended eyes. The meagre light revealed in the cuffs links of a peculiar device. The fingers clutching the branch were as familiar.

Weigall forgot the slippery stones, the terrible death if he stepped too far. He pulled with passionate will and muscle. Memories flung themselves into the hot light of his brain, trooping rapidly upon each other's heels, as in the thought of the drowning. Most of the pleasures of his life, good and bad, were identified in some way with this friend. Scenes of college days, of travel, where they had deliberately sought adventure and stood between one another and death upon more occasions than one, of hours of delightful companionship among the treasures of art, and others in the pursuit of pleasure, flashed like the changing particles of a kaleidoscope. Weigall had loved several women; but he would have flouted in these moments the thought that he had ever loved any woman as he loved Wyatt Gifford. There were so many charming women in the world, and in the thirty-two years of his life he had never known another man to whom he had cared to give his intimate friendship.

He threw himself on his face. His wrists were cracking, the skin was torn from his hands. The fingers still gripped the stick. There was life in them yet.

Suddenly something gave way. The hand swung about, tearing the branch from Weigall's grasp. The body had been liberated and flung outward, though still submerged by the foam and spray.

Weigall scrambled to his feet and sprang along the rocks, knowing that the danger from suction was over and that Gifford must be carried straight to the quiet pool. Gifford was a fish in the water and could live under it longer than most men. If he survived this, it would not be the first time that his pluck and science had saved him from drowning.

Weigall reached the pool. A man in his evening clothes floated on it, his face turned towards a projecting rock over which his arm had fallen, upholding the body. The hand that had held the branch hung limply over the rock, its white reflection visible in the black water. Weigall plunged into the shallow pool, lifted Gifford in his arms and returned to the bank. He laid the body down and threw off his coat that he might be the freer to practise the methods of resuscitation. He was glad of the moment's respite. The valiant life in the man might have been exhausted in that last struggle. He had not dared to look at his face, to put his ear to the heart. The hesitation lasted but a moment. There was no time to lose.

He turned to his prostrate friend. As he did so, something strange and disagreeable smote his senses. For a half-moment he did not appreciate its nature. Then his teeth clacked together, his feet, his outstretched arms pointed towards the woods. But he sprang to the side of the man and bent down and peered into his face. There was no face.